COURT OF THE TETRARCH

BOOK TWO

# WIFE OF
# CHUZA

KATRINA D. HAMEL

Published by Long Walk Publishing
Alberta, Canada

Map Illustration by Cay Danielson

Wife of Chuza : Court of the Tetrarch Book Two / By Katrina D. Hamel — 1st ed.

1. Christian Historical Fiction 2. Biblical Fiction

ISBN: 978-1-9990338-6-6

*For all the women in ministry who dare
to serve the Lord with all their
hearts, souls, and minds*

# Herod's Family, as Mentioned in Wife of Chuza

Antipater (an Edomite) married Cypros (a Nabatean)

Antipater and Cypros had five children, including Herod and Salome
Salome and her second husband Costabar had two children, Antipater and Bernice

Herod married ten wives and had fourteen children

By his wife Doris, Herod fathered:
Antipater (executed days before Herod's death)

By his wife Mariamne I (descendant of Hasmonean royalty), Herod fathered five children including:
Alexander (executed by Herod, and the father of two children)
Aristobulus (executed by Herod and had four or five children with Salome's daughter Bernice, including Herod, Agrippa, and Herodias

By his wife Malthace (a Samaritan), Herod fathered:
Archelaus (named ethnarch, before being exiled by Caesar)
Antipas (who became tetrarch)
and Olympias (who married her cousin and had one daughter, Mariamne, who married Herodias' brother, Herod)

By his wife Cleopatra, Herod fathered:
Philip (who became tetrarch)

By his wife Mariamne II, Herod fathered:
Herod, who married his niece Herodias, the daughter of Aristobulus
Herod and Herodias were the parents of one daughter, Salome

Herod had other wives and children, but as I do not name them in this book, I have not included them here. You can find a more complete family tree, including the many marriages within the family, on my website, katrinadhamel.com.

# Timeline of Historic Events

40 BC Herod named King of the Jews by the Roman Senate

37 BC Herod achieves military control of his territory

29 BC Herod executes his beloved wife Mariamne on suspicion of adultery

27 BC Caesar Augustus named Emperor

20 BC Herod starts massive renovations of the Jewish temple

9 BC Aretas IV made king of Nabatea

7 BC Herod executes his sons Aristobulus and Alexander

4 BC Herod executes his son Antipater

4 BC Herod dies

4 BC Archelaus becomes ethnarch, Antipas and Philip become tetrarchs

6 AD Archelaus exiled and Roman prefects rule his territory of Iudaea, which includes Judea, Idumea (Edom), and Samaria

14 AD Augustus dies

14 AD Tiberius becomes Emperor of Rome

23 AD Tiberius' son and heir, Drusus, dies suddenly

[25 AD This story begins]

26 AD Pilate becomes the fifth prefect/governor of Iudaea

27 AD (approx) Antipas divorces his wife and marries Herodias

28* AD John the Baptist arrested

28* AD Jesus begins ministry

*Biblical scholars debate these dates, some of which argue for an earlier date of 26 AD, and others place Jesus' ministry within 30-36 AD.*

# HISTORICAL NOTES

*Herod's Name*
In the Bible, there are four individuals using the name Herod. For clarity, I call the second Herod by his name, Antipas.

*King, Tetrarch*
Biblical authors sometimes give Antipas the title of 'king', such as Mark 6:14, though he was not a king like his father Herod, but a tetrarch, as mentioned in Matthew 14:1 and throughout Luke's gospel. A tetrarch ruled a quarter of a territory or was a subordinate prince, and he was under the authority of the Roman government.

*Israel*
The name 'Israel' for the land may be anachronistic for this time period, but I felt that in some places, it added clarity for modern, western readers. A document from the 5th century BC gives 'Palestine' as the name for the general region. Within the New Testament, the land is often mentioned by its various territories, such as Galilee. Judea was the name of a specific territory, but also of a larger area ruled by the Roman governors. Often clarified by using the Latin name 'Idumaea', this territory encompassed Judea, Samaria, and Idumea (Edom).

*Historical Accuracy*
I did my best to represent the practices and traditions of the time, and to present them in a way that will appeal to a modern reader. I acknowledge that my research may be in error, or disputed now or in the future. The dates given for historic events are debated and are simply used within this book to help situate you on a timeline. Please keep in mind that this is a work of historical fiction, and not intended for academic purposes.

Map Illustration by Cay Danielson

*But seek first His kingdom and His righteousness,*
*and all these things will be added to you.*
Matthew 6:33

# PROLOGUE

7 BC

"Is it over?" Bernice gnawed at her raw nail, wincing at the taste of blood.

Salome swept into Bernice's chambers, her robe whispering along the polished floor. She checked the hallway for listening ears and shut the door. Her lips curved with triumph. "It is finished," she said.

Bernice nodded once, then her stomach heaved. She stumbled for the washbasin, convulsing as her gut emptied. Hunched over the bowl, she panted, the smell of her own bile burning her nose. She swiped the back of her hand across her lips. Her mother held out a cup, her face emotionless. Bernice swished a mouthful of wine and spat it out, then drained the goblet.

"Careful, or you'll bring that up too," Salome said dryly.

"How did they—" Bernice hesitated. Maybe she didn't want to know. "How did Aristobulus die?" Salome studied her face, calculating. Bernice tried to stand taller, but she could not match her mother's queenly bearing.

"Strangled," Salome said at last, and Bernice's knees wobbled.

She squeezed her eyes shut and envisioned Aristobulus' purple face, his bloodshot eyes. She pulled a sharp breath, turning from the image.

"It needed to be done," Salome said.

"I know. It's just..." She couldn't explain her churning emotions to a woman who had seen two husbands executed without a qualm. "Nothing."

"Herod sent the bodies to be buried." Salome filled a cup for herself. "All this... unpleasantness... will soon be over." She took a deep drink.

Bernice's lower lip trembled. Now that it was over, she struggled to remember why. Was it not enough that Salome smeared Aristobulus' mother with tales of adultery and had her executed?

Bernice strode to the window where the afternoon was tipping toward twilight. Somewhere out there, men were hauling her husband's body away. The last Hasmonean princes would never see another sunrise. She jerked her attention from the hazy light.

"My children," Bernice said, pressing her hands to her stomach. "They will not suffer because of this. You promised."

"Yes, yes." Salome swept her hand to brush off Bernice's fear. "My brother will not harm his grandchildren. We shall bring them before Herod in a day or two, to stir his pity. They shall have fine marriages and estates—when the time comes."

"So what do we do now?"

"We?" Salome raised her eyebrows. "We will do nothing."

Bernice pushed a hair off her damp forehead. She should be relieved to escape her mother's intrigues, yet now that their goal was complete, she felt bereft. Rudderless.

Salome chuckled, a low rumble in her throat. "I will let Antipater celebrate with his mother tonight. His imagined throne is all but gilded." Her chilling laugh jarred Bernice's bones. "We shall see if his dreams are as solid as he believes."

Two of Herod's heirs were eliminated. If Salome had her way,

Antipater would fall next. But Herod had other sons, and Salome must allow one of them to claim the throne.

Bernice cleared her throat. "What will you do?"

"I will wait." Salome walked in a slow circle around her daughter, sizing up Bernice from head to toe. "Some plants shoot up quickly, give their fruit for a season, and fall away. Others take years to produce a crop, but they feed you for a lifetime." Bernice wondered which she was. "We must sow our next seeds carefully," Salome's voice rasped in a chilling whisper. "Someday, we shall be free."

Bernice caught the simmering rage beneath her mother's cold exterior. Though Herod listened to Salome's counsel, he ruled her every breath. He had forbidden her from marrying the one man she desired—perhaps the only person Salome ever truly loved.

The men of her family might be born to lord over their subordinates, but the women had their own sources of power. Her mother taught her that.

Heat rushed through her veins as Bernice finally allowed herself to feel her victory.

Salome saw her acceptance and answered with a nod of satisfaction. She set down her cup and strode to the door. "I am weary from this day's work," Salome said. "We shall speak more tomorrow."

"Yes, mother."

Alone in her chambers, Bernice wrapped her arms around herself, knowing no one else would hold her tonight.

She wandered to her bed, trailing her fingertips over the fine linen, remembering when Aristobulus took her into his arms for the first time. She had been so young. So in love. His years in Rome gave him a refinement that set him apart from other men. She bore him three sons and a daughter and believed she could never be happier.

But her happiness ended when Salome told her that Aristobulus and his brother were scheming to kill their father and seize his kingdom. It was her duty to thwart the evil plot.

Bernice sank onto the soft bed. No one could blame her for the death of the beloved princes, and she wasn't the only one to accuse her husband. Herod's questioners tortured countless men to gather proof that his sons planned to murder him.

Bernice bit her lip. She had done the only reasonable thing in turning over her husband.

A knock saved her from her dark thoughts.

"Come," she said.

One of the nursemaids bustled in, a deep V between her brows. "Is Herodias in here?" she asked.

"No, of course not," Bernice said.

"I've caught her playing in your clothes before." The nursemaid gestured at the wardrobe. "May I?"

Bernice nodded, unable to speak. The nursemaid opened the carved cedar doors.

"For shame!" the nurse exclaimed. "Making me look all over the palace when you know it's time for your supper."

Bernice rose on shaky legs as her eight-year-old daughter stumbled out of the wardrobe, one of her mother's scarves wound about her waist. Two fat tears tracked down her deathly pale cheeks. Bernice's mouth dried.

"What is the matter?" the nursemaid said, giving Herodias a little shake. "I have hardly scolded you." Herodias glared at her mother, chilling Bernice to her core. The nursemaid looked between the mother and daughter in confusion.

Bernice gave a weak smile. "I shall bring her to the nursery in a moment." The nursemaid hesitated, then nodded, leaving them alone. Bernice shut the door, drawing a breath before turning to face her child's accusing eyes.

"Papa is dead?" Herodias whispered. Bernice's chest tightened with pity. She remembered her own tears when Herod executed her father for sheltering his enemies.

Bernice knelt before her daughter, peering up into her face. "I told you this might happen, remember? After your grandfather put them in prison?"

Herodias' gaze flickered back and forth on hers. "Then why aren't you crying?" she accused. "Did you want Papa to die?"

Bernice struggled for an answer, inching closer on the cold floor. "I'm going to tell you something my mother told me, all right?" She took her daughter's icy fingers in hers. "A little discomfort now will reap a plentiful harvest later. Do you understand? This will all work out for our good."

Herodias jerked her hand away. "You told me that Papa was supposed to be a king. I would be a princess. Now what will I be?"

Bernice frowned in frustration. How did the child remember a conversation from years ago, a promise given in happier times?

"You will have all you desire, I promise you. You are part of a great family, descended from two priestly lines, and with royal blood."

Herodias screwed up her face, stamping her foot. "I don't want to be part of this family. They killed my papa! I hate you! I want my papa!"

She raced from the room, leaving Bernice kneeling on the floor, grasping at air.

She betrayed Aristobulus for all of them, to give her children a better future. Someday Herodias would understand her mother did everything for her good.

# ONE

28 AD
WINTER

A determined beam of sunlight filtered through the ornate screen, painting Chuza's arm in a glowing tattoo. Joanna propped her cheek on her wrist, her dark hair spilling over her shoulder in a tussled wave. Her husband faced away from her. The blanket had slipped to reveal his smooth back, and she watched the rhythm of his breath, memorizing the sound.

The moment was gilded by second chances. Her sickness had stolen precious moments like these, and now that she was healed, she yearned for the joys they had missed. It wasn't all she longed for.

Today was the day! She would journey to find the incredible prophet, the man filled with God's spirit—a healer and teacher. She stretched her strong calf muscles and wiggled her toes, eager to return to the one who made her well.

But she wasn't gone yet.

She slid closer, the radiating warmth of Chuza's body reaching her before she wrapped her arm around his chest, curling against his back. Stirring at her touch, he rolled toward her, squinting as the light struck him across the face, glinting on the golden earring that proclaimed to all that he was a bondslave.

"Good morning," she murmured, planting a kiss on his lips. "I need to get up soon. The others will be at the gate within the hour."

His arm tightened, pinning her to his chest, his leg snaking around both of hers. She laughed as she halfheartedly tried to escape. They were the same height, but Chuza easily kept her snared.

"Not yet," he said, his voice rough with sleep. He nuzzled against her neck, his lips dancing along her throat before meeting hers. Joanna returned his passion with equal measure. With amusement, she remembered a time when she thought the steward was cold and unfeeling. How wrong she had been.

Too soon, she disentangled her limbs from the bed covers. Chuza reluctantly released her to slip from the bed, and she shivered in the winter chill. She peeked over. He was watching her dress, his bare chest tempting her to return to his arms.

She tossed him a teasing grin. "This is a role reversal now, isn't it? The staff will gossip that their steward is lolling about in bed."

"I have never 'lolled' in my life," Chuza said, lifting his brow. "They'll be more astonished that the steward's lazy wife has roused herself so soon after sunrise." Joanna snatched his tunic off the floor and threw it at his face, and he chuckled.

He pulled the garment over his head and his demeanor shifted. His shoulders tightened as he wound his belt around his waist. Joanna's months in bed had nothing to do with laziness. She cleared her throat. Perhaps it was too soon for jokes.

She had teetered closer to death than she liked to admit. Now, only a week after her miraculous recovery, she was leaving Chuza behind. He said he understood, but perhaps he was burying his feelings again. She dragged a comb through her tangled hair with more force than necessary. If he could just come with her, everything would be perfect.

She twisted the strands into a braid. "I'll only be gone a few weeks," she reminded him. A few weeks passed quickly.

Chuza jerked a nod.

She kept her tone light. "And if someone asks, you're going to tell them I went home to check my vineyard?"

"Yes," he said flatly. "Please visit, so you don't make me a liar." Honorable, as always.

Joanna tied the braid with a string, pressing her lips together. Leaving was her choice, but this parting was more difficult than she expected.

She crouched by her chest of clothes and rummaged to the bottom, withdrawing the purse hidden among the folds. She opened the drawstrings and peered at the hefty pile of gold coins, her reward from King Aretas for returning his daughter to Petra.

"How much do you plan to give?" Chuza asked, his voice neutral. He had never asked her to hand over the small fortune, insisting she deserved it after everything Princess Phasaelis put her through.

"I'm not sure," Joanna said. She shook out a handful. "I don't want to look like I'm showing off."

He glanced at the glittering pile and raised his brows. "That should provide for a good while. If they spend it wisely."

"I'm sure they will," Joanna said. She had seen those the prophet surrounded himself with—common men and women in simple clothes. They must be used to stretching a denarius. She wrapped the coins in a handkerchief and tucked them into her satchel.

Chuza reached for the office door, and her stomach twisted with the realization she was really leaving. She flew across the small apartment, throwing her arms around him. He returned her embrace stiffly, but then softened, drawing her closer.

"I will miss you," Joanna said. She pulled back to look him in the eye. His dark brown hair curled over his brows and ears, and his trimmed beard emphasized his fine nose and gentle expression. She had never felt so eager to go and so desperate to stay in her whole life, and she had no idea how to put her tumbling emotions into words.

"I love you," she said.

"And I love you," he replied, the corner of his mouth lifting. They shared a lingering kiss, one that Joanna wished would never end.

Chuza pulled the door open. A chilly draft from the office swirled into their private chambers and stirred Joanna's wool robe around her ankles. She and Chuza shared a somber glance. The room was a blatant reminder of his obligations and responsibilities to the tetrarch, a ruler who would not take kindly to a prophet moving through his lands.

Joanna retrieved her bag and scanned the first home she shared with her husband. They would have rooms in Antipas' other palaces, but despite enduring months of illness within these four walls, this room would always hold a special place in her heart.

She met Chuza's questioning eye and drew a breath. A prophet with the spirit of Elijah beckoned. It was time to go.

Leah leaned on the wall outside the office. The thirteen-year-old wore traveling clothes, and her shoulder-length hair was pushed back by a scarf. She scanned Joanna's face, assuring herself that her mistress hadn't relapsed.

"I packed some food," Leah said, gesturing to a bag at her feet. "Nothing fancy, but it will serve."

Joanna chuckled. "As long as it's not bone broth, I'll eat anything." If she never saw another bowl, it would be too soon.

Leah's lips curved in a tiny smile. "Thanks for letting me come along this time."

Joanna squeezed her thin shoulder. Leah would never forgive her if she was forced to stay behind again. Joanna only hoped that the journey would not be too difficult for the young woman. After tomorrow, they had no idea where they would sleep, or if they would find shelter from the winter rain. Joanna bounced on her toes. Somehow, not knowing what lay ahead only heightened her sense of adventure.

The trio crossed a large hall and entered the central courtyard of the palace. A colonnade protected ornate doors that led into opulent halls and apartments fit for royalty. Manaen waited for them, leaning against a pillar and warming himself in the sun. His lengthy beard and prayer tassels were a sharp contrast to Chuza's fashionable clothes.

"Ready?" Manaen asked, tugging the scarf on Leah's head. She straightened the cloth with a scowl that did not quite reach her eyes.

"We're just waiting on Susanna," Joanna said, adjusting her bag so the strap crossed her chest.

"Are you implying I'm late?" A woman's teasing voice made them all turn. "Good morning, my friends," Susanna said, striding past the guards at the gate. Older than Joanna by a decade, Susanna was the only friend Joanna boasted in court.

Joanna hurried forward to hug her, and the two women linked arms and strode through the gateway to peer over the tidy city of Tiberias. Beyond the city walls, the Sea of Galilee spread before them, sparkling in the morning sun. The hills surrounding the lake wore their brown, winter mantles, dotted with short trees and dark green brush. White gulls swooped over the shoreline in search of breakfast.

Joanna's heart soared with the birds. She drew an invigorating breath, grateful for freedom after months of illness. A week ago, she feared she would never be strong enough to walk to the market, never mind march across the countryside.

"I'm glad Jaban agreed I should delay my return," Susanna said. Waiting for his permission had postponed their departure by a few days. Her gaze grew distant. "But I miss my boys. I hope they'll understand why I'm returning to the prophet first."

Joanna squeezed Susanna's arm. "Of course they will. They'll be excited to hear about your adventures." Joanna's tone grew

11

teasing as she said, "Who knew their old mother led such an interesting life?" Susanna gave a burst of laughter, smacking Joanna's shoulder. Joanna was grateful the official's wife could join them again. The first time was for healing. Now, they would give aid and learn.

Joanna said, "We'll be back before they know it." She wasn't sure if she was reminding Susanna or Chuza, who hovered behind them.

Manaen strode past, his steps jaunty as he whistled a tune. Leah fell in step and Susanna hurried to catch up.

Joanna turned to her husband. The palace guards stood at attention over his shoulder, braced by their spears. She twined her fingers in his.

"Be safe," he said, his eyes warm with meaning.

"I will," she promised. She gave him a last, discreet peck on the cheek. "I'll be back soon."

They did not break their gaze until her hand slipped from his. She looked over her shoulder as she hastened after the others, but on the third glance, he was gone. She strode with her chin lifted. The pain of a temporary separation was worth the reward of witnessing a man whose power rivaled the great prophet Elijah.

Chuza did not linger in Tiberias. In record time, he packed his scrolls and his writing materials in a wooden trunk. He gathered up his clothing, lingering on the feminine touches Joanna wrought on what had been an austere room. Her box of belongings was ready for him to take along, and he clung to the tangible promise of her return.

He understood that she wanted to support the man of God. He couldn't deny a prophet's unyielding pull on a woman who yearned to serve the Lord. But knowing didn't make parting easier. He dumped the last roll of papyrus in the chest and slammed the lid.

Within two hours of Joanna's departure, he had broken his fast, given final orders to the small staff who maintained the palace in Antipas' absence, and arranged for a cart and a pair of armed guards. While servants loaded the luggage, Chuza turned to the stables.

"Leaving for Jericho, my lord?" one of the young grooms asked as Chuza strode forward wearing thick sandals and his woolen cloak. With a curt nod, Chuza fetched a measure of grain and hooked a halter and lead rope on his shoulder.

He marched to the paddock where his bay gelding was grazing.

"We were all pleased to hear of your wife's recovery," the youth said, jogging in his wake. Chuza's lips pressed together. "It happened so quickly too. The guards didn't see her go. Did she visit the new healing baths?"

"No," Chuza said.

"A doctor in town?"

"No." Chuza's tone lowered in warning. He shook the jar of grain, the sound traveling across the paddock until Celer's ears perked up. Celer trotted to the fence, and Chuza offered him a handful. His shoulders softened as velvet lips tickled his palm. Time with his old friend always lifted his spirits.

"I saw your wife leaving this morning," the groom said. "Where is she going?"

Chuza drew a breath for patience as he opened the gate and led Celer through. The groom looped the latch into place.

"She's checking on her vineyard," he said, infusing enough ice into the statement that the groom shrunk in his sandals. "Not that it's any of your business."

The groom realized he had overstepped. "Yes, of course, my lord. Forgive my manners. We are all mighty glad that she's recovered. Praise God."

"Praise God," Chuza agreed. He turned his back on the prying youth and brought his horse to the stable. As he brushed Celer's ruddy hair and swung the saddle into place, he worried rumors might already be flying across Galilee. The miracle was undeniable, and he couldn't blame the staff for their curiosity. If he had believed Manaen's report, perhaps he could have found a way of taking Joanna to be healed without drawing attention.

With a flush, he remembered how he swept aside Manaen's insistence that the man from Nazareth was genuine, leaving his wife no choice but to sneak away in the middle of the night. Now he believed, but he could do nothing about it. He could only imagine what wonders Joanna would witness over the next weeks. Chuza tamped his emotions down before they could grow into envy. He was honor-bound to serve Antipas, and serve him well.

Leading Celer back outside, he gave his foot to the groom and swung into the saddle. He prayed the rumors about Jesus of Nazareth would remain in Tiberias. The tetrarch's court was not ready for what they meant.

He urged Celer forward with a squeeze of his knees and a click of his tongue. The guards and the cart rumbled behind him. They left the city and took the southern road, loyalty to his master warring against his faith. He didn't want to lie to the man he spent thirty years serving, but he couldn't allow Antipas to throw another prophet in prison with John.

# TWO

J oanna kept her word and went to the vineyard first. She led the way down the road, paused in her favorite spot, and drew a contented sigh. It had been too long since she beheld her home. Beneath the deep blue sky, the rolling hills shifted to tidy, trellised rows of grapevines, protected by a stone wall and twisted thorns. The brown valley pooled around the vineyard like spilled wine, the seeded fields waiting out the cold winter months.

Susanna and Manaen paused with her, but Leah dashed ahead. By the time they arrived, Tirzah was hurrying out of the house, a toddler on her hip and Leah in her wake.

"Joanna!" Tirzah said, holding out one arm so Joanna could step into the half-embrace. "You look so wonderful, I can hardly believe it."

Joanna introduced Manaen and Susanna to the hired woman who maintained Joanna's ancestral home, filling it with laughter and children again. "These two were instrumental in my healing," Joanna said, giving Susanna an affectionate smile.

"Nonsense." Susanna waved her words away. "It was you who

helped me, remember? It was your faith that led me to Jesus' feet."

"Jesus?" Tirzah furrowed her brow, then looked between the women, understanding brightening her eyes. "Do you mean Jesus of Nazareth?"

"You know about him?" Joanna asked in surprise.

"Know about him?" Tirzah laughed. "Everyone knows about the prophet from Nazareth. He turned water into wine at a wedding in Cana and raised a boy from the dead in Nain—if you believe the stories."

Joanna shared a knowing glance with Susanna. Those rumors pulled her from her bed when the physician insisted she was too weak to travel. Together, she and Susanna endured the jostling ride, believing that Jesus held the miracle that others could not offer.

Susanna said, "If he healed us with a touch of his hand, turning water to wine should be easy."

Joanna raised her eyebrows and crossed her arms. "Hopefully not too easy, or he'll put me out of business." The others laughed.

"Whoever thought we'd live to see such things?" Tirzah shook her head, lifting her eyes and her free hand to the sky.

Her simple acceptance made Joanna's heart sing. Her people were ready for this. After generations of exile and foreign rulers, it was time for God to restore Israel's blessings.

Tirzah hitched her youngest child higher on her hip. "We should tell David you're here."

"Why don't I go find him?" Joanna said. She was eager to see her home and walk the familiar paths she had trod since her first toddling steps.

Tirzah said, "Alright. I'll start supper if Leah will help me with this wiggly one." Leah's expression softened, and she held out her arms for the boy.

While Tirzah led the others into the house, Joanna strolled to the field to find David, her skirts swishing around her legs. Speaking with the foreman who served her father was like stepping back in time. Promoting him to the steward of her vineyard had been a wise choice, and it was clear he and his wife cared for the property as if it was their own.

Nostalgia burrowed deep as they made their rounds. Her childhood was painted on every tree and rock, and on the storeroom where Amichai's destruction changed everything. The shady building was nearly empty now, the wine already delivered to their clients across Galilee. Joanna ran her thumb over the seal on a clay amphora, tracing her family's mark with pride. She and David were continuing her father's legacy, despite her brother's political ideology.

David went into the house, but Joanna wasn't ready to rejoin the others. She collected pruning shears and wandered down the rows alone, trimming the old vines so the new growth could thrive. Her father's voice echoed in her mind, teaching her which branches to cut. She blinked back tears.

She had been too ill to accompany her sister and mother when they brought Ira's bones from their temporary resting place and placed them in the family tomb. No doubt Dalia told everyone that Joanna could have dragged herself from her sickbed to attend the burial.

Joanna's chest tightened at the pain her siblings inflicted the past few years with their assumptions and accusations—even calling her a traitor to her face. She snipped a branch with a scowl. Her father had praised her faith, but ever since Joanna joined the tetrarch's court, Dalia and Amichai couldn't see her for who she was. They only saw the stain of Antipas' unrighteousness.

The sun sank, tinting the sky vibrant orange and pink. A cool breeze teased a strand of hair from her braid, and she let her hands grow still as she surveyed her childhood home. It was as if time stopped here. And despite what Dalia said, Joanna hadn't changed either. She still longed to serve the Lord in some tangible way.

She trimmed another vine, her lips pressed together with determination. Someday Dalia and Amichai would see her for who she was—and regret every accusation they hurled at her.

Joanna, Manaen, Susanna, and Leah left the vineyard early the next day, their breath like smoke, the grass crisply white along the dirt road. The sun struggled to break through the clouds, and chilly air permeated their thick woolen clothes.

They followed the reports and made their way to an obscure town amid fields of tilled and seeded crops, the cluster of houses barely large enough to warrant a synagogue. The overcast sky was low and gray. Other than chickens scratching in a yard and a dog slinking around the corner, the place was eerily empty.

"Where is everyone?" Leah asked. "Are you sure this is the place?"

A man hurried up the road, carrying a child on his back.

"Peace be with you," Manaen called. The man didn't break stride as he approached them. "Have you seen the healer, Jesus of Nazareth?"

"Not yet," the man said, then gestured with a flick of his head. "He's in the synagogue. I'm bringing my daughter to meet him."

Joanna offered the child a smile, but the girl ducked into her father's shoulder.

"We'll come with you," Manaen said.

The man nodded in reply, passing them to enter a stone building, the largest structure in town. In a small community, the synagogue served not only as a place of prayer, but a school, record building, and guest house.

They neared the doorway and Joanna heard the hum of conversation. The farmer pulled on the wooden door, and a familiar voice swirled outside and enveloped her.

"Jesus," Joanna whispered, the name sweet on her tongue. Leah tensed, tugging on her lower lip.

The farmer left the door open and they stepped through. It appeared the whole town was crammed shoulder to shoulder inside. The locals filled tiered seats built along the wall and sat on the floor, crowding right up to Jesus' feet. It was a mixed audience, with white hair over creased faces, and the soft bodies of young children curled on mother's laps, sharing shawls for warmth. Men tanned from hard labor focused on the teacher's seat as raptly as scholars, rather than farmers, masons, blacksmiths, and shepherds. And she knew why.

Jesus sat on the teacher's seat with a scroll unfurled in his lap, illuminated on both sides by clay lamps. The flames cast his skin and hair in an amber glow while he spoke with confidence and passion, as if God whispered in his ear, telling him what to say.

Joanna jumped at a tap on her shoulder. Susanna beckoned her to follow as Manaen led the women to find an empty place. A family squeezed closer together so the four of them could sit on the floor, tucking their robes under them.

Jesus was proclaiming the kingdom of God, and Joanna drank in his words like a deer in the desert. He spoke in parables, telling them what the kingdom was like instead of speaking directly about it. She didn't fully understand what this kingdom of God was, but the phrase alone was enough to kindle a fire in her belly.

Jesus closed the scroll and the man from the road stepped forward, holding his daughter.

"Rabbi," he pleaded, "will you heal my daughter? She cannot move her legs. She has been paralyzed from birth."

Leah strained to see better. A shiver rippled through Joanna, not just for what Jesus could do for the crippled child, but what a miracle would do for Leah's broken faith.

Jesus set the scroll on the altar and reached for the little girl. No longer shy, she leaned out of her father's arms. Jesus held her on his lap and she nestled against his chest, toying with the tie that closed his robe.

"Hello, little lamb," Jesus said. He peered around the room. "My friends, the kingdom of heaven belongs to ones such as this." He placed a large hand on her hair, and she tipped her face to watch while he blessed her. Jesus dropped a kiss on her forehead, picked her up, and set her on her feet. She stepped toward her father.

The room gasped as one.

Startled by the noise, the child threw herself into her father's chest. He wrapped her tiny frame in his thick arms, his body shaking with sobs. Men and women leaped to their feet, crying out in astonishment.

Joanna and Leah scrambled to avoid being trampled. Joanna pulled Leah closer, her vision blurring with wonder and joy. Leah stared up at her mistress. "This is why you wanted to return?"

"Yes." Joanna laughed, torn between watching the celebrations and Leah's dazed expression. "And this is just the beginning."

Through the narrow windows, the sky turned black. The community left for their homes, seeking food and mulling over Jesus' message and his miracle. The last person drifted away and Joanna seized her moment to hurry forward. She hesitated as the glow of the flickering lamps highlighted shadows under Jesus' eyes. A disciple stepped closer, ready to intervene, but Jesus waved him aside.

"Joanna, wife of Chuza," Jesus said with a welcoming smile.

He remembered her!

"Rabbi," she said, unable to say more around the tightness of her throat.

Jesus nodded at Susanna and Manaen. "You've returned."

"We want to learn whatever you will teach us, Rabbi," Manaen said, and Joanna murmured her agreement.

Jesus seemed pleased. "Then follow me."

He leaned sideways to peer behind the trio. Leah hung back. Jesus beckoned to the young woman, and to Joanna's surprise, Leah stepped closer. "And welcome to you too, my daughter."

"You don't look like a rabbi," Leah said. Joanna choked on a startled laugh.

"No?" Jesus' brows lifted over twinkling eyes. "And what does a rabbi look like?"

"Angry." Leah refused to look at him.

Jesus said, "Not all teachers are bitter like the one you met in Alexandria."

The young woman jerked to stare in his face, her lips parting. Joanna stepped closer to her ward. Somehow, Jesus knew more about Leah's past than Joanna did.

"He was wrong about you," Jesus said.

"No." Leah dropped her chin to her chest. "He was right. I deserve to go to hell."

Susanna and Joanna shared a shocked glance. Jesus lowered himself to one knee, peering up into Leah's down-turned face.

"You sinned, my daughter, but that does not define you." Jesus tilted his head until her eyes met his. "Repent, and you will be forgiven."

"Some things are unforgivable," Leah said. She took a step back, her expression shuttered.

Joanna hoped Jesus would press Leah and make her understand that she was still part of God's chosen people. But he rose to his feet. He squeezed Leah's shoulder and beckoned to a woman standing among a group of men. Threads of silver wove through her black hair, glinting in the lamplight. Crescent dimples framed her large mouth. She caught Joanna's eye and stepped forward, the dimples deepening.

"My name is Maryam," she said. "These are my sons, James and Joses." She gestured to a pair of young men in their twenties. At the sound of their names, they straightened, and James clasped Manaen's hand, nodding in welcome.

Joanna glanced back. Jesus slipped outside, flipping his mantle over his head.

She wondered what was it like to be him. He was filled with power, yet he took the time to welcome them and speak to a reluctant young woman. Jesus was a little younger than Chuza, but while Joanna's husband was one of the most powerful men in Galilee, Chuza's authority and responsibility were dwarfed next to a prophet of the Lord.

She realized Manaen was introducing her as the wife of Chuza, Antipas' steward. Her smile faltered as three pairs of eyebrows rose over doubtful eyes. She drew herself up to her full height, heat crawling up her neck. Whatever these people thought about the tetrarch, she and Chuza served the Lord.

"We brought money to help support Jesus," Joanna said, hoping to shift their focus. "Who do we give it to?" The others relaxed.

James turned and called, "Judas!"

A handsome man detached himself from his conversation across the room.

James chuckled at Joanna and leaned forward as if sharing a secret. "He has a head for numbers, so we put him in charge of the money, whether he likes it or not."

Judas caught the end of James' remark and gave him a patient smile. "I'm happy to help, however I can."

Joanna dug in her satchel and pulled out the handkerchief. Untying it, she held out the coins.

"Gold?" Judas' eyebrows shot up and he gave a low whistle. James and Joses leaned forward, jaws slackening.

Joanna's sense of inferiority shifted to pride as she tipped the coins into Judas' hand.

Susanna also handed Judas her money, a generous number of silver denarii. Judas' eyebrows rose even higher.

Maryam nudged her eldest. "And you were worried women wouldn't have enough to do, hmm? It seems there is much to be done besides making your supper." James snapped his jaw closed, and Maryam nodded approvingly at Joanna and Susanna. Joanna felt an instant liking for her.

"Speaking of supper," Maryam said. "I should help the others." Her smile encompassed Susanna and Joanna, and she tipped her head to Leah, who kept hidden a half-pace behind her mistress. "Would you three be willing to pitch in?"

"Of course," Susanna said.

Joanna followed Maryam into a small courtyard, hoping to find a way to help with the least amount of damage.

A cluster of women gathered around a bed of glowing coals, stirring two cook pots. Joanna sensed peace among them. A camaraderie. Something she feared she would never find among the women in the tetrarch's court. She shook off the moment of self-pity. She knew what it was like in Antipas' palaces before she married Chuza. But, she admitted to herself, she hadn't realized how lonely it would be.

The newcomers were put to work and Leah's skill was quickly noticed.

"Your mother taught you well," Maryam said, watching Leah's deftness with a blade.

Leah hunched. "My mother is dead. Michael taught me."

Maryam stammered for a response, and Joanna intervened. "Michael is the head cook for Herod Antipas. Leah learned a few things in his kitchen."

"So you are a cook's apprentice," Maryam said, her smile returning. "A worthy trade."

Longing gleamed in Leah's eyes for one brief moment, but she shrugged and scraped the dates into the pot. Joanna blinked in surprise. Despite Joanna's promise that she could choose her own future, Leah hadn't mentioned wanting to pursue a trade. But then again, the stoic girl was hardly forthcoming. Leah refused to be freed from the bond of slavery, seeming to prefer the protection of a legal contract rather than trusting that Joanna would provide for her out of kindness.

Joanna began kneading a mound of dough at a polished table,

her palms sinking deep. She understood the longing in Leah's expression, to dream of a future she wasn't sure she could have. Joanna had ached to do something for God since she was a child. She smiled to herself, remembering lofty hopes of becoming like Deborah, Elijah, or the wise woman who counseled King David. As much as she would love to be counted among the great prophets, to do miracles and hear God's voice, she would settle for a smaller role. When she married Chuza, she dreamed of the good they could do together.

Her smile faded. So far, she and Chuza hadn't been able to do anything. They hadn't even been able to keep Antipas from arresting John the Baptizer.

She gave the dough a heavy punch, the smack reverberating around the courtyard. Susanna raised her brows in question, and Joanna ducked her head, her cheeks warming.

Violent, selfish men had ruled for too long. Perhaps it was time for them to be swept aside. Joanna followed the daring thought. If Chuza and she served a godly king, they could do so much good, and no one would cast suspicious glances at them ever again.

She grinned, liberally dusting her dough with flour before turning it over. It was a pleasant dream, but perhaps that was all it was. She needed to know more about the kingdom Jesus proclaimed.

Jesus' words reverberated in her mind. *Follow me.*

Her time with the disciples was short. She would have to absorb as much as possible so she could share it all with Chuza. If the kingdom of God was coming, maybe there was a way she and Chuza could hurry it along.

# THREE

Chuza hunched his shoulders against the cold, driving rain, tugging his hood forward. Macherus loomed ahead of them, a city on a hill. The fortress crowned the summit and surveyed miles of countryside—the fringes of the Nabatean wilderness to the east, and the Dead Sea to the west. Perched on the edge of Antipas' borders, this desert city was now the unwilling residence of the prophet John.

Antipas rode at Chuza's side, his neck bent. The tetrarch's body slave rode on the other side, the young man's face deathly pale as he shivered. Guards flanked them, ready to defend their master, though no other travelers braved the lonely, muddy road.

They risked bad roads and winter weather. They left Herodias seething in Jericho because her husband once again journeyed to hear a man who dared to call their marriage a sin.

Their horses plodded under the city gate, where miserable guards saluted Antipas as he passed. The streets were nearly empty, the sensible residents warm within their houses. Streams of water rushed off roofs and funneled into underground cisterns. The earth was sodden now, but in a few months, the soil would crack beneath the blistering heat of summer and this rainwater would keep the citizens alive.

Antipas' small retinue picked their way uphill, the road snaking as it approached the palace-fortress. Chuza sighed with resignation. He hadn't wanted to come along, but Antipas insisted. Chuza had been Antipas' slave since he was six—maybe seven. Time clouded his exact age, but after three decades together, Chuza suspected he understood Antipas better than any man. They were friends, though the sharp lines of master and slave never fully eroded.

He had been chosen to accompany Antipas to Rome over two years past, when Antipas stepped from his prescribed path and fell in love with his brother's wife. Chuza shifted in the saddle as if he was sore, but it was his conscience that pained him. Antipas had brought Chuza and not his foster-brother Manaen, who would have condemned Antipas' decision to divorce his wife, the Nabatean princess, Phasaelis.

And now Antipas dragged Chuza along while he visited the imprisoned Jewish prophet. Despite the chill, Chuza's face burned. He despised being the friend Antipas could be himself with, the one who witnessed Antipas' selfishness and disdain for the faith he was supposed to uphold. But Antipas did not fear his steward's censure, and that made Chuza a choice companion.

Just outside the palace gates, they passed a clump of bedraggled men. Rain dripped from their hems and the ends of their long beards. Belatedly noticing Antipas' approach, a palace guard jerked to attention, swinging his spear at the waiting men. "I told you to leave! You will not see your prophet today!" They refused to budge.

Chuza winced beneath the heat of their glares, and one spat on the ground as Antipas' party passed. It seemed the disciples' fervor had not faltered with John's imprisonment. Chuza had a sudden image of Joanna standing amid the dripping men, her hair plastered around her face, her expression accusative. He shook his head, loosening icy raindrops to trickle under his hood and down his neck. Joanna was far away. Her prophet was safe, and Chuza would do everything possible to keep it that way.

They dismounted inside the gate and grooms led the horses to the stables for a well-deserved rub-down. The housekeeper bustled forward, eager to please. He bowed. "There are fresh towels in the bathhouse, my lord."

Antipas beckoned to Chuza, and the two men entered the dim, delightfully warm room. A hidden furnace warmed the Roman bath, piping steaming water into a tiled pool.

"I've been dreaming about this moment all day," Antipas said, tossing aside his sodden clothes and stepping into the deep water.

Chuza followed him in, a sigh of relief escaping as heat covered his tense shoulders. Servants entered, bringing dry clothes and waiting by the wall.

The men soaked for several minutes as the water lapped in the peaceful chamber.

"You've been moody," Antipas said. Chuza glanced over. The tetrarch's head lolled back against the tile. "You think I should avoid the prophet. Just like my wife."

Chuza flinched at the comparison to Herodias. She was no Jezebel, but neither was she a godly woman.

"You confess with your own lips that he is a prophet," Chuza said.

"And?" Antipas' tone warned Chuza to tread carefully.

Chuza wiped his damp forehead. "Is it... right to keep a man of God imprisoned?"

"I'm keeping him safe!" Antipas said, sloshing upright. Tension thickened the humid air. "Herodias isn't the only one offended by him, or haven't you heard how he called the Pharisees and Sadducees a brood of vipers? They would rather stone him than listen to him."

"But he's a prophet. How can he speak to the people when he's locked—"

"You think they deserve his message more than I do? More than the tetrarch of Galilee and Perea?" Antipas' nostrils flared. "The prophets of old came before kings. Am I not a king in purpose, if not title?"

Chuza hastily shifted tactics before Antipas' temper boiled over. "Are his words helpful to you?" The waiting servants straightened, eager for gossip. Only the prison walls were privy to whatever Antipas and the prophet discussed, though theories abounded.

Antipas' expression eased. "Truthfully, I hardly understand a word. His speeches are... perplexing." He grinned and leaned closer. "I'm sure there is truth in his messages—if I could just puzzle them out of the prophetic rhetoric."

Chuza frowned. "So you will keep the prophet to yourself?"

Antipas fixed him with a steady eye. "God has not intervened, and so I have to think he approves of my keeping John safe. He is fed, sheltered, and his followers attend him. Can anyone accuse me of cruelty?"

Chuza opened his mouth to say more, to insist it was still wrong, but his words crumbled beneath Antipas' challenging stare. It was the same unfaltering glare that cowed Chuza throughout his life.

"They cannot," Chuza said.

"Exactly." Antipas let his head tip back and his eyes close. "So stop your brooding. I brought you to examine the housekeeper's accounts and keep me company. Don't dampen my mood. The weather is doing a thorough job of that already."

Chuza had soaked long enough. He rose, the water streaming in rivulets, and toweled off.

"A massage, my lord?" a servant said, his expression inscrutable.

"Not today," Chuza said. Though it would be a relief to knead the knots from his shoulders, he couldn't relax until they were far from Macherus.

He dressed in his dry clothes and stepped into the courtyard. Braziers flickered under the sheltering colonnade as the rain drove into the open space. Chuza skirted puddles and made his way to the housekeeper's office.

The housekeeper rose in surprise when Chuza entered, bowing to reveal his thinning crown. "You wish to go over the accounts tonight, my lord?" he said. "I thought you would refresh yourself after your long journey."

"Better to complete tasks before taking pleasure, don't you think?" The housekeeper tensed under the subtle rebuke, and Chuza warmed with perverse satisfaction, then guilt. Just because he was under Antipas' thumb didn't mean he needed to demean the staff. "You keep excellent accounts," Chuza said. "This should not take long.

The housekeeper relaxed and led Chuza through the palace expenses, referring to his meticulous records. The stacks of ledgers grew on the desk. Chuza listened with half his mind while the man lamented the rising cost of wheat and difficulty in procuring good oil.

Antipas must be with John by now, he thought, imagining a flickering lamp illuminating the prophet's face. He had never met the prophet, but he would bet money that the baptizer looked like his followers. But with eyes that blazed with fire.

Chuza realized the housekeeper was watching him expectantly. He cleared his throat. "I'm sorry. What was that?"

"Antipas often pledges a charitable gift when he comes to Macherus to entertain his friends," the housekeeper said. "I know this visit is brief, so I wondered whether he would offer one on this occasion."

"Oh yes," Chuza said, sitting upright, possibility filling his veins. "Antipas will be pleased to show favor to his citizens. What does the city need most?"

The housekeeper hesitated. "Well, the city could use more reservoirs for water, but—"

"Commission the work."

"It will be quite expensive."

"It is a vital need," Chuza said, feeling better than he had in

29

hours. "Antipas will shoulder the total cost."

"That is wonderful, my lord!"

Chuza smiled to himself. Antipas didn't respect his steward's opinion on relationships or spiritual matters, but he allowed Chuza free rein over his finances. If he couldn't make Antipas pious, he would at least make him generous.

Chuza stood and peered out the window. The rain carried the faint scent of roasted meat and his stomach rumbled. "I'm sure Antipas is getting ready to dine," he said. "We can finish this tomorrow."

"As you wish."

Chuza swept from the office and back to the courtyard. His mood faltered as Antipas emerged from a doorway and handed the guard his lamp. There had to be a way to nudge Antipas onto the proper path, a life of righteousness. Once Manaen returned, the two of them would plan the way forward together.

Antipas saw him approach and smirked. "Ah, I see time with a ledger has soothed you. Come, my friend. Let us determine if the cellar boasts anything worthwhile." He took Chuza's arm and they went inside, Antipas steering the conversation to safer topics than imprisoned prophets.

# FOUR

29 AD
SPRING

J oanna hitched her bag higher on her shoulder amid the hum of conversation. It was time to go home. Her feet itched to return to Chuza's side, but she couldn't shake the frustration that she hadn't found the answers she needed about the kingdom of God. If only Jesus was more like Chuza, with a clear plan laid out in orderly steps. Chuza would have maps, an itinerary, a budget... She chuckled to herself, affection for her husband warming her chest.

She scanned the small crowd of men and women, those who dropped everything to stay with Jesus. They were a motley group from many backgrounds, yet none of them faced the suspicious glances that drifted her way—just because her husband served Antipas.

The rest of her traveling party said their farewells and picked their way toward her. Despite her lack of answers and the constant internal pressure to show she was just as devoted to righteousness as any of them, it had been an amazing few weeks. Jesus moved from place to place, healing and teaching. He called the people to repent for the kingdom was near. Yet, he seemed in no hurry to confront the unrighteous rulers who plagued their homeland. Jesus was laughing with the sons of Zebedee, and concern furrowed her brow. The prophets of old brazenly accused kings to their faces. Some repented. Others had not.

Manaen, Susanna, and Leah joined her at the edge of the crowd. The four from the tetrarch's court turned and strode down the Galilean road that would lead them to Tiberias, then on to Jericho.

Joanna peeked over at Leah. The young woman hummed to herself as she tramped through the brown grass. Leah broke off a long stem and whipped it like a feeble sword, lost in her own world. She was another reason Joanna wished they could stay with Jesus. Rather than drawing nearer to the miracle worker, the girl preferred to watch Jesus from afar—perhaps to discourage him from revealing any more of her past.

Joanna burned to know what Leah had done to warrant such hateful words from a rabbi, and why Leah wouldn't accept forgiveness or her birthright among God's people.

Joanna's father shaped her mind and heart with scripture. The stories of her people buoyed her through trying times and devastating loss. If Leah could sit at Jesus' feet, Joanna knew she would be comforted and healed. But if they remained, Joanna couldn't be with her husband. The push and pull of opposing desires drew a sigh from her lips.

She peeked to the side. Manaen's forehead was a stack of creases.

"Wishing you didn't have to escort three women to Jericho?" Joanna asked.

Manaen twitched in surprise. "Of course not," he said. "We started this journey together, after all."

"But now what?" Joanna asked. They had seen Jesus and given him money, but nothing had changed. The kingdom of God was little more than a pretty thought. Susanna met her eye and Joanna voiced the gnawing question. "What do we do now?"

"I am going to rejoin them," Manaen said with a resolute nod. "I'll see you both home, then I will return to Jesus."

"I am happy for you." Susanna patted his arm.

Joanna turned her face to study the horizon, wrestling against her frustration. Manaen could go where he liked, but Chuza needed permission to leave Antipas' side. Which meant if Joanna wanted to be with her husband, she couldn't be with Jesus. It wasn't fair that she had to choose.

The breeze rustled the grass, accompanied by the hum of insects and the soft trill of birds. They passed other travelers and greeted them with words of peace. Susanna and Manaen chatted, but Joanna remained silent, contemplating the problem of Antipas.

Their journey took them through the hills that surrounded the Sea of Galilee, emerging in Magdala and turning south around the shore. The road hugged the water's edge, leaving more room for homes and crops.

Susanna invited them to spend the night at her home, but Joanna only half-listened, her thoughts roving ahead. A prophet declaring a kingdom of God would sow chaos in the court. Lines would be drawn. And Antipas might refuse to let Chuza stand on the side of righteousness.

In the open fields and rural towns of Galilee, Jesus' ideals seemed not only possible, but natural. But now she was coming back to harsh reality, where there were unbelieving men and women to be served and everyday tasks to be completed. Joanna wasn't sure how she could commit to Jesus' teachings while living in the real world. Her worries swirled around in her head, making it ache.

The next day they left Tiberias through the southern city gates and took the road following the Jordan River, veering into Antipas' other territory, Perea. They stayed overnight in an inn, then spent their second night in the province of Judea. Early on the third day, they approached Jericho. The vast city was divided into two sections, with a road spanning the short distance between the old portion of the city and the new.

Susanna led them to her in-laws' home in an affluent district. Generational houses stood two or three stories tall, shaded by palms and sycamore trees. Servant girls chatted, balancing water jars on their hips. Laughter from a children's game down the street caught Leah's attention, and baking bread watered Joanna's mouth. They stopped at a pale house with double doors.

Before Susanna knocked, she pulled Joanna into her arms.

Joanna clung to her. "I feel like it's all over," she said.

Susanna offered a comforting smile. "We can bring Jesus' teachings with us, wherever we go."

Joanna understood the sentiment, but carrying Jesus' teachings in her heart wasn't the same as living them out among those who believed. Years ago, Susanna warned Joanna against showing Antipas up in piety. She couldn't even recite the blessings in front of the tetrarch.

Susanna knocked on the door and pushed it open. The servant gasped when he saw her, and as Susanna stepped into the portico, her name reverberated off the walls and feet came running.

"Susanna is here!"

"Mother, you're back!"

Joanna smiled, knowing Susanna's joy would be complete as she reunited with her family.

The remaining trio pressed on to the palace, and Manaen stopped a stone's throw from the main gate.

"You won't even come in to rest?" Joanna asked.

"Not this time," Manaen said. "I don't want to speak with Antipas. Not yet."

"Isn't he going to wonder where you've gone?"

Manaen tugged on his beard. "You, more than anyone, know why I can't tell him, and I don't wish to lie."

"Of course," she said. But Antipas couldn't remain oblivious to

Jesus' presence forever. With a nod of farewell, Joanna and Leah went on alone.

Joanna cast a last glance over her shoulder before entering the massive southern wing of the palace. Jesus walked the windblown fields of Galilee while Chuza was constrained by gilded halls. Drawing a deep breath, she deliberately put aside her frustration. She summoned a servant to lead her to Chuza's office. Trailing after the young man down long hallways, they skirted a maid scrubbing the floor on her hands and knees. Fragrant incense sweetened the air, mingled with polished furniture and the clean scent of palace gardens that beckoned from every window. Deeper within the palace, someone plucked at a lyre. The familiar scents and sounds rekindled Joanna's everyday concerns.

The servant stopped by a carved door. Joanna entered, Leah in tow. Chuza bowed over his desk as Michael pointed at a sheet of papyrus with his thick, scarred hands. The grizzled cook, barrel-chested and with thinning hair scraped back into a ponytail, looked more like a retired soldier than a master of delicacies.

Michael looked up first, his wide face splitting when he saw Leah. "Finally! Some decent help for my kitchen!"

Chuza jerked in alarm. His startled expression shifted to joy.

Unable to wait, Joanna rushed forward, throwing herself into her husband's arms. His embrace wound around her, tight and warm, and she inhaled the scented oil in his dark curls. A missing piece of her heart slid back into place. She cupped his bearded face and poured her emotions into a kiss.

Remembering they were not alone, Chuza drew back. He cast a sheepish grin at Michael, who had averted his gaze.

"Hello, Leah," Chuza said.

Leah replied with equal politeness, and Joanna pursed her lips, realizing two people she held dear barely knew each other. She stored that problem away to deal with later.

Joanna studied her husband's cluttered desk. "What task have we so rudely interrupted?" she asked with a teasing smile.

"Antipas just returned from Macherus," Chuza said, his expression sobering. "Herodias wants a feast tonight." Chuza held out a list. "What do you think?"

She scanned the menu, her eyebrows rising at the long list of delicacies. "A feast fit for a king," she said, nodding at Michael in compliment.

"The ingredients cost a king's ransom," Michael said. "But Herodias wants only the best. She hopes if he won't stay for her charms, he'll stay for his stomach." He winked at Leah and the girl twisted her lips in amusement.

Joanna turned to her husband. "Are Antipas and Herodias arguing?"

"A little," Chuza admitted. Michael snorted in disagreement, and Chuza shot him a warning look.

Michael raised his hands in surrender and stepped toward the door. He spoke to Leah, "Come find me once you've settled in. I'll need your help."

Leah nodded, her eyes sparkling.

Chuza tilted his head as the cook disappeared into the hallway. "Why does he need you?" he asked Leah.

Leah's humor dissipated, and she shrugged. "He's joking."

Joanna hid a smile. Chuza prided himself on knowing everything that happened in the household, yet he was apparently unaware that Joanna's maid was in the kitchen every chance she found.

Chuza moved to the door. "I'll show you to our room."

"How long are we staying in Jericho?" Joanna asked.

"Herodias is pushing for a move. She was excited to reacquaint herself with the city of her youth, but I think she's ready to create distance between Antipas and Macherus."

Chuza led the women from his office and down the soaring halls. They turned down a narrow hallway, with windows opening on one side, overlooking a lush courtyard. Dressed in elegant robes, a small group of women wandered amid the palms, arm in arm. Joanna's stomach flipped. This was her first time visiting Jericho as Chuza's wife. Would any of Antipas' extended family remember Phasaelis' companion?

Chuza opened a door and showed her a modest sitting room with a low table and couch. She walked through another doorway and into the private bedchamber. An intricate rug lay beside a bed covered with fine linens. A screen dappled the window, and a small mirror hung on the plastered walls above a vanity and chair. One of her robes hung on a hook, waiting for her. Chuza must have put it there. Her chest warmed, and she gave him another kiss.

"There is an attached maid's chamber," Chuza said proudly, leading them back into the sitting room. He opened a small door and showed them a tiny room with a soft couch.

"It's perfect," Joanna said.

But Leah stared into the room silently. After an awkward moment, Leah glanced between Joanna and Chuza.

"Does this mean I must continue as your personal maid?" Leah asked.

Chuza shot Joanna a confused glance, but Joanna seized the chance to show Leah kindness. She had saved Leah from the slave market, but the girl had repaid that debt many times over.

"No, of course not," Joanna said, taking Leah's hand and pulling her to sit on the couch. "I made you a promise, remember?"

Leah hesitated. "So I can choose?"

"You are my maid in name only," Joanna said. She leaned closer. "I think you should begin a trade. Perhaps as a groom in the stable? Or a blacksmith?" She squeezed Leah's spindly arm as if testing for muscles. Her teasing was rewarded when Leah covered a smile with her fingers. "No? Well then, I think the position of apprentice cook would suit you very well."

Leah's hand dropped from her lips, and her beaming smile was like the sun breaking through a winter storm. Joanna blinked with wonder. She would have given the girl anything she asked for, just to catch another glimmer of the soul Leah kept hidden away.

Leah shook off the smile and cleared her throat. "Well, cooking isn't what I had in mind," she said with a mock frown, "but if you think that's best." Chuza jerked his neck in confusion, and Joanna laughed. She rose.

"I'm sure you'll learn to like it," Joanna said, winking. She took Chuza's hand and pulled him from the room.

"What was that about?" Chuza asked.

Joanna led him to their bedchamber, keeping her voice low. "It's what she wants."

"If you're sure." He cast a doubtful look back at Leah's room. "Will Michael agree?"

"Of course." Joanna flicked her wrist, dismissing his concerns. "He has practically hired her already, or did the all-seeing steward not notice?"

Chuza lifted his eyebrows but accepted the teasing.

Joanna trailed her fingers over the robe on the hook. Her current attire was thick and serviceable, but in dire need of the laundress.

"Go back to work," she said. "Leah and I will bathe, and then I'll speak to Michael."

Chuza gave her one last peck on the cheek and left. Joanna and Leah followed a moment later. As they walked along the wide hallway, familiar voices drifted from somewhere out of sight. Joanna glanced down at her travel-stained robe and made a fist to hide her dirty fingernails. She straightened her back before they rounded the corner.

Herodias and Olympias strode arm in arm, thick as thieves and twice as analytical. Their eyes swept over Joanna like an icy wind. Joanna and Leah bowed.

"She's back," Olympias said, her lip twisting in amusement at Joanna's appearance. "This time with a maid of her own." Leah stepped closer to Joanna.

"We were so pleased to hear about your recovery," Herodias

said with a sweet smile. "Yet, instead of rejoicing with your husband, you ran back home. Is married life not quite what you expected?"

Joanna matched Herodias' honeyed tone. "I needed to check my vineyard. Chuza agreed I should go." She wished she could reveal her real purpose and wipe the smirks from their faces.

"Hmm." Olympias raised her brows at Herodias. "I guess we had it backward. Perhaps it is Chuza who finds his marriage bed... lacking."

The women snickered and Joanna narrowed her eyes. There must be juicier sources of gossip than the steward and his wife.

"We must celebrate your recovery," Herodias said. She fixed her cold gaze on Joanna. "You and Chuza shall come to the feast tonight." Her tone conveyed this was a command, not an invitation.

Joanna hesitated. Chuza had never expressed a wish to dine with Antipas and his wealthy friends, and her release from Phasaelis' side freed her from the courtly maneuverings that set her teeth like sour wine.

But she couldn't refuse Herodias.

Joanna bobbed her head in a bow. "Thank you. We will be pleased to attend."

"Excellent," Herodias said, then delicately covered her nose. "I suggest you... freshen up first." Tittering, she and Olympias continued their promenade.

Joanna's cheeks flamed as she stormed away.

Leah hastened to catch up. "What was that?"

Joanna sighed. "Women like her say one thing, but their eyes tell the truth. She will never forget that I helped Phasaelis escape."

They entered the large bathhouse, the damp, cavernous room echoing with emptiness.

Joanna piled her soiled clothes on a bench, considering what Herodias' resentment could mean. If Herodias dug too deep, she would unearth Joanna and Chuza's support for Jesus. That would be far more tantalizing gossip than a failed marriage.

39

Frustration rising, Joanna filled a raised basin and scrubbed at her skin until it was red. She stepped into the steaming water and fully submerged, tiny bubbles tickling as they chased each other to the surface. While just as overwhelming, palace politics were even more heated than this pool.

# FIVE

Joanna sat in her best peplos, turning her head before the mirror. A hairdresser had secured intricate braids with a needle and black thread. Joanna carefully scratched between the tight plaits, already missing her usual braid.

Chuza burst into the room and hastily changed his clothes, his brow creased. Joanna helped him smooth the neckline of his robe, determined not to show her nerves and add to his anxiety.

"Did Herodias say why she wanted us at the feast?" he asked.

"She thought we should celebrate my recovery," Joanna said with forced casualness.

Chuza nodded briskly. "We'd better go. We're already late."

The couple hurried to the dining room, their arms linked. Joanna shoved down churning emotions that kept trying to crawl up her throat. This shouldn't be any different than past feasts. Yet, in those times, she had been a princess' companion, unworthy of any more notice than the murals on the walls. Now it seemed she must serve as amusement for the tetrarch's new wife. Her pride rankled at the thought.

Chuza leaned closer. "I'm pleased to see Herodias welcoming you back to court."

Joanna made a vague noise in her throat.

"I don't understand why I'm so nervous," Chuza said with an awkward chuckle. "I know everyone in the room. And it'll be nice to have Manaen in court again."

Joanna stiffened. "I forgot to tell you. Manaen went back to Jesus."

Chuza stared at her. "Why?"

"He wants to learn more."

"Learn more? Manaen is a scholar already!"

"Yes, but Jesus' teachings are different," Joanna said. "I can understand why he wanted to stay." The image of Jesus sitting among the open fields of Galilee filled her mind like a breath of fresh air, but she pushed it aside. She was in the palace now.

Chuza's gaze probed behind her words, but they had reached the doors to the dining hall. A pair of servants swung them open, and the melody of conversation poured out.

"We'll talk later," Chuza said, and his strain smoothed into a pleasant smile.

They strolled into the room side by side, as if they belonged among the wealthy men and women of the court.

Antipas sat on a couch, leaning forward as he boasted with his friends. Herodias draped against him. She laughed too loud when Antipas made a mild joke, and he raised his eyebrows.

Joanna turned her face to hide a smug smile. Phasaelis used to vie for Antipas' attention, and the more she tried to be close to her husband, the more Antipas pulled away. But Herodias wasn't usually so clingy. Antipas' visits to the prophet must be more threatening than Joanna realized.

"Chuza!" A man came forward, his palms spread in pleased surprise. "I don't think I've seen you at one of these gatherings before." He eyed Joanna with curiosity.

"Herod, this is my wife, Joanna," Chuza said. He leaned toward Joanna. "Herod is Herodias' brother. He's married to Mariamne, Olympias' daughter."

Herod inclined his head to Joanna. "Blessings for your continued good health," he said. Before she could thank him, he fixed Chuza with an expectant look. "Have you heard from Manaen?"

Chuza's expression didn't flicker. "He has not written to me. I'm sure he is still with his friends."

Herod clicked his tongue and stepped closer. "That's a shame. We could use him here." He tilted his chin to Herodias and Antipas.

Chuza followed his line of sight. "Yes, we could," he said, and sighed.

Joanna walked with Chuza in a circuit of the room, her arm hooked in his. He knew everyone by name, and they all had a word for Antipas' steward. She had never seen him in an environment like this. She hadn't realized how well-known he was, or how powerful he could be—if power was what he sought. But he seemed content to serve rather than be served. Jesus would appreciate that about him. She squeezed Chuza's arm, wishing she could pull him away from these people and show the disciples how wonderful he was.

Meanwhile, the other wives studied Joanna, narrowed eyes raking over her clothes and hair in silent judgment. She prayed she would not embarrass herself.

When it was time to eat, the guests were divided by gender and seated by rank. They reclined on couches arranged on three sides, leaning on bolsters as servants passed platters. Joanna had the lowest place, beside a snow-haired woman who ate like it was an assignment.

Joanna found the selection staggering after the bread and lentil stew of the past few weeks. She chewed a brined olive and closed her eyes with pleasure.

Herodias' voice cut through the atmosphere like an ax.

"You're not talking about the prophet again, are you?"

Antipas stiffened and faced her, his eyebrows meeting. "And if I am?"

"His words are meaningless," Herodias said. "He is a charlatan. A fake."

Silence fell over the guests.

Antipas studied her over the rim of his cup. "Then why are you so concerned about what he says?"

"I'm not," Herodias said, tossing her hair. "I just don't see why you must bore your guests with his ramblings. It's not like he's the oracle of Delphi." She tittered, glancing around the room, welcoming others to share in her joke. But everyone else averted their gaze.

Herodias caught Joanna watching, and her eyes blazed. "Care to honor us with your opinion, Joanna?"

Joanna's mouth dried. Her hope that the question was rhetorical faded as all eyes turned her way. Aligning herself with either spouse could spell disaster. But Joanna hadn't spent two years in court for nothing.

"Who is the oracle of Delphi?" she said, widening her eyes innocently.

Herodias took the bait and sneered. "Sometimes I forget you're only the daughter of a Galilean vintner."

This time, others did join Herodias in laughter. Joanna looked away, tugging at the neckline of her peplos, playing up her real embarrassment. While it was better to look like a fool than an enemy, she knew precisely who the famous oracle was, perched on her stool over noxious vapors, conjuring obscure phrases that passed as prophecy. She peeked at Chuza and his answering smile was sympathetic.

The guests' amusement faded, and Herodias glared at her husband, all pretense of humor lost. "John is a desert dweller who thought he could make a name for himself by provoking religious fanatics. Your continuous visits bolster his prestige among his disciples."

Antipas let her dig her own pit. "So?"

"So?" Herodias' voice rose an octave. "The man is inciting rebellion against you. His followers are spreading his lies across your lands. You shouldn't visit him. You should have him executed!"

Herodias and Antipas locked eyes and their guests studied the food before them.

Joanna's mouth turned to dust. Herodias wanted to kill John? She darted Chuza a shocked glance and shared his dismay.

Silence stretched, and no one moved.

Antipas turned to the man next to him and inquired about a stallion he had for sale. The man stammered a reply and the feast stuttered back to life.

Herodias' neck reddened at Antipas' summary dismissal. She leaned toward Olympias, and the two of them muttered. Joanna saw it with misgiving. According to rumors, Olympias helped plot the downfall of Antipas' half-brothers and uncles. If this family could kill their own, nothing would hold them back from executing a man from the desert.

Joanna drained her cup, and the watered wine strengthened her resolve. She surveyed the room, seeing past the wealth and ease. This family should not, could not, be the rulers of her people. She and Chuza were entwined in the tetrarch's court as tightly as if bound by chains, but there had to be a way to prove her and Chuza's dedication to God was greater than their loyalty to Antipas.

But those thoughts veered into seditious territory.

"Are you going to eat that?" a petulant voice broke into her plans. Joanna sighed and slid the platter over.

"I can't believe Manaen left again," Chuza said. He stormed across their room, dragging off his robe. He threw it on the floor and flopped to sit on their low bed, cradling his head in his palms. The view outside their window glowed with moonlight. "Antipas needs his guidance. After everything Antipas sacrificed to marry

45

Herodias, we can't have another unhappy marriage tearing the court apart."

Joanna felt no sympathy for Herodias. "Antipas and Phasaelis fought for a decade and it didn't hurt anyone—except each other."

Chuza raised his head. "She didn't have Herodias' connections in court. If Herodias stirs up the family, we will have trouble."

Joanna picked up Chuza's robe and draped it over the chair. "Do you really think Herodias will move against her husband just because he won't execute a prophet?"

"Herodias' primary concern is her name and the honor of her marriage. But the rest of the family watches for instability in Antipas' rule. There are others willing to take Antipas' place, you know." He fiddled with the hem of his tunic.

Joanna unhooked her necklace and placed it back in her small jewelry case. "What will Manaen do that you can't? He tried to keep John out of prison and failed."

"Things are different now. Antipas doesn't see John as a threat anymore. He believes in him, in his own way. There must be some way we can use that to set John free. Or at least keep him alive."

"If there is a way," Joanna said with full confidence, "you will find it."

Chuza's expression grew pained. "But I haven't. I need Manaen. He'll see a way through this mess. I will write him, insist he come home."

Joanna hesitated. "I'm sure he wants John to be safe. But I don't think he'll come back anytime soon."

"Why? How many miracles will it take to sate his sense of wonder?"

"It's more than the miracles," Joanna said. It was difficult to explain to one who had not seen him. "Jesus' teachings are ..." She struggled for the right word. "Powerful. Challenging. But not just that. It's like he sees something the rest of us can't. He doesn't just know what the scriptures say, but why. Listening to him feels like hearing the beat of God's heart."

Chuza's expression darkened. "You wish you were with Manaen, don't you? He's pursuing a prophet you admire, while I'm serving a man you despise."

Joanna flinched. She hadn't realized her warring desires were so obvious. But Antipas' behavior was not her husband's fault. She sat beside Chuza, her voice softening. "That's not what I mean."

"Isn't it though?" Chuza jerked away to stare through the window. He leaned against the frame, his muscles taut. "You wish you married a man with freedom, who serves who he wants, goes where he wants. You don't think I wish the same?" He tossed an angry glare over his shoulder, and she blinked. "Antipas listens to Manaen. And Manaen has abandoned us when we need him most."

Joanna stood too, her resolve settling. "We aren't powerless. There are things we can do."

He fixed her with a sharp stare. "Like what? I'm not plotting against my master."

"Not plotting. Preparing. If Jesus confronts Antipas like the prophets of old, he will insist John be freed."

Chuza's brow twitched with concern. "Jesus is coming here?"

"Well," Joanna hesitated, "he hasn't talked about it, but what else can he do? All the great prophets spoke to kings."

Chuza's reply was dry. "Yes, but not all of them were successful. I fear that if Jesus tries to reproach Antipas, he will face the same fate as the Baptizer. I need Manaen's help to sway Antipas first, get him heading in the right direction."

Despite the tetrarch's flaws, Antipas still held a place in Chuza's heart. "What if Antipas won't change?" she said carefully. "What if to bring the kingdom, Jesus needs to sweep aside the unrighteous rulers? Like Pilate." She paused. "And Antipas."

Chuza stiffened. "What are you saying?"

"I'm saying that if lines are drawn, we need to be on the right side."

Chuza kneaded the back of his neck. "How? You will flee the

47

court like Manaen?"

Joanna weighed her words. Balancing her roles and desires would take all of her skill, or everything she held dear would crumble in her hands.

"Eventually, I want to go back," she admitted. "I want to give more money." And she needed to learn more about the kingdom if she and Chuza were going to help it arrive. "But if you honestly think Antipas can change, maybe there are things we can do here."

Chuza nodded, grasping at actionable steps. "Antipas isn't ready for a confrontation with Jesus. We must try to deflect Antipas and Herodias' attention. Smother any rumors that make it to the palace. Antipas trusts me to be his ears, but I can filter what he hears." He hesitated, and she could see his honor warring inside.

She said, "Perhaps I can keep Herodias occupied with embarrassing me, instead of plotting against John." Her chest heated at the thought.

Chuza grimaced in sympathy. "You handled her well."

She winced. "I'm afraid the court believes you married an empty-headed idiot."

Chuza took her hand, giving it a squeeze. "Anyone with any sense will understand your answer. And voicing your opinions wouldn't have freed the Baptizer." He was right, yet that didn't make the humiliation easier.

"So that's the plan then," Joanna said with a nod. "We stall for time and give Antipas a chance to change." And Jesus time to gather supporters. Arresting Jesus would be a lot trickier if the people were on his side.

Chuza watched her pour water into the basin and wash her face, the tension draining from his shoulders. He returned to sit on the edge of the bed.

"It's almost Passover," he said. "I thought we would share the meal with your family."

She cringed, her sister's sneer filling her mind. "I didn't think you would want to do that, considering..."

Chuza lifted his eyebrow. "Considering your sister thinks I'm a traitor?"

Joanna grimaced. Dalia made no secret of her disgust at Joanna's choice to marry Chuza and stay in the court. "We don't have to spend the festival with them."

"So we share it with a court that casually discusses whether a prophet of God should live or die?" He dragged a hand through his hair, setting the curls on end. "Don't you think Leah deserves a Passover among a proper family?"

Joanna opened and shut her mouth. Chuza deserved a proper Passover just as much as Leah, yet her family felt like a poor offering. Miriam would be delighted to see them, but Dalia was suspicious and Amichai was off somewhere with his zealot friends, doing who knew what. But surely her broken family was better than the court.

"All right then," Joanna said. "We will spend Passover with my family."

Chuza's shoulders relaxed. "Thank you." She hoped he would not regret his request.

She unwound her belt. Chuza came to stand behind her, loosening the ornate pins that gathered her peplos at her shoulders. It was a maid's task, but Leah was fast asleep in her own chamber, worn out from her new duties. The soft garment slipped to the floor. Chuza's hands trailed over the thin linen tunic she wore underneath.

"I missed you," he said, his voice husky with desire. She turned, and he cupped her face with one hand, his other arm wrapping around her waist.

"I missed you too," she said, her lips softening as he brushed them with his thumb.

"How much?" he said. His brows rose in anticipation. She drew him closer, eager to demonstrate.

# SIX

Joanna squinted against the mid-morning sun as she, Chuza, and Leah picked their way through the teeming streets of Jerusalem. The ancient city was built on a slope, with Herod's Palace and the upper city on the west, and the temple raised on a massive platform to the east. The Antonia—a bulky fortress that housed Pontius Pilate's soldiers—hunkered against the courtyard of the temple compound like an unwanted suitor, its towers leering at the Jews worshiping below.

Jerusalem was a city at odds with herself. The palace of the cruel King Herod opposed the crumbling remains of the beloved King David. Humble Lower City dwellings shrunk below the spacious homes of the Upper City elite. Greek culture in the open-air theater challenged the sermons preached in the temple courts. The pious steps of the Pharisees whispered before the stomping tread of Roman soldiers.

The splinters within Joanna's family echoed that conflict. Her parents had staked their place in the middle ground, increasing their wealth by selling wine to Antipas' court while holding firm to the laws of the Lord. Amichai refused that compromise. Instead, he veered onto the path of the religious fanatics, eager to push Roman influence from the promised land. At any cost.

Joanna believed she was doing the right thing by marrying a righteous man in Antipas' court, but Dalia saw it as a betrayal. John's arrest surely bolstered Dalia's confidence that Joanna was supporting sinful men—which wouldn't make for pleasant Passover conversation.

She knocked on Dalia's front door. Muffled voices filtered through the thick wood. The latch was thrown and the door swung open to reveal Dalia's beaming face. Joanna's heart gave a beat of joy at this unexpected welcome, but Dalia's expression flattened. "Oh, it's you."

Joanna's heart shriveled. She thrust her basket forward. "You didn't tell me what to bring, so Leah selected a few delicacies from the palace kitchen."

Dalia accepted the gift as if Joanna offered an adder. "Is it clean?" she asked, her nose crinkling.

"Of course," Leah said, bristling beside Chuza.

Dalia didn't look convinced. "Well, I guess you better come in." She pivoted on her heel, leaving them to make their own way.

Joanna cast Chuza an apologetic glance. Maybe it wasn't too late to turn back. But Chuza gave her an encouraging nod and stepped into the narrow room, an addition to the ancestral home. Steps led to the upper levels, and sunlight shone from the door leading into the central courtyard.

The sounds of a joyous family reunion formed a lump in Joanna's throat. Her memory roved over festivals when traveling with her siblings was a carefree adventure. She remembered the fun of reuniting with cousins she hadn't seen for months and the sense of belonging.

The trio strode past baskets and bundles tucked in every available space and entered the sunny courtyard. A hush fell. Even the children stopped their play to see who had arrived. Joanna's cheeks warmed. Chuza wore an unreadable expression to hide his embarrassment, but Leah scowled openly at the stares.

"Joanna!" Miriam called, breaking the silence as she rose to her feet. The love in her voice was a balm after Dalia's coldness. Joanna hadn't realized how much she missed her mother. Miriam wrapped her in a hug, and Joanna and Chuza's names were passed around the courtyard like appetizers.

Miriam reached for Chuza next, and he kissed her cheek with only a hint of awkwardness.

Miriam cupped Leah's face with her palms. "You've grown. How lovely you are becoming!"

Leah blushed but didn't jerk back from Miriam's touch.

Clapping her hands together, Miriam summoned the pack of children, her two little grandchildren among them. "My dears!" she said, claiming their attention. "It is nearly time for the festival of unleavened bread. The Lord has commanded that no yeast can be anywhere in our house. Do you think we've found it all?" She tipped her head in question.

The children jumped up and down, shouting, "No!"

"Hurry, see if you can find any!"

The children raced to find the hidden bread, and Leah watched them disappear.

Joanna leaned toward her. "Did you want to help look?"

Leah twisted her brows in disgust. "I am not a child anymore. I was just... remembering."

For the hundredth time, Joanna wished Leah would be more open about her past. Even if her family was gone, there had to be someone, somewhere, who missed her. But Leah insisted she was alone.

While children tore through the house like a pack of wild animals, Miriam settled Chuza amid the other men. They eyed the steward with curiosity, and Joanna crossed her arms tightly against her chest, praying this day would pass without incident.

She drew a breath and turned to her mother. "Can we help with the meal?" Joanna asked.

Miriam smiled, but as she opened her mouth, Dalia interjected.

"Oh no," Dalia said, waving her away. "You are our guest. Sit and rest."

Joanna and Leah sat on the cushions Dalia offered, but Joanna saw her sister give other women tasks. Her cheeks heated at the forced solitude.

The children ran back into the courtyard, hollering and holding up the offending loaf. One little girl cried, disappointed she hadn't been the one to find it. Miriam ripped the bread into pieces and dolled them out, every bite vanishing in seconds. There would be only unleavened bread for the next week.

As the children returned to their games, the women's laughter in the kitchen complemented the lower hum of masculine conversation in the courtyard. Joanna peeked over at Chuza. He was doing his best to take part in another family's concerns. His effort made her love him even more.

Joanna and Leah sat for the next hour, conversing among themselves. When the men rose to attend the temple sacrifice, Joanna prepared to go with them, determined to escape. Chuza came to her side, and she slipped her hand into his.

Alexander brought the lamb from its pen. The children all rushed to say goodbye to the yearling, burying their fingers in its clean wool.

Joanna drew a relieved breath as they left the house and joined the throng on the busy street. Other families were making their way to the temple, leading their sacrificial lambs. The noisy river of people descended into the Lower City before climbing the steps up to a temple gate.

They passed the high walls and entered the Court of Gentiles, and the noise reverberated off the thick stone. Passover brought Jews from all over the known world, and pilgrims created islands in the crowd's current as they craned their necks, trying to absorb everything at once.

Sheep sellers passed lead ropes to men who scowled at the premium price. Money changers sat at their tables, exchanging foreign coins for the Jewish shekel, the only currency deemed suitable for temple donations. The crowd shuffled, muttering apologies while they bumped shoulder to shoulder, the air thick with the call of trade and the bleating of lambs and people trying to speak over both.

Joanna made sure Leah was on her heels as they wove their way into the Court of Women. Behind the tall walls, the noise of business dimmed and the relative quiet was a relief. Joanna hooked her arm in Chuza's and leaned against him.

The deep blast of the shofar echoed across the city. The Levites stood on the steps and began their songs as the first round of sacrifices began. Joanna caught glimpses of priests throwing lamb's blood against the smoldering altar. Curling smoke rose high into the sky, blackened by the fat and organs that were offered to the Lord. As the ceremony continued, the priests' white linen became more and more splattered with crimson. Deep channels prevented the stone floor from becoming slick, but the priests could not perform their duties without staining their robes with the blood of lambs.

In short order, men began shuffling down from the inner court, the meat wrapped in lambskin to carry home.

Leah rushed forward to pet the sheep before Dalia's father-in-law took the yearling up the steps to the Court of Israel. She returned to Joanna's side with flushed cheeks, and Joanna smiled. The young woman was growing, but hints of the child remained.

As the dark smoke spiraled and cooked meat mingled with sweet incense, Joanna traversed the scriptures that told of the first Passover. How simple it must have been, each man sacrificing his own lamb for his extended family, the wives cooking unleavened bread as they prepared to be led from captivity. Yet, at its conception, this night was a choice between life and death. Without the blood of the lamb smeared on their doorposts, the angel of death would have claimed the Hebrew firstborn along with the Egyptian. The Passover had been the final miracle—when Pharaoh was broken, Egypt was crushed, and the Israelites walked free. They became more than slaves, and God affirmed their birthright.

Many prayed for another miraculous rescue, for their enemies and the idolaters to be swept aside by God's righteous vengeance. Joanna wanted freedom too, and she wouldn't say no to a miracle. She scanned the crowd, wondering if Jesus was somewhere here, looking ahead to the future and the restoration of Israel.

Their weeks in Jerusalem passed slowly. Chuza made no inroads in his attempts to convince Antipas to free John. Herodias took every chance to show her disdain for the steward's wife and forced the other women to scorn Joanna's company. With Susanna away from court and Leah in the kitchen, Joanna was left without feminine companionship. She poured her energy into helping Chuza as his scribe, yet loneliness crept into her life. She even missed Phasaelis. The princess was spoiled and self-absorbed, but she had been a friend. Joanna and Chuza were like an island in the Great Sea, surrounded by dangerous waters that no one wanted to cross.

# SEVEN

29 AD
SUMMER

They arrived in Sepphoris after days of travel in the summer heat, a dusty caravan of horses, covered carts, and wagons of luggage. The city perched upon a hill, within easy distance of Cana and Nazareth.

Joanna dismounted from the cart in the stable courtyard and stretched. Leah stumbled down after her, rubbing her aching back. For the space of a breath, Joanna could imagine she was still Phasaelis' companion, a hostage for her brother's crimes.

"I'll scrounge up a bed in the maid's quarters," Leah said, grabbing her bundle. Chuza had warned them that his chambers in Sepphoris were small—too small to include Joanna's maid. "Do you need my help with anything?"

"You can go to the kitchen," Joanna said. "I might find you later though, so we can talk about... things." Leah was already walking away, pushing through the crowd of grooms and servants rushing to serve their masters.

Joanna pressed her lips together wryly. Well, hopefully Chuza would think her plan was clever.

Joanna strode through familiar hallways, her fingers knotted in her palla. She wanted to arrive before her husband, to tuck away the painful memories that steeped this palace and make space for better ones.

The office door was open. She entered the austere room. One wall was taken up with cubbyholes for Chuza's scrolls. A window illuminated his small desk, the polished surface unusually tidy. No mat softened the floor, though there was a couch she knew too well.

She sat on that couch while Chuza insisted Amichai's sedition implicated Joanna's whole family. Chuza had demanded Joanna stay as a hostage to ensure her father did not support Amichai's band of revolutionaries. Joanna could still see the pain on her father's face, his helplessness to stand against Herod Antipas' steward.

Joanna purposefully reframed the memories around the truth and her current situation. Despite the unpleasant memories, this room set her feet on a new path, and she believed good came of it, beyond giving her a husband she could love and admire.

She strode to the doorway at the rear, curious to see Chuza's bedchamber.

He was right, it was tiny. A low bed hunkered beneath a plain cover, hooks lined one wall, and a little table provided a place to eat. A solitary window offered sunshine, the cheeriest aspect in the room. The sparseness was inappropriate for a man of Chuza's influence, but Chuza had never sought the trappings of power. She raised her brow. He could at least have added a bit of color.

A shuffling sound alerted her to an arrival. She stepped back into the office to direct the servant on where to set their luggage. Joanna began unpacking, planning how to turn this dismal space into a proper home.

Chuza strode into the room, carrying the small chest with his most important documents. The warm scent of sunshine and horse followed him in. He nestled the locked box beside his desk. "Getting settled?" he asked.

"I am," Joanna said as she shook wrinkles from one of his robes. "But perhaps I shouldn't unpack everything."

Chuza froze, his gaze roving over her face. "What do you mean?"

She prayed he would see things her way.

"It's nearly harvest time on my vineyard," Joanna said. "I don't think anyone would consider it odd if I went home for a few weeks. A month even. To ensure the wine is properly blended and stored."

Chuza began putting away his scrolls, and she watched his mind at work. He spoke slowly. "But that's not what you plan to do."

Joanna stepped closer, lowering her voice. "I think I should return to Jesus. Bring more financial support. I'm sure what I gave before is long gone." Chuza didn't reply, and she drew a breath. "I've been mulling over what I learned last time, and I have questions only Jesus can answer." Still, he was silent, showing her his unreadable steward's mask. "Maybe you could come with me," she said, tipping to catch his eyes. "Antipas let you visit my vineyard before."

Chuza shook his head and her hopes fell. "Antipas was gone from Galilee for too long, he'll never approve a request to leave. I have meetings with tradesmen, accounts to go over, budgets to approve…" He rubbed the back of his neck and sat at his desk, studying her face. "What's it like, being with him?" he said wistfully.

She gestured to his scrolls, some of which held their scriptures. "It's as if the prophets of old have come to life. Remember how we wished to see the stories firsthand? To witness Elijah call down fire, or David strike down Goliath? All our lives, we have read about men of God, but now there is one walking our land."

Chuza's shoulders sagged. "You make it sound wonderful."

Joanna's heart tugged with sympathy. She went to him, and he pulled her to sit on his lap. "Jesus holds the answers we need to plan for the future," she said, setting her arm around his shoulder. "When is the kingdom of God coming and what will it be like? We can't prepare if we don't know what to do."

Chuza sighed. "If I was free to go with you…" he trailed off, leaving the rest unsaid.

Bitterness against Antipas rose in her throat like bile. After three decades of service, Antipas should free her husband. It was the only way to release Chuza from his vow. But perhaps it was too much to expect from a selfish ruler occupied with his own happiness.

Chuza squeezed her waist. "A month at harvest time shouldn't raise any eyebrows." He gave her a smile. "And now I won't have to worry about you being lonely while I'm catching up on work."

She studied his face, wondering if he was hiding his emotions from her. "You'll be alright while I'm gone?" she asked. His silence tugged on her heartstrings. She leaned closer, her lips teasing. "Perhaps I will kidnap you."

Chuza gave her a rueful smile. "As fun as that sounds, no. Don't worry about me. I'll be busy."

Joanna rested her cheek against his hair. Life would be easier if she didn't feel this pull to follow Jesus. Simpler. But only until the kingdom came in force. Oblivious peace came at a high price if everyone thought she and Chuza supported Antipas' sinful ways. And, she admitted to herself, she needed to get away from Herodias for a while. A few side-glances from the disciples were nothing compared to the outright animosity in the court.

*Follow me.*

All her life she had wanted to be called by God, and maybe he was calling her through Jesus. For what purpose, she had yet to discover, but she wouldn't find it in the tetrarch's court.

Joanna found Susanna the next morning and the women embraced tightly.

"How are your boys?" Joanna asked as they took seats in Susanna's suite. The sitting area was elegant and far larger than her and Chuza's room.

"They are well, and back with their usual tutor." Susanna smiled. "It is as if I was never ill."

"I'm happy for you," Joanna said. She scanned the room, making sure they were alone. "Now that things are settled, would you like to see Jesus again?"

Susanna hesitated. "What did you have in mind?" It wasn't the excitement Joanna hoped for.

"I plan to join the disciples during the grape harvest. I'll be gone a month."

"For so long?" Susanna toyed with the fringe on a nearby cushion. "I don't think Jaban would want me to leave again."

Joanna fought back disappointment. It was hard to imagine taking this journey without her friend. She leaned forward. "Will you ask him?"

Susanna's expression softened. "He likes me by his side. We are both expected to attend the upcoming feasts. Besides, it's not as easy for me to slip away without drawing notice, and Jaban won't want to lie. Truth be told, he finds it odd that so many women follow a prophet. He is more... traditional... than Chuza, I think."

Joanna knew she was unusual, but her spiritual instruction veered from the womanly sphere long ago. Perhaps that was why some rabbis tried to keep women focused on specific scriptures. Give a woman a little knowledge and households would be disrupted, with dishes unwashed and beds unmade. Total chaos. A smile teased at her lips.

Susanna leaned forward and placed her hand on Joanna's forearm. "There are many ways to serve the Lord."

"Of course," Joanna said. "I don't doubt your faith, and I'm happy you are content." She glanced to the door. "Chuza will be busy for weeks catching up on work. I'm sure he won't even miss me."

Susanna lifted her brows. "Now that I can't believe. I've known Chuza for many years, and he is a different man since he married you. You have brought light into his life."

Joanna made a face. "Sometimes I fear he got more than he bargained for."

Susanna chuckled. "A clever man needs a wife to match. You challenge him. Force him to grow. I don't think he would have been satisfied with anything less."

"I just hope I don't get him in trouble," Joanna said. Chuza still hoped Antipas would change, but Joanna feared Antipas' reaction when he discovered his steward subsidized a prophet—at least by proxy.

Susanna squeezed Joanna's wrist. "I'm glad he supports you going," she said. "I will expect you to tell me everything. Every single word." Joanna swallowed a pang. She was more than happy to recount her experiences, but it wasn't the same as sharing them.

"Before I forget," Susanna said, moving to a side table, "I've told a few friends about my healing." Joanna stiffened, and Susanna held up her hands to allay Joanna's fear. "They aren't part of the court, don't worry." She unlocked a small box and withdrew a purse. She offered it to Joanna. "We all want to give something to help the rabbi continue his good work."

Joanna accepted the heavy pouch. "I'll be sure he gets it."

"I will see what other funds I can raise, and I am saving my allowance from Jaban." Susanna looked down at her clothes. "I wonder if he even notices that I haven't bought anything new in months."

They shifted to lighter topics and Joanna reveled in the feminine conversation. She loved Chuza, but talking with a husband wasn't the same as chatting with another woman. She could have sat with Susanna all day, but Susanna was supposed to join the other wives in Herodias' rooms for the midday meal. Too soon, Joanna stood to go, the purse in her hand.

"When do you leave?" Susanna asked.

"David will write me when they begin the harvest. It shouldn't start for a week or two."

"Then you'd better make the most of your time with your husband."
Joanna laughed. "I'll try, but I bet he's already buried in ledgers."
"Oh, I'm sure you'll think of some way to distract him." Susanna
gave a roguish wink. Joanna pretended to be scandalized, her hand
pressed to her chest.

Joanna strode back through the palace halls, and loneliness returned
to follow her. The other women would share a meal, gossip, work
on their handicrafts, or play games.

Joanna lifted her chin. She should be grateful for Herodias' scorn.
It cut her out, but it also left her free to rejoin Jesus.

# EIGHT

Joanna stood near the gateway of the Sepphoris palace, clutching the strap of her satchel. A heavy purse of her and Susanna's coins nestled inside, proof of their support for the prophet. Perhaps it would be enough to dispel any lingering suspicion about Joanna's intentions.

She drew a deep breath of the fresh morning air, but the cloudless sky portended scorching heat. Ideal for crushing grapes. Not for long walks.

She gave her husband a stern look. "Make sure you take breaks to sleep and eat."

Chuza chuckled. "I somehow managed to stay alive before we were married, you know."

"I'm not sure how," Joanna said wryly. More than once in the last week, she had to drag him away from his desk and order him to take a meal. She had given Michael strict instructions to send him food at regular intervals, whether he asked for it or not.

Leah hurried forward, stuffing last-minute additions in her bag. She cast a longing glance over her shoulder. Joanna wasn't the only one torn between two worlds. She knew Leah wanted to be elbow-deep in sauces and dough, but there was more to life than work.

A familiar figure strode across the cobbles and Titus joined their little group. He was in his early twenties, his handsome face marred by a broken nose that was never properly set. He had exchanged his guard's uniform for a simple tunic and cloak, but his short sword hung in a sheath at his hip. Between his weapon and his cropped hair, anyone could tell he was a Gentile with Roman connections.

Joanna's stomach tightened with unbidden memories, but she shook off the ill feeling. Nothing that day had been Titus' fault. He might be a foreigner, but he protected her and Phasaelis during the riot, witnessing the worst day of her life. His discretion earned the steward's attention.

Chuza had commissioned Titus to escort the two women. To avoid unwanted questions about his absence, his other business was to gather a report from the centurion based in Capernaum.

Titus grinned at Joanna, offering a small bow. Leah folded her arms, raking him from head to toe, unimpressed. He winked at her, and she turned away with a sniff.

"Ready?" Titus asked.

Joanna turned to Chuza. Her stomach twisted like a wrung cloth, torn between wanting to go and wanting to stay. Chuza peered deep into her eyes and swallowed hard.

Titus seemed to sense the emotional tension. He clapped Chuza on the shoulder. "Don't worry," he said. "I will bring them safely there and back."

Chuza's grin appeared forced. "I will hold you to that," he said. He drew Joanna a step away. She pressed her lips together, tears threatening to fall. She hated saying goodbye.

He held up his finger in mock chastisement. "Enough dawdling," he said. "Don't you know I have work to do? Get out of here."

A laugh escaped. "I love you too," she said. She took a few steps before turning back. His encouraging nod tugged at her, but Jesus' words echoed in her mind. *Follow me.*

She realized Titus and Leah were watching and cleared her throat. Fixing a determined smile in place, she strode past them, leading them away from the palace.

Leah caught up to her. "Ease up, Joanna. Your face will scare children. Don't you want to go?"

Joanna let the smile slide off her face and sighed. "I do. But I want to be with Chuza too. I hate having to choose."

Leah's eyebrows rose. "That's why I'll never marry," she said with the determination of youth. "I will do whatever I please." Joanna cast her a doubtful look, and Leah smirked. "Of course, if you and Chuza ever stood toe-to-toe, I'd put my money on you."

Titus chuckled in their wake.

Joanna strode onward, muttering under her breath. She had just gotten used to surly Leah, now it seemed impertinent Leah was taking her turn on stage. Joanna hoped whatever version emerged next would finally be willing to reveal Leah's past.

They planned to spend the night at Joanna's vineyard, though Titus' presence created an unexpected hitch. Tirzah drew Joanna aside, and they both glanced back at the soldier. He swung his arms awkwardly as three little boys stared up at him in awe.

"A Gentile?" Tirzah's hushed voice was accusing.

Joanna explained in an undertone. "He came here from Antioch to learn more about the Lord."

Tirzah's eyebrows shot up. "And he decided Antipas' household was the place to be?"

Joanna winced, wondering if Tirzah thought the same about her place in the court. Her reply was defensive. "Perhaps soldiering is all he knows."

Tirzah pursed her lips as she considered. "If he's a God-fearer, he can eat with us," she said at last, "but please ask him to sleep with the goats. There is plenty of hay in the loft."

Joanna flushed at asking Titus to bunk in the barn.

Tirzah nudged her. "I will give him good blankets. He will be just as comfortable there as in the house. But I don't want my boys to spend more time with him than necessary."

Tirzah's eldest boy was nearly ten, the ideal age to dream about adventure. Few men claimed more adventures than a soldier traveling the world.

"I understand," Joanna said. "And we will leave at dawn."

Tirzah gave her a grateful smile. She turned to the kitchen, and Joanna blew a stray hair from her hot face. She couldn't believe she had overlooked the difficulties of traveling with a Gentile. She picked at her fingernail.

Titus might be a God-fearer, but his position enforced Roman laws and taxes on the citizens of Galilee—not exactly a man rural Jews would welcome. Her reputation was unsteady at best, and now the disciples would see her arriving with a Greek soldier at her side.

The next day, the trio arrived at the freshwater sea. Alternatively called the Sea of Galilee, Lake of Gennesaret, or the Sea of Tiberias, even a body of water couldn't remain neutral anymore.

They took the pass to Magdala, a bustling city that salted the daily catch and shipped it far away. They traveled the northern road, leaving the city behind for shorn fields of wheat and barley dotted with farmhouses.

A lone man with a basket of tools approached. At the sight of Titus' sword, he averted his eyes, but Joanna hailed him.

"Peace be with you," she said. He slowed but did not stop. "Have you heard any news about Jesus of Nazareth?"

He jerked his thumb back toward Capernaum. "He's in town. But the crowd would be better served by returning to work, if you ask me. Next thing you know, they'll be lowering cripples through roofs again. I don't mind the pay, but..." he shrugged, holding up his tools.

Joanna thanked the man as he sidled past, giving Titus a suspicious glare before hurrying on his way.

"Well, he was friendly," Leah said, twisting her eyebrows.

Titus said, "At least we found out where your prophet is. I'll take you there at once."

Joanna imagined the stony stares Titus would receive if he approached a crowd of Jews inflamed with religious fervor. She needed a tactful way to avoid embarrassment—for both of them. She said, "Once we're in sight, you are free to continue on to your centurion. We can find the disciples on our own."

Titus mulled that over. His gaze turned after the wary stranger, then down to the weapon beneath his fingertips. Understanding flickered in his eyes, and they dimmed. "Alright."

Leah shot her a dirty look, but Joanna knew this was best for all of them. Maybe if Titus left his sword at home, he could have gone unnoticed, but the blade seemed as attached to the soldier as his arm.

They strode past hills that drew away from the road, the summer grass sprinkled with wildflowers in the fertile basin surrounding the lake. Joanna didn't want to make Titus feel like an outsider, especially when she knew him to be a good man. But sometimes others couldn't see past appearances to the goodness inside. She fidgeted with the strap of her bag. Maybe no one would see past her and Chuza's connection to Antipas' court either.

To Joanna's surprise, Leah struck up a conversation with Titus. Realizing the girl was trying to smooth over his hurt feelings, Joanna's conscience prickled.

"Where is your family, Titus?" Leah said.

"Antioch," Titus said. "My father is a merchant, and my brother works with him."

"Why don't you?"

Titus shrugged, the sparkle returning to his eyes. "Ever since I was a boy, all I wanted was to stand for what is right." He chuckled at the memory. "It earned me a few black eyes, but also a good number of friends. One day, I defended a young woman from an older man."

"Did you win?"

"I lost. Badly," Titus said with a self-deprecating grin. "But a city guard intervened and took both the girl and me to her father's house. Her father admired my bravery, even though I didn't have the skill to back it up. In thanks, he paid my admission to train in a ludus, giving me access to skilled masters. I planned to join the army, but I found myself needing to leave Antioch in a bit of a hurry."

"Why?" Leah asked. Joanna looked over, curious.

Titus shrugged. "For reasons that no longer matter."

"But why come here?" Leah pressed. "What drew you to Israel? You could have gone to Rome, or Egypt, or even Gaul. Why serve the tetrarch of Galilee?"

Titus chuckled. "You ask pressing questions for one so young."

Leah scowled. "I am nearly fourteen."

Titus swept her a gallant bow that was too full of good nature to be offensive. "My apologies, my lady."

Leah shook her head at him, hiding a smile and gesturing ahead. "I think we're here."

Capernaum appeared on the horizon. Sturdy piers thrust themselves into the water and shallow-keeled boats bobbed while fishermen washed their nets. The town was smaller than Magdala, but the noise of eager crowds traveled on the wind. The name of Jesus danced from lip to lip as the inhabitants abandoned their work to exclaim over a miracle. Titus stepped closer to the women, his brow lowering.

"I'm not leaving you alone in this," he said. "I will take you to your friends before I find the centurion."

Joanna began to protest, but Titus wouldn't rest easy until he knew they were safe. With a sigh, she snapped her jaw closed.

They wove through the packed streets, Leah following so closely she dislodged the heel of Joanna's shoe. Titus hovered, his eyes scanning the crowd. They passed the synagogue, an impressive building of dark basalt stone. It seemed too grand for a town of this size.

Titus leaned closer to speak under the noisy crowd. "Marcus the centurion commissioned the synagogue."

Joanna lifted her eyebrows. "Why did he do that?"

Titus' expression was veiled. "He loves your nation. He believes in your God, and he built this synagogue to show his goodwill. Though I don't know if he's welcome to pray there." His gaze held hers for a moment, laced with accusation, before dropping away.

Joanna rubbed her nose, staring over the crowd. What did he expect her to say? Committed converts joined in worship, but until a Gentile took on the ritual of circumcision, he would remain on the fringes of Jewish society.

"Does that woman need help?" Titus' concern interrupted her thoughts.

Joanna followed his line of sight to a narrow alley. A woman hovered in the shadows, wringing her hands as tears slipped down her cheeks. Noticing their attention, she jerked and retreated deeper into the shadows.

"Wait!" Joanna called over the crowd. She broke into a jog and darted between the houses.

The woman turned, holding her hands up. "Don't come any closer!" she cried out. "I am unclean!"

Joanna skidded to a halt, scanning the woman. The woman seemed in good health, if rather pale.

Joanna glanced over her shoulder. Leah and Titus watched from the street. "You seem upset. I just want to help."

71

"No one can help me," she said. She shook her head, releasing a fresh river of tears. "Except maybe *him.*"

Joanna didn't need to ask who she meant. She held out her hand. "Come on, I will take you to him."

The woman stared, her eyes luminous in the shadowed alley. "You know him?" she whispered.

"I do," Joanna said, her heart surging at being able to make that claim. "He healed me."

The woman wiped her cheeks with her palms. "From what?"

"A wasting disease. The physicians could do nothing to help me."

The woman barked a harsh laugh. "I know what you mean."

Joanna reined in her curiosity with difficulty. "Jesus will heal you, if you believe he can. All it takes is faith."

The woman looked away, and Joanna strained to hear her words. "I don't know if I believe. I want to, I really do, but my hopes have been dashed before. I don't trust my own judgment anymore."

Joanna took a small step closer. "Then trust mine. He can do it." The sounds of the crowd beckoned from the sunny street, but the woman stepped deeper into the dark alley. Joanna pleaded with her. "Don't let this chance pass you by."

The woman drew a shaky breath. "I just need a moment. You can go. Please."

Her tears had stopped, and her voice was stronger. Hesitating for a moment, Joanna nodded and walked back to where Titus and Leah waited. She stepped into the sunlight and prayed the woman would find her courage.

They wove their way down the street and the crowds thickened, a sure sign they were drawing close to Jesus.

A man shouted in panic. "Let me pass! I must reach the rabbi!"

Ahead, the man forced himself through the crowd, others stepping back to give him room. He wore an embroidered cap, askew and bent, and his prayer shawl dangled from one shoulder.

The crowd solidified, and Joanna could not get close enough to overhear, but in a few moments, they were moving again. Joanna rose on tip-toes, using her height to full advantage, peering over heads and finally catching sight of Jesus among his disciples. Her heart skipped a beat with excitement.

The wealthy man was leading Jesus down the street. The crowds stepped on each other in their eagerness to see where they were going.

A bystander called ahead. "What's happening?"

"Jairus' daughter is grievously ill," a voice called back. "He's asked Jesus to come to his house."

Joanna grabbed Leah's hand, giving it a squeeze. Perhaps they would see another miracle today. Joanna grunted as she collided with the man in front of her. The crowd had stopped.

"Who touched me?" Jesus demanded.

The people drew back, leaving a circle around Jesus. Jairus looked frantic at the delay.

"Who touched me?" Jesus asked again, and the crowd fell silent, no one willing to admit they touched the rabbi.

Peter leaned toward his rabbi, clearly embarrassed. "Master, the people are crowding and pressing on you."

But Jesus was insistent. "Someone touched me. I felt power go out of me."

Joanna sucked a breath as the woman from the alley stepped forward. She fell at Jesus' feet. "It was me," she gasped. "I touched you." Her voice was clogged with tears, and her next words came out in a sob. "I was afraid. I thought if I could just touch the fringe of your robe…" she trailed off.

A lump of pity rose in Joanna's throat as the crowd waited for Jesus' judgment.

Jesus' expression softened. "Daughter, your faith has made you well. Go in peace."

As she sagged with relief, a man elbowed into the crowd from the opposite direction, his outer tunic torn. He looked at Jairus.

"Your daughter has died," he said. "Don't trouble the teacher anymore."

Jarius paled. "No," he said, his face crumpling. "No!"

The people murmured in sympathy. Far away, the mourners began their keening. The familiar sound stung her eyes.

Jesus gripped Jairus' shoulder. "Don't be afraid. Only believe, and she will be made well." Jarius stared at the woman at Jesus' feet and nodded. He and Jesus moved on.

The woman remained bent double on the road, the crowd parting like a river around a rock.

Joanna stopped. She reached out, hesitating for just a moment, then rested her palm on the woman's back. The woman flinched, jerking up her tear-stained face. Her expression eased with recognition. Joanna took her arm, raising her to her feet.

"You did it," Joanna said, offering a wide smile.

The woman looked away. "I tried to believe, like you said. If he would touch a leper, maybe he would touch me." She glanced at Titus, and two spots of color bloomed on her cheeks. She lowered her voice. "I have suffered twelve years with a hemorrhage."

Joanna blinked in shock. "Twelve years!"

The woman nodded, pressing her lips together, a decade of suffering shining in her eyes. "I went to him, but the crowd was so close. I felt like I was drowning, I couldn't breathe. And when I nearly reached him, I fell. I saw the fringe of his cloak. The moment I touched it, I felt something. Something like… like…"

"Like light entered you?" Joanna whispered. She remembered God's Spirit burning away her sickness.

The woman's expression softened. "You know."

The crowd had disappeared around the corner, leaving the four of them alone in the street. The woman gave a damp smile. "Time for me to go home," she said, nodding once. She drew a sigh that plumbed a well of weariness and then smiled. "My life can begin again."

"You'll be alright?" Joanna asked.

The woman tucked her hair behind her ears, straightening her shoulders for the task ahead. "Oh, yes," she said. "I have dreamed of this moment for years. I know exactly what I'm going to do first." She strode away, her chin high.

Joanna turned back to the others, and Titus' eyes probed hers with an unspoken question. They made their way after the crowds, but he remained quiet.

"Did Jesus really touch a leper?" Titus asked at last.

"I guess he did," Joanna said, trying to gauge if he was intrigued or disgusted.

Titus' mouth worked, chewing on words he couldn't express. "Once we catch up to your friends, I'll head to the centurion's estate."

Leah tugged on Joanna's sleeve and raised her eyebrows in a sharp hint. Joanna's conscience smote her. Knowing how it felt to be regarded as an outsider, it felt wrong to inflict the same brand on Titus.

"Maybe you should stay," Joanna blurted. "Meet Jesus of Nazareth." Jesus touched lepers and the unclean. Perhaps Jesus would accept a Gentile soldier trying to find faith.

Titus wouldn't meet her eye. "Maybe."

They approached a noisy crowd packed by a large house. Jairus hoisted his daughter on his shoulder as he danced on the spot. She was only a little younger than Leah, smiling shyly at the attention.

It was impossible. Yet it was real. "She's alive," Joanna said, her pulse racing.

Titus shook his head, his eyes wide. "How?"

"The power of God," Joanna said.

Leah spun around and marched a few steps away, her hands clenched by her side. Joanna and Titus shared a confused glance.

Joanna stepped closer, and Leah stiffened. "You mean she was healed by God's favoritism," Leah said. She turned to face her mistress, her large eyes accusing. "Her father is obviously some kind of religious leader. Is that why his family gets this miracle?" The unspoken implication hung in the air. Leah lost her entire family, yet God had not intervened.

Joanna struggled for an answer. She had grappled with a similar question, wondering what would have happened if Jesus was there when her father died. She wanted to explain that sometimes God offered miracles, and other times he let things be, but everything she thought to say sounded shallow.

Joanna was ashamed to feel relieved when Manaen saved her from answering, hurrying up with a friend in tow. Manaen mussed Leah's hair in his usual way, but the girl jerked away. Manaen raised his brows at Joanna. She gave a slight shake of her head.

"Have you met Cleopas?" Manaen asked, patting the shoulder of the man at his side.

Joanna introduced Titus, and she didn't miss the suspicion that passed over Cleopas' face as his focus was drawn to Titus' weapon.

Peter strode past, beckoning to the men. "We're going to my house. My mother-in-law insists on feeding us all."

Cleopas and Manaen followed him at once, but Titus hung back, wrapping white knuckles around the hilt of his sword. Joanna's pity surged. He had witnessed Tirzah's hesitation at hosting him in her home. He saw the man's distrust on the road, caught Joanna's hints, and surely noted Cleopas' suspicion. Titus might be a God-fearer, but he wasn't one of them. Not really. He took a step away.

"I better get going if I want to report to Marcus before the sun sets," he said. He gave Joanna a wide yet empty smile, and marched away.

Joanna opened her mouth to call after him, but she couldn't assure him a warm welcome among the disciples. Jesus might be ready to touch lepers and unclean women, but not everyone could look past years of painful history with Rome. Or, she admitted with a pit in her stomach, overlook her connection to Antipas' court. She avoided Leah's dark stare and fell in Manaen's wake, allowing Titus to walk the other way. She had her own biases to overcome.

# NINE

His office door opened and Chuza glanced up from his work, ready to scold the servant for neglecting to knock. He saw who entered and jerked to his feet.

"My lady," he said with a small bow. "How can I help you?"

Herodias swept into the room. Chuza waited while her sharp eyes cataloged the wall of scrolls, the large Persian rug, and a colorful tapestry.

"Your office is smaller than I expected for a man of your position," Herodias said. "Though better decorated than they led me to believe."

Chuza chose not to point out Joanna's influence on the decor. He gestured to the side table. "May I pour you some wine, my lady?"

She nodded, taking a seat on the couch and arranging her robe. Herodias accepted the cup and took an appreciative sip.

She crooked her brow. "From your wife's vineyard?"

"We have a long-standing contract."

"How fortunate for her," Herodias said. Her false sweetness set his teeth on edge. "Any news about her harvest?" The thirst for gossip glinted in her eyes.

"It is a joyful time," Chuza said, avoiding a straight answer. "I have fond memories of Joanna's attentiveness to both the work and her staff."

"I suppose a man like you would choose an industrious wife." Herodias laughed. Chuza kept his face blank.

Herodias cleared her throat and set her cup to the side. "Let's get down to business. I want you to arrange a betrothal between my daughter and Philip."

Chuza blinked. "Your daughter Salome?"

"I have no other."

"To Philip? Antipas' older brother, Philip?"

Herodias folded her fingers in her lap, patient in the face of his confusion. "The tetrarch of Batanea and Iturea, yes."

Chuza needed a cup of wine after all. He moved to the sideboard as he attempted to gather his thoughts. King Herod's family was famous for their intermarriages, but this proposal was awkward. The prospective groom was older than the mother-in-law. The last time he saw Philip was during Antipas and Herodias' wedding. Philip was tall and handsome—for a man of fifty-five. Salome couldn't be over sixteen.

He darted a glance at Herodias. "The age gap is quite significant."

Herodias waved away his concerns. "Philip's mannerisms remind me of my—of Salome's father. She can be a flighty thing, and his calm maturity will steady her. As for Philip, a young wife will be a blessing to him in his later years."

Chuza's mind dashed ahead, trying to foresee Herodias' plans. Philip had ruled long and well, and his tetrarchy was secure. It was possible that Herodias simply sought a promising future for her daughter and potential grandchildren. But the marriage would also keep Philip from forming any other attachments, ones that would complicate who inherited after he was gone. Currently, Antipas was the natural choice.

All this raced through Chuza's mind in seconds. He gave Herodias a polite smile. "And how can I help?"

"Go to Philip and present the idea to him. If he agrees, you have your master's full confidence to arrange the contract to mutual satisfaction. I want everything settled before my daughter arrives. A betrothal will make a lovely surprise, don't you think?"

Chuza was not sure Salome would agree.

"I should speak to Antipas first," Chuza said.

Herodias' expression darkened. "You doubt my authority? I assure you, Antipas wants what's best for my daughter." She held his gaze in silent challenge.

"Very well. If Antipas can spare me, I will go to Caesarea Philippi and present the offer."

Herodias rose with a rustle of fabric, her smile back in place. "Excellent."

Chuza bowed, and she glided from the room.

He drained his cup. Herodias regained her standing in the royal arena with her marriage to Antipas, but the victory was not enough to placate her. She seemed determined to claw back the future she and her siblings lost the moment Herod executed their father. Chuza shuddered to think of the political turmoil she could create.

He returned to his desk, uncomfortable with the shifting dynamic in the court. He hadn't appreciated a complacent master until it was too late.

Pulling a wax tablet closer, he began drafting a betrothal contract. At least a trip would help pass the time until Joanna's return.

Chuza rode away from Caesarea Philippi, the signed betrothal secure in his satchel. He and Philip had set the wedding date for one year from now. Herodias would be happy.

It was a relief to leave Philip's capital behind. The ancient site was lined with temples, all large and beautiful—and woefully pagan.

Like the rest of Philip's domain, the city was a melting pot of cultures, and it was only by the tetrarch's indulgent, peaceable nature that they could live in harmony together.

Chuza shifted in the saddle, knowing that would be the place Salome called home. He did not know the depth of Salome's religious instruction, but she was Jewish by birth. Was it right to marry her to a man who allowed a pantheon of gods?

The city fell away behind him, and Chuza was determined to set aside his concerns and enjoy the long ride through Philip's territory. It was more than he could claim for the silent guard in his shadow. The man grumbled against the unrelenting sun in the cloudless sky.

With such company, the day crawled by. Heat shimmered over the road. Chuza's back grew damp, and he pulled his hat forward to shield his eyes. At midday, he purchased freshly picked figs from a farmer and ate the tender fruit while they rode, licking the juice that dribbled down his wrists, sweet as honey.

It was late afternoon when he stopped at the Sea of Galilee. Chuza soaked a scarf, draping it around his neck. Celer drank deeply of the fresh water and nudged Chuza's shoulder, hoping for some of the grain in his saddlebag. Chuza squinted at the busy lake. Some of Jesus' disciples were fishermen, Joanna said. They should be hauling in their nets, but they had given up their livelihood to follow a rabbi. Their choice seemed irresponsible, yet he felt a twinge in his core, a wish that he was equally free.

Chuza had just enough time to make it to Magdala before nightfall. He knew he should push on, but perhaps he could discover his wife's whereabouts. Maybe even talk with her. Once the idea was planted, it was impossible to ignore.

Chuza stopped at the centurion's estate on the outskirts of Capernaum. A servant offered to hold Celer's reins, and Chuza asked after Titus.

The boy grinned as if he knew the cheerful soldier well. "He's exercising with the soldiers behind the barracks," he said.

Chuza gave his satchel to the guard and strode around the villa toward a rectangular dwelling with a passageway through the center. His curiosity was piqued by the clack of wooden swords and grunts of exertion.

He entered the practice area and scanned the groups of men in short tunics. Muscles gleamed with sweat as they thrust weapons at each other or hacked at one of the splintered dummies. Chuza drew their notice, conspicuous in his expensive robe. He folded his hands and swallowed unwanted feelings of inadequacy at the masculine display. He had trained for life in court, not a battlefield.

Titus glanced over and twisted his wrist, spinning his sword in an effortless circle, grinning. Tossing his weapon to a waiting slave, he snatched a towel and wiped his face, his hair damp against his flushed skin.

"Chuza!" Titus called. "I wasn't expecting you. Have you come to collect your wife?"

Chuza drew him away from the practice courtyard and listening ears.

"Where is Joanna? If you're here, I'm assuming they're still in Capernaum?"

Titus shook his head. "Jesus has gone to Chorazin. I was going to accompany them, but Manaen assured me he would keep an eye on Joanna and Leah."

Chuza pressed his lips together. He had intended Titus to remain closer to Joanna than this. Titus studied his expression, then looked down at his hands, rubbing them unnecessarily with the towel. "I find it difficult to stay near the disciples. Being Greek, I am… out of place among them."

"You are a God-fearer," Chuza said with a frown. "Are you not righteous enough to wander the countryside?"

Titus flushed. "Don't worry about her safety. She travels in the company of many women, and there are capable men to protect them. I keep tabs on their whereabouts, and Chorazin is not far.

There's been no trouble—well, not counting some disgruntled Pharisees."

Chuza studied the hills turning dusky in the twilight. Chorazin was just a couple of hours away, but in the wrong direction. He sighed with resignation and turned to the soldier. Titus' cheerful personality pulled on him like a current.

"Would you like a drink, maybe something to eat?" Titus offered.

The fig had been hours ago. "Yes," Chuza said, surprising himself. "I would like that."

Titus inclined his head, looking pleased. "Come on," he beckoned. "There's always bread and beer in the hall."

The guard's ears perked up, and Titus obligingly invited him to join. Chuza wished he hadn't. Thankfully, Titus noticed Chuza's reluctance, and when they entered the cool, shadowy dining hall, Titus steered the guard to a pair of soldiers tossing dice. The guard settled in with them, rubbing his palms together.

The remaining pair filled mugs and sat opposite each other at a long wooden table. Chuza took a sip of his barley beer, wiping off the residue that clung to his beard.

"She is well," Titus said, reading Chuza's mood with uncanny ease. "Jesus draws a large crowd with his miracles and wise words. She seems to enjoy being a part of it. Last time I saw her, she was rambling about the Sabbath being for man, not man for the Sabbath. Whatever that means." He chuckled.

"I'm glad she's happy," Chuza said, but he rubbed at an ache between his ribs. He hoped Joanna would learn all she needed this time.

As Titus took a deep draft from his cup, Chuza cleared the emotion from his throat.

"So," Chuza said, his voice a little rougher than usual. "What caused a young man to leave Antioch?"

Titus cast him an amused glance. "Does every Jew find it odd that I would come to Judea?"

Chuza worried he had offended the soldier. "If you'd rather not say—"

Titus laughed. "I am only teasing. Leah was also quizzing me about my past. As I told her, I had to leave the city."

"Why?"

Titus grinned. "The usual reason. A woman."

"Now I must hear the whole story."

Titus rose to refill his cup. "You will be disappointed. It is a short one. I fell in love with my patron's daughter, and he caught us in a rather, uh, compromising situation."

Chuza lifted a brow, and Titus raised his hand as he slid back into his seat. "I didn't include that detail in my tale to the women. Her father's patronage only extended to my training as a soldier, not to my becoming his son-in-law. I couldn't watch the woman I loved given to another man. So I left."

"But you did not join the army."

They both glanced over as the dicing men roared at a good toss. He and Titus shared a grin that softened the ache inside Chuza's chest. He couldn't remember the last time he sat with a friend like this.

Titus said, "I was going to. I planned to sail to Lycia and enlist there. I booked passage and boarded the ship with a horse and my armor. My patron wrote me letters of recommendation."

"So why—?"

"I met a rabbi," Titus said, and answered Chuza's startled expression with a grin. "There were some... unsavory characters on the same voyage. I don't know if you've witnessed the animosity some have toward your people—"

"I have."

"Well, I couldn't let them push an old man around. The rabbi was grateful for my help, and while we sailed, we talked. I'll admit, I was feeling pretty bitter about life. I asked him questions about his God, planning to shred his monotheistic faith to pieces with my reasoning." Titus looked sheepish. "My misery desired company, it seems." Chuza gave him an understanding nod, and Titus continued.

"He was not afraid of my arguments. His calm assurance that he was one of God's people by birthright was new to me. My family provided offerings to the gods, but I never felt the gods cared for mortals beyond what we could give them." He waggled his eyebrows, refusing to be serious. "Perhaps I was an easy target for a sermon, alone and heartsick."

"So what then?"

Titus leaned his elbow on the table and rubbed his jawline with his forefinger. "We parted ways in Lycia, but I booked passage for Caesarea Maritima. I wanted to visit the temple the rabbi described with such reverence. I rode to Jerusalem. No one warned me your country was so dusty. I thought I would choke on the way and become food for the birds."

Chuza chuckled. "Was it worth the ride?"

"As a Greek, I couldn't enter the inner courts, but I saw the gleaming white marble and gold and stood where I could hear the songs of your priests. I smelled the sacrifices and the incense." Titus trailed off, his expression unusually thoughtful for the young soldier. He leaned forward. "Something... called to me. My soul stirred in a way I had never experienced."

A shiver rippled along Chuza's skin.

Titus said, "I spoke to a man willing to teach me the commandments I must follow to be righteous. A God-fearer. When I learned Antipas' captain of the guard was recruiting men, I applied at once, wanting to stay close to the temple. And that is my story." He leaned back.

Chuza took a long drink. He couldn't imagine not living under the commandments, or not knowing from his youth that he was part of God's chosen people. "How do you find our laws?" he asked.

"They seem practical. A path to an honorable life."

"And do you like our history? The stories? We draw much of our wisdom from the lives of the patriarchs and our ancestors."

Titus lifted his shoulders. "I only know a few."

"But you must have heard them in synagogue."

"I haven't gone," Titus admitted. "I wasn't sure which ones accept uncircumcised God-fearers, and I do not know the benedictions or the prayers..."

"I will help you," Chuza said, stunning himself with his impulsive offer.

"Would you?" Titus smiled. "I have been following the seven laws the man gave me, but I still don't feel God's presence in my life. Not like my first time in the temple."

"I don't know if I've felt the Lord's presence in the way you describe," Chuza said. "I'll admit, sometimes he seems very far away. I have never experienced the Lord as he appears in the scriptures. Never heard his voice, never felt his hand guiding me. Perhaps that is my fault, however."

Titus glanced over his shoulder. The men were crowded around the dice, jeering and teasing one another.

"Is that why Joanna wants to be near the prophet?" Titus said, too low to be overheard. "To experience the God of your stories?"

Chuza spun the mug in his hands and nodded. "Our people haven't received a great prophet in hundreds of years."

"And now there is one walking and talking and performing miracles."

Chuza leaned closer to Titus, resting his forearms on the table. "Have you seen any?"

"Miracles? I have. Have you?"

"He healed my wife, and that is enough for me to believe in him."

"But not enough to go see him for yourself?"

Titus had struck a sore spot, and Chuza struggled to keep his tone low. "Of course, I want to see him, but that action would have consequences. Word would spread if Herod Antipas' steward visited a miracle-working prophet." He pressed his palms into the rough wooden tabletop. "Antipas will learn about the Nazarene and everything he can do."

Titus mulled that over. "But wouldn't it be better coming from you?"

"He is not ready. He will react… badly, I'm afraid."

"How do you know?" Titus asked.

The image of John's disciples in Macherus rose in Chuza's mind, their stares accusing him. Herodias' anger wasn't the only reason John was in prison. Antipas reveled in having a prophet of his own, a direct connection to the supernatural.

He drew a sigh. "I've known him all my life."

Titus considered, then nodded. "I'm sure you know what is best." He turned the conversation before the others noticed their whispers.

But Titus' words niggled at Chuza. He feared he was being a coward, letting a prophet walk the land without trying to see him. He tipped back his mug and drained it. As Antipas' steward, he had learned that practicalities must overrule desire. Someday, when the risk was less, he'd go.

Chuza returned to the palace without seeing Joanna, afraid that if he approached her among the disciples, he wouldn't be able to stifle the rumors that would fly to the palace. He wasn't ready for his master to learn about Jesus. Not while Antipas kept a prophet in prison.

Chuza knew that Joanna secretly wished Antipas would be pulled from power. Maybe she was right, that life would be simpler if they served a righteous man. But until the kingdom she believed in was in place, fully and completely, powerful men weren't going anywhere.

And Chuza's life was tied to Antipas. If Antipas refused to repent and was forced to step aside, there was a good chance he'd drag Chuza down too. But there was no sense in worrying about it yet.

So far, Jesus was content in the fields and the synagogues. Until the prophet marched on the palaces, Antipas—and Chuza—were safe.

# TEN

29 AD
AUTUMN

The summer ended in a whirlwind of feasts and courtly games, enough to satisfy even Antipas' craving for constant pleasure. To Chuza's dismay, the palace began whispering about Joanna's extended absence. According to gossip, the steward's marriage was unhappy and Chuza sent Joanna away. Rumors started by Herodias, no doubt.

Chuza was clearing off his desk when quarreling voices drifted through his closed door, drawing nearer. His pulse leaped with recognition and he grinned like a fool.

"You can't call him Jovian. It's too familiar," Joanna said.

"But he asked me to!" Leah insisted. "He's our friend."

"But he's also a Gentile, and you're a young Jewish woman."

"What does that have to do with anything?"

"People will talk."

Leah snorted. "I'm not interested in him romantically. That's the truth."

"What does truth have to do with gossip? People will say whatever they like, and Jews do not marry uncircumcised Gentiles."

Leah's snap response was right outside his door. "If that's the case, then they'd be foolish to assume, wouldn't they?"

The door opened, and Joanna and Leah drew up short under Chuza's amused expression. Two flames ignited on Leah's cheeks, and she muttered something about going to the kitchen. She disappeared with a whirl of hair, and Joanna unhooked her traveling bag from her shoulder, dropping it to the floor as she rushed to Chuza.

Joanna's kiss melted the ache in his chest.

He drew back and studied her, his arms encircling her waist. She looked healthy. She smiled, joy radiating from her tanned face, though he detected notes of weariness as well.

"So?" he asked, clearing thickness from his throat. "Was it everything you hoped for?"

Joanna chuckled. "You have no idea. The things I have seen! You wouldn't believe half of them. And his teachings—" she shook her head in wonder "—I've never heard anyone so wise. I see everything like it's for the first time. There is so much I didn't understand before."

Her eyes begged him to press for details, but he asked, "Has Manaen come back?"

Sympathy flickered as she said, "No. I'm sorry."

Chuza turned to hide his hurt, stepping out of her embrace and returning to his desk, sorting a stack of receipts. "I was hoping for his help."

"What? Why? Has Antipas learned about Jesus?" Her expression was half excited, half fearful.

Chuza said, "He and Herodias have been feasting and entertaining. He's been too busy with his friends and his horses to care for anything beyond his own courtyard."

"If Antipas is so distracted, perhaps you could just release John."

Chuza barked a pained laugh. "I wish. Between Herodias' hatred and Antipas' belief that he's doing John a favor, the prophet won't be free anytime soon."

Joanna crossed her arms, shaking her head. "How can you stand it? How can you serve men and women like them?"

The question stung. He rose, plucking scrolls from the shelves and stacking them in his traveling chest, his fingers clumsy. He brought everything he was to his role as Antipas' steward. What if her time with Jesus made her ashamed of him, too?

He stiffened as Joanna's arms encircled him from behind, knotting at his waist. She laid her cheek against his shoulder. "I'm sorry. I didn't mean to hurt you. You are a good man." She squeezed him for emphasis. "I can only imagine what you could accomplish if you served an honorable king."

He placed his hands on hers. "What would that be like, I wonder? To serve a ruler both powerful and wise?" Joanna was silent, and he turned in her arms. They were almost the same height, and she could meet him eye-to-eye.

"I know you love Antipas, despite his faults," she said. "Everyone can see that you're doing your best to serve Antipas and God."

Chuza's stomach tightened. "I feel like I'm failing them both."

Joanna glanced back to the doorway. "I think you need to talk to Antipas about Jesus. Prepare him."

His stomach sunk with foreboding. "For what?"

Her gaze still averted, she said, "It would be better coming from you I think." Her large eyes met his. "Some are calling Jesus the Messiah."

The word hung between them, and Chuza realized he was holding his breath.

"The Messiah?" Chuza choked on the title. For generations, his people had looked forward to a promised messiah, a man who would sweep away their enemies and restore Israel to the glory it enjoyed during the days of David and Solomon. But it had always been a vague dream, not something he expected to happen in his lifetime. "So it's confirmed then. Jesus is more than a prophet?"

Joanna lifted her shoulders, her eyes hopeful. "He hasn't taken on the title, but he hints at it. What if he's not just preparing us for the kingdom, but planning to lead it?"

Chuza blinked, trying to foresee the future. By itself, the title 'Messiah' would be enough to rouse Antipas' suspicions. He shook his head. "We can't tell Antipas yet. As long as he focuses on himself and his court, Jesus can gather supporters. Heal. Teach." Chuza couldn't watch his master throw Jesus into jail, proving Antipas was everything Chuza feared he could be.

Joanna's brow furrowed as she studied his expression. "Alright," she said. "But don't you worry about what will happen when Antipas finds out you kept this from him? What if he punishes you?"

A strand of hair had loosened from her braid. Chuza tucked it behind her ear and stroked her soft cheek with his thumb. "That is a problem for another day," he said. He slid his hand down her arm to bind their fingers together, purposefully setting his worries aside. "Right now, I am more interested in pleasant thoughts."

"Care to share?" She tilted her head, teasing.

"It would be my pleasure," he said, and pulled her into his arms.

The sun hung low, casting golden light through the window. Joanna's cheek lay on Chuza's chest, and he trailed his fingertips over her back. The moment was perfect. Peaceful.

He said, "Two years of marriage, yet we've had so little time to be... like this."

Joanna did not reply. He wondered if she had fallen asleep, but then she sighed, her breath warm on his skin.

"I know how you feel."

The sounds of the palace outside their door beckoned him back to work, but he ignored them. "Did he say when the kingdom will come?"

She lifted her head, shifting to rest on her elbows. "He talks like it's soon, yet all he wants is for us to repent. To love our neighbors. Our enemies."

"Our enemies?" Chuza said in surprise. "Is that even possible?" A revolution couldn't be based on a teaching like that.

"Half of what he asks us to do seems impossible. Yet, the Spirit of God is working through Jesus, and it's not something we can ignore."

If only he was a free man, able to walk away from Antipas whenever he wanted. He snipped the futile wish before it grew into discontent.

"Your devotion to the Lord is one reason I fell in love with you," he said, "but I miss you when you're gone. Perhaps I'm being selfish." He hated the petulance in his tone.

"No," she said, resting on his chest again, her wavy hair covering his shoulder. "You've supported me—and Jesus. Even if it leaves you alone."

He swallowed hard, and she ran her fingers over his chest.

After a long silence, Joanna said, "Is Antipas planning on spending the winter in Tiberias?"

"Why?"

"Well, if Jesus is still living in Capernaum, it is an easy boat ride from the palace. I could go back and forth, rather than disappearing for weeks at a time."

"Will that be enough for you?"

"I don't know," she said. "Will it be too much for you?"

"Maybe. I guess that makes it a suitable compromise then? Neither of us fully satisfied."

"Is that how diplomacy works?" Joanna teased, sitting up and pulling the covers around her shoulders. "No wonder there are so many wars."

Chuza chuckled, then grew serious. "We can make this work, right? Everyone whispers that our marriage has failed, but they're wrong. Aren't they?"

Her eyes danced, and she leaned closer, stopping inches away, her lips tantalizing him. "Completely and unequivocally wrong."

He grabbed her, growling playfully, and she shrieked with laughter. It was the best sound in the world.

# ELEVEN

## 30 AD
### EARLY SPRING

Chuza strode through the Tiberias palace toward Antipas' quarters, his fist opening and closing. It had been a long winter, with his stomach clenching whenever Antipas summoned him.

The days of Antipas' oblivion were growing short. Joanna reported that Jesus sent twelve disciples to go into the cities, preaching about the kingdom of God. Jesus had even given them the authority to cast out demons and heal sickness. Chuza shook his head, imagining twelve men like Jesus marching across Galilee. News of the prophet from Nazareth would spread like wildfire, and it would burn its way into Antipas' sequestered life of wealth and ease.

Then Antipas would demand to know why Chuza waited to tell him. If Jesus made any messianic claims, Herodias would twist Joanna's clandestine visits into insurrection. His insides writhed at the thought.

He knocked on Antipas' door. A servant swung it open. Antipas was lying on a couch, his head in Herodias' lap. Chuza cleared his throat at the intimate display, and Antipas sat upright, his expression unabashed.

"Ah, good," Antipas said. "I want your help." He shifted to stand, but Herodias pulled him closer, demanding a kiss. Chuza looked away.

After a moment, Antipas moved to the sideboard, picking at the artfully displayed food. "I want you to plan a feast for my birthday. It's my fiftieth, and it should be grand. It's an opportune time to remind the Jerusalem nobles and elders about my successful reign."

"You will celebrate in Jerusalem, instead of one of your own palaces?" Chuza asked in surprise.

"Why not?" Antipas raised his brow. "It was my father's palace. Am I not his son?" Chuza folded his hands and didn't reply. Antipas turned to his wife. "Shouldn't Herod's heirs enjoy the palaces of their childhood?"

Herodias nodded. "It is our birthright."

Chuza bowed. "As you wish. I shall begin the arrangements at once."

"Draw up your plans," Herodias said, "but bring them to me for approval."

Chuza glanced at his master for confirmation, and Antipas gave his wife a questioning look.

She batted her eyelashes. "I want to make sure your birthday is perfect."

Antipas softened at once. "Of course." He nodded at Chuza. "You two can plan it together. I look forward to what your partnership produces."

Chuza bowed, and when Antipas flicked his fingers in dismissal, he showed himself out. Chuza puffed his breath through his lips as he walked the lavish halls of the Tiberias palace, his sandals loud on the marble floors. A birthday celebration seemed innocent enough, but he could not forget the single-minded determination Herodias displayed in Rome.

Joanna tipped her face to the warm breeze. The boat sliced through the waves, rocking her seat. Her mind was full of what she had seen. Men weeping, freed from the burdens of a lifetime. Women dancing, uninhibited. Elders angered by Jesus' teachings.

But now Tiberias loomed ahead, towers casting long shadows over the shoreline as their boat made its way to dock. Unless someone stuffed Antipas' ears with wool and put him in a box, he would hear about Jesus any moment.

Joanna glanced back at Leah and pursed her lips. The young woman sat on a bench, staring dully across the water. Joanna had been confident that more time with Jesus would help Leah open up, but she had withdrawn even further.

Joanna leaned over to whisper to Susanna. "What do you think is bothering Leah?"

Susanna cast a glance over her shoulder and sighed. "Maybe it's time you pushed her to talk about her past."

The small boat bumped against the dock, and the women disembarked with the other passengers. They entered the city gate and began making their way through the streets. Leah lagged, and Joanna drew her arm through Susanna's so she could murmur in her ear.

"I've tried talking to her, but she gets so upset. After everything she's suffered, I can't cause her more pain."

Susanna pressed her lips together. "When Asher was a boy, he broke several fingers in a fall. The physician had to set them before bandaging the hand. I've never heard such screams." Susanna shuddered. "But without the initial suffering, he would have been maimed for life."

Joanna understood, but she still hesitated. "What if she hates me for pushing her to talk?"

"She might, yes," Susanna said, and Joanna looked at her in alarm. Susanna chuckled. "Youth are governed by their emotions. She might lash out. Say words that cut deep. But I think your bond is strong enough that she can express herself without irreparable harm to either of you."

Joanna hoped she was right.

They parted ways at Susanna's door, and Susanna gave her an encouraging nod. Joanna slowed to walk beside Leah.

"You've been quiet," Joanna said as they turned onto the road that led to the palace.

Leah nodded, her expression fixed on the way ahead. "I'm trying to decide how to tell you I won't be visiting Jesus anymore."

Joanna drew a sharp breath. "Why not?"

"You wouldn't understand."

Joanna's ire rose, despite herself. "Why wouldn't I?"

"Your life has been simple."

"Where have you been?" Joanna said. "Have you not seen the difficulties in court? The troubles with my family?"

Leah averted her face. "But you still have a family."

Joanna flinched, heat crawling up her cheeks at her insensitivity. She was tempted to let the matter drop, but she couldn't let Leah stumble in darkness without trying to help.

Praying she was doing the right thing, she cleared her throat. "Why don't you tell me about your family?"

"I lived with my parents, my younger brother, and my twin sisters. I told you."

"And no one else? No aunts or uncles? Grandparents? Cousins?"

"No," Leah said, but a flicker across her eyes hinted at a secret.

"Did you have relatives in another house? Another city?" Joanna asked. She tried to coax her with teasing. "Or did your parents spring from the dust of the earth?"

Leah glowered and a long minute dragged by. Finally, she muttered, "On the other side of Alexandria."

Joanna's hope surged, then contracted with guilt. "So you do have people missing you. Who might have been searching for you all this time? Oh, Leah! They must think the worst."

Leah shook her head, her jaw set. "I told you the truth. No one is looking for me."

"But—"

"The synagogue cast us out." Leah jerked to a halt and wrapped her arms around her body like a shield. "Is that what you need to hear?"

Joanna stared. She hadn't known what to expect, but certainly not this. "Why?"

"Because my father did not follow the laws. He worked on the Sabbath and ate unclean meat with his friends. He didn't want to be a Jew!" Tears gathered on Leah's dark lashes, but like the lancing of a boil, she could not stop. "When my grandfather confronted him, he would not repent. So the synagogue shunned us. My mother lost all her friends and I couldn't play with my cousins. We moved out of my grandparents' house and to a new neighborhood. As we walked away with all our belongings, my grandfather cursed us." Joanna's throat constricted as Leah's lip trembled. "He said the sins of the father would fall on the children. And they did."

"That's not what he meant," Joanna said, and tried to gather the girl into her arms.

Leah jerked out of reach.

"Isn't it though? My memories are fading, but my grandfather's face is as clear as day. He wanted us to suffer." She sniffled and wiped her nose. Joanna winced in sympathy. No wonder Leah felt like an outcast. She believed herself cut off from God's people even before she lost her family.

"So what happened?"

"We moved to an insula. It was dirty. Too full. A sickness spread and many died, including my family. My grandfather's curse fell on us, and swallowed my family whole."

"I'm so sorry," Joanna said, her mind heavy as she imagined Leah as an eleven-year-old girl, helpless to save her family, cut off from relatives who could help her, cut off from her people, her faith. A tear slipped down Joanna's cheek, and she did not wipe it away when Leah glanced over.

"I used the last of our money to give them a proper burial," Leah said bitterly. "The landlord came by, demanding rent. He didn't know my father was dead, and I didn't tell him. I went out, trying to find work. I passed a synagogue and men were discussing sending tithes to the temple in Jerusalem."

Leah was quiet for so long that Joanna wondered if she would continue.

Leah's voice was little more than a whisper as she said, "There was a backdoor. I slipped in and found the money in a chest. I had a handful when he caught me. He slapped me. Hard. When I gave the money back, the rabbi told me I was a wicked girl who would burn in hell for stealing from God."

Joanna's skin prickled like an icy breeze swept off the sea. God granted the rabbi a chance to help an orphan, but instead, he spewed words of hate.

"He dragged me outside and handed me to a city guard. The guard asked me about my family, and when he learned I was alone, he didn't take me to a magistrate. He took me to the market and sold me as a slave, pocketing the coin. He never looked back."

It was a moment before Joanna could speak. "Why didn't you tell me this before?"

Leah shot her an incredulous glance. "Would you have accepted a thief into your home, into Antipas' palaces? I hoped by serving you well, I could start over, but I am cursed. I will bear my family's sin forever."

"No—"

"You don't know the sin that fills my soul." Leah pressed her fist to her chest, tears shaking free as she spat her confession. "Sometimes

I lay awake at night and burn with hate at my grandfather. At my father. The rabbi. At the guard and my first master. I think the hate will swallow me whole and drag me to the depths of Sheol."

Joanna was at a loss for words. She knew Leah's stoic manner concealed a depth of emotion, but this was overwhelming. She fumbled for the right words. "Jesus said that if you repent, you will be forgiven."

Leah scoffed. "Repent? I have tried to put aside my hate, but it has become a part of me." She turned and stared across the lake. "Jesus also said by the measure we judge others, we will be judged." She shook her head slowly. "Jesus is the Messiah, and he is bringing the kingdom of heaven. But not for me."

Before Joanna could answer, the young woman spun away, running toward the palace. Joanna could do nothing but watch her go, knowing her clumsy efforts made everything worse.

Joanna's feet dragged on the road. Since that first moment in the slave market, she had wanted to rescue Leah. "What do I do now, Lord?" Joanna whispered. "How do I help her?"

No answer rode in on the wind.

She rushed through the palace halls, turning her damp face away from curious stares. Chuza wasn't in his office, so she flopped to sit on her bed. She would give Leah some space. If Leah didn't want to see Jesus, Joanna couldn't make her. She dropped her face into her palms, failure pulling her down like a millstone.

"Joanna?" Herodias' voice sang from the office.

Cringing, Joanna wiped her face and strode out of her bedchamber, giving Herodias a bow.

"Yes, my lady?"

"I thought I saw you come in here," Herodias said, her smile triumphant. She scanned Joanna's face, widening her eyes in false sympathy. "Anything the matter?"

"Everything is fine," Joanna said, attempting a serene smile. "Did you need something?" More likely she came to witness Joanna's tears.

"I wanted to let you know I've had word from the coast. My

daughter's ship has arrived in port, and she is making her way to Jerusalem. She will join us for Antipas' birthday feast."

Joanna forced herself to smile. "How lovely for you."

Herodias inclined her head. "I know you flitter about Galilee like a bird, but I wish for you to remain with the household until her arrival. She is often emotional, and could use someone with your experience to make her feel at home."

Joanna was confused. "My experience?"

"As a companion." Herodias' eyes narrowed.

Joanna stiffened, and Herodias' sweet expression returned. "You needn't attend her all the time, of course. My daughter has never left Rome and you will help her get her bearings. You understand."

Joanna wasn't sure she did, but she inclined her head. "I will do what I can, my lady."

"Excellent," Herodias said, and left the office.

Chuza entered a moment later, frowning in concern when he saw Joanna's face.

"What did she say to you this time?" Chuza said, turning to stare after Herodias.

"She wants me to help welcome Salome."

Chuza blinked with surprise. "You?"

Joanna laughed mirthlessly. "She has finally found something good about my time serving Phasaelis. I think she expects friction when her daughter arrives and doesn't want to take the brunt of it. Or she's just showing her superiority by ordering me about."

"Perhaps," Chuza said, his expression doubtful.

"At this moment, I don't care what her small-minded reason is."

Chuza's eyes roved over her tear-stained face. "Then why—?"

Joanna recounted her conversation with Leah.

Chuza tipped his head. "So you're going to let her remain behind when you visit Jesus?"

Joanna's already thin temper threatened to shatter. "Let her?" She scowled. "I didn't drag her there."

"She hasn't seemed very enthusiastic the last few weeks."

Joanna narrowed her eyes. Leah and Chuza seldom spoke, yet now he thought he knew better? Seeing her expression, Chuza held up his hands in surrender. "We'll help her past this, all right?"

Her ire dissolved, replaced by the hope that she wouldn't have to solve this problem alone. "We?"

Chuza took her hand. "Just don't ask me how."

# TWELVE

Two weeks later, the Jericho palace disgorged its guests. Servants secured the packed carts with practiced movements and thick ropes. The grooms led the horses from the stable, hooves clattering on the cobbles, their long tails swishing. Antipas' carefree friends and family laughed in the shade, eager to celebrate Purim and the tetrarch's birthday. Heads turned as a cart rumbled into the courtyard.

Chuza had been pinned by one of Antipas' cousins, but his complaints faded as Chuza studied the unexpected arrival with a frown, noting its odd construction. He strode toward it, ignoring the angry protest of the man behind him.

The cart was, in fact, a cage, not unlike those he had seen transporting bears and lions. Someone had lashed a rough cloth to the top, providing its passenger with shade. As Chuza neared, he saw it was not a terrifying beast inside, but a man sitting cross-legged on a mat, all knobby knees and sharp angles. Dressed in a shaggy garment of camel hide, his overgrown beard and hair floated about his head in careless snarls. Shadows made camp under his eyes, dark against skin long deprived of sunlight. His piercing gaze made Chuza shiver involuntarily.

"Who is this man?" Chuza demanded, though, in his sinking heart, he knew.

The guard shrugged his shoulders, his leather armor creaking. "It is the baptizer, John."

"But why is he here?" Chuza asked, dragging his palms down his bearded cheeks. What was Antipas thinking? Surely half of Jericho had seen John rolling by, his followers too. Now they would flock to him and insist on his release, or incite a riot.

"I summoned him," Antipas said, interrupting Chuza's frantic thoughts. Chuza jerked around to face his master. Antipas was dressed to ride, his tunic belted under a waistline that had thickened considerably since his second marriage.

Chuza swallowed. "Why didn't you inform me?"

Antipas laughed, flicking a hand at Chuza's expression. "Because of how you'd react. You would have talked me out of it."

"But why?" Chuza asked, dropping his tone so the guards would not overhear.

"Herodias insisted that I stay away from Macherus." Antipas lifted his brows in mock solemnity. "So I brought him to me."

Wrapped in her palla, Herodias swept forward. "What is going on?" she said. Her lip curled in a hiss as she beheld the prophet. "Why have you allowed this man to behold the light of day?"

"Peace, my love," Antipas said, shrugging at her shock. "He is in a cage. I have not released him. Yet." Chuza knew Antipas only teased her, but Herodias paled. She spun and stomped away.

"Will you really bring him to Jerusalem?" Chuza said. "What will the people say?"

Antipas clapped a hand on his shoulder. "Don't worry so much. You'll go gray before your time." He strode back to the others, signaling his groom to lead his gleaming mount forward. Turning at the last moment, Antipas called to the guard. "Fall into the procession."

"Yes, my lord," the guard said in return. Chuza scowled at him, and the guard lifted his palm in a shrug. Herodias spat to ward off evil spirits as she rejoined the other women. They leaned toward her, eager for information.

Chuza clenched his fist by his side. This was a bad idea, one he would have strongly counseled against. But he couldn't properly serve as the steward if Antipas kept him in the dark.

He fixed his glare on the guard. "I'm going to fetch more cloth," Chuza said. "Keep him hidden." He took a step, then hesitated. "And I will send food and wine to sustain him on the journey. Ensure that he receives it."

"He won't drink it," the guard said, then winced as his partner elbowed him. "But we would appreciate some wine, if you've got it."

Chuza sighed, striding away to complete these unexpected, last-minute tasks. He met Joanna coming out of the palace. She took one look at his face and placed her fingertips on his arm. "What's happened?" she asked.

He explained, and her eyes widened.

"Will he parade John through the streets?"

Chuza shook his head. "I think he's only trying to make a point with Herodias. He wants to show that he's not under her thumb. I won't let him cause a riot."

Her expression eased. "I know you won't."

Joanna was so confident in his abilities. If only he felt the same.

They celebrated Purim in Herod's Palace, ignoring the empty halls across the verdant courtyard where the rooms were always ready in case the Judean governor deigned to visit the city. But Pilate did not consider Purim a festival that warranted his presence.

The irony was that Purim celebrated a revolution. The court gathered to feast and recount the story of the brave duo Esther and

Mordecai, who faced down a king and overturned the order to kill all the Jews. The royal court booed and hissed and stamped their feet whenever the storyteller said the name "Haman". The men drank wine until they could not tell "Haman" from "Mordecai".

It was a festival suited to Antipas and his retinue, and they celebrated the ancient victory late into the night with performances and songs. Chuza sent servants into the city with bread and watered wine for the poor, given in Antipas' name.

Despite his bluster, Antipas quietly locked John in the palace dungeon. Antipas liked to tease Herodias that he would show him off as entertainment. Ignoring Chuza's warnings, Antipas behaved as if it was all a game.

Chuza's neck and shoulders stiffened with painful knots as he concealed an even greater prophet moving unchecked through Antipas' lands.

Three days before the planned birthday party, Joanna received a summons. She followed the servant to Herodias' apartment. Elegantly appointed, it boasted plush couches and delicate tables cluttered with pretty knick-knacks. A lute was set aside with the air of recent use.

"My daughter has arrived," Herodias said as Joanna gave a formal bow. "I want you to be here to welcome her."

"Of course, my lady," Joanna said. "I am honored you asked."

Herodias assessed her, probing for insincerity as Joanna kept her face neutral, hiding her curiosity to know what sort of woman Herodias had raised.

They turned as the door opened. Joanna immediately identified Herodias' daughter. She was her mother's miniature, with the same heart-shaped face and dark curls. A demure maid with flaxen hair followed a half-step behind. The two girls bowed before Herodias, neither smiling. The men behind them were alike in height and face, though there were decades between them. A father and son, Joanna thought.

"You've come at last, my darling!" Herodias gushed, rushing forward to wrap her daughter in an embrace.

"Hello, Mother." Salome's arms were rigid by her side. Herodias kept her arm around her daughter as they faced the men.

"Thank you, my friends, for escorting her here," Herodias said. "She is precious to me, as you know." She stroked Salome's cheek, and Salome's face twitched before she brought it under control.

The older man nodded approvingly at this maternal display, but the younger one clenched his jaw, challenging the truth of Herodias' claim. Salome met the young man's eyes, her lips parting with unspoken words. Joanna's stomach sank. It seemed love had traveled from Rome as well.

"Come, sit! Rest after your long travels," Herodias said, bustling and cheerful, gesturing at the couches. She turned to Joanna. "Will you send a message to the kitchen?"

There was a maid waiting in a corner, her station more suited to running errands, but Joanna matched Herodias' smile and stepped out. The second Joanna left the room, she stuck out her tongue, venting the frustration she could never show.

Herodias was determined to see her humbled, but she would float above the pettiness untouched. Like a child whose tantrums go unheeded, Herodias would lose interest.

The next morning, Joanna knocked on a familiar door. It was Phasaelis' old room and Joanna recognized Herodias' subtle barb.

Salome's maid ushered her in, bowing her golden head.

Salome reclined on a couch, the picture of wealthy displeasure. It reminded Joanna so much of Phasaelis that she could not suppress a memory-filled smile.

"What are you smirking at?" Salome demanded, narrowing her eyes.

"Nothing," Joanna said. "It is a pleasant day."

"Is it?" She sighed. "I hadn't noticed."

"Well then," Joanna slipped into her old role like a worn pair of sandals, "let's walk in the courtyard so you can decide for yourself."

Salome stood up, brushing a hand down her lavender peplos. Her hair was braided and curled to frame her face. "Very well. There is nothing else to do in this backward city, anyway." She cast a pointed frown at her maid.

They walked side by side, the maid trailing them momentarily before slipping away. The remaining pair stepped into the groomed garden, lush with flowers, leafy shrubs, and palms.

As their sandals crunched on the gravel path, Joanna wondered if Herodias had told Salome about the betrothal. Not wanting to spill the news, she tread carefully.

"I'm sure Jerusalem feels strange after living in Rome," Joanna said. "You must miss your father." Salome turned away, but not before pain shifted across her delicate features. "It is hard to leave home," Joanna said. "I know I struggled when I first joined Antipas' court."

Salome cast her a measuring glance. "Mother says you were a maid."

Herodias would say that. But Joanna refused to be baited. "I was the chosen companion of the princess. Phasaelis and I were good friends."

Salome sniffed. "Well, I don't need a companion. I won't be staying long, anyway."

"Oh?" was all Joanna dared to respond.

Salome tossed her head as if sensing Joanna's doubt. "Papa was entertaining several offers for my hand before I left. He will write and ask me to return." A blush painted the girl's cheeks.

Joanna remembered the sparks between Salome and the young man and her curiosity surged. "Your escort looked like men of rank," Joanna said.

Salome peeked in her direction. "Melchus' daughter, Livia, is my best friend. They are an honorable family. Not of the equestrian order," Salome admitted, "but they've risen through their business dealings. I'm sure Lucius will raise their name even higher.

"Lucius is the son then, the younger man I saw yesterday?"

"Yes," Salome said with a secretive smile. "When my mother summoned me for her husband's birthday, Papa asked them to escort me to this dusty, ugly city in the middle of nowhere."

"It is the city that holds our temple," Joanna said, unable to allow that insult to pass. "You are a Jew by birth, and Jerusalem deserves greater respect on your lips."

Salome reassessed her. "Of course," she said, her expression now veiled. "I am grateful to have the chance to complete my *one* pilgrimage to the holy city."

Joanna did not miss her emphasis, but let it slide. The girl was young, homesick, and feeling uncertain about her future.

Footsteps crunched on the gravel and the maid rejoined them, carrying a shawl. "I thought you might be chilly, mistress," she said, though the spring sun was warm.

"How thoughtful of you." Salome glanced at Joanna as she draped the cloth over her elbows. "This is my maid, Helga. My mother bought her for me before she left for her wedding." Joanna tried to smile at the maid, but the young woman didn't lift her eyes.

Joanna turned at a footstep from the opposite direction. Lucius wandered on the path ahead, and he noticed the women with over-done surprise.

Joanna shot Helga an accusing look, and the girl's pale skin flushed scarlet.

"Salome!" Lucius' cheek dimpled with a smile. "Out enjoying

this beautiful morning?" As Salome brightened like the rising sun, Joanna's misgiving grew. Herodias needed to tell her daughter about Philip. Today.

"It's impossible to stay inside on a day like this." Salome fluttered her lashes. "Why don't you walk with us?"

Lucius offered Salome his arm, leaving Helga and Joanna to follow. Joanna tried to be a good chaperone, but Helga became very chatty, asking questions about the household in accented Greek, preventing Joanna from overhearing the whispered conversation happening in front of her.

They wandered for half an hour until a slave summoned the women. Salome parted from Lucius regretfully, trailing her fingers on his forearm. He caught her hand and brought it to his lips. Joanna saw it with misgiving.

Joanna followed Salome into Herodias' room. She blinked at finding Chuza standing over Herodias' shoulder as they studied a sheet of papyrus.

"Yes, this menu is better," Herodias said. "More fashionable, don't you think?"

"I agree," Chuza said, his gaze flicking to Joanna. "Michael is confident there is time to prepare these extra dishes. His staff is purchasing ingredients as we speak."

"Excellent. Now we just need to confirm the entertainment," Herodias said, ignoring Salome and Joanna. "The dancers and acrobats have arrived?"

Chuza met Joanna's eyes before nodding. Joanna remembered the scantily clad dancers from a previous party. The salacious women would please Herodias' worldly husband, but they would not make a good impression on the city elders.

Herodias nodded with satisfaction and handed him the papyrus. "My daughter shall also dance."

"Me?" Salome said, and Herodias rose to acknowledge her, holding out a hand that would not be refused.

"But of course!" Herodias said, bringing Salome closer. "You have danced for your father before. How is this different?"

Salome's eyes sparked like flint. "Antipas is *not* my father."

Herodias' demeanor cooled. "He is my husband, and I want to show the city a united family."

"I am not a little girl anymore," Salome said. "People would think it odd if I dance."

"Nonsense!" Herodias said. "A young woman pleasing her new step-father will warm their hearts."

Salome's lip curled with practiced stubbornness. "I won't do it."

Herodias spoke to Chuza in an undertone, as if Salome was not in the room. "Mark her down to dance after the acrobats."

Chuza hesitated, then nodded, not wanting to be caught in a squall. Herodias dismissed him with a flick of her hand, and Joanna moved to follow.

"Remain here, Joanna," Herodias said, sitting once more on her couch. Joanna shot Chuza a hidden, exasperated glance, then sat across from Herodias. Salome flopped onto the chair furthest from her mother.

"Salome, I have the most delightful news," Herodias said, beaming. "You are betrothed."

Joanna swallowed as Salome sat upright.

"Betrothed?" Salome said, all petulance gone. Hope shone in her eyes.

Herodias practically sang, "To Philip, the tetrarch of Batanea and Iturea." Herodias clapped her hands together with glee. "We have already signed the contract. You will be married this autumn. Isn't that wonderful?"

Salome stiffened, her mouth opening in confusion. Her longing gaze turned to the door.

Herodias frowned. "Aren't you happy, my dear?"

Dragging her attention back to her mother, Salome's eyes filled with tears. "I cannot marry him."

"Of course, you can. It is a better match than I ever dreamed possible for you."

"But he's older than your new husband!" Salome leaped to her feet, fists clutched by her side. "He's an old man!"

Joanna studied her knotted fingers, pity rising. Philip could not compete with the dashing Lucius.

Herodias' eyes narrowed, and she gestured at Salome to sit. After a moment, the young woman obeyed.

"Yes, he is a bit older than we'd like." Herodias wobbled her head as if this was a minor problem. "But he has vast territories and is a capable ruler." She lowered her voice. "His revenues are more than a hundred talents a year." She raised her eyebrows as if that would be enough to sway any woman. "You will be a powerful woman, my daughter, and your sons will inherit a generous portion of my grandfather's lands, lands that rightfully belong to our family."

"Sons?" Salome choked as she imagined coupling with a man old enough to be her grandfather.

"We are the descendants of two priestly lines and of royalty, are we not? Should we not reclaim our place as heirs?"

Joanna loosened her fingers from their white-knuckled grip before they lost sensation. Herodias was so eager to salvage her inheritance that she'd ride over her daughter's happiness. Joanna glanced between the women, wondering why she was privy to this conversation at all.

Salome drew herself up. "Mother, I cannot marry Philip. I am in love with another man. Lucius asked for my hand, and Papa and Melchus were negotiating the betrothal before we left."

Herodias scoffed. "A youthful infatuation, and not even a worthy one. Lucius' family is not on our level."

"But Mother, I love him!"

Herodias' nostrils flared with annoyance. "What does love have to do with it?"

Salome's eyes flashed. "Didn't you divorce Papa and marry Antipas because of love?"

Herodias darted a glance at Joanna, and Joanna couldn't resist raising her brows in question.

Herodias made a noise in her throat. "Yes, I married Antipas for love. But I was careful where I gave my affection, wasn't I? Affection grows where you nurture it. You must decide to love Philip, and you will."

She gestured to Joanna.

"Did you love your husband before you wed?" Herodias asked. Now it was Herodias' turn to arch her eyebrow.

Joanna's stomach tensed. Herodias would turn her answer into fodder for the insatiable palace gossips.

"I respected and admired him," Joanna said. "I wanted the life we could have together. And I love him now." The affection that seeded their marriage bloomed as Chuza opened his heart to her, revealing the sensitive side he kept hidden from others.

Herodias looked pointedly at Salome, and fat tears slipped down Salome's face. She threw herself at her mother's knee. "It is too late. I love Lucius! Papa will support me. He actually cares about me. You cannot make me marry against my wishes."

Herodias cringed away from her daughter's tears. "Stop the theatrics, foolish girl. I have no intention of sending you to Caesarea Philippi bound and gagged. You will go of your own accord. If you think carefully, you'll see Philip is your best choice."

Salome's head reared back. "Never. And I'll run away if you try to force me." Her lips trembled.

Herodias smiled, but it was as chilly as winter frost. "My dear child, you may love Lucius, but does he feel the same? If you had no dowry, no connections to further his business, would he marry you still?"

Salome hesitated, color climbing up her neck. "Of course he would," she said.

Herodias smiled serenely. "As long as you're sure." She let that hang in the air like a bird of prey and then stood, beckoning for

Salome to follow her into her private chamber. "Come now, let's discuss your dance for Antipas."

Salome enunciated each word with care. "I don't want to dance."

Herodias pursed her lips, tipping her head to the side as she considered. "Agree to this, and I will give Lucius a chance to plead his case."

Joanna blinked, trying to figure out what Herodias was up to.

Salome searched her mother's face, looking for the trap. "You'll give him a proper audience? You're willing to change your mind?"

"I only want what's best for you," Herodias said, smoothly deflecting the question. "And you dance so prettily. Remember the ribbon dance you performed for your father? If you do well, Antipas may even grant you a gift."

Salome brightened with possibility, and Herodias grinned like a cat with a mouse. She swept through the doorway and into her private chambers, her daughter in tow.

Joanna drew a breath as she escaped back into the hall. She needed to share this conversation with Chuza, but more than anything, she wanted his arms around her. Not everyone could boast they had a marriage of love.

# THIRTEEN

Twilight fell on the night of Antipas' birthday. Braziers blazed in the courtyard but Joanna hovered in the shadows, watching the trickle of guests become a flood as men and women climbed the palace steps. Her time in the palace had dulled the impressiveness of the tetrarch, but the prestigious guests were a stark reminder of his power. Sadducees chatted with the leading men of Jerusalem. Pharisees moved in tight clusters. The influential wives of the city tried to outdo each other, their robes draping in every hue of the rainbow, their throats and ears glittering with jewels.

Herodias and Antipas waited inside the great hall to receive guests and accept their gifts. Joanna craned her neck, scanning for Herodias' daughter. She expected to find her hanging around Lucius, but she was nowhere in sight. Poor Salome. Herodias' ambitions were set on a man higher in station than the merchant's son, but Philip? Joanna shuddered. She could not imagine marrying a man three times her age.

The courtyard emptied as the guests made their way inside the vast dining hall and Joanna's stomach growled with hunger. The kitchens would be bursting with enough tantalizing dishes to feed an army. But Leah was there.

She twirled her sash around her finger. Leah avoided her presence since Tiberias, and Joanna tried to give her the space she wanted. But they couldn't dance around each other forever.

After the coolness of the evening, the kitchen was uncomfortably warm. Long tables stood in ordered rows, almost hidden by platters of delicacies. The kitchen staff feverishly added final garnishes.

Leah was easy to spot among the controlled chaos. She stood on a chair holding a long wooden spoon, directing the serving staff as they crowded forward for the trays.

"Yes, the cakes, take them," Leah urged. "And the refills of wine."

The servers scooped up the items as she directed, hurrying out the door. Michael, his face coated with a sheen of sweat, approved the roasted lamb and then checked the slab of beef, calling for more sauce.

As the trays vanished, Leah saw Joanna's approach. Her expression flattened. She hopped off her chair and wiped the back of her hand across her forehead.

"Chuza sent you to check on us?" Leah frowned.

"I wanted to see you," Joanna said. "And maybe get a taste of what you're serving. It smells like manna from heaven."

Leah's lips softened at the praise, and she led Joanna in a lap around the room, snatching samples until she had a hefty plateful. She thrust it at Joanna without a smile.

"Will you sit with me?" Joanna asked.

Leah hesitated, then gestured to the kitchen courtyard.

"Where do you think you're going?" Michael said with a glare.

Leah scowled in return. "Don't I deserve a taste after slaving the past few days?"

Michael shook a thick finger. "You have fifteen minutes to eat, you hear?"

"You'll be lucky if I come back at all!" Leah said. She smirked as she flounced away. Michael grinned at his protege's back and gave Joanna a wink.

The courtyard ovens radiated heat, and the two women found a bench and set the dish of food between them.

Joanna picked up a cake filled with gooey fruit and bit into it with an appreciative murmur. Finally, Leah smiled. They ate silently for a few minutes.

Joanna began on a safe path. "You love working in the kitchen, don't you?"

"I do." Leah nodded, her focus fixed on the food. "I love how Michael shows me how to combine ordinary ingredients into something amazing."

"I feel a little like that when I'm with Jesus," Joanna said. "The way he uses simple stories to teach life's greatest truths."

Leah stiffened, dropping her half-eaten cake on the plate. "Why do you always do that?" She crossed her arms.

Joanna blinked in confusion. "Do what?"

"Turn every conversation into some sort of moralizing lesson. You ask me about my life, but it's just to sneak in what you really want to say." She threw up her hands. "I'm more than a problem for you to fix."

"Of course you are!" Joanna said. Leah had to see how much Joanna cared, but Leah shoved the plate away.

"You can't see me as anyone other than a slave girl you rescued. An orphan with a tragic history."

Joanna flinched. That might be partly true. But she had so many hopes for this young woman, if only Leah would accept her help. "I—" Joanna began, but Leah overrode her.

"Have you ever considered that your insistence that I deal with my past makes me feel worse? Maybe I'm content to stay as I am."

"You were so depressed—"

"I'm not now, am I?" Leah said, sitting taller. "I'm happy apprenticing under Michael."

But Joanna wanted Leah to find more than a trade. She wanted her to take her place among the chosen people. Again she tried to explain. "But with Jesus we—"

"With Jesus, I am constantly reminded that I'm not good enough, and I might never be." Leah narrowed her eyes in challenge. "Maybe I'm more like my father." Joanna stiffened and Leah crossed her arms. "You are ready to hang your entire future on a man of God, but you've never seen how they can turn on you. One day, you'll let Jesus down, and your whole life will fall at your feet."

Joanna stared. It was hard to see past the skinny, frightened child from the slave market, too full of pain to even crack a smile. But this young woman thrummed with complex emotions. For the first time, Joanna realized she might not be able to help her. And Leah didn't want her to try.

"My lady?" a voice broke into the strained silence. Helga stood in the doorway, wringing her fingers.

Joanna cleared the emotion from her throat. "What is it?"

"It's my mistress," Helga said. "She doesn't know I'm here, but I need help."

"Now?" Joanna glanced at Leah's averted face, then back to the maid. "Is she ill?"

"No," Helga said, squirming with discomfort, "She's, uh, she's well, but you need to stop her."

Joanna looked at Leah again, unspoken words suspended between them.

"Go. I need to get back to work," Leah muttered, storming into the kitchen.

Joanna exhaled a long breath through her nose. She nodded at the fair-haired maid.

Helga hastily led the way to Salome's rooms. She cast Joanna a last, pleading glance, pulled the door open, and they stepped inside.

Joanna expected something dramatic, but Salome sat on a couch, wearing a loose robe. Cosmetics lined her eyes, and her hair tumbled in styled ringlets.

She looked up at Joanna's arrival, her face void of expression. "What are you doing here?"

Joanna raised her brows at Helga, confused.

Salome rolled her eyes. "My maid doesn't want me to dance tonight."

"This isn't the dance your mother planned for you," Helga said.

Joanna frowned at Salome. "What is she talking about?"

"There's been a change," Salome said, her dark eyes flashing. "Though it is none of your concern."

A knock drew their attention to the door as a servant called, "It's time!"

Salome rose. She kept her eyes fixed on Joanna as she let the robe slip off her shoulders to pool on the floor. Joanna gaped. Salome wore a sheer garment of white Egyptian linen. The gauzy cloth covered her from neck to ankle, but it revealed every contour of her body.

"You can't wear that," Joanna said, heat blazing in her cheeks. "Everyone will see you!"

"I don't care," Salome said. She strode to the door.

Joanna's mind scrambled. "Lucius is there. What will he think if you appear dressed like that in front of everyone?"

Salome's eyes narrowed. "Didn't you hear? He withdrew his offer this morning."

"But…" Joanna struggled to keep up. "Why?"

"Don't you understand?" Salome tipped her head with a mirthless smile. "To my papa, I am a daughter. To my mother, I am a tool. One she will use to carve out the future she wants. My betrothal to Philip, this dance—" Emotion choked off her words, and she blinked rapidly before she marred her kohl-lined eyes. Despair seeped into her voice. "I have no life. I am an extension of hers. Let her feel my shame, because I will not."

Joanna recognized this dance for what it was. Revenge. With malicious compliance, Salome was turning her mother's game against her, but Joanna feared it was not Herodias who would pay the price.

Salome jerked open the door and marched toward the side entrance of the hall.

Joanna hurried after her. "Please reconsider," she begged as the servants stared at Salome. "I know you're upset about the betrothal, but is this how you want to be remembered in Jerusalem?"

"I hope word of this spreads far and wide."

Joanna reeled, trying to understand why the girl would throw away her future. They approached the servant's entrance to the hall and a parade of scantily clad acrobats filed out, bells jingling from their long braids, their chests heaving with exertion. Salome strode into their midst.

"I hope rumors reach Caesarea Philippi," Salome said. "When Philip hears, he won't allow my name to be uttered in his presence."

Joanna faltered a step. So this was more than revenge. This was a plot to escape her fate.

Salome spoke to the musician. He nodded and ducked inside. The beat of a drum vibrated like a heartbeat, and the crowd quieted. Joanna's mind spun. Salome shook back her curls, stubborn pride in every line of her lithe body. She stepped into the hall, placing each dainty foot with precision.

Joanna retreated a few paces, pressing her icy hands to her cheeks. She hadn't believed Salome would do it. Herodias would be furious when she saw her daughter. Joanna should have pinned Salome to the ground, hollering for a guard to lock her in her room.

At last, the drum stopped, and the hall erupted with raucous cheers. Cups bashed on the tables in approval. Joanna didn't know whether to sag with relief that it was over, or cry.

Summoning her courage, she peeked through the doorway. Salome stood before Antipas. The tetrarch reclined on a dais, beaming and surrounded by prestigious guests. Joanna leaned to the side to catch a peek of Herodias. To her astonishment, Herodias regarded her daughter with victorious pride.

Antipas heaved himself to his feet and spread his arms wide. The guests quieted. "A fine dance," he said, his words slurred by wine. "Superb! You have delighted us all. Please, dear girl, ask for anything you wish. Up to half my kingdom, ask, and it shall be yours."

It was the promise Xerxes made to Esther. Joanna flinched at his choice of phrase while the guests murmured at this extreme generosity. Salome paused, turning to her mother. Herodias nodded.

"All I desire," Salome said, clear and strong, "is the head of John the Baptizer, given to me on a platter."

Shock pulled the air from Joanna's lungs. An audible gasp rippled through the room. Drunk young men cheered approval. The tetrarch slumped back onto his couch, the blood draining from his face as his darting eyes sought an escape.

There was no way Salome would have asked for this gift without prompting. Joanna couldn't believe Herodias' daring, her willingness to risk her husband's love to satisfy her jealousy. Salome waited, shifting from one foot to another, every movement radiating sensuality.

Joanna prayed Antipas would refuse, but everyone had witnessed his promise. He couldn't back out without embarrassing himself.

Herod Antipas stood. His voice wobbled as he called to his guards, "Send word to the prison. I order John the Baptizer beheaded, and his head brought as a gift to Salome."

Joanna stared, her mind refusing to comprehend as several men in the crowd cheered. Her hope flickered as Chuza rushed to the dais. He spoke in Antipas' ear, and Antipas shook his head as if in a dream. Herodias preened, callous to her husband's distress. Surrounded by admirers, Salome flirted shamelessly.

Chuza fled the hall, his head bowed. He almost collided with Joanna as she stepped forward. Their eyes met, a thousand words passing, and then he grabbed her hand and pulled her into his arms. A long, disbelieving moment draped around them like a smothering blanket.

"Did he change his mind?" Joanna whispered into his neck.

"No," Chuza said flatly.

She pulled back to study his face. "Can we stop it?"

Chuza grunted, refusing to meet her eyes. "It's too late." He drew a shaky breath and his words came roughly. "All these years, and he still refuses to listen to me." His gaze met hers, despair shining from the depths. "I have loved and served him most of my life. I never believed this is the ruler he would become. I thought he would be different."

Joanna's heart broke as tears trickled down Chuza's face.

# FOURTEEN

Chuza's stomach still hadn't settled. Voices pushed against his consciousness while his mind replayed the grisly scene—John's head oozing gore, hair matted around his yellowed face, his eyes half-lidded and glazed. The spirit of God, gone. Chuza's fingers tightened on the wax tablet. He never imagined Antipas could do it.

The tetrarch sagged on a plush couch in his Jerusalem quarters, his eyes dull and clothes rumpled. Herodias sat stiffly by his side.

Melchus cleared his throat as his eyes darted around the tense room. His weight shifted backward like a soldier facing an overwhelming foe, anxious for the call to retreat.

Herodias broke the stilted silence, attempting a warm smile. "Thank you again, my friends, for delivering my daughter. I trust you will pass her message along to her father?"

Melchus nodded, his gaze shifting for a split second to his son. Lucius' white knuckles clutched a leather-sheathed scroll. It contained Salome's declaration that she no longer needed her father's assistance in procuring a betrothal. Herodias stole that right from her ex-husband as well.

"We will, my lady," Melchus said, and nudged his son.

Lucius' face was like stone. "Yes, my lady," he said through his teeth.

Herodias nodded at Chuza. He scooped the heavy purse from the side table and offered it to Melchus. The man seemed torn between delight at its weight and distaste at what it meant.

"I'm grateful we part so amicably," Herodias said. "I would have been grieved to lose years of friendship over something so... inconsequential."

Lucius' jaw worked as he glared at the woman who thwarted his happiness. Melchus bowed, murmured blessings for good health, and led his son away. Chuza could not bring himself to care about the young man's disappointment. They would return to Rome, back to climbing the social ranks, and Lucius would find another pretty woman to soothe his heartbreak and bolster his family name.

Herodias reached for her husband's hand. Flinching at her touch, he jerked to his feet and stormed from the room.

Chuza could not pity his master any more than the heartsick youth. Back in Rome, he tried to warn Antipas about Herodias' scheming nature, but Antipas was blinded by her warmth and charm.

Herodias kept her seat, her lips pressed together as the servants stared at the floor, pretending they hadn't witnessed the awkward scene.

Chuza stepped forward, showing nothing but practiced neutrality. "Will there be anything else, my lady?"

Herodias' attention flicked to him, nostrils flaring before she smiled again. "Yes. I am a little concerned that Philip might feel some—" she paused delicately "—doubts when he hears about my daughter's performance. Go to Caesarea Philippi with gifts. Assure him that we are still very much interested in the marriage." Her voice lowered as she leaned forward. "Do not fail me."

Chuza inclined his head.

"And take your wife," Herodias said. Surprise almost dislodged

Chuza's neutral expression. "I want a woman's report to soothe Salome's nerves about her future home. Be sure Joanna gives a glowing one." She flicked her hand in dismissal, and he bowed and left the room.

Chuza strode to his and Joanna's shared quarters, his movements clipped. A headache stabbed at his temples. Herodias faced the heavy task of making Antipas love her as before, but Chuza grimly prophesied she would succeed. Murder and intrigue were bread and meat in King Herod's house. Antipas may have avoided such manipulations during his reign, but he was no stranger to political games. Time would fade his bitterness, and Herodias would be there, pouring tenderness and grandiose dreams in his ear.

Chuza let himself into his office. He tossed his tablet on his cluttered desk, barely noticing Joanna's attempts at organization. He stuck his head in their private quarters and found Joanna cross-legged on their bed, elbows on her knees as she hunched over a scroll. His back ached even considering sitting in such a fashion.

Joanna glanced up, a sharp crease between her eyebrows. She straightened and gestured at the words. "I needed a distraction. John wasn't the first prophet hated by a queen." The stories of Elijah were her favorite.

Chuza sat beside her, rubbing her back. She leaned toward him, her head landing on his shoulder. She sighed.

"I'm not doing any good here," she said. "Herodias and Antipas will never change. What if everyone blames us, accuses us of not stopping them?" If she sensed his dismay at her words, she didn't show it. She sighed. "I should return to Jesus."

Finally noticing his tension, she looked at him in question. "I don't think so," he said. "Not with things as they are. Not with Herodias…"

"Killing prophets?" she finished his sentence darkly.

"She requested you come with me to Caesarea Philippi."

Her eyebrows rose, then eased with understanding. "Shoring up the betrothal?" She gave him a wan smile. "At least it'll get us out of the palace." Chuza nodded. He was eager to escape the court as well.

She shifted to face him, holding one of his hands in both of hers. "I can't believe Herodias actually did it. I mean, I knew she was dangerous, but what will she do to us when they learn we kept Jesus a secret?"

Chuza's headache flared painfully. "We knew the danger before," he said, kneading the back of his neck. "This just makes it more real."

Joanna moved to sit behind him, replacing his hand with both of hers. Silence hung in the room as she worked at his knotted muscles.

"We're in this together, right?" she said. "Supporting the kingdom of God?"

His inadequacy gaped wide. "I failed to save John," he said. "We must keep the situation from getting out of control when Antipas and Herodias hear about Jesus."

Her thumbs rubbed small circles, triggering sparks of pain in his temples as the knots loosened.

"I have no idea how to influence Herodias," she said. Her voice turned dry. "We both know how well I did leading Phasaelis to righteousness."

"Your influence on the princess was greater than you know."

"I pray you are right." She sighed, and Chuza realized they had both struggled with instilling faith in the tetrarch's court.

He said, "Perhaps if you help Herodias secure Salome's happiness, she will—"

"Stop seeing me as her enemy?" Joanna interrupted wryly.

"It can't hurt to try."

"Salome loved that young Roman, you know."

"Herodias is set on this union," Chuza said. "Our job is to make the transition as smooth as possible. I think when you meet Philip, you'll see he has the makings of a good husband."

"Then why hasn't he married before?"

"He has spent a lot of time serving his citizens. I'm sure it is time-consuming, with all their variances and political needs."

Her hands stilled. "I don't fully agree with this betrothal. But I will help you."

Chuza eased away, his neck and his emotions soothed. He faced her. "I appreciate that."

Joanna smiled. "We will find a way together. Through everything."

He rose, pulling her up with him and pressing her to his chest. If they were leaving tomorrow, he had much to prepare. He drew back. "So, how do you feel about riding horseback?"

He smothered his grin as her jaw dropped.

"You're joking, right?" she said. He strode back into his office, systematically replacing fears with plans, chuckling as her voice followed him, rising in pitch. "Right?"

# FIFTEEN

They left Herod's Palace as the sky faded from gold to pink to pale blue. They rolled through the wide city gate and Joanna took her first full breath in days. She felt odd leaving Leah behind, but the grizzled cook would keep a careful eye on his young apprentice.

As they rumbled through the countryside, Joanna drew back the curtains on the canopy to allow fresh air and conversation to circulate. Chuza rode nearby. He made it look easy, and she wondered if it was as hard to stay in the saddle as he made it sound.

A soldier drove the cart, the reins loose in his hands as the mules placidly followed Titus' sorrel gelding. Titus whistled a jaunty tune, yet one hand often strayed to the hilt of his sword.

Jerusalem was soon far behind them, and the terrain continued its descent. The trail narrowed as it entered the ruddy cliffs of the Jericho Road, and sharp embankments forced them to ride in single file. The sun scorched the earth and heat rose in shimmering waves over the ground.

The steady swaying and the crunch of gravel beneath the large cart wheels were hypnotic. Shaded by a canopy and bolstered with an extra cushion, Joanna let her heavy eyelids close.

A faint whistle invaded her sleepy thoughts. Her brow furrowed. It was a sound she heard many times in her childhood, adventuring with her brother in the hills behind their house. It was the song of a leather sling, spinning through the air.

Preparing to launch a pebble at deadly speed.

She had only a split-second to cry out a warning before a sickening smack hit the driver of her cart. His head snapped sideways as he yelped in pain. His hand jerked to his neck, and he withdrew bloodied fingers. Her mind urged her to react, but she was frozen in her seat, unable to even scream.

At the same moment, Titus' mount reared, whinnying as rocks pelted his hide. Titus flailed, trying to keep his seat. Before he caught his balance, a trio of men rushed from a crevice with spears, shoving them at the horse's face. Titus was thrown to the ground and spear points swung within inches of his throat.

Men leaped out from behind Chuza with undulating shouts, trapping the travelers on the narrow strip of road. Chuza struggled to rein Celer under control. The cart driver stood up, yanking his short sword free.

"I would reconsider if I were you," a man's voice echoed through the cavern, punctuated by the whirring of a dozen slings.

Galvanized by the voice, Joanna stuck her head out of the cart to peek up. Men lined the cliff wall, their faces covered by scarves, pinning their captives with glares and the threat of rocks hurled with lethal force.

"Get down," Chuza hissed. Joanna slid to crouch, but the canopy was a flimsy shield.

"Toss your sword!" a bandit yelled, and after a moment's hesitation, the cart driver dropped his weapon in the dust. "And you!"

It took a moment for Joanna to realize he was speaking to Chuza. Chuza's shout was tight. "I'm unarmed."

"Really?" the man asked, and he laughed. "Off your horse then."

134

Chuza hesitated, and Joanna's pulse pounded in her ears like waves. Chuza leaned forward, swung his legs over the saddle, and dropped to the ground. A man swathed in dusty cloth yanked Celer's reins from his hands, and Chuza clenched his empty fist.

"Search the cart," the voice commanded from on high.

Panic twining up her throat, Joanna hastily climbed out the back, scurrying near to Chuza. One of the bandits glared as he passed them, then clambered in the cart. With a rattle, he opened the wooden chest in the cart and released a string of colorful curses. Clothes were flung aside. Her favorite palla unfurled, floating over the edge of the cliff, a blaze of pink before it was lost to the dust and the vermin that made their homes in the rocky cliffs. Finally, the thief found the small money bag.

"Is this it?" He peered into the purse. "Three guards for this paltry amount?" He shook his head at his friends, then eyed Joanna. "Who's she?" he demanded. "Is she worth three guards?"

Joanna's legs weakened, and Chuza stepped in front of her.

"Two guards, and one unarmed fool," a masked man corrected in a lazy drawl. He sauntered through the others, stopping before Joanna and Chuza. The mask could not disguise the fine line of his nose or his intense eyes. As they stared each other down, he tugged his scarf down.

"Amichai!" she gasped.

His friend darted a glance at him. "You know this woman?"

Amichai's lips twisted with amusement. "She's my sister." Hooking his thumbs in his belt, he added, "And this is her husband, Antipas' steward."

"Antipas' steward!" The exclamation echoed up the cliff.

Joanna stepped between her husband and her brother. Chuza growled and gripped her arm, trying to tug her backward. But this was her family. Amichai wouldn't go through her to hurt Chuza. Would he?

"Let's take him then!" the men said. "Antipas would pay a hefty ransom."

"No!" Joanna cried out at the same moment Amichai raised his hand for silence.

"Not worth the trouble or the price on our heads," Amichai said. He peered up at the cliff heights where a man crouched to hear. "Barabbas! The spoils are negligible. Let's move on."

The leader nodded and disappeared. While Amichai pinned his sister beneath a glare, the guard and Titus were relieved of their swords and belts.

"So you're a highwayman now?" Joanna said, unable to help herself. Chuza's grip tightened on her arm.

"A freedom fighter," Amichai corrected, his eyes narrowing. "Taking down Roman supporters." The threat closed her mouth. The men retreated, spears bristling and slings whistling warning from the heights. The bandit tossed Celer's reins, and Chuza hastily grabbed hold of his horse, running a hand down Celer's ruddy neck.

Amichai drew his mask back up, and it muffled his voice as he said, "I'd rethink your allegiances, sister. You might not be so fortunate next time."

He hurried after his friends and disappeared into a narrow cave. The whirring stopped, and a heavy silence hung in the air.

Titus scrambled to his feet, cursing. As Titus examined his horse for wounds, the driver clambered into his seat, muttering bitterly and beckoning for Joanna to get inside.

Joanna trembled as she tugged herself free of Chuza's grip, unshed tears burning as she tried to gather up the tossed garments.

A hand captured her wrist, and she turned as Chuza pulled her into his arms. They hugged for a long moment, neither willing to put words to what might have happened.

They made the remainder of the journey silently and with grim speed, alert to any hint of trouble. The sooner they were off the Jericho Road, the better.

Joanna breathed a sigh of relief as they rolled into the palace courtyard in Jericho, the sun sinking low in the sky. Chuza reported the highwaymen and a patrol was dispatched, though everyone knew the bandits were long gone amid the warren of caves and cliffs.

Chuza called for hearty food to be brought, but Joanna insisted all she wanted was a bath. She slipped down the familiar corridors like a shadow, ducking her head, hoping to avoid conversation.

In the bathhouse she struggled out of her dusty clothes, fighting tears and frustration. She rinsed off in the basin, the water turning murky as she sloughed herself clean, water spilling everywhere. As she sank into the hot bath, her adrenaline drained away and she shook violently, her limbs boneless. If Amichai hadn't intervened, the men might have taken her. Or Chuza. Or killed them all.

Yet, Amichai's intervention wasn't enough to make her glad he had joined the highwaymen. She knew he followed violent men, but she hadn't realized... How many times had he done this? How often did his sling sing before a rock struck true? She shuddered. This couldn't be the way to Israel's freedom.

Amichai's cold accusation about her allegiances rose in her mind. He had grown up with her and seen her love for scripture, her love of the Lord. Did he really think she had thrown her faith away?

Joanna shifted her mind to practicalities. She needed to keep this misadventure from Herodias' attention. The tetrarch's wife would be delighted to spread the news that Joanna's brother had turned to criminal activity, and the disciples would be shocked to learn that Joanna was related to a highwayman. She shook her head. Only four people knew that her brother was involved with a band of thieves. And that was how it needed to stay.

# SIXTEEN

They were a noisy procession as they traveled around the inland sea. Joanna rode with the presents for Philip, her feet crowded by the pottery, glassware, and trinkets Chuza had gathered from Tiberias and packed in straw-filled baskets. Behind her cart, a white stallion was fastened with a sturdy rope, tossing his long mane. Chuza was confident these generous gifts would appease the tetrarch.

Titus led the way on the smooth road. Extra guards lent a sense of security, and the pleasant scenery set Joanna at ease. The crops in the fertile basin grew tall in the late spring sunshine, hinting that Passover and Pentecost were near.

She felt conspicuous riding through Magdala in a covered cart, surrounded by Antipas' guards. Amid the clopping of hooves and jingling of tack, she wondered if everyone thought she was one of Antipas' lackeys, sent to do his bidding. She shifted in her seat, knowing that wasn't far from the truth.

She drew a sigh and her nose crinkled against the fishy aroma. They were passing the pebbled beach where men and women gutted the night's catch, gulls shrieking for the offal.

Their procession continued around the lake, past Capernaum, until they reached the northern edge where Philip's tetrarchy claimed a sliver of shoreline. His territory, sprawling between Jewish Galilee and Gentile Decapolis, was mostly Greek descendants, with a heavy sprinkling of Syrians and Arabs. Joanna scanned the land with curiosity as they left Galilee behind.

They rode past the city of Bethsaida and took the road north. After a night in an inn, they continued up through verdant, marshy territory. Joanna breathed deeply, tasting the humid air with its green scent.

As they neared Philip's capital, she studied Caesarea Philippi with interest. The city connected trade routes from Syria, heading west to the coastal cities of Tyre and Sidon, and south to Tiberias and Jericho. As they rode through the wide city gate, they passed a caravan of camels burdened with wares and guarded by men wearing turbans and dark glares.

They made their way down paved streets, past multiple temples to false gods and one to honor the emperor. Crowds milled and men met in conversation under the perfumed smoke of offerings and incense. Residents strolled toward a famous cave, the source of the river that watered this entire region. It bubbled up from under the mountain, a well so deep none had plumbed its depths. She hoped to see it for herself, despite its long history as a base of pagan worship.

They paraded through the palace gate and into the front courtyard. She and Chuza freshened up and a servant brought them to a receiving room to prepare their gifts. As she helped Chuza display the items on a side table, she mentally cataloged the size of the room and its decor. Herodias would demand the most minute of details.

Another servant opened the door and Philip strode into the room. Joanna blinked with dismay. Chuza had described Philip as handsome, but Salome's betrothed wore wrinkles on his brow and liberal streaks of silver at his temples. His expression was mild, and though he was tall, his elegant robes couldn't hide a comfortable paunch. He was not ugly, but he could not compare to Lucius.

Careful to avoid revealing any of these thoughts on her face, Joanna bowed with her husband.

"Chuza!" the tetrarch said in a familiar tone, striding forward to clasp Chuza's wrist, clapping him on the shoulder. "Back so soon?"

Joanna did not envy her husband's position.

Chuza said, "I have brought gifts, my lord, from your brother and his wife." He swept out his hand to show the display. "They are eager to promote happiness between you and their daughter, Salome. We have also brought a stallion of good breeding stock."

Philip's eyebrows rose. "My brother is generous. I wasn't expecting presents—at least until the wedding." He drew a palm down his beard. Chuza hesitated, and Philip waved dismissively. "We can discuss business after we have eaten." He turned to Joanna with a smile. "And after you've introduced this lovely woman."

"This is my wife, Joanna, daughter of Ira the vintner."

Philip inclined his head. "We are blessed by your presence." Joanna bowed in return. At least she could give Salome a glowing account of his manners.

The servant reappeared at the doorway and caught his master's eye.

"Ah, the meal is ready," Philip said. "Let me escort you in." She allowed the tetrarch to lead her into an elegant triclinium that was fragrant with blooms and adorned with murals.

Philip was an attentive host, and the conversation flowed faster than the wine. Chuza and Joanna shared an awkward glance as the server placed a platter of meat. Neither wanted to ask if it had been offered to idols. Joanna picked at her food, waiting for Chuza to introduce the reason for their visit.

But it was Philip who broached the subject. "So, my brother had a birthday celebration in Jerusalem, I'm told."

Chuza nodded. "It was well attended."

"Yes, the rumors have flown ahead of you." Philip held up his hand and ticked off his fingers. "Important guests. A feast. Entertainment. And an execution. My father would approve." His smile grew wry.

Chuza cleared his throat, his expression carefully controlled. "Yes, John the Baptizer is dead."

Philip selected a bit of meat. "Did the prophet's death cause any unrest?"

"Not yet," Chuza said.

Joanna's throat tightened. It wasn't right. A prophet's death should not go unmarked.

"I had heard my brother was rather fond of him," Philip said. "What changed?"

Chuza drew a breath. "His head was a reward for Salome's dance, my lord."

Philip twitched in surprise, then chuckled. "I see Herodias hasn't changed one bit."

"I must tell you," Chuza said, "Salome's dance created a stir. Some have said it was too provocative."

"Salome is young, yes?" Philip smiled indulgently. "As long as she comes to me a virgin, I do not mind a little... youthful display. Dancing would certainly enliven my court." He winked at Chuza.

Joanna's cheeks warmed and she studied her cuticles as Philip continued. "Tell my brother I accept his gifts and await my bride. If she is as biddable to me as she is to her mother, I foresee a happy future."

"Yes, my lord," Chuza said.

Philip held his cup out so a servant could refill it. "I am glad you caught me before I leave. In a few days, I will begin the summer progress through my lands. Many of my subjects are nomadic, with ancient customs. I find it is best if I go to them in order to pass judgment and make myself known."

"Your willingness to become the ruler your people expect has served you well," Chuza said. "Your territories have been at peace."

"It is the Roman way," Philip said, his tone ringing with confidence. "Tolerance is the mark of higher civilization. Acceptance of religion especially. Too many wars have ravaged this land in the name of a god."

Joanna could not catch the words before they escaped her lips. "You mean our God?"

Philip's smile was patient. "My mother was a good Jewish woman, and I learned our history at her knee. I know how we battled our way to claim this land from the Canaanites and the Philistines, citing purity as our ambition, pretending it was not an instinctual need to establish a kingdom and a name for ourselves."

Ignoring Chuza's pointed gaze, Joanna leaned forward. "The Lord promised the land to Abraham. He commanded Joshua to conquer it."

Philip shrugged. "Perhaps. There is truth to every legend. In my Roman education, I learned about many conquerors. Each was appointed by a god or helped by one. Israel is not unique."

Joanna's lips parted with the craving to set him straight, but Chuza shot her a warning glance. She clamped her mouth shut.

Accepting her silence as agreement, Philip held out his hands, as if welcoming all to come to him. "Rome allows all religions to flourish, as long as they harmonize with the government." He nodded at Chuza. "I salute my brother's ability to keep the peace with so many Jews in his territories. I am fortunate to have a more... tolerant population."

Chuza gave a tight smile, but Joanna's skin crawled. Perhaps it was a mercy that Salome was raised in Rome. Joanna couldn't imagine living with tranquility among idolatry, where truth was a matter of opinion.

The next day, Philip led them on a tour of the palace and the city, showering Joanna with attention as he showcased the best parts of his domain. She made as careful an examination as the taxman.

Maybe if she pleased Herodias in this, she wouldn't care that the steward and his wife supported a prophet from Galilee. The hope was slim, but better than nothing.

# SEVENTEEN

Joanna and Chuza departed Caesarea Philippi with their guards. In a few months, Salome would arrive as the new wife of the tetrarch of Batanea and Iturea. It was an excellent position for a girl with noble blood running through her veins, but Joanna frowned at the discrepancy between the bride and groom. Philip was healthy now, but past his prime. As Salome blossomed into womanhood, her husband would grow old.

They journeyed without incident to Bethsaida and spent the night in a large inn, busy with locals and travelers. A matronly woman served hearty food and their choice of beer or wine, while the innkeeper plucked songs from his lyre.

The next morning, a torn harness delayed their departure, and it was midday before they could resume their journey. Chuza pushed them to make up the time, but a large party of travelers clogged the road. They barely passed one group before they rode up on another. Joanna wondered if the travelers were journeying to Jerusalem for Passover, but they were too excited, considering the miles still ahead of them. The wagon driver muttered at the reduced pace.

At a point between Capernaum and Bethsaida, the group in front of them left the road, striding into the empty field with a single-minded purpose. Joanna's pulse jumped with understanding. She leaned from the cart to confirm her suspicions.

"Where are you going?" Joanna called to a middle-aged woman.

"To see Jesus of Nazareth," the woman returned.

Joanna's heart surged. "Stop the cart!" she said. The driver drew up on the reins with a frustrated growl, but she didn't care. This was too good an opportunity to let pass.

Chuza rode up as she hopped onto the road, resolution settling in her bones.

"Do you need a personal moment?" Chuza asked from horseback.

"Jesus is here," Joanna said. "That's where everyone is going." She waited for his reaction, hoping he would see the blessing of this chance encounter.

Chuza stared after the crowd, calculating their options. Foreseeing difficulties instead of blessings. Joanna rested her hand on his leg.

"This is your opportunity to see him," she said. "I know you're worried after what happened with John." She paused to ease the quiver in her voice, and his mouth thinned. She gripped his leg. "But you can't let that hold you back. Let's go to Jesus. We're in this together, remember?"

The conflict warred on his face as he glanced at the guards. They would surely report this deviation from the itinerary. His gaze drifted over Joanna's full cheeks, her strength—her health a testament to Jesus' power. Chuza nodded once, and Joanna grinned. She had waited for this moment long enough.

Chuza leaned forward to dismount and Titus trotted up. "What's going on? Why have we stopped?" His gaze followed the crowd disappearing into the hills and he looked at Joanna for confirmation. She nodded, and Titus raised his brows.

"It's time I see him for myself," Chuza said.

Titus grinned. "Finally."

Chuza shot him a glare, and Joanna caught the undercurrents of a previous conversation between them.

"I'm sending the guards ahead," Chuza said. "I don't want to cause a scene."

Titus swung off his horse to land beside them. "Send the other men along, but I am coming with you." Joanna's eyebrows shot up.

"You think we need an armed guard to meet a prophet?" Chuza asked.

Joanna opened her mouth to protest, but Titus shrugged. "Jesus is not the one I'm worried about," he said. "I have seen what happens when your people gather. Antipas will have my head if harm befalls his steward."

Chuza and Joanna locked eyes, remembering the riot that killed her father. Joanna squeezed her husband's fingers.

"The crowds have been peaceful with Jesus," she said. "We'll be safe."

Chuza considered. "Come along," he said to Titus. "But keep your sword out of sight. We don't want to look like we're asking for trouble." Joanna would have preferred Titus leave the weapon behind altogether, but the blade seemed sewn to his hip.

Titus tugged a plain brown traveling cloak from behind his saddle and swung it around his shoulders, letting it hang over his leather armor and sword. Chuza and Titus handed their reins to the confused guards and commanded them to go on ahead and secure lodging.

Joanna, Chuza, and Titus left the road as the wagon rattled away with their personal luggage. She smothered a giggle at so many men guarding her favorite robe.

She turned her face to the hills of swaying grass dotted with wildflowers. They strode forward with no idea of their destination, forced to trust those who walked ahead.

They crested a hill in the wilderness, and Joanna gasped. The trickle of people pooled into a vast crowd in the thousands, mirroring the vastness of the Sea of Galilee gleaming behind them. She had never seen anything like it. Chuza jerked to a stop and stared, his mouth falling open, and Titus' hand twitched toward his hip.

Joanna's pulse skipped at sharing this incredible moment with Chuza, but his expression was uncertain, as if the numbers were a threat rather than a sign of God's movement. She reached for his hand, and he fell in step beside her. Joanna searched for familiar faces in the crowd, for Jesus' disciples and her friends. It seemed impossible to find anyone among the sheer mass of people, but the trio picked their way forward, careful to stay together.

Her attention skipped over curious expressions and focused on those celebrating. A father danced with his small son on his shoulders. An elderly couple sang in harmony, hands clasped, tears washing down their faces. Joanna jerked back as a pack of children cut through their path. The leader's face was aglow with delight, his bare feet pounding on the grass as his friends urged him on. "Run Joshua, run!"

A man stared at his hands, rotating them front and back. A mother unwound bandages from her wiggling child, weeping with relief. A man was turning a jig on his worn mat. Everywhere Joanna turned was evidence that the Spirit of God was working through Jesus.

She sensed that Chuza was overwhelmed, but she pushed on, excitement growing. As they drew to the heart of the crowd, bodies jostled them on every side. Sweat, spices, and the pungent tang of sheep assaulted her nose. Joanna thanked God for her height, or else she would have been helpless to see her way forward.

Finally, she spotted Jesus on a slope. Hands touched him on every side, desperate for a brush with the divine. He bent his head to a pleading woman, setting his palm on her shoulder as he nodded at something she said.

"There he is," Joanna said, pointing. Chuza followed her finger, and he stared for a long minute.

"I'm not sure what I was expecting," he admitted.

"He looks like your average Galilean, doesn't he?" Titus said. "Until you see what he can do."

Joanna furrowed her brow. The disciples were strangely absent. They usually kept the crowd back and helped bring the sick in some semblance of order. But today Jesus seemed alone. Protectiveness surged in her chest. She needed to help him.

They pushed forward, taking long minutes to cross a few feet.

"Rabbi!" Joanna called. Jesus followed her familiar voice and gave her a smile, though grief shadowed his eyes. She sucked a breath. He must have heard about his cousin, John. Yet, here he was, without his disciples and swamped with crowds.

He answered her unspoken question. "I came here to pray," he said, speaking over the crowd. "But they are like sheep without a shepherd."

Even in his sorrow, he put the people above his needs. "Where are the others?" she asked, wincing as a woman stepped on her toes.

"Back in Capernaum," Jesus said. Someone called his name, and Jesus moved on.

Joanna turned to Titus. Jesus shouldn't have to do this alone, especially not while carrying his grief. "Will you get word to the disciples?" she asked. Titus glanced between the thick crowd and the couple he came to protect. "We will be fine," Joanna said. She waved him away, but Titus looked at Chuza for confirmation.

Chuza nodded, and Titus gave him an encouraging slap on the shoulder. The Gentile wove through the masses, vanishing in seconds. Joanna turned to Chuza. He was trying to make himself as small as possible.

"We should help," she said. "Let's stand on either side of Jesus and give him a little space to work." Chuza's eyes widened, staring at the pressing crowds, and Joanna leaned closer. "Just be kind. Some are desperate for healing, others need hope. Be compassionate, but firm."

"You've done this before?" Chuza asked, grunting as an elbow jabbed his ribs.

Joanna tried to hide her nervousness with a smile. "Sort of." Usually, she was one of dozens of disciples, all working together.

Chuza drew a shaky breath and nodded. They stepped closer to Jesus, holding up their arms as they flanked the prophet, keeping the crowd back.

"Give the rabbi a little room," Joanna said, her voice wavering. She cleared her throat and spoke louder. "Give the prophet space to move!"

The people eyed her, wondering who she was to order them about. But one by one, those in front ceased their pressing. Joanna glanced over her shoulder at Chuza, her husband mimicking her motions. Pride surged in her chest. Finally. They were helping Jesus together. She prayed this was a peek into their future.

Without hands clutching at him, Jesus could reach those who needed him most. He caught Joanna's eye and nodded with gratitude. She bobbed her chin in response.

They stayed with Jesus as he moved among the crowds. She wondered what Chuza was thinking, seeing limbs restored, blindness cleared, ears unstopped, tumors gone, sores vanished, and invisible diseases brushed away.

As hours passed, Joanna sagged with weariness and hunger. Her throat was parched from asking others to wait, just for a moment. The prophet would speak to them. Just wait.

At last, she spotted Peter clearing a path, the rest of the disciples in tow. At the same second, Titus approached. His gaze roved over her face in concern and Joanna wondered if she looked as exhausted as she felt. The twelve moved into their customary places around Jesus, working as extensions of their master's will. Joanna dropped her arms and drew a breath, glad for the respite. Chuza hastily made way for Andrew, as if afraid of being chastised for presuming to help their rabbi.

"Joanna!" Maryam pushed closer, her crescent dimples deepening. "You're here!" She scanned Joanna's face and held out a wineskin. "You look like you could use this."

Joanna gestured to Jesus. "He needs it more than I do."

"He's being taken care of," Maryam said. Joanna glanced over as James pressed a wineskin into Jesus' hands.

Joanna took several mouthfuls of the watered wine. She passed it to her husband. Maryam followed the gesture, her eyebrows raised.

"This is my husband, Chuza," Joanna said as he took a grateful drink.

"Antipas' steward," Maryam said, assessing him. Joanna stiffened, but Chuza didn't retreat from the scrutiny. Maryam's expression softened. "Welcome," she said.

Joanna puffed a breath of relief. Chuza noticed and shot her an exasperated look, but he didn't understand how important it was for them to be accepted among Jesus' disciples.

"Thank you," Chuza said, and handed back the wine.

Maryam nodded and rejoined the others. Jesus had chosen her son James as one of the twelve, and Joanna knew how proud she was. But how did his brother feel at not being sent out? Her throat twinged with sympathy. She had waited her whole life for God to use her, and as yet, she remained in the background. But once Jesus brought the kingdom, she and Chuza could serve him everyday.

"Manaen is here," Chuza's voice rumbled near her ear.

Manaen spotted them as they approached, and his joy at beholding the steward brought a flush to Chuza's cheeks. Manaen bounded to them, weaving through the crowd.

"You've come!" Manaen exclaimed, gripping Chuza's upper arms with both hands. He stared into Chuza's face, then pulled him in for an embrace.

"Just for today," Chuza said.

"You say that now." Manaen wagged a finger. He chuckled, but

Chuza looked pained. Manaen planned on spending a few weeks with Jesus and disappeared for over a year.

"How is everyone?" Joanna asked. She lowered her tone, searching his eyes. "They've heard about John?"

A cloud of grief passed over Manaen's face. "Yes. One of John's disciples came to us this morning while we were in Capernaum. Jesus is understandably upset." Not only Jesus' cousin, John was also a fellow prophet.

Joanna asked, "What's he going to do?"

Manaen flapped his hand at the people. "This, I guess! He went off on his own, seeking solitude to pray. Peter's young sister-in-law heard a great crowd had found Jesus, and we came after him."

Joanna looked at Titus, eyebrows lifting in question. He nodded, and Joanna mouthed, "Thank you."

"You know how he is," Manaen said. "He can't leave the people to fend for themselves, no matter how his heart is breaking."

"And you?" Chuza asked, sizing up the man who had been his mentor and ally. "How do you feel about John's beheading?"

Manaen caught the unspoken challenge, the question of his loyalty to the one he called brother. His face remained gentle. "I grieve for Antipas," he said, gripping Chuza's shoulder. "The wife he thought would bring him happiness has heaped trouble upon his head. I fear what Herodias will do when she discovers an even greater threat walks her lands."

Their eyes turned to the vast crowds. Thousands of men, plus women and children, had flocked to Jesus of their own volition. His fame had spread far. All of Galilee and Judea would know his name—including Antipas.

# EIGHTEEN

Chuza's robe clung between his damp shoulder blades like the claustrophobic press of the crowd. He watched the twelve men who surrounded Jesus. Whatever they had been before, their one responsibility was to learn and imitate their master. If only life was so simple.

Joanna took his arm. Though worn out from the day's effort, she looked as if she belonged here. She slipped so easily between her role in Antipas' court and her time as a disciple. Chuza envied her fluidity.

Miracles were happening through Jesus' hands, but Chuza's focus kept skipping away to scan the masses, wondering how he would explain any of this to Antipas. The sheer numbers alone could be construed as a threat.

A cluster of Pharisees was not lost on him either. The sect stood as a symbol of righteousness to the Galilean people, and here they were, supporting Jesus. He squinted, sure he recognized at least one man as a well-known teacher—no, two. Nicodemus. Joseph of Arimathea. Wealthy, influential men.

Chuza studied Manaen from the corner of his eye. He tried to understand Manaen's choice to abandon Antipas. Perhaps this was the worthier way. No middle ground. No need to omit the truth. But the thought of breaking his vow was like vinegar in his stomach.

"God, what do I do?" he murmured a breath of prayer.

"What was that?" Manaen asked, leaning closer.

"Nothing." Chuza waved his words away. He finally had his mentor by his side and could seek the counsel he craved for months, but now he feared Manaen held no answers for him.

"Let's find a place to sit," Joanna said, drawing a peaceful sigh. She beamed at him as they retreated from the heart of the crowd. "How did it feel? Serving?"

Manaen looked at Chuza in surprise, and Chuza's shoulders hunched. All the things he had accomplished as steward, yet fending off eager crowds made her glow with admiration. "I offered crowd control, nothing more."

"Nothing more?" Titus said, holding out his arms in exaggerated insult. "If I knew you valued my skills so slightly, my friend—"

"You know what I mean," Chuza growled, and Titus grinned.

Chuza led the group until the masses thinned and they found a patch of grass. Joanna folded her legs to sit. Chuza glanced around, seeing others doing the same. The resting crowd kept their faces toward Jesus, as if loath to leave this hill, this moment when the harsh realities of life were undone, one by one.

The afternoon slipped away. Chuza stayed deep in his own thoughts while the other three chatted. His stomach rumbled, and he scanned the dusky horizon. They hadn't brought food, and a few mouthfuls of wine would not sustain him. They must leave soon or it would be difficult to make it to a city before dark. Chuza nudged Joanna, and she frowned in disappointment at his expression.

"Not yet," she said, reading his mind.

"I think he's done," Chuza said.

Jesus had withdrawn into his circle of disciples. One of them swung his arm at the vast crowd. Another brought a young boy forward. The child stared up at Jesus' face with awe, holding up a basket. Chuza's chest warmed. The boy was offering the hungry rabbi his lunch.

Jesus rested his palm on the boy's head, then spoke to his disciples. They nodded and fanned out.

"Sit down!" one bellowed. "The rabbi asks you to sit!"

The people hesitated, then sat down, staring expectantly up the hill. Jesus held the food and blessed it. He reached inside and broke off a piece.

"Bring me baskets," Jesus said. The disciples scrambled to follow his order, and Chuza sat taller, trying to see what was happening.

Jesus set the broken bread into the basket, and a minute later, a woman moved through the crowd, offering the contents to those near her. Other disciples joined, picking their way among the masses. Jesus hadn't put more than a mouthful in each, yet they walked as if carrying a heavy load.

Chuza's brow furrowed as Jesus sent another basket away. Chuza followed its progress until it stopped before him. He stared at the pile of bread. This was impossible. In a daze, he took some. It was soft in his hand and yeasty in his mouth, like a loving mother baked it for her son.

Chuza chewed, calculating the cost of the flour and the oil, the fuel to heat a hundred ovens, and the sheer organizational skills needed to bake so many fresh loaves. Yet these crowds came spontaneously, and they were in the middle of nowhere. Jesus created food for them from a small boy's lunch. His mind spiraled at the incredible wonder of it.

Titus leaned closer, waving his crust of bread. He spoke in an undertone. "A king who can heal his army and feed thousands from mere morsels would rule the world."

Chuza's stomach dipped at the unexpected truth. A ruler who multiplied food meant a nation immune to famine. Combined with his healing abilities... no hunger, no sickness, no cripples... was it true? Was Jesus the Messiah they had been waiting for, the one to surpass even the mighty King David and his son Solomon?

He wasn't alone in his thoughts. As the disciples gathered up the baskets of leftovers—leftovers!—whispers blew through the crowds, and soon some were speaking aloud.

"We should make him king."

"Yes, let him be our king!" other voices took up the call.

The crowd milled, and women drew their children close, retreating from men whose eyes flashed with excitement. Chuza jerked to his feet, pulling Joanna up with him. Their hunger sated, the people were eager for something else to happen.

Titus stepped closer, his hand slipping beneath his cloak, his sword at the ready.

Chuza looked at Jesus and blinked in surprise. He was sending his disciples away. They trickled down the slope, hurrying to the Sea of Galilee. The sudden departure caught the crowd off balance, and Jesus seized the moment to speak to them, his voice echoing over the hills.

"Go home," he said, firm but kind. "Go back to your homes."

The zeal of the crowd cooled, and they drifted away, blinking as if rousing from a strange dream.

Chuza exhaled a breath that unwound the tension in his shoulders.

"I need to go," Manaen said. Before Chuza could protest, Antipas' foster-brother raced across the fields after the disciples. It was clear where his allegiances lay.

Joanna, Chuza, and Titus made their way to the road, joining the river of people.

"I didn't think anyone could stop revolutionary fever once it started," Titus said. His fingers were still wrapped around the hilt of his sword. "I thought they'd make him king by force."

"But what is he waiting for?" Joanna said, then blushed as they stared at her. "There are thousands of men here."

"Enough for an army, you mean?" Chuza raised his brows. "You've never supported your brother's violent politics."

Joanna rolled her eyes. "That's different. Amichai is venting his anger. Jesus could be the Messiah we've all been waiting for."

Chuza understood her reasoning, yet it was uncomfortable to consider the implications. When rulers were deposed, they were either executed or exiled. If Antipas was exiled, he could force Chuza to go with him. Would Joanna leave the promised land and a prophet of the Lord to follow an unrighteous tetrarch into exile? Fear dug under his ribs.

Chuza cleared his throat. "So you'd support Jesus if he marched on Jerusalem right now and pulled Antipas from his throne?"

She hesitated, as if sensing his churning emotions. "Antipas isn't God's chosen king."

"You know that for certain?" Chuza said. "The Herodian sect supports his rule."

Joanna looked at him like he was crazy. "He hasn't fulfilled the prophecies. His lineage isn't from David, and we live and breathe by the will of Rome."

"His father rebuilt our temple," Chuza said stubbornly. "Herod united our lands for the first time since Solomon. Didn't some rabbis say only the Messiah would do that?"

Joanna frowned. "Herod also killed thousands of Jews for trying to follow God's commandments. He built temples to false gods and emperors." She leaned toward him. "Are you defending Herod as a righteous ruler? Do you really think Antipas is the king God wants for us?"

Chuza pressed his lips together and puffed out a sigh. Despite everything Antipas had done, loyalty to his master lingered, like a splinter under his skin. "Herod was cruel," Chuza said, "and Antipas has... lost his way. There has never been a perfect king. Even David and Solomon had grievous flaws. Jesus heals and teaches, but he shows no interest in politics. Is he the kind of man to lead our nation?"

Titus strode beside Chuza, his face grave. "If Jesus challenges Roman authority, it'll mean war. The emperor will send Syria over your borders to force you back in line." He glanced around him. "The crowds might fight for Jesus, but can they win against trained soldiers?"

Joanna set her jaw. "Moses was a prophet, and he freed our people."

Chuza nodded. "But will Jesus do the same?"

Joanna hesitated. "I don't know, but he must have come for a reason."

"But what is it? To call our people to turn back to God, or something more?"

They shared a glance, neither of them able to answer.

A wind rose, sweeping over the lake and sweet with coming rain. Dark clouds scuttled past the rising moon. Shadowed fishing boats transported the disciples on choppy waves, the men heaving against the oars. He wouldn't want to be on the water tonight.

He realized Joanna had stopped on the road, her palla billowing around her body as she stared after the ships with longing. Jealousy prickled along his arms. He couldn't compete with miracles, or with those who gave up everything to follow a prophet. If it came down to a choice, perhaps she would choose them over him.

"Come on," Chuza said, his voice rougher than he intended. When she still hesitated, he became sarcastic. "Unless you plan to swim out and join them?"

Her eyes flashed at his tone. "Fine," she said, and strode toward Capernaum, her long legs setting a pace that required the men to catch up. The wind whipped Chuza's hair into his eyes and tugged on his clothes as if chastising him for his roiling emotions.

They pushed on to Magdala, and Joanna led them to an inn she knew. At the gate, she spoke to a burly man named Samuel. When Joanna introduced Chuza as her husband, the innkeeper's wide face broke into a grin.

Assured that the steward and his wife were situated, Titus said good night and left to rejoin his fellow soldiers at an inn that accommodated Gentiles.

The wind vanished in the sheltered courtyard of the inn. Despite the late hour, the tables were crowded with patrons, many of whom seemed to be discussing Jesus of Nazareth. Samuel led Joanna and Chuza up a staircase to the second story, where private rooms with beds and locked doors were prepared for wealthy guests.

Chuza fished coins from his belt. Samuel accepted them with a bow of his bristly head and said, "I shall have water sent up so you can wash, along with hearty food and wine." He flushed sheepishly. "Though my cellars do not boast the best vintage in Galilee anymore."

Joanna twisted her lips into a wry smile. "A problem that we can remedy, my friend."

Samuel shook his finger at her. "You are your father's daughter," he said, and laughed. "I hear your vineyard is flourishing."

"Thanks to the Lord," Joanna said.

Samuel raised his palms skyward and shook his head in agreement. He shut the door behind them.

Chuza exhaled his first full breath in hours. The wind whistled through the roof tiles, but the four walls of their room sheltered them and confined Joanna to his side. His wife's spirit was like a new-broke mare, yearning for the freedom that a life with Jesus offered. His inadequacy pressed on his chest.

There was a knock at the door, and Joanna opened it to accept a pitcher and towels. Another serving girl bore a tray of steaming stew, round loaves of bread, and a jar of wine.

As Chuza set the food on the table, Joanna filled the basin. Dipping one end of a towel into the water, she wiped her face, sighing at the pleasure of removing the dust from her skin.

Chuza's chest heated at the sight of her, his pulse thrumming like David for Bathsheba on her roof. In a quick stride, he was standing behind her, his hands brushing down her waist to her hips.

Joanna cast a glance over her shoulder, her dark eyes teasing. "Worried I'll use all the clean water?" she asked innocently. She dipped the cloth again and wrung it with her strong fingers. Turning, she washed his face, the water wonderfully cool. He pulled her closer and his lips covered hers. She melted against him, the cloth hitting the floor with a splat. The tightness in his ribs loosened. In this moment, she was his. All his.

Hours later, Joanna awoke, Chuza's steady breathing at her back. She guessed it was an hour from dawn, the darkest part of the night. The wind howled around the building as if determined to pull the inn to the ground.

And then, suddenly, it was still.

Joanna instinctively held her breath to listen. After a moment, she slipped from the warm bed to pad across the floor. She unlatched the shutters and pushed them open, peering over the city of Magdala that slumbered below. The clouds were dissipating and the low-hanging moon cast a pale glow over the smooth water. Freed from the storm, silhouetted boats bobbed peacefully.

The night air raised goosebumps on her skin and she shivered, rubbing her bare arms. Her husband's presence coaxed her like a fire's warmth, beckoning her under the covers and into the comfort of his embrace. Yet part of her pulled outwards, out to wherever Jesus had found haven, moving where the Spirit sent him.

Another shiver shook her limbs, and Joanna hurried back into bed, her muscles easing as she tugged the blanket higher. Through the open window, stars emerged in the inky sky as the clouds cleared.

She and Chuza hovered in the peaceful moment between night and day, but they could not stay. The sun would rise and the cost of their secrecy would be due. John was barely in the tomb and another prophet had captured the people's hearts, drawing thousands to him. She wanted to feel overjoyed, but instead, she feared what would happen when they returned. Both she and Chuza had lied by omission. She supported Jesus financially. She had succeeded in showing everyone that the steward's wife supported Jesus, but now she must pay the price.

Joanna swallowed hard, picturing Antipas' anger and Herodias' cruel satisfaction as they charged her as a seditionist.

It would be safer if they didn't return to court, but Chuza would never abandon his vow. He believed his friendship with Antipas was enough to keep them both safe, and she hoped he was right.

She rolled over, studying the contours of her husband's face in the pale light. She had made a promise too, to be Chuza's wife, no matter what troubles life brought their way.

"He wants to serve you, Lord," Joanna whispered a prayer. "Show him how. Help him know what to say to Antipas and keep us safe from Herodias. And give me the courage to stand beside him, come what may."

She still believed they would do great things together. They just had to survive the tetrarch's court first.

# NINETEEN

Joanna was relieved to put the cart behind her as she disembarked in front of Herod's Palace in Jerusalem. She knuckled her lower back with a grimace as servants unloaded her and Chuza's chest of belongings.

She and Chuza strode together across the courtyard, their steps clipped with nervous expectation. A servant hastened to them, his face pinched. Joanna stepped closer to her husband.

"What is it?" Chuza asked the servant with admirable calmness.

"Antipas is in a terrible state, and his wife is no comfort to him," he said, dry-washing his hands.

"Why? What happened?" Chuza asked.

The servant leaned closer. "There are rumors of a prophet, and Antipas insists John has risen from the dead."

Chuza locked eyes with Joanna. Her stomach swooped as she nodded. It was time.

Chuza turned to the servant. "I will wash and change my clothes. Tell him I've arrived and can give an accurate report about this prophet."

Joanna couldn't let her husband face this alone. "Is Herodias with him?" she asked the man. Chuza frowned at her.

"She is," he said. "Though he refuses to speak with her."

"Then I will come too," Joanna said. Chuza opened his mouth to dissuade her, but she shrugged with exaggerated nonchalance. "I have a report to make." One that would hopefully serve as a distraction.

A few minutes later, they were striding to Antipas' suite of rooms. "Do not say too much," Chuza muttered under his breath. "I have given this conversation a good deal of thought."

Joanna looked down at her nails, picking at a cuticle. He was worried about what she would say, but Chuza's sense of honor and loyalty had been tested for over a year. Once he broke his seal of silence, anything could flood out.

He saw her uncertainty. "I have decades of experience dealing with Antipas," Chuza said. "Trust me, I know how to manage his fears."

They paused before Antipas' doors and the servant swung them open. The tension in the room drove through her like a winter wind. Herodias and Antipas sat as far from each other as possible without one of them crawling out the window. Antipas' flushed face and red eyes were a sharp contrast to Herodias' cold stare.

Antipas rose to his feet as Chuza and Joanna bowed. "Finally!" he said. He thrust his cup at the servant, sloshing the wine. He hurried forward to clasp Chuza's hand with shaky fingers. "Someone I can trust."

Herodias bridled.

"Tell me how I can serve you," Chuza said.

"They say you bring me a report on this prophet," Antipas said, his eyes wide with constrained fear. "Is it John? It is, isn't it? He's come back to life and will incite the people against me!"

"No, my friend," Chuza said. "It is not John."

"I shouldn't have released the body to his disciples," Antipas said, pulling away from Chuza and dragging both hands through his hair.

"I should have buried him where I could find him. To know."

"It is not him," Chuza repeated. "I saw the prophet with my own eyes, and it is not the baptizer."

Antipas hesitated. "You're sure?"

Chuza guided Antipas to his couch, encouraging him to sit. Joanna detected echoes of their first relationship—Chuza as the body slave, seeing to his master's every need, Antipas as the young tetrarch, trying to rule his people in the wake of rebellion and discontent.

Chuza took a low-backed chair. "This new prophet is from Nazareth," he said.

"South of Sepphoris? In the hills?"

"Yes," Chuza said. "He is John's cousin."

"The rumors speak of miracles," Antipas said, searching Chuza's face. "Even his followers heal and cast out demons. He can raise the dead. He called bread out of heaven and fed five thousand."

Chuza hesitated, and Joanna's muscles strained to keep her expression neutral.

"It is true," Chuza said.

Antipas stared, digesting the statement. A frown stole over him like a shadow, transforming his whole demeanor. "If it is true, I want him brought here," he said. "I want to see a miracle."

Joanna's stomach plummeted to her feet.

Chuza shook his head. "I do not think that would be wise, my lord."

Antipas scowled. "Why not? Why should the masses behold spectacles while the tetrarch of Galilee and Perea is left in the dark?"

Chuza pulled his seat closer. "You remember the stories of prophets in the scriptures. Did they bend to the will of kings? If this new prophet refuses your invitation, what then?"

"I can make him come." Antipas leaned back in his seat, nostrils flaring. Joanna twisted her sash around her finger, cutting off the circulation to her fingertips.

"Yes, you can drag him here with soldiers," Chuza said. "But how will the people react if you seize this miracle-worker by force? They remember what happened with John."

Antipas glared at Herodias, who had the decency to swallow hard.

"No, you cannot push the people now," Chuza said. "We cannot have riots or trouble, especially so close to Passover."

"I just want to see one miracle," Antipas whined with the petulance of a child.

"You must wait for him to come to you," Chuza said.

Herodias' voice cut through the room. "But don't some claim this prophet is the messiah?"

Chuza half-turned to her, his expression revealing none of his inner thoughts.

"If that's true," Chuza said, "he is a strange one. The people were ready to make him king—" Antipas drew a sharp breath, but Chuza held up his hand "—but he refused. He sent them home. He does not gather men to fight. I saw those he keeps close to him. They were commoners, fishermen even."

Herodias jeered. "His closest allies reek of fish?"

"They are his disciples," Joanna said without thinking. Three sets of eyes turned on her. Chuza shot her a warning look. She cleared her throat. "He teaches them."

"And what does he teach them?" Herodias' brows rose nearly to her hairline.

Joanna shrugged her shoulders as if the words of Jesus were a mere nothing. "He speaks like the sages, hiding truth in parables. He compares faith to farming, sheep, yeast, and... fishing."

Herodias' eyes narrowed with suspicion.

Chuza took the conversation back in hand. "There is no need for concern."

"But there might be in the future," Antipas pressed.

"At least wait until after Passover," Chuza said. "You don't want trouble while Pontius Pilate is in Jerusalem."

Antipas' lips tightened. "Very well, but employ your web of contacts. If there is the barest whisper of revolution, you must inform me."

"Of course."

"That brings up another concern," Herodias said. "How long have you known about this prophet, steward?" Joanna had to remind herself to breathe.

Antipas furrowed his brow at his wife, then looked at his right-hand man. Joanna was impressed with Chuza's self-control.

"I've been watching his progress for many months," Chuza said. He folded his hands as if keeping track of prophets was within his purview. "The Nazarene goes from synagogue to synagogue, speaking about righteousness. He is spiritual, not political. None of his teachings slander Rome or your rule, my lord."

Joanna's pride rose at her husband's shrewd skill, but Herodias sneered. "And we should trust your word?"

Antipas scowled at her.

Chuza kept his attention on his master. "You have entrusted me with great responsibility. Your coffers are full. Your estates are thriving. Your people are content and at peace. Can any man accuse me of neglecting my duties?"

Antipas smiled at him, though it was a little muddled by wine.

Herodias' lip curled in disbelief, but Chuza steered the conversation to safer ground. "While I'm here, I wish to say that my wife and I were very pleased with Philip's hospitality. He was honored by the gifts and eagerly anticipates his bride."

Herodias' posture eased a fraction.

"Yes," Joanna said, grasping at Chuza's hint. "I have much to report, my lady."

Herodias hesitated, torn between sowing seeds of bitterness and gathering the fruit of her efforts. She rose with a rustle of fabric. "Come, Joanna. Let's go to my room so you can tell me everything." She bowed to Antipas, her voice chilly as she said, "If my husband will excuse me?"

Antipas waved Herodias away without looking at her. Herodias' jaw clenched and she swept from the room. Joanna fell in step beside her, casting a worried peek back at her husband.

Herodias summoned Salome to her chambers, and the young woman drifted in like a storm cloud. Joanna's sympathies for Salome's situation resurfaced.

"Rearrange your face, if you please," Herodias instructed her daughter coolly. She gestured that Joanna should sit. Joanna chose a soft seat, but could not relax.

"Now," Herodias said, settling her robes around herself. "Tell my daughter about her future territory, the city, and the palace. And her betrothed, of course."

Joanna shared her attention between mother and daughter, careful to speak well of Salome's future without exaggerating. She didn't want to give false hope, but she attempted to soothe the young woman for losing the man she loved.

Herodias pressed for more details, but Salome sat as if carved from marble, her face set in grim acceptance. When Joanna had plumbed the depths of what she had seen, Herodias smiled sweetly at her daughter.

"Just think, my girl," Herodias said. "All of that shall soon be yours."

"How thrilling," Salome said sarcastically. "My star shines just a little less than yours. Am I not right, mother?"

Herodias studied her daughter with narrowed eyes. As Philip's wife, Salome would not hold the wealth or prestige of her mother.

Herodias sighed at Joanna, leaning forward as if confiding a secret. "I wish my family would see how much I have done for them. My daughter will marry a tetrarch. My brother and his wife are safe from his debtors—"

"Living in a desert fortress," Salome interrupted, her hands bunching into fists. "You truly believe my uncle is happy? Do you think he still laughs, throwing back his head, his eyes dancing? Does he throw lavish parties like he did in Rome? Is he now entertaining the local people with his charm and wit?" Her accusations flowed easily, and Joanna blinked. She had never met Herodias' brother Agrippa, but Chuza told her he had been popular in Rome—until his debts cut off both his powerful friends and his extravagant lifestyle.

Herodias' voice coiled like a viper. "For now, it is enough that he is safe. I have not forgotten my brother, nor the honor he is owed because of our heritage. The blood of my father, who should have inherited all of this—" she waved her hand as if encompassing the palace, the city, the land "—will rise again. We will reclaim what was stolen from us."

Joanna stared. What was Herodias plotting? Herodias flushed beneath Joanna's assessing gaze. She cleared her throat and rose to her feet, signaling Joanna to rise as well.

"I've kept you long enough," Herodias said. "I'm sure you wish to rest after your journey. Perhaps later you can take a walk with my daughter. Passover is fast approaching, and she needs to be educated on its significance."

Joanna looked at Salome in confusion. "You haven't celebrated the festival before?"

Salome folded her arms, bitterness in every line of her body. She gave Joanna a mirthless smile. "Back home, Mother was embarrassed to be a Jew. But now she waves her history like a banner." She fixed her mother with a heartless stare, her voice rising in pitch, mocking. "Poor, deposed, princess Herodias. Isn't that right, Mother?"

Herodias swelled with fury. Joanna mumbled a few incoherent words and made her escape as Herodias unleashed her tongue on her daughter.

The sound of raised voices faded as Joanna strode to the kitchen. She was unhappy with how she and Leah had left things. Somehow, they needed to patch their friendship and move forward. After facing

Herodias, talking to Leah should be easy, but as she pushed open the door, Joanna swallowed her nerves.

The palace kitchen was in a state of organized bustle, everyone slicing or stirring or kneading. Michael leaned with one scarred hand on a scrubbed wooden table, hovering over Leah's shoulder as she formed a delicate shape with dough. Leah's brow furrowed with concentration as she pinched in one place, then picked up a pair of small shears and snipped in another spot.

At Joanna's approach, Leah glanced up, her expression unusually open as she did what she loved best. She picked up the dough and held it out so Joanna could see. A little bird nestled in her palm.

"It's beautiful," Joanna said, and Leah set it on the tray with the rest of its flock. She picked up a bowl and brushed the dough with a beaten egg.

"It's perfect," Michael said, puffing out his chest. "As is everything that comes from this girl's hands." Two maids giggled at the gruff man's tenderness for the orphaned young woman, but Joanna gave him a grateful nod.

Leah finished preparing the tray and picked it up, balancing its weight with practiced hands as she moved toward the courtyard. Joanna followed. Leah peered into an oven, examining the low bed of coals. With a nod of satisfaction, Leah slid the heavy tray inside and kept watch over her creations, tucking a stray hair behind her ear.

"You're doing well?" Joanna said.

"I am." Leah's tone was guarded. "How was your journey?"

Joanna filled her in on their nerve-wracking encounter on the Jericho Road and how they stumbled into Jesus.

"So Chuza finally saw him," Leah said, her expression neutral. "That must make you happy."

Joanna nodded, but she twisted her belt around her finger. "Antipas and Herodias have learned about Jesus."

Leah's cold facade cracked. She glanced about for listening ears.

"Do they know you were following and supporting him?"

"Not exactly," Joanna said. "Chuza handled Antipas like a potter handles his clay, shaping the truth in a pleasing way."

"So you're still lying to them," Leah said.

"We haven't lied about who Jesus is."

Leah raised her brows in disbelief. "So you told them he's the Messiah?"

Joanna flushed. "Jesus hasn't declared himself yet."

"But that's who you believe him to be."

"I hope he is. God has gifted him. What better man to lead us?"

Leah fell silent. Her hand shielded by a rag, she slid the tray out, inspected the golden birds, and pushed it back in. She darted a glance at Joanna. "Are you thinking of rejoining Jesus?"

Joanna nodded. "Eventually. Chuza needs my help here." Her emotions churned as her heart pulled in two directions. Neither choice was free of consequences.

Leah removed her creations and strode back to the kitchen, leaving Joanna to follow or not. One by one, Leah plucked the golden bread off the tray. As she set the last bird aside, she blew on her fingers, her hazel eyes sizing up her mistress.

"So you do care," Leah said. At Joanna's questioning look, she added, "About Chuza."

"Of course I do!" Joanna said, startled by the accusation. "It was never about picking one over the other."

"It looked like that to me."

Joanna made sure the other maids were too busy to overhear. "I can be both. Wife and disciple."

Leah looked doubtful. "You're going to get both of you in trouble. Chuza can only shape the truth so far before it collapses in his hands. How long will you push your luck?

"We're trying to do the right thing," Joanna said.

Leah leaned her hip on the work table, folding her arms. "You really think you can make a difference? That Jesus needs you? You're just one woman."

Leah had poked a sore spot. Besides giving money, Joanna hadn't done anything. The old yearning raised its head. All her life she had desired to be used by God, yet her prayers still went unanswered.

Leah tilted her chin to the side. "Is your need to support a prophet more important than your life here?"

"Of course," Joanna said, then flushed as Leah stiffened. "What I mean is that my devotion to God is foremost. Above everything. It should be for everyone."

Leah's mouth puckered. "And how do you know this is what God wants from you?"

Joanna winced at the hard edge behind Leah's challenge, wavering for an answer. She had never heard God's voice. She had never received a call beyond Jesus' invitation: *Follow me.*

"I don't know," she admitted, and Leah's eyes narrowed. "But if I keep showing up where God is working, surely my time will come."

"So that is why Jesus healed you?" Leah said, challenging her. "To work for him?"

Joanna blinked. "What? No. I think he healed me because he wanted to. He sees broken things and wants to fix them."

Leah's jaw clenched. "Like you want to fix me?" Leah was as adept at twisting Joanna's words as she was at creating culinary delicacies.

"I want to help you," Joanna corrected. She reached out a hand, but let it fall to her side. "I don't understand everything you're feeling, but I am trying." Leah grew still, and Joanna pressed on. "We should talk again. Soon. You can tell me more about your family. Your grandfather. I promise I won't start moralizing again." She twisted her lips into a rueful smile.

"I doubt talking will help," Leah said, tossing her head. She met Joanna's eyes and her shoulders lost some of their tension. "But it might be nice."

Joanna accepted the olive branch, no matter how tiny. "I'd like that."

"Later," Leah said, pushing away from the counter and brushing off her fingers. "I need to get back to work."

Joanna reached around her and snagged one of the golden birds, laughing as Leah tried to slap her hand. Joanna hurried from the kitchen with her prize and the hope that she and Leah could recover their friendship.

# TWENTY

Joanna watched her husband resume his duties as if nothing had changed. Twice, Antipas summoned Chuza to soothe his fears. Each time Chuza assured the tetrarch that John was dead and it would be imprudent to arrest Jesus for curiosity's sake. Joanna and Chuza shouldered the role of unwilling actors, feigning normalcy while knowing the spiritual and the physical world were weaving together in Galilee.

Chuza kept his wife's support of Jesus hidden, but Joanna feared the palace gossips would finally connect her disappearances with the famous prophet. If Jesus declared himself the Messiah, everything she had done, every proof of her support, would be weighed against her loyalty to Antipas.

As days slipped by in the friendless court, Joanna grew homesick for the camaraderie of the disciples and the feeling that God was nearby. One morning she decided to walk to the temple alone, drawing her palla over her hair.

She was halfway across the aqueduct bridge when the tromping of hobnailed sandals and the rattling of wheels drew her against the stone balustrade to peer below. A procession marched down the city street, the lead riders bearing the standards of Rome. Joanna sighed with grim acceptance. The governor had come to Jerusalem.

Joanna squinted as the sun glinted off golden shields borne by soldiers. Pilate had never brought anything like them before. A knot of Pharisees glared at them before hastening away. Joanna's stomach clenched with misgiving.

An ornate carriage rolled behind Pilate, requiring four horses to pull its bulk. Instead of turning to Herod's Palace, the procession rumbled under the bridge. She crossed to the other side of the road as they pulled into the courtyard of the Antonia and disappeared from view.

Joanna hastened into the temple complex, trotting across the intricate tile and up the steps to peer down into the outer court of the Antonia. Pilate nodded in approval as soldiers arranged the shields flanking the doorway. Satisfied, he went to the carriage and opened the door, holding out his hand. To Joanna's surprise, a woman stepped out. Pilate brought her fingers to his lips, then led her into the fortress.

Suspecting trouble was brewing, Joanna hurried back to the palace. As she neared the gate, she realized she wasn't the only one rushing to share the news. The Pharisees from the street spoke to a guard, who nodded them in. Joanna slipped into their wake before veering to Chuza's office.

Sticking her head in the door, she found him hunched over his desk.

"Better hurry," she said. "There's trouble."

His mouth pressed into a line. "What happened?"

Joanna recounted Pilate's unusual arrival as they made their way to Antipas' receiving hall. A servant met them.

"Antipas just sent me to summon you," he said, glaring reproachfully at Joanna.

Chuza quickened his pace and Joanna followed. Antipas' receiving room was moderate-sized, with a raised dais for Antipas' throne. His advisors and friends stood nearby. Antipas' shoulders were taut, and Joanna wondered if his tension arose from the Pharisee's report, or because Herodias stood in his shadow, pretending she was still his trusted wife.

The Pharisees turned at the sound of Chuza's approach and gave him respectful nods. Joanna slipped to the side of the room, where she knew she'd be forgotten.

Antipas tented his fingers beneath his chin. "Tell my steward what the shields proclaim."

One of the Pharisees cleared his throat, his voice ringing angrily across the room. "They are inscribed with the names of Pontius Pilate and Emperor Tiberius, calling the emperor 'the son of god'."

Joanna's stomach swooped in dismay. Pilate was a fool, carrying such words into a Jewish city. Chuza's shoulders stiffened. He considered for a moment before answering.

"In Roman lands," Chuza said, "it is a common honorific for Caesar. Perhaps Pilate does not realize how offensive it is to our people."

"Oh, he knows," Antipas said, spinning his large ring with his thumb. "He's provoking the crowds. Goading me. Hoping I'll take issue with the title and give him reason to complain to the emperor about my disloyalty."

Chuza clasped his hands behind his back, so only Joanna could see their tight grip. His voice was calm. "He can't want trouble. It would reflect on his rule as well."

"I'm not so sure," Antipas said. "He's staying in the Antonia, a more defensible position."

Chuza glanced at Joanna. "Pilate has brought a woman with him, likely his wife. Would he have brought her if he planned to endure a siege?"

"He's brought Claudia with him?" Antipas leaned back as he took in this new information.

Chuza continued. "He displays the shields, though they are only visible to those who peer into the Antonia's courtyard, which Jews are unlikely to do." Most Jews avoided the fortress like it was a den of lepers. "I agree he is pressing his position, but I don't think we can say he's spoiling for a fight."

Antipas glanced around at his friends. "What do you think? Should I confront the governor?"

One man spoke up. "On what basis? As the steward pointed out, it's a common title for the emperor since Augustus. If you say it is not true, you insult Emperor Tiberius."

The Pharisees bristled and their leader drew himself up. "Tiberius has given us freedom of worship. He allows us to gather money for the temple without interference, and he asks us to offer sacrifices on his behalf. Would he condone Pilate inflaming the people over words on a decorative shield? They serve no purpose other than to prop up the governor's vanity. They must come down."

Antipas considered, brushing a knuckle over his lips, the ring catching the light. He inclined his head at the Pharisees. "Tiberius would not want trouble over a trivial matter. But—" he stretched out his palms, "as yet, there is no trouble."

One of the Pharisees opened his mouth to argue, but then closed it again.

"Perhaps the people will let the shields pass," Antipas said. He leaned forward in his seat, pinning them with his gaze. "Especially if their leaders keep silent."

The Pharisees muttered at letting the golden shields remain unchallenged, but Antipas' retinue was nodding.

Herodias murmured, "Wise decision, my lord."

Antipas ignored her. "Let us wait and see. If trouble arises, we will discuss this again."

The Pharisees bowed stiffly and swept from the room. Joanna could sympathize with their displeasure. A shiver trailed over her skin as she remembered the deadly repercussions of Pilate's other political blunders.

Antipas rose from his throne, but Herodias held out her hand.

"My lord," she said, and he paused as she hurried to stand before him like a supplicant, bowing low. "While your advisors are gathered, I wish to put an urgent matter before you."

Antipas' lip curled, but he resumed his seat with a curt nod.

"My sister-in-law has written to me in great distress," she said. "My brother, Agrippa, has been living in the fortress of Malatha for many months. Withdrawn from society as he is, and without a hope for a change in fortune, he has become depressed."

Antipas' expression showed no sympathy for a man forced to flee Rome to avoid debtors' prison.

Herodias pressed on, emotion filling her voice and drawing pity from her audience. "He has been so grateful for your support and friendship, which you graciously offered. Yet, placed so far from all his family, he has despaired. He speaks of taking his own life."

A few men murmured in sympathy as Herodias clutched her hands to her chest. "Please, my lord, to preserve my brother's life, and to save his wife and children from grief, I ask that you move him from Malatha and give him a position in your kingdom where he could do some good. Let him serve as the mayor in one of your cities."

Antipas' lips puckered at handing over the rule of a city, but a quick glance showed the idea found favor with his friends.

Herodias lowered her chin, and her voice softened with emotion. "Herod became more than a grandfather to us when our own father was... taken." She glossed over the fact that it was Herod himself who executed his son as a suspected traitor. "I think Herod would want more for his grandson than destitution in the desert. He would desire all his descendants to hold positions of power, for the honor of his name, and in memory of his glorious rule."

"Well said," a man cheered, and others nodded.

Antipas sighed. "Which of my cities would you give to your

brother's tender mercies?"

Herodias tipped her head to the side. "Isn't the mayor of Tiberias retiring?"

Antipas stiffened. Tiberias was his capital city. His pride and joy.

Herodias wasn't finished. "As some of your subjects still refuse to enter the city, despite its beauty, it would be a good place for Agrippa," she said. "He can find the middle ground. He observes the Jewish faith, yet has moved in the highest Roman circles."

"It is a shame his powerful friends cannot aid him now," Antipas said dryly.

She ignored that statement, but her cheeks colored. "Your help would mean a great deal to him," she said, pausing for a heartbeat before adding, "and your wife."

Antipas considered for a long time, the silence stretching to the point of awkwardness. Finally, he beckoned Chuza over, and the two of them conferred for several minutes. Joanna knew that neither man held any respect for Agrippa.

Antipas turned his attention back to his wife, displeasure cutting into the creases of his brow. "Very well," he said. "Let us hope Agrippa fares better in his position as mayor than he did with his ventures in Rome."

Herodias beamed as if he offered Agrippa the entire kingdom. "I will write to Cypros," she said. "This will give my brother a reason to live again."

Joanna drew back as Herodias hurried from the room, triumph glowing in her eyes.

As Antipas heaved himself to his feet and began chatting with his friends, Chuza returned to Joanna's side, his cheeks stiff. "I remember when Antipas promised to never gift Agrippa a bronze quadran. Now, he gives him his favorite city." He shook his head in disbelief. "We need to be careful. Herodias clearly knows how to play the court. If she learns about your time with Jesus, she could turn everyone against us. Even Antipas' regard for me might not be enough to keep us safe."

Joanna's stomach sunk, but before she could answer, Antipas called Chuza over. Joanna slipped from the hall, praying she and Chuza could find their way forward with both honor and lives intact. Antipas might need Chuza's counsel, but if he would not listen to him, both men were wasting their breath.

The sight of Salome interrupted Joanna's grim musings.

"There you are," Salome said with impatience. "Mother insists that I familiarize myself with the coming festival." She tossed her curls and folded her arms. "Apparently, it's of some importance."

Joanna raised a brow. "You could say that." She drew a deep breath, trying to clear her concerns away. Despite Herodias' scheming ways, Salome should understand her heritage. "Let's go to the temple and I will show you what to expect," Joanna said. "I can tell you the story of the first Passover."

As Joanna crossed the aqueduct bridge for the second time that day, explaining the Exodus to the young woman at her side, she remembered another woman she tried—unsuccessfully—to teach about faith. Phasaelis had been argumentative and jaded. To the Nabatean princess, the purpose of religion was to sway the gods' fickle moods. Sacrifices were a bribe to receive blessings. Joanna left the princess in Nabatea with no sign she had influenced Phasaelis to a greater understanding of the one true God.

Salome, however, became fascinated by the story of Moses and Pharaoh. Joanna was shocked to discover Salome had never heard it before. Gratitude for her upbringing made her reach over to tuck Salome's arm under hers. It was like strolling with a statue at first, but as Joanna chatted and smiled, the young woman gradually relaxed. Joanna took her time showing Salome around the temple complex, taking her as far into the Court of Women as they could go, pointing out the large altar, and telling her about the sacrifices.

As Salome listened with genuine interest, Joanna's spirits lifted.

Maybe she could accomplish with Salome what she failed to do with Phasaelis. Perhaps God would use her to lead Salome to faith. The idea made Joanna's heart swell with longing.

# TWENTY-ONE

While the city muttered at John's beheading, Herodias and Antipas sequestered themselves in the palace. Joanna doubted the couple would attend the sacrifices for fear that the people, full of Passover fervor, would rise against them.

Whispers of a prophet from Nazareth swept the streets like the winds of spring, but Jesus did not appear. Joanna's emotions lurched from hope that he would show up and anxiety about what would happen if he did. Between Pilate's golden shields and Antipas beheading John, Jerusalem was on edge. If the people decided a prophet could lead them to freedom, Jesus would be declared king—whether he was ready or not.

The day of Passover arrived. Joanna and Chuza dutifully prepared to fulfill their festival tradition. As Dalia opened the door, Joanna cringed at the now-familiar stare, feeling like a beggar at a banquet.

"Where's your maid?" Dalia demanded.

Joanna fixed a smile in place. "Spending the feast with friends." Leah outright refused to come, and she tried to convince Joanna to do the same.

"Hmm," Dalia said, pursing her lips. She held the door open. Joanna puffed out her breath, wishing she had listened to Leah.

The women were arranging the tables in the courtyard, laying out dishes and lamps while half a dozen children helped with various degrees of skill. Miriam greeted Joanna with a hug, then sent her to the storeroom for more wine. Joanna gritted her teeth as Dalia followed her into the small room, shutting the door and pinning her beneath a suspicious frown.

"Why aren't you pregnant yet?" Dalia asked without preamble. Joanna blinked in shocked silence. "There's a rumor that the steward's wife disappears to her vineyard for weeks at a time, avoiding her husband and his bed."

Joanna flushed. It seemed Herodias' malicious rumors had escaped the court and spread far enough for Dalia to catch them. Hugging the amphora of wine to her chest, Joanna lifted her chin. "I love Chuza," she said. "We will be blessed in the Lord's timing."

Dalia studied her. "And there's another rumor. That the wife of Chuza was among the disciples of Jesus. Some say he healed you, and you support him out of your means."

This rumor was more favorable to her character, but more dangerous if it reached the court.

Dalia searched her face and grinned with triumph. "So it's true. You are supporting this new prophet. He really healed you? Then why did you let us assume that you simply recovered?"

Those painful days felt like another life, one she was not eager to revisit. She met her sister's suspicious eye. "That winter when I wrote Mama, telling her I was sick, I didn't say how serious it was." She shuddered, remembering the fevers, weakness, nausea, and crippling headaches that leeched the life from her bones.

"Why not?" Dalia said, crossing her arms.

"If Mama knew, she would have tried to visit me at the palace. I didn't want to put her in the middle of our arguments again."

Dalia narrowed her eyes. "Why should I believe you?"

"Well, you can believe what you like," Joanna said, her ire rising, "but Jesus healed me. Since then, I have traveled with him and supported him with my money. Witnessed him heal and proclaim the coming kingdom of God."

Joanna braced for her sister's reaction, but Dalia simply leaned against a shelf. "I guess your story is less crazy than some reports going around. Like feeding five thousand men from only a few fish and loaves. Or raising people from the dead." She grinned.

Joanna stared, realizing she and her sister were of one mind for the first time in years.

Dalia lowered her voice. "Amichai thinks Jesus might be the one they've been waiting for."

Joanna clutched the amphora tighter. Of course, anything Amichai said, Dalia would accept. Joanna opened her mouth to retort but then shut it again. Perhaps the messenger didn't matter if Dalia heard and believed.

Dalia saw Joanna's inner turmoil. "Does Chuza know you've been to see Jesus?"

Joanna was tired of defending her and Chuza's righteousness. "He supports me," she said with more volume than necessary. "He's witnessed Jesus for himself. Chuza is a man of faith, no matter what you think."

Dalia considered for a long moment, then nodded, a new gleam in her eye. "This is good. I will tell Amichai that you and Chuza support the prophet. Perhaps, when the time comes, you can help topple Antipas' rule from the inside."

Joanna stiffened. "Amichai is making plans?"

"He's here in the city, with some of his friends. They hoped Jesus would come and the revolution would begin."

Joanna's stomach flipped at the word. After her conversation with Titus and Chuza, the repercussions of a revolution felt all the more real. "If Jesus isn't here by now, I don't think he's coming for Passover."

"Me too," Dalia said, her lips quirking as the sisters agreed for the second time. Dalia picked up a tray of dried fruit, bestowing a conspiratorial smile Joanna hadn't received in years. "We'd better get back before Mama begins to worry we strangled each other." They both chuckled.

Her hand on the door handle, Dalia fixed Joanna with a stern eye. "I told you Amichai is in the city because I trust you. We're on the same side, right?"

Joanna hesitated, remembering the men on the Jericho Road and the whistles of their slings. But maybe, if her brother had a chance to listen to Jesus, wisdom would hone the edge of his national pride into a tool Jesus could use.

"Yes," Joanna said. "We are."

Dalia smiled again, and memories washed over Joanna. She and Dalia had shared chores, played together, and whispered secrets in the night, little moments that sweetened her childhood. Though she wouldn't admit it aloud, Joanna cried like a baby the first night she slept alone after Dalia's wedding. They had been at odds ever since Joanna joined Antipas' court, but perhaps Jesus could bridge the distance.

Joanna followed Dalia from the storeroom with the wine, delivering the amphora to her mother. Miriam glanced between her daughters and softened with relief. Joanna's cheeks warmed with guilt. For too long, Miriam had watched her children live with animosity toward each other.

Dalia invited Joanna to join her and the other women in the kitchen. Chuza overheard, and he raised his brows. Joanna smiled, her eyes promising to tell him everything later.

At first, the other women were confused at Joanna's inclusion, but they followed Dalia's lead. Welcomed among the chatter and busy hands, Joanna blinked back tears of relief. Maybe years of exclusion were finally over.

Her and Dalia's reconciliation rolled away a burden Joanna had borne for years. Her steps felt lighter, the world seemed brighter. But not everyone in the palace was as cheerful. Salome moped in the palace courtyard. Joanna, feeling unusually buoyant, asked the petulant girl to walk with her to the temple. Together they crossed the Upper City.

They drifted around the temple courts, Joanna walking slowly so she could catch the whispered rumors. Jesus had disappeared, though the sources differed as to why. Some said he feared confronting Antipas. Others insisted the religious leaders were tired of him trampling on tradition and were turning against him.

Salome interrupted Joanna's eavesdropping.

"Can we go up there?" Salome said. She gestured toward Solomon's Colonnade.

They took the stairs to the second story, passing rabbis teaching their disciples. They ascended to the third level and peered over the temple courts. Lingering incense sweetened the breeze as Joanna surveyed the temple's gleaming white marble and gold. She scanned the city, her gaze drawn to Herod's Palace, where Chuza was busy at work. The Mount of Olives spread in the east, verdant with silvery-leafed trees.

Salome was unimpressed with the view. She gestured to the eastern tower, built on the outer edge of the city wall. "I don't suppose we are allowed up there," she said. The terrain sloped away, making the pale tower seem impossibly high when seen from the ground.

"No," Joanna said. "That's where the priests blow the shofar. Only the watchmen can go up."

"What a shame," Salome said, her expression flat. "If I threw myself from there, I would be certain of a swift death."

Joanna gripped the girl's arm with white knuckles. "What are you talking about?"

Salome's eyes puddled with tears. "It'll be months before I receive word from my father—maybe longer. By then it will be too late to stop this marriage. But even if he could fly to my side, he would not interfere. He always bends to Mother's ambition." Salome stared across the horizon and a tear tracked down her cheek. "My uncle had the right idea. Sometimes suicide is the only escape."

Joanna reeled, plumbing her limited experience for advice. "Have you told your mother how you feel?"

Salome scoffed. "Oh, yes. But she says I'm being dramatic. Mother doesn't believe I'd actually do it." Her lips trembled, and she pressed them together. "She'll help her brother, but not her daughter. You know why, don't you?" She turned her dark eyes to Joanna. "Because I am a woman. My purpose is to marry the right man, support him in all he does, and produce sons. I am a tool in my mother's hand, used to further her fortune. In Rome, it's no different. Women are wed in business mergers as if we were ships or stock. Our wombs are our worth."

Denial rose in Joanna's throat. She squeezed Salome's arm. "That may be how the world works, but that doesn't make it true. My father valued me for myself. He educated me like a son, and he was proud of my faith and understanding."

Salome peered at her through damp lashes. "Then you were luckier than most." She fanned her hand over the scene below. "Even your temple places us in a lower position. You told me that we aren't supposed to go past the Court of Women, except for a special sacrifice. Yet the men can go whenever they like."

Joanna paused. She had discussed the issue with her father before, struggling with the exclusion. In the original tabernacle, there was no division, just one large courtyard for everyone. Hannah met the priest Eli right by the tabernacle door.

As time passed, the separation between the genders had grown —by tradition rather than God's command. Perhaps it was because women were exempt from adhering to all the laws because of their role as mothers. Fear that a menstruating woman might defile a priest became a reason to keep them all away. Joanna's memory roved over the woman with the hemorrhage who touched Jesus, receiving healing and praise.

"There are distinctions, yes," Joanna said, "but God sees us all. Our worship is no less worthy than a man's. Our sacred texts celebrate women who served the Lord as prophetesses or wise women who counseled kings."

And Jesus welcomed women as his disciples. He listened to women, healed them, praised their faith, and accepted their support.

But Salome was right. Not everyone saw them in that way. Joanna felt a pressing on her heart, an urge to tell the depressed young woman about Jesus, to give her hope and worth. Before she lost her courage, she spoke carefully.

"There is a prophet who values women. He calls them to repent and watch for the kingdom of God, teaching them along with the men."

Salome looked doubtful. "Do you mean Jesus of Nazareth? Have you met him?"

Joanna hesitated. She could lie and protect herself, but this young woman was desperate, even suicidal. Salome needed to find value in herself, outside her role as an unwilling wife.

Joanna nodded, and Salome's eyes widened. Salome leaned closer, whispering, "You've seen the one everyone is talking about? Witnessed his miracles?"

Joanna nodded again, her heart hammering against her chest.

Salome set her hand on Joanna's arm. "Tell me about him."

Joanna prayed she would do Jesus justice. Salome would depart for Caesarea Philippi soon, and she might not get this opportunity again. As they stood overlooking the temple and Herod's Palace,

Joanna told Herodias' daughter about Jesus.

Salome absorbed every word. When Joanna finished, Salome tilted her head. "So, those women you spoke of, who gave generous sums of money, were you one of them?"

Joanna's chest swelled with pride at being one of the women who supported Jesus. A small part of her mind warned her to keep her role quiet, but this was the tangible expression of her devotion and proof that women were of value, even outside the home. She didn't want Salome to think she was bragging, so she flicked her wrist dismissively.

"We feed Jesus and his disciples so they can continue their work," Joanna said, "but it is more important that we sit as students and learn."

Salome rested her hand on Joanna's. "Thank you for talking to me," she said. "To be honest, I don't know why you care. You hardly know me." Her cheeks grew pink. "I wish my mother was more like you." The praise warmed Joanna from the inside out.

As they returned to the palace, Joanna prayed she had accomplished with Salome what she failed to do with Phasaelis. But, she realized, Phasaelis had never heard about Jesus. He made all the difference. The proof of his power brought history to life, and the miracles of Moses and Elijah became tangible and real. If miracles were real, then God was real. And if God was real, then he would fulfill his promises. Restoration was coming at last.

# TWENTY-TWO

Joanna jerked awake in the dark bedchamber. "What have I done?" She sat up, her fist pressed against her lips. Moonlight spilled through the window screen as she replayed her conversation at the temple, trying to remember every expression, every word Salome said. Salome's distress had been real. Joanna was sure of that. The girl was as helpless as a sparrow in a storm. But even if Salome hadn't been playing on her sympathies, Joanna risked too much by trusting Salome with her secret.

"God, did I do the right thing?" Joanna whispered. Surely there was little danger in talking about Jesus now that he was known in the palace, but confessing her support was another matter entirely. She groaned. Why had she admitted to giving Jesus money?

Her past mistakes taunted her. Years ago, her pride in her own wisdom pulled her from home, and perhaps factored into her father's untimely death. Now her determination to be seen as righteous might have put her and Chuza in danger.

She needed to talk with Salome again. In the morning she would find her and see if Herodias' daughter had taken her for a fool.

Joanna slept fitfully, and when she woke, bright sunlight bathed the room. Chuza was already gone. Berating herself for over-sleeping, Joanna threw on some clothes and braided her hair. She shoved her feet in her sandals and strode to Salome's suite.

Salome's maid opened the door.

"Is Salome awake?" Joanna asked.

Helga nodded. "She's walking in the garden with her mother."

Joanna's throat tightened. Maybe she was already too late. She spun to go, but Helga leaned forward. "Thank you, my lady, for whatever you said yesterday. She was like a different person this morning. You are her only friend here."

Some of Joanna's fear drained away. "She considers me her friend?"

"Oh, yes!"

She wanted to believe Helga, to hope that Salome would not betray her confidence. With effort, she gave a smile.

Joanna turned for the center of the large courtyard, where groomed paths wove through thick greenery. She would stroll in and catch Salome's conversation. Perhaps she was worrying over nothing, but she needed to be sure.

Joanna stepped into the garden, trying to appear innocent while walking on the quiet edge of the gravel path, her ears straining. She paused as she heard lowered voices on the other side of tall ferns. Herodias and Salome. She held her breath, and Salome's petulant tones filtered through the dense brush.

"I can't marry him, Mother. Please, don't make me!"

Herodias' response was tight. "Someday you'll understand that minor discomfort today will reap a plentiful harvest tomorrow. For both of us. The world is a harsh place for women. It is time you learned how to use what little we command to secure our future. Yes, I'll admit that this marriage benefits me, but it does even more for you."

Salome sniffled, and Joanna pictured her tearful face. After a few moments, she heard Salome's hesitant voice. "What if I helped you another way?"

"What are you talking about?"

"I could be your eyes and ears here. I already have information that you need—if you still want Joanna thrown out of court."

Joanna's limbs turned to stone.

"Then tell me."

"Not until you call off my betrothal."

Herodias laughed mirthlessly. "I'll consider it."

"Promise me."

"Tell me, and I will decide if your help is worth offending Philip."

Joanna didn't dare breathe, didn't dare move, lest they realize she was eavesdropping.

After a heavy silence, Salome huffed out her breath. "Joanna hasn't been spending her time at her vineyard. She follows the prophet from Nazareth."

"If the rumors are true, so does half of Galilee," Herodias said.

"Yes, but she's given large amounts of money to help him."

Joanna's trembling hand covered her mouth. This couldn't be happening.

Herodias' voice thickened with smothered excitement. "Hmm. That is a little something more."

Salome's anger rose. "You know this evidence will cast suspicion on her loyalty. First, she helped Phasaelis escape. Now she secretly supports a man many call their savior. What else could you need to get rid of her?"

Joanna's muscles quivered, but fear of discovery kept her in place. Herodias answered with a malicious smile in her voice. "And what about the steward? Does Chuza know what his wife is doing?"

"Chuza? I don't know. She didn't mention him. Everyone says Chuza is unswervingly loyal to Antipas."

"So they do," Herodias said dryly. "Recent matters have shown me that Chuza's influence over Antipas is stronger than I first believed."

Salome took her chance at a jab. "Stronger than yours, you mean."

Herodias ignored her. "But he can not be as perfect as he seems.

If Joanna is any sort of woman, she has tainted Chuza with her revolutionary ideals already. That is why he keeps Antipas from arresting the Nazarene, and why he constantly reminds Antipas about John's execution—keeping him bitter toward me." Her voice became a hiss. "Antipas should come to me for advice. I should be his greatest support. His confidante. But I can't as long as the steward has his hooks in him. "

"But how can—"

Herodias was practically cackling with glee. "We will arrest Joanna, then bring her before Antipas on charges of sedition. She will implicate Chuza."

"Joanna would never do that." Salome's staunch belief offered a sliver of comfort.

"You must repeat everything you told me when I have Joanna brought to Antipas. Your testimony should be enough to warrant a more... thorough line of questioning."

"Wait..." Salome sounded strained. "You wouldn't... torture her, would you?" Sweat beaded on Joanna's upper lip, but she didn't dare wipe it away. Salome's voice rose with panic. "I thought you just wanted her to leave court!"

Herodias' sickly sweet voice set Joanna's teeth on edge. "And that is why you still need your mother's guidance. Joanna has been a thorn in my side, but now she will rid me of an even greater problem. Antipas does not trust me, so if I accuse his most trusted friend, he could turn against me."

"So he'll turn against me instead?" Salome snapped.

Herodias' voice was soothing. "Only for a moment. When Joanna confesses that Chuza has been secretly supporting our enemies, Antipas must lean on me for comfort, and you will receive praise."

"But why must I testify?" Salome said. "She was trying to help me. As a friend."

Herodias laughed. "If she thought she was your friend, you're not as helpless as I feared. You'll make a wonderful addition to Philip's court."

"Philip's—! But you promised!"

Herodias scoffed. "If your information results in arrests, we'll talk. We must work quickly, before Joanna flitters off once again."

As soon as Joanna heard the crunch of their steps on the gravel, she fled, berating herself for her foolishness. She had placed her fate in the hands of a child.

Bile rose in her throat as she considered what kind of torture Herodias had in mind. As much as she hoped she would withstand, the weakness in her knees warned her that the questioners' methods could make anyone confess to anything.

Joanna burst into Chuza's office. It was empty. She dug her fingers into her hair, and a groan ripped from between her teeth. She had no idea how quickly Herodias would implement her cruel plan. Guards could already be on their way.

The door creaked open behind her, and she jumped, whirling around.

Chuza strolled into his office. She burst into tears, throwing herself into his arms.

"What's wrong?" he asked in alarm. She clung to him, but he pulled back, his brow creased with worry. "What happened?"

As fast as she could, she explained everything. Chuza grew pale.

She wiped her cheeks with her sleeve. "What do we do?" she whispered.

Chuza drifted to his desk. He hunched, his fingers splayed on his accounts and correspondence. He shook his head, thinking. Planning.

But time was running out. She saw only one way forward. She swallowed hard. "You can't leave, but if I'm gone, Herodias won't be able to touch you."

He jerked his head up, stricken. "So you'll just leave the court? Forever?"

The word stabbed at her heart. "Not forever," she said. "Just until Herodias forgets her anger."

Chuza scrubbed his face with his palms. "Where will you go? Your vineyard?"

She could hide at her vineyard, hoping that her sudden disappearance would give Herodias pause. Maybe a delay was all they needed for Herodias to come to her senses. But the idea of going home to sit in shame and embarrassment spread tingling heat across Joanna's face and neck. She would have to tell Tirzah that her foolish pride had ruined everything.

"I could rejoin the disciples," Joanna said.

Chuza stiffened, but if Joanna had to flee, she needed to preserve a measure of dignity. "I have friends there. I'll be safe. And I can continue to support Jesus." Chuza still didn't answer, and she set her trembling hand on his arm. "I don't have a lot of time. We need to decide."

"Do you even know where he is?" Chuza said, his expression pained.

"No," Joanna admitted. "But I know someone I can ask in Capernaum."

He groaned. "So you'll walk back to Galilee? Alone?"

Joanna flinched. He was right. She didn't have Manaen to accompany her, and she couldn't ask Susanna. "I'll take Leah," she said, but then shook her head. Leah might see it as her duty, but she would resent Joanna for taking her away. Panic tightened Joanna's throat. It seemed she would truly have to go alone.

Tears slipped down her cheeks and Chuza pulled her close. "She actually said she'd torture you to get to me?"

Her stomach writhed. "She did. Her jealousy knows no bounds."

He drew a breath, and she felt his resolve settle. "Then you must go. I'll ask Titus to take you."

"You can't. If Herodias finds out, it could cost him his job. We can't be responsible for that."

Chuza growled in frustration, and Joanna cupped his face with her palm. "Lots of pilgrims are leaving the city. I'll find a family and ask to travel with them. I'll be safe, I promise." Anxiety fluttered her pulse, but she tried to stifle it. He took her hands, his eyes closing with resignation.

"Alright," he said, barely above a whisper.

Precious minutes had already passed. Joanna hurried to their bedchamber and snatched up her satchel, shoving items inside. She exchanged her thin sandals for sturdy shoes and tossed her traveling cloak around her shoulders. Stuffing all of her money at the bottom of her bag, she left the room without a backward glance.

Chuza was waiting for her in his office, his arms limp by his side. She kissed him, long and hard, tears burning in her eyes. "I love you," she said and wrenched the door open. She couldn't hesitate.

She flipped her cloak up to cover her hair and strode across the courtyard, afraid that at any moment someone would shout her name. She paused at the gate and dared to look back. Chuza stood alone. A sob jerked up her throat. She rushed down the palace steps, tears blinding her. This was her fault. The slap of leather echoed off the cobbled road, and she fled into the city, trying to outstrip her guilt.

She always intended to return to Jesus, but not like this. Not fleeing like a criminal, leaving pain in her wake.

Memories of her brother's sudden disappearance jarred her bones as she jogged toward the city gates, a stitch pulling at her side. She was running away, just like him. She flicked that thought away. No, not like Amichai. She fled to save herself from the questioners. She escaped for Chuza's safety, to keep him from being pulled into conflict with Antipas. All because of Herodias.

Joanna knew she should pray that Herodias would repent, but in her burning heart, she wanted Antipas' wife to suffer. She must pay for what she did to John. Face the repercussions of her manipulation, her self-serving pride, and her ambition that would sacrifice her daughter and destroy the one man who loved Antipas more than he deserved.

# TWENTY-THREE

Chuza pinched the bridge of his nose, squinting gritty eyes as he stared without comprehension at his tablet. Two days had passed since Joanna left. Within an hour of her escape, a soldier came to his office, insisting Joanna go with him. While it was satisfying to send him away empty-handed, Chuza wrestled with knowing Herodias was plotting to hurt them.

Ironically, Herodias' petty rumors became a shield. Whispers spread that Joanna left in a huff, and Chuza hadn't even attempted to go after her. Chuza leaned back in his chair, his muscles aching from tossing and turning through the night.

Even if Herodias suspected Joanna had rejoined the disciples, she had no proof that Chuza knew Joanna funded the prophet. All he needed was enough time to placate Herodias' jealousy—painful as that task would be.

A knock roused him from his grim thoughts, and he tossed the wax tablet away with relief.

"Come," he called, his voice rougher than normal. Titus strode in, out of uniform.

"Come in!" Chuza repeated with more enthusiasm, standing up. "Please sit down. Will you take some wine?"

"No thanks," Titus said, holding up a large hand. "I've just come from the tavern. That's actually why I'm here."

Chuza studied his grim expression. "What happened?"

"Bad news, I'm afraid. I overheard a group of Galileans talking. I couldn't catch everything they said, but they're definitely planning to take down those golden shields. Tonight. The way they were talking, they consider this a holy battle. A mission for God."

Chuza's stomach clenched, understanding the anger that fueled the Galileans, yet abhorring their violent tactics. "Thanks for telling me."

"That's not all," Titus said. He hesitated, working his mouth. "I recognized one man. Joanna's brother, Amichai." Chuza sagged into his chair, groaning, but Titus plowed on. "I thought Joanna would want you to know. Maybe you can stop him before he gets himself killed. Because there's more."

"More?" Chuza said weakly.

Titus nodded. "After the Galileans left, two men rose to follow. On a whim of suspicion, I followed them. After seeing where Amichai and his friends are staying, they went to the Antonia."

"Spies," Chuza muttered, and Titus nodded, his lips pressed into a line.

"Pilate will know that they're coming," Titus said. "They'll be walking into a trap."

Chuza jerked to his feet and peered through his window, circling his tight shoulders while trying to decide what to do—what Joanna would want him to do. Her relationship with her brother was complicated, but she would want Amichai safe. He turned.

"Could you take me back to that house?" he asked.

"I can," Titus said. "Are you going to warn or arrest them?"

Chuza strode to the door. If Amichai's friends were followers of Barabbas, they deserved prison. Maybe worse. But he couldn't be responsible for arresting Joanna's brother. Her family would never forgive him. "Let's try talking first. I just hope he'll listen."

Titus led him through the twisting warren of streets in the Lower City until they reached a nondescript, two-story house. Chuza knocked. The woman who answered insisted her guests were at the evening sacrifice.

Chuza and Titus shared a glance and turned for the temple. Chuza's only interaction with Amichai was on the Jericho Road, but that encounter was enough to show that the young man was calculating. Zealous. But hopefully open to reason.

They wove a path through the packed courtyard, scanning groups of men dressed in the garb of rural Galileans. Finally, right near the entrance to the Court of Women, Titus pointed.

"There," he said.

A group of men led a yearling lamb. Amichai was among them, wearing a rough robe that had seen better days.

Chuza drew a deep breath and pushed forward. "Amichai?" he called, hoping Titus was wrong and Joanna's family wasn't caught up in trouble again.

Amichai recognized them. "Chuza," he said, his lip curling in disdain.

"I must speak with you," Chuza said. He stepped away, beckoning Amichai to follow. Joanna's brother glared with cold suspicion, his eyes flicking to Titus, but he moved toward Chuza as his friends disappeared into the inner courts.

"I know you're planning to remove the shields," Chuza said, casting his gaze around for listening ears. "Pilate knows it too."

Amichai leaned back and crossed his arms. "Who told him? You? Or your friend here?" He thrust his chin at Titus and sneered. "I thought that was you at the tavern."

Titus glowered. "I overheard you, but I wasn't the only one. The others returned to the Antonia with what I can only guess is a report on your plan."

Amichai's brow furrowed, and he looked over his shoulder. His friends were no longer in sight.

Chuza leaned to the side until he caught Amichai's attention. "If Pilate knows, you are doomed to fail."

"Says who?" Amichai stood taller. "Didn't Jonathan take down an entire army with just his shield-bearer?"

"He knew God's hand was with him. Are you so confident?"

Amichai wavered, giving Chuza hope, but before he could press his point, angry shouts filled the air. Chuza sucked a breath as the stone floor vibrated beneath his feet. Roman soldiers marched forward in hobnailed sandals, brandishing weapons, forcing their way through the balustrade that separated Gentile from Jew. Men tried to bar their path, but the soldiers shoved them aside so they could enter the Court of Women.

"Those two at the front," Titus said, his low voice cutting through the clamor. "They were the spies."

Amichai blanched and lunged to rejoin his friends, but Titus and Chuza grabbed him, straining to keep the young man from running into danger. Women and children fled as men shouted in outrage. Amichai tried to twist away, but Chuza tightened his grip. He would protect this hot-blooded youth for his family's sake.

Screams rent the air, and the fleeing crowds increased. White-robed priests poured from their quarters, running to the temple in protest at the sacrilege.

"Blood! Blood mingling with the sacrifices!" an elderly man screeched over and over, his eyes giant orbs as he ripped at his snow-white beard with both fists.

Chuza cringed, frustration and rage coursing through his veins. The soldiers killed them without trial? Pilate was a fool.

Chuza and Titus wrestled Amichai back until, finally, the young man sagged. Titus heaved, forcing Amichai to leave with them.

Once they were free of the complex and back on the streets, Amichai jerked himself away and whirled to face his brother-in-law.

Chuza braced, expecting Amichai to strike him, but the younger man looked away, his chest heaving.

"I appreciate your warning," he said begrudgingly.

Chuza grimaced. "I wish I was in time to warn all of you."

"Those shields still need to come down," Amichai said. "Now more than ever."

"Just... give me some time," Chuza said, spreading his hands. Antipas would have to reconsider his stance on the shields now. "I'll see what Antipas can do to help. He is friends with Caesar Tiberius."

Amichai's nostrils flared. "I know."

"Perhaps, this time, that connection can be in our people's favor," Chuza said, though even he barely dared to hope.

The next day, the whole city muttered about the soldiers marching into the Court of Israel, striking down unarmed men. According to rumors, their blood mingled with the sacrificial blood. Some said God must hate the Galileans if he allowed their deaths to pollute the temple.

Chuza took his report to Antipas' room and described what he had seen, leaving out any mention of Amichai. Herodias, Antipas' silent shadow, absorbed every word, her sharp eyes narrowed in concentration. Chuza's skin crawled under her scrutiny.

To Chuza's relief, Antipas was infuriated by Pilate's disregard for the Jewish temple and the way he slaughtered men from another jurisdiction without trial.

"He's a fool, a blood-thirsty fool!" Antipas raged. At least they could agree on that.

"You must do something," Chuza said, praying that Antipas would heed him. "You and Emperor Tiberius are friends. He might listen to you."

"Yes, my love," Herodias said, resting slender fingers on her husband's arm. Antipas cringed away from her touch, but she pretended not to notice. "By writing to the emperor, you pave the way to replace this foolish governor."

"She's right," Chuza said, avoiding Herodias' eye as he pointedly sided with her. "And you will win the favor of the people."

Antipas slouched back in his chair, his brow furrowed. He propped his elbow on the armrest and rubbed his large ring over his lips as his eyes drifted. He nodded. "I shall write to him immediately. Summon a scribe. I will ask Philip to send letters as well."

"Philip?" Herodias frowned.

Antipas glared at her as if she was a half-wit. "The sons of King Herod must stand together. I have many half-brothers and cousins, a powerful force Tiberius can employ, if need be."

"But none of them are like you," Herodias purred. "If your father's proper will had been honored…"

Antipas' eyes flashed. "The will that named me sole ruler, or the one that declared your father would be his heir?"

Herodias' gaze darted to Chuza, glaring at him for witnessing Antipas' rebuke. It was time to retreat. He bowed. "I will send for a scribe."

He turned and was nearly struck by the door as a servant barged into the room, panting.

"My lord!" the servant wheezed. "The High Priests are coming. I told them to wait, that you'd receive them in your audience chamber when you were ready, but—"

"We're already here," Annas' deep voice droned, entering the room before him. Chuza stepped back. Annas wore a snow-white robe under an elaborate coat in brilliant shades of blue, purple, and green. He leaned on an ornate walking staff like an overdressed shepherd with his flock, leading Caiaphas, his son-in-law and the current High Priest, and a retinue of others, all members of the Sadducee party, all dressed with equal pomp.

Antipas glowered at Annas' breach of protocol, but he remembered himself and rose to greet the High Priests with the proper respect. Antipas was a tetrarch, but they served the one true God.

"So, Herod Antipas, tetrarch of Galilee and Perea," Annas drawled the title. "What will you do about this mess?"

Antipas folded his hands, his smile tight. "I will write Emperor Tiberius. I was about to summon my scribe when you arrived."

Caiaphas frowned. "Letters to the emperor? That will take weeks to have any effect."

Annas grunted in agreement. "Surely you could do something more immediate?"

"I can't order Pilate to take them down," Antipas said. "He is the governor of Judea, not me."

"But the insult..." Caiaphas drew an incensed breath that fluttered his long beard. "Those were your subjects he killed. Men from your jurisdiction. Yet you stand there so calmly?"

Antipas' jaw tensed. "There are ways to handle this properly. They are just shields. They are not in the temple, but in a courtyard the people avoid. Find some perspective and employ your patience."

"The people may riot!" Annas stamped his long staff on the floor.

"Then you must see that they don't," Antipas said. "We shall have to trust in your powerful influence." His twitching lip hinted at a sneer, and Annas and Caiaphas shared a frown.

A younger priest piped up. "Once news of this insult spreads..."

Antipas spoke with forced calmness. "We must keep the peace." He fixed his gaze on Caiaphas. "Your position may depend upon it, and more immediately, your use of the vestments for the next festival."

Caiaphas folded his arms, his eyes flashing. Pilate kept the sacred vestments in the Antonia, held as ransom against the priesthood. The position of High Priest had become a political tool to be doled out to whoever the governor thought worthy—or compliant.

Antipas took his seat again, fixing the priests with an unwavering glare. "I will write to the Emperor, but I must be careful not to insult him or Pilate. Meanwhile, you need to restrain the people."

The priests reluctantly agreed that there was nothing else to be done. With sour expressions, they swept from the room.

Antipas slouched in his seat and Herodias patted his arm, murmuring praise for his wisdom.

Antipas spared her a mere glance. He rubbed a hand over his smooth jaw. "The sooner this is dealt with, the better."

Chuza saw the letters dispatched by mounted messenger to the coast, with money to hire passage on a fast vessel bound for Rome. Then there was nothing to do but wait.

# TWENTY-FOUR

## 30 AD
## SUMMER

Joanna stood to the side of the road, squinting against the dust as the caravan continued without her. A young woman gave a nervous wave as they left Joanna behind, totally alone. The caravan pushed on toward Cana, and Joanna turned to the Sea of Galilee and straightened her shoulders with deliberate unconcern. There was still plenty of light. Still time to reach Capernaum. She would be perfectly fine all on her own.

Lengthening her stride to eat the distance, she ignored her tired feet and the ache in her thighs. She threw back her palla, letting the wind blow through her hair and cool her face.

Twilight was descending as Joanna reached Capernaum, the lake gleaming with shades of purple. Her rumbling stomach protested the late hour, but worse was the anxiety fluttering in her core. Maybe no one could tell her where Jesus was.

She stopped and drew a deep breath in front of Peter's house. Light spilled through the open door. Joanna leaned against the frame and called a greeting.

Tamar came forward, and her eyes widened in surprise. "Joanna!"

she said. "What are you doing here?" She gestured for her to enter.

Joanna brushed the mezuzah and ducked under the low doorway. Tamar's son sat at the table with an oil lamp, a wax tablet spread open and a stylus in his hand. His older sister, Hannah, looked up from kneading dough. Joanna surveyed the quiet room. The large house sighed with emptiness, missing the noisy disciples and the sounds of Jesus' teaching. Joanna gripped the strap of her bag, feeling like an intruder.

"I'm looking for Jesus," Joanna said. "Do you know where he is? Please, I've come a long way."

Tamar's smile was gracious. "You must be exhausted," she said, sliding past the question. "Let me get you something to drink." She went to the table and poured Joanna a cup of wine. Joanna sipped it. The finish had a sour note, but it soothed her throat. Tamar glanced behind Joanna. "Has your Roman guard come with you again?"

Joanna hesitated, unsure what answer Tamar would prefer. "No. It's just... me."

Tamar's eyebrows rose, and Hannah's mouth fell open.

Joanna flushed, clutching the simple cup. "I need to rejoin the disciples." She heard the desperation in her tone and forced herself to smile.

Tamar's gaze wavered, and she caught her bottom lip between her teeth. "They'll come back, don't you worry. In the meantime, you are welcome to wait here." Joanna was sure Tamar knew something, but for some reason, Peter's mother-in-law didn't trust her. Joanna looked down at her expensive robe, a symbol of her connection to Antipas' court, to the man who killed John the Baptizer. No wonder this rural housewife hesitated to help her.

But she couldn't go to her vineyard in disgrace. Not when a single word from this woman would take her back to Jesus.

"If you know where they are," Joanna begged, "you have to tell me." She saw at once she had come on too strong. Tamar's expression clouded. "I'm sorry," Joanna stammered. "I just wanted—I just need to—" Her words failed.

Tamar came closer. Her head only made it to Joanna's chin. "You are not yourself today," she said, tipping her face up, her face gentle. "What's troubling you?"

Her compassion brought tears to Joanna's eyes, but it was too humiliating to confess that her pride in giving money to Jesus had gotten her and Chuza into deep trouble.

Tamar set her hand on Joanna's arm. "Don't worry about it tonight," she said. "You will stay the night with us. Things always look brighter in the morning."

It wasn't the answer Joanna sought, but at least she had a place to sleep. "Thank you," she said.

"Can I get you something to eat?"

"I'm starving," Joanna confessed, and Tamar looked pleased.

"I will find you something right away."

Joanna removed her palla and bag. "Can I help?"

Tamar smiled. "Perhaps you would help my son with his lesson?" The boy's gaze flicked between his mama and this unexpected guest.

Joanna brightened. The boy ducked his chin, but Joanna knelt next to him at the low table. She surveyed what he had written. "Ah, the prophet Hosea," she said. "A worthy passage. Will you read it to me?"

As she helped him correct his work, Joanna eased into the cozy atmosphere that permeated the home. It had been years since she experienced an evening like this, with a family gathering to complete simple chores without political fears or looming responsibility. It felt good. But Joanna didn't know how to replicate this peaceful environment within her own little household. Especially now, when she couldn't return.

When the stars spread across the sky, Joanna lay in an empty room. One of Peter's robes hung on a hook and her throat ached with loneliness for Chuza. Their parting had been so sudden, and there was no planned date for her to return. And it was all her fault. She rolled away, pulling the blanket over her head.

If she could find a way to help Jesus, maybe it would fill the hole in her chest that echoed like an empty vat.

The next morning, Joanna rose early, itching for answers. Tamar ignored her guest's fidgeting. She served a hearty breakfast and took her son to the synagogue for his lesson. When Tamar came back, she invited Joanna to walk to the well, leaving Hannah grinding grain. They passed a group of women hauling their laundry to the lake shore, chatting and laughing like a flock of contented hens. Joanna's focus drifted after them.

"Why are you alone, Joanna?" Tamar asked. "Where are your friends? Your escort?"

Joanna faltered, heat creeping up her neck. "I couldn't bring anyone," she said. "Not without getting them in trouble, too."

Tamar peeked sideways. "Too?"

Joanna shifted her water jar to the other hip. Tamar was going to think she was a fool, but there was little point in hiding her shame. "I told the wrong person that I support Jesus," she said flatly. "Now Herodias wants to charge me with sedition and force me to implicate my husband."

Tamar slowed her pace. "So you can't go back to Antipas' court? To your husband?"

Joanna winced. "Not unless Chuza finds a way to appease Herodias."

Tamar stopped, her eyes probing. "Appease her how?"

"I don't know," Joanna admitted.

"What if Herodias wanted you to report on Jesus in exchange for letting you rejoin your husband?"

Joanna stared. "What? No!" Her insides withered as she realized

Tamar thought was capable of betraying Jesus. "Chuza and I want to support Jesus. We believe he is a prophet of the Lord, maybe even the Messiah." She drew a breath, trying to slow her racing pulse. "Chuza will find some other way to make things right. I know he will."

Tamar pressed her lips together, and Joanna berated herself. She bumbled the entire conversation, and Tamar had no reason to trust her. Guilt rose in her throat, demanding release.

"I messed up in Jerusalem," Joanna blurted, rubbing her eyes roughly. "I thought I was doing something good, telling Salome about Jesus, but my pride ruined everything." Her voice broke as she struggled to hold back tears. "I just wanted her to see that I'm not like Antipas and Herodias. That Chuza and I are good people. Giving money is proof of that, right?"

She drew a shaky breath. "What if I was blinded by my need to be used by God? My desire to have a purpose, to feel like I'm important in God's eyes? I'm starting to realize that is its own kind of vanity."

Tamar glanced at her, but did not reply. They uncovered the well and filled their jars. Joanna's stomach was in knots as she hoisted the heavy jar onto her hip. Self-loathing prickled in her eyes. Maybe Tamar was right not to trust her.

When they were halfway back, Tamar paused and glanced around. "They've gone to the region of Tyre and Sidon," she said.

Joanna fumbled her jar, splattering droplets of water. She stared at the other woman, confused.

"Yes, you messed up," Tamar said. "You should have told Salome about Jesus and kept your good deeds out of it. You don't need to prove your goodness, you need to show God's." Tamar fixed her with a stern, motherly glare, and Joanna nodded meekly.

"But now I can't go back—"

"You can't undo your mistakes," Tamar agreed. "But you can learn from them. Even great prophets had to run from their enemies."

"But they were running for doing the right thing. Standing up to kings. Not for—" Joanna blushed "—blabbing about their good deeds."

"Your greatest vanity is assuming that you can do something so wrong that God can't turn it to good." Tamar gave a confident nod and continued walking, but Joanna was rooted to the road.

She wanted to believe Tamar was right. That God could transform her mess into something worthwhile. She had no idea what good could come of being chased from her home, but she would rather hope for good than battle regret.

But Tyre and Sidon? The comfort from Tamar's encouragement faded before the difficulties ahead. She'd have to journey all the way to the coast of the Great Sea, to a region she had never visited. Alone. To find a man who might not want to be found.

Tamar turned back, reading the worries that were surely written on her face. "There is no shame in waiting. You can stay with us until they return."

It was tempting. Tamar's home was a comforting reminder of Joanna's childhood, when life was simpler. She could rest and recover. But she shook her head. Joining Jesus wasn't just about making up for her shameful mistake, she wanted to offer him support and learn more. Tamar was right. Joanna didn't need to prove she was a disciple, but somewhere, deep inside, she still heard his call. *Follow me.*

Maybe she could just follow Jesus without her own agenda, forgetting what everyone thought about her. The idea felt like a breath of fresh air in a stagnant room.

She gazed down the road. "I must find a caravan heading to Tyre."

Tamar didn't seem surprised by her determination. "You're more likely to meet one in Magdala," she said. "My brother-in-law Zebedee could take you in his boat."

Joanna grinned. She had met Zebedee before, a barrel-chested man with a booming voice, father to two of the twelve. Jesus called James and John the Sons of Thunder, an apt nickname for Zebedee's boys.

They went down to the shore mid-morning and found Zebedee sorting his catch with his hired men.

He glanced up as the women approached. "Piddling," he said with disgust, waving a thick hand at his half-filled baskets. "Hardly worth the trouble of delivering to Magdala."

Tamar gestured to her guest. "Perhaps a passenger will make your trip worthwhile." Zebedee scanned Joanna, then nodded with recognition. Tamar leaned closer to him. "She's trying to join a caravan going to Tyre."

He hesitated. "I can give you a ride to Magdala, but that's as far as I can take you."

Joanna smiled. "I understand. I know an innkeeper who will help me plan my next steps."

Tamar hugged Joanna goodbye. The wind toyed with Joanna's hair as she watched Zebedee sort his catch. She helped him lug the smelly baskets to a boat moored at the pier. Joanna clambered aboard and he shoved off, the shallow-keeled craft bobbing as he stepped in. He set the sail and gripped a long oar, steering the craft and working in tandem with the wind.

The shoreline slipped by, pleasant farmland hedged by rising hills. Joanna looked ahead to find Zebedee studying her.

She gave him a wan smile. "You think I'm foolish for trying to find them on my own, don't you?"

Zebedee pulled twice on the oar before answering. "I see a hunger in your eyes," he said. "My sons looked the same when Jesus called them. For many weeks, I wondered why Jesus didn't ask me. Then I wondered if I was foolish for not going along when Naomi did. But someone has to keep the business afloat and pay our taxes." He smiled wryly. "It's not as important nor as wondrous as traveling with Jesus, but it is my duty, and my little sacrifice allows my family to serve."

Joanna turned her face away. Her husband had sacrificed as much as Zebedee, if not more.

Tears threatened, and she hastily changed the subject. "Why do you think Jesus left?" she asked.

"A rest, perhaps?" Zebedee shrugged. "He's been teaching and healing for a while now. It's got to be draining."

Joanna hadn't considered that. "Rumors in Jerusalem say he's hiding. That he stirred up too much trouble."

Zebedee laughed, the sound rolling over the water. "Ah yes, he did a bit of that, didn't he?" He wobbled his head back and forth, considering. "I can't speak for Jesus, but if I was to guess, I'd say he wanted to take his disciples away from the fickle crowds and their expectations and contrary opinions."

"He wanted some quiet so he could teach them?"

He shrugged and dragged on the oar again. "Could be. I suppose you'll find out when you reach them." His confidence that she would actually find Jesus buoyed her spirits.

At the Magdala pier, Zebedee took her hand in his large ones, looking her in the eye. "May God bless you and keep you," he said, speaking as if he meant it. It reminded her of her father, and she smiled gratefully.

She made her way through the bustling town to Samuel's inn. The innkeeper promised to inquire about a caravan on her behalf. After paying for a private room, she shut herself inside, drained physically and homesick for her husband.

Four days later, Joanna joined a merchant caravan heading for Tyre, a line of camels, wagons, armed guards, and a few other travelers like herself. The others chatted among themselves, but Joanna kept her lips shut. Half the people would condemn her connection to Antipas' court, and the other half would judge her for following Jesus.

After a few days of sulking, she realized she was falling back into her folly. It didn't matter what they thought, it mattered what God thought of her. As night spread over the countryside like a warm blanket, she moved out of the firelight. She spent an hour on her knees, pouring out her worries about finding Jesus and her anxieties about Chuza. She asked forgiveness for her failures and for another chance to serve the Lord, a way to share her love between a prophet and her husband. Despite Herodias, there must be a way to be both—a wife and a disciple.

By the time Joanna wrapped herself in her cloak to sleep, the night had grown chilly and she was emotionally depleted. Yet beneath her exhaustion was hope. She didn't know how to fix the mess she was in, but God did.

And if he chose not to intervene... well, a long walk never hurt anybody.

# TWENTY-FIVE

Joanna drew in the salty air of the Great Sea for the first time, a briny smell that made her nose tingle. Though curiosity tempted her to escape the crowds and find a view of the water, Joanna kept with the caravan as they maneuvered down Tyre's busy streets.

Tyre was as foreign as she expected, with statues of gods along the thoroughfare, the bronze shiny from being rubbed for luck. Insulae were everywhere, rising above the city four stories tall, laundry flapping from residential windows, and shops bustling on the ground floor. Government buildings with imposing facades loomed over the road as men entered on important business. Women promenaded, their hair styled in the latest fashion. Carriages rattled by, litters were carried by slaves, and a horse left a steaming mound on the cobbles. A cacophony of languages filled the air, and as the streets grew closer together, the tangy stench of bodies, refuse, and open sewer made Joanna draw her palla over her nose.

They reached the market, and the caravan leader nodded at Joanna, their business completed. Joanna turned in a slow circle, overwhelmed by the crowds and the streets flowing in all directions. She didn't know where to even begin.

Her stomach rumbled, and she grinned. First things first. She stopped at a booth and bought a loaf of bread.

The baker's rosy cheeks and broad smile invited conversation. In Greek, Joanna asked, "Do you know about a Jewish prophet? One famous for miracles?"

The woman looked at her in surprise. "Ah, you mean the Nazarene? My neighbor walked to Galilee to see him. He claims he saw signs from God, if you believe such things."

Joanna's pulse leaped. "Have you heard if he is here? In Tyre?" Joanna pressed.

"Here?" the woman said, doubtfully, and Joanna nodded. The woman shook her head. "I haven't heard anything about that, but it's a big city."

Joanna gave a half-smile, disappointed. "I'll keep asking, thank you."

She ate her bread as she walked, scanning the street for friendly faces, stopping to ask women and children if they had seen a prophet. The public latrine was a surprisingly good place to catch the local gossip. Joanna eavesdropped as the women chatted side-by-side, but Jesus' name was never mentioned.

She passed temples to pagan gods and followed the road to the northern shore, filling her lungs with clean air. Twilight brushed the water in dusky shades, the painted surface rolling rhythmically with white-tipped waves. She puffed out a sigh, discouraged despite the natural beauty spreading before her. If Jesus was in Tyre, he kept himself hidden.

Joanna gazed past the port with its fleets of ships and toward Sidon. The prophet Elijah had also fled from a king and his wife, living with a widow and her son. Despite a famine, God cared for them all.

Bolstered by the ancient story, she strode to the market, searching for the baker. She was closing up her booth, and most of her bread was gone.

"You again?" the woman said with a cheery smile. "You didn't find your prophet?"

"Not yet," Joanna admitted. "I was wondering if you could point me to a reputable inn."

"For you, by yourself?" The woman puckered her brow. "There isn't any." She scanned Joanna up and down. "Tell you what," she said. "If you help me close my booth and take my things home, you may spend the night with my family."

Joanna hesitated, worried this was a trick to get her alone and rob her blind. The woman smiled. "I'm Portia. I'm a widow, and I live with my parents. You'll be quite safe, I assure you."

Joanna was still leery, but the invitation seemed better than sleeping in an inn. She helped gather up the unsold product and assumed responsibility for one of the enormous baskets. Portia led her down the streets to an insula, and as they climbed the stairs, the sounds of multiple families hummed behind walls. Portia's family claimed four rooms on the third floor.

When Portia introduced her to an older couple, Joanna felt a little better. She wondered what Chuza would think about her trusting strangers and Gentiles, but right now, she was just grateful for their hospitality. Joanna shared their evening meal and fell asleep on a borrowed pallet, confident that God was watching over her.

The next morning, she awoke to an empty room and the rich, yeasty fragrance of fresh bread. Following her nose, she took the stairs to the street level of the house. Portia and her parents were pulling pans of baking from a row of enormous ovens. Housewives gathered around the counter, buying fresh bread for their families. Some paid a fee and handed over pots, gossiping as Portia's father slid them into an oven to bake. The little bakery bustled, but Portia noticed Joanna and gave her a fresh wheat cake and a welcoming grin.

As the morning rush waned, Portia began loading up baskets.

Wanting to repay Portia for her generosity, Joanna mimicked her hostess as Portia hefted a basket in each arm, hooking them on her hips to ease their weight. Her arms ached by the time they arrived at Portia's market booth.

Portia held out a large loaf. "For your help," she said with a flourish.

"My help? I should pay you."

Portia waved away her words. "If you haven't found your prophet by nightfall, I'll be here."

"Thank you for everything," Joanna said, sniffing the bread appreciatively. Portia nodded before a customer approached, demanding her attention.

Tucking the loaf in her satchel, Joanna wandered again, this time making her way down residential areas with narrow roads. She paused as a woman rushed down the street, sandals slapping on the cobbles as she pushed around others. Joanna hesitated, scanning for danger, but no villain followed in the woman's wake. Between her gasping breaths, the woman began shouting.

"Circe? Circe!"

"Mama!" A girl raced out a door. The child was perhaps ten years old, still wearing her nightclothes. "Mama! I'm better!"

The words drove into Joanna's heart as the woman burst into sobs, falling to her knees as the girl threw herself into her mother's arms.

"He did it." The woman wept, running her fingers over her daughter's cheeks and smoothing hair from her brow. "He said you would be healed, and here you are!"

An aged servant followed the child. "Where have you been?" she asked with fists on her thick waist. "Her fever broke not half an hour ago. I guess you didn't need to find the prophet after all."

The mother laughed, shaking her head. "Foolish woman, it was the prophet who did it. I found him."

The servant blinked, then noticed Joanna and a few curious

neighbors watching. She flushed and flapped her apron. "Get off the ground before you ruin your robe," she chided. "Come inside. You're making a scene."

"Wait!" Joanna called. She rushed forward, hopping over sludgy water congealing in the street. "Was it Jesus of Nazareth who healed your daughter?"

The woman stood up and tucked her child against her side. "Yes, it was. I wasn't sure if he would help a Phoenician, but he did. He saved my Circe." She looked down into her daughter's face with adoration.

Joanna's heart skipped like a young goat. She was so close! "Where is he?" Joanna asked breathlessly.

"He's just left the city," the woman said, pointing east. "If you hurry, you might catch up."

"Thank you," Joanna said, impulsively hugging the startled woman. She raced down the street. It couldn't be coincidence that she wandered down the right road at the right time. God had answered her prayers and brought her back to Jesus.

She sagged with relief when she spotted the crowd of disciples ahead, more than a mile out of the city. She jogged to catch up. As she drew nearer, she noticed their reduced numbers. The last time she saw Jesus, thousands surrounded him. He had either lost considerable popularity or these were the select few he chose for special instruction. She slowed her steps, trying to catch her breath. She came all this way, but she suddenly felt like she had shown up to a feast without an invitation.

One woman turned her head, sensing Joanna's presence. It was Maryam, walking with her sons. "Joanna?" she said in surprise, and the group stopped. Joanna hurried forward, her face hot, and stammered her explanation.

Maryam's jaw dropped. "You came this far on your own?"

Joanna laughed, shrugging as if the overwhelming stress of her journey was a mere inconvenience. "Don't think I'm going to let you out of my sight again." She scanned the group, trying to hide her apprehension. Jesus smiled as he came forward, and her fear drained away.

He gripped her shoulder with his strong fingers. "Welcome, Joanna, wife of Chuza."

His acceptance was more satisfying than a cup of cold water on a hot day. Joanna dared to peek at the others. They seemed willing to welcome a woman who walked across Galilee to find them. Her cheeks warmed with gratitude, and she sent up a hasty prayer of thanks to God for guiding her safely.

Jesus resumed his brisk pace, and Joanna fell in beside Maryam, wondering where Jesus would go next. Her chest contracted as she thought about Chuza, wishing he was with her, praying he was alright.

# TWENTY-SIX

Chuza studied the report. Antipas' letters to Tiberius were successful. The golden shields had finally disappeared, and it seemed Pontius Pilate set them up in the temple to Augustus in Caesarea Maritmea. Another loss for the governor. Chuza's lips tipped with grim satisfaction.

Chuza tossed the slip of parchment aside. All that anger and blood for nothing. Antipas helped the people manage Pilate, but it was a temporary patch on a leaking cistern. Something big needed to change, and soon.

Someone knocked on his door.

"Enter," he said, without looking up from his work. One of the kitchen staff brought in his supper tray. His appetite soured at eating alone yet again.

The serving girl slipped into his room and set the tray on his low table. His cheeks were stiff as he offered a tiny smile, and she left as wordlessly as she arrived.

He rose and stood in the doorway to his Sepphoris chambers, staring at the steam that wafted from the dishes, vanishing without a trace. Joanna's chest of belongings sat unopened, her absence haunting him like a shadowy presence.

She had written him, an unsigned document from a messenger who didn't know her name. She found her friends and hoped he could find a way for her to come home. His throat burned with inadequacy. He couldn't make peace with Herodias when she only saw him as a threat to her power, and Antipas' continued animosity toward Herodias wasn't making it any easier.

Chuza walked up to the tray of food but didn't sit. He wondered if Leah prepared it. He guiltily realized he hadn't given the young woman a thought over the past weeks, occupied with his work and his worries about Joanna. He shouldn't be so self-involved.

Joanna told him once that she hoped Jesus would repair the damage inflicted by Leah's heavy loss. Chuza rubbed his chest and wondered if a prophet could truly cure a broken heart. Perhaps time was the greater remedy. And friendship.

He thought back to his boyhood years, when Antipas made him feel like he belonged and was valued. He had looked up to Antipas like a favorite uncle, or a brother. Antipas tempered the jagged hole his family carved when they left.

Tears prickled in his eyes despite himself. His grief for his family dimmed with the passing decades, but it lingered like an injury he learned to ignore. Why didn't they come back, like they promised? Had he done something to warrant his abandonment, or did some terrible fate befall them?

Their faces rose in his mind, veiled by the passage of time. He closed his eyes and focused, trying to remember the details, his mother's eyes. He remembered smiling for her, trying to be brave, yet already regretting offering himself in his brother's stead. He relived the gaping hole in his middle, the burning in his throat as he swallowed back a plea he refused to utter. *Come back, Mama! Don't leave me.*

He wanted to be a hero, to save his mother more anguish and

not wail like his brother. Rael was older, the firstborn, the natural choice to stay with Antipas. Chuza was sure Rael would be grateful for what Chuza had done, but he never came back. His brother disdained Chuza's sacrifice, and that truth hit Chuza like a fist. He gave up everything for them, and not one of them cared enough to return.

Tears slid in hot rivers, and for the first time in decades, Chuza didn't tamp his feelings down. He let them rise, and a sob jerked from his throat. The dam broke, and the sobs became violent. He roared out his pain at being traded away and forgotten. Somewhere in his grief, he realized he wept for this newest loss—his wife. He believed Joanna would fill the emptiness, the place in his heart where a family belonged, but he sent her away too. Now she might vanish with the rest.

An hour passed as he released his pain in a torrent of tears. As the waves of grief softened, he shifted into prayer.

"God, you are the only one that stayed with me through it all," he whispered. "You're the only one with me now. Manaen left, Joanna is gone, and Antipas never became the family I craved. I am alone, Lord. What do I do?" His hands pressed the throbbing wound in his chest. "What do I do?"

*Leah*

The name rose like the ghost of a whisper, not a sound he could hear, but clear as a shofar blast. With it came a sense that the Lord had spoken. He sucked in a breath, relief and wonder pouring into him. God heard him. God saw his sacrifice and offered comfort. And with the name, flowed understanding.

Leah needed a family, too. Chuza could give her what had been stolen from him. He could treat her as a daughter, give her a home and everything they had both been denied. God was telling him that by caring for her as his own child, he could heal them both.

But Chuza had no idea how to be a father. Inadequacy rushed down his limbs, replacing his wonder and weighing him down.

This wasn't like having a baby, where he could learn little by little as the child grew. Raised among Herod's family, Chuza had little experience with a loving family, and Leah was a young woman with a harsh past. What was God thinking, giving this task to him? He dragged his hands through his hair. He must have misunderstood.

But the silent shofar blast still vibrated in his chest, the sense that God had spoken to him. He put aside his worries for a moment and reveled in the feeling. Perhaps this was what Titus felt that day in the temple, a call strong enough to change the course of his life. Chuza couldn't just ignore it.

Conviction returned and he wiped his face on his sleeve. This was just a task like any other. He remembered the first time he negotiated a contract. The first time he hired a staff member. He hadn't known what to do then, but planned the steps and carried them through. This situation, although rather unusual, could be approached logically too.

But how to begin? He couldn't charge into the palace kitchen and tell Leah that he was adopting her as his daughter. He choked out a nasally laugh at the idea, picturing her scoffing expression.

No. Though God had prompted Chuza, this needed to happen on Leah's terms. She hardly knew him. He had treated her as his wife's friend, Joanna's ward, Joanna's project. But now Joanna was gone.

Perhaps that was where he should start. He would show Leah that she could rely on him as she relied on Joanna. Prove that he was an ally in the court.

He looked down at the congealed meal. He picked up the tray and strode to the kitchen. Leah was washing dishes with the other women, her sleeves rolled past her elbows. Nervousness rattled the dishes on his tray, but he kept his face calm.

She studied him, her eyebrow curving as she beheld his untouched food. "Not to your standards?" she asked.

"I'm afraid I was too... occupied to eat while it was hot," he said sheepishly. "Is there something else?"

Leah made a face, but stepped back from her basin and dried her hands. "I'm sure we can find something."

He watched as she prepared him a new platter with cold meat, cheese, sliced fig, and crusty bread. She held it out, and he set it on the table. Her eyes widened as he sat on one of the serviceable benches, the plain wood smoothed by thousands of occupants over decades.

"Sit with me," Chuza said, and Leah's lips parted in confusion. "I have been eating alone too long," he said. "Please, Leah, do me this favor."

Leah hesitated, then slid beside him, glancing at the other staff, who cast sneaky peeks at the unlikely pair. She scooted farther away.

Chuza ignored the others. "How was your day?" he asked.

"Fine," Leah said.

Chuza would need to try harder. "What has Michael been teaching you?"

Leah crossed her arms, leaning on the table. "You're interested in becoming a cook, steward?"

Chuza waved a hand. "Perhaps I am. What should I learn first?"

Leah assessed him, her lips quirking. "The first thing you must learn is to forget everything you think you know."

He shot her a doubtful look, and her tone became arch. "If you want to be my apprentice, you must put aside your pride and your self-sufficiency. You must become…" her gaze drifted "… like a fresh wineskin. It's the only way I can pour my knowledge into you without you bursting." Her eyes flicked back to him, pretending solemnity. "You're stretched thin with your own ideas of how things are done. You must be ready to learn what the master teaches, your mind as supple as a child's." She fixed him with a stern stare. "That is why masters do not take apprentices who are forty!"

The maids burst into laughter, then ducked their heads as they realized they were laughing at Antipas' steward. Chuza chuckled to put them at their ease, unexpectedly pleased when their shoulders relaxed and they shared grins with Leah.

It seemed Leah possessed a sharp sense of humor, and she used it to remind him of his place. But though his cheeks warmed, her teasing reprimand was not laced with cruelty. It might be interesting to spend more time here, getting to know this young woman.

A smile still playing on her lips, Leah poured him a drink. He took the cup, casting her a measuring glance over the rim. "How did you think of that analogy?" he asked. "The wineskins?"

She sobered, picking at a crack in the wooden table. "Jesus," she said. "Though he was talking about the kingdom of God, not cooking." She glanced up, gauging his reaction. He realized she was treading carefully around his feelings, shielding him from reminders of his wife's absence. It seemed a sensitive heart lived beneath her stoic exterior.

He gave her an encouraging smile. "Can you explain how it applies to the kingdom of God?"

"Maybe," she said, "though I'm not sure I understand it myself. Jesus is wise, and I am just… me."

She spoke about her time with Jesus and Chuza listened. When his plate was empty, Leah stood to resume her duties. He rose with her.

"Could I eat here again?" he asked.

Leah furrowed her brow. "You're the steward. You can eat wherever you like."

"But you wouldn't mind?"

Leah shrugged, folding her arms. "Just don't expect me to drop everything to keep you company."

"Wouldn't dream of it," he said, and grinned.

Making friends with Leah was a slow process. Chuza began eating his supper in the kitchen every day. He didn't ask her to sit with him again, but instead, he sat nearby while she worked. Day by day, he learned a little more about her. He admired her work ethic and her sharp mind. The other maids liked her, and Michael doted on her like a daughter. Chuza envied the cook's natural ability. There were still moments when he doubted his conviction, and Michael seemed much better suited as a father figure. But Chuza knew, deep inside, that God wanted him involved in Leah's life for some purpose. Perhaps, all together, he, Joanna, and the kitchen staff could fill the void carved by the family Leah lost.

One afternoon, Titus stopped by his office, asking if there was any word from Joanna. Touched by his thoughtfulness, Chuza invited the soldier to join him in the kitchen instead of eating with the men in the barracks.

Soon both Titus and Chuza were fixtures in Michael's kitchen, taking their evening meal at the long table. Chuza and Titus would often play board games late into the night, the kitchen staff dwindling, the air rich with bread and spices. On those occasions, Leah would sit nearby, and they would all laugh like old friends.

Chuza came to treasure Titus' friendship. Since Manaen left, Chuza didn't have many opportunities for male companionship. Not with someone who considered him an equal.

It surprised Chuza to discover Leah couldn't read, considering all her time with Joanna. He began instructing her on her letters, bribing her with the recipes and shopping lists she could read for herself.

The three of them attended synagogue every Sabbath, Chuza explaining history and laws and guiding them both through the traditions. Leah withdrew during these lessons, but Titus' under-standing grew in leaps and bounds. He still hesitated to take on the full rites of Judaism, but Chuza could be patient. If the Gentile meant to adopt the ways of God's people, he needed companions to learn from, and friends to welcome him into God's family.

But, despite what he offered, Chuza was one who needed this most.

The chance to mentor, to lead someone to righteousness. Investing in Leah and Titus was a balm on a wound he hadn't wanted to uncover for a long, long time.

As Chuza lay on their bed, Joanna's side cold and empty, he prayed for her, as he did every night. His yearning for her had not waned, but he stopped praying for God to bring her home. He asked the Lord to use his wife as he saw fit. It was easier to fall asleep that way, giving Joanna into the Lord's hands. Otherwise, the ache for her presence would swallow him whole.

# TWENTY-SEVEN

## 30 AD
### AUTUMN

Chuza hesitated halfway across the stable courtyard, unsure whether he should intervene. Herodias swelled with anger as she loomed over her daughter. Salome was dissolving into tears, and her maid shrunk in her shadow.

"Everyone is waiting on you," Herodias hissed at her daughter, sending shivers up Chuza's spine. "You are humiliating yourself, carrying on like this. Antipas is becoming impatient."

Salome stood trembling another second then wordlessly clambered into the cart, releasing a sob. Her maid scrambled after her. Herodias stormed away to climb in another cart, and Salome jerked the canopy closed, hiding her tear-streaked face. The cloth couldn't muffle the sounds of her distress, and Chuza's insides squirmed.

Chuza pressed his lips together as he joined Antipas, who observed the whole scene from atop his horse. Antipas looked troubled. He leaned toward his steward as Chuza checked Celer's girth.

"Young women are usually nervous before their wedding, right?" Antipas asked.

Chuza cast him a look. "How would I know?" he muttered. "My

wife didn't cry."

Antipas grunted. "Mine neither."

Chuza offered his foot to the groom and swung his leg over the saddle, settling his robe around his legs. Antipas gave the signal and the procession moved out, the grim atmosphere more suited to a funeral than a celebration.

Leah was watching from the palace gate. Chuza waved, warmed by the wide smile illuminating her face. He noticed Titus waving at Leah too, and he chuckled knowingly. Leah lifted her hand momentarily before ducking her chin, hurrying back inside as one of the other guards teased Titus about the pretty young woman.

Unwillingly, Chuza's focus was dragged to Salome's cart. Leah was only a year younger than Salome. He pictured Leah on her way to an unwanted marriage and tightened his grip on the reins.

As they left Sepphoris and crossed the valley, Antipas' mood grew oppressive. Of late, the tetrarch regressed to his old ways, surrounding himself with friends and masculine conversation, shutting his wife out. But now, as they journeyed to Caesarea Philippi in this intimate grouping, Antipas' depression had nowhere to hide. Chuza cleared his throat. Countless times over the years, he served as Antipas' confidante, and he slipped easily into the familiar role.

"Want to talk about it?" Chuza asked.

Antipas shot him a glance, then smiled wryly. "What is there to say? Herodias tricked me, yet claims to still love me. She still won't apologize, insisting she had John killed for our good."

Stifling his own emotions, Chuza gave his master a sympathetic nod. "She shouldn't have gone against your will." He hesitated to say more, in case his words got back to Herodias.

"I'll just be glad to get her daughter out from under my roof," Antipas said sharply. "I can't believe I fell for her charms." Chuza wasn't sure whether Antipas spoke about Salome or Herodias. Perhaps both. "And now," Antipas' voice rose with disbelief, "she manipulated me again, and her idiot brother is the mayor of Tiberias. With a generous allowance, of course." He glowered. "I hope he bungles it, so I can have him kicked out." He turned to Chuza, his face dark as a storm cloud. "How am I supposed to find any peace this winter if Agrippa is walking the streets? He'll be at our council meetings too, ugh!"

Chuza sensed Antipas didn't actually want advice, just a listening ear. And the clopping of hooves was steadying. Calming. The tetrarch glanced over. "I suppose your marriage hasn't been what you expected either, has it?"

Chuza adjusted his seat to hide his discomfort. "How so?"

Antipas gave him a patient look. "Your wife spends more time in her vineyard than your bed. We haven't seen her for months."

Chuza shrugged with pretended nonchalance. As he hoped, the rumors Herodias planted about his failed marriage diverted attention from Joanna's true location. "It's a good vineyard," he said. "She keeps it profitable."

"Well, that's good. For your sake," Antipas said charitably. Chuza turned away and raised his eyebrows at the sky. Antipas granted him a small stipend, but it was far less than he would have paid in wages if Chuza wasn't his bondslave.

After a long pause, Antipas made a comment about a flock of sheep near the road, and Chuza's shoulders eased. The tetrarch had never been interested in Joanna. Even Herodias had not mentioned Joanna's name the whole summer. It helped that Salome kept her mother fully occupied. The staff caught Salome crying in odd places, and for once Herodias was suffering the brunt of gossip.

The squeak of cartwheels brought his mind back to the present. Chuza hoped Philip would be kind to his young bride. Perhaps, once she was free of her manipulative mother and enjoying the privileges of a tetrarch's wife, Salome would grow content, even happy. Her future home was beautiful, she'd have servants to attend to her, and estates to visit. God willing, she'd soon have a child to fill her heart and arms.

On his own wedding day, he assumed he'd be a father within a year. He glanced over his shoulder, back to Sepphoris. What if his friendship with Leah was the closest he came to a child of his own? He hastily faced forward. He would find a way to bring Joanna home. Somehow.

Celer's hooves drummed a steady beat. The leather of his saddle creaked, and the late summer air was rich with baked grass and the chorus of insects. Lost in the soothing symphony, he let his mind roam after Joanna and their uncertain future.

Joanna sat on a marble bench in the shade of a palm tree, watching the traffic churn on the street. After more frustrating interactions with the Pharisees, who continued to test Jesus despite all he had done, Jesus brought his disciples to Caesarea Philippi, a place she never expected him to visit.

The disciples were investigating the Gates of Hades, the cavern beneath the mountain where water bubbled from a bottomless spring. She had no desire to play sightseer again, so instead, she sat and observed the locals going about their business.

A shift in the city's mood drew her attention down the road. A procession was drawing a crowd. With a swoop in her gut, she realized it was Antipas' household, delivering Salome to her husband.

Bitterness at the girl's betrayal lay on her shoulders like a scratchy shawl, but it was threaded with pity. Salome used every trick to escape a marriage she didn't want, yet here she was, rolling inexorably forward.

Joanna drew behind the trunk of the palm tree. The guard was imposing as it tramped by, and she noticed Titus's distinct profile. Next came Antipas and a few of his friends. Chuza rode beside his master. The sight of her husband widened the persistent ache in her core, and she folded her arms against her ribs.

The carts rolled by next, their canopies closed. Salome must be in one with her mother. Joanna pictured Herodias' smug expression, and her lip curled.

As the procession rumbled toward Philip's palace, Joanna stepped into the street, staring after her husband. Around her, gossip was already dancing from lip to lip, the people anticipating their tetrarch's marriage and the gifts he would send into the city.

Joanna wavered, glancing back to where she left the disciples. They would be busy for a while yet. Drawing her palla over her hair, she strode to the palace. There must be some way she could talk with her husband without alerting Herodias. Maybe if she passed a message through Titus, Chuza could meet her. Her pace quickened.

She paused before she reached the gate, worried someone would recognize her. When she realized she was becoming a topic of conversation between Philip's guards, she threw back her shoulders and marched up to the gate, hoping she was not being a fool.

"I need to talk to one of Herod Antipas' guards," she said primly.

The men shared a glance and smirked. "I'm sorry," one said, "but for those kinds of visits, you'll need to visit the side gate."

She blinked. Those kinds of visits? Understanding dawned and her cheeks flamed at their assumption. She tried again. "He's a friend. If you could just pass along a message—"

The guard rolled his eyes. "Look, woman, if you want to talk with one of the men, go around to the side, alright?" He jabbed a thumb in the proper direction.

She stared at him, indignation drawing her up to her full height. For a split second, she considered naming her husband and seeing the crass man disciplined, but her better sense won out. With as much dignity as she could muster, she strode in the direction he indicated, ignoring the jeering amusement behind her.

She found the gate and a guard who regarded a woman's solitary arrival as a matter of course. Though he repeatedly insisted he relayed her message, it was an hour before Titus appeared, his brow furrowed with confusion, scanning for the mysterious woman who summoned him.

"Titus!" she called, hastening forward.

His eyebrows shot up as he saw her. Glancing over his shoulder, he hustled her away from listening ears. He frowned in disapproval. "Do you know what you look like, coming to this gate alone?"

She bristled. "Well, I do now," she said. "I couldn't help it. Can you tell Chuza I'm here?"

"Of course." His gaze softened. "He'll be glad to see you're all right. He's been missing you, you know."

Joanna gave him a measured look. "You talked about me?"

Titus nodded. "Leah misses you, too. We've all been wondering where you were. If you were safe." Joanna had a hard time picturing Chuza, Leah, and Titus gathering to talk about anything, never mind her.

"Can you hurry?" she said, fidgeting with her belt.

"Sure, but Chuza shouldn't meet you here," Titus said, his neck reddening. "It would hurt his reputation, and yours, I suppose, if people thought he entertained a—"

"I get your point," Joanna said. "Tell him to come to the Augustus temple. There's a grove there, where we can talk without prying eyes."

Titus nodded. "I'll find him right away."

As Joanna waited near the lush garden, her nervousness grew. She figured out how to meet her husband, but she had no idea what to say. Now that he had time to mull over what happened, he might be angry with her.

She spotted Chuza and wrung her fingers at the sharp crease between his brows. Their eyes locked and Joanna's knees weakened. The months of separation crashed against her at once, and she burst into tears. Chuza hurried forward, pulling her into a private nook where leafy branches shielded them from a casual passerby. Joanna went into his arms, burrowing against his neck, inhaling his familiar scent. He held her, his arms warm and strong. After a few moments, she sniffled, wiping her eyes on her sleeve.

His voice was hoarse. "I missed you. I can't believe Herodias has forced us apart."

Joanna barked a bitter laugh. "She hates me for serving Phasaelis. We should have realized she'd become jealous of your relationship with Antipas."

"So what now?" Chuza said, dragging his hand through his hair.

Joanna twisted her fingers in her belt. She hoped he would come up with a plan by now. "I don't know how to fix this," she admitted. If only she could turn back time and do it all over again. "Maybe if I go to the vineyard, you can visit me there. Like you used to."

Chuza shook his head, and her hopes fell. "The rumors of our failed marriage have become a shield. If I visit you, Herodias could use our relationship to implicate me—even without your testimony."

They were well and truly stuck. Joanna blinked rapidly. "So I can't go back to the court, and you can't leave."

Chuza groaned in frustration. "Maybe I should just tell Antipas why you left. He's already bitter at Herodias. If I can get him on our side, she won't be able to touch us."

"Do you really believe that?" Joanna was unconvinced. "She's made him do things he doesn't want, even while he hates her."

He puffed out his breath. "Like with Agrippa." They shared a solemn look.

"What if you help them make peace?" Joanna said. "If they stop fighting, Herodias might forget about you."

"I've been trying, but it won't remove the fact that you've been supporting Jesus of Nazareth. She could still have you banished from court—or arrested."

It all felt impossible.

"What if you just left right now?" she asked, gripping the front of his robe. "Come with me. We'll run away. Please." Even as she begged, she saw his answer in the deepening lines of his brow.

He stared into her eyes as his voice cracked. "I want to be with you, but I vowed to serve Antipas. I made a promise before the Lord."

Joanna's fingers loosened, and she studied the ground at her feet. "You're too honorable for your own good."

"Do you regret marrying me?" he whispered, and her gaze flew up.

"No!" she cried out. "I love you." She cupped his cheek, smoothing his beard with her thumb. If only love was all they needed to be together. "But I don't know how we live with Herodias."

"I will find a way," he promised, placing his hand over hers and drawing it to his heart. "We'll be together again." Joanna was comforted by the steady beat beneath her palm. He gave her a small smile. "Leah misses you."

Joanna raised her eyebrows. "So Titus informed me. I didn't realize you and the Roman were so close."

Chuza chuckled. "We're a strange bunch: Leah, Titus, and me. Outcasts, you might say. Three souls without their families, so we've made one of our own."

Joanna struggled with the word, fighting a rising tide of home-sickness. But she didn't want to burden Chuza further. "How is Leah?" Joanna asked, to hide her emotions.

"She's as prickly as a thorn sometimes, but I can see why you care so much about her," he said, grinning in a fatherly way.

Joanna's heart turned over with a surge of gratitude. She shouldn't be surprised that he was filling the gaps she couldn't, caring for the orphaned girl while she was away. It was the kind of man he was.

"I'm glad you're looking after her," Joanna said.

"Well, it wasn't my idea, exactly." Chuza admitted. He told her how it began, and her mouth fell open. "I don't know exactly what

God wants from me," Chuza said, "but I know that he wants us involved in Leah's life."

The call aligned with God's command to care for widows and orphans, but on a deeper level, God knew Chuza craved a family, a chance to influence and lead and protect. She sent up a prayer of gratitude, thanking God for giving Chuza purpose in her absence. But he shouldn't have to do it all alone.

Joanna asked, "Would Leah like to come with me for a while?"

Chuza hesitated. "I don't think so. She talks about Jesus often, his parables especially. But she felt a lot of pressure when she was with... Jesus."

His pause touched a sore spot. "You mean when she was with me," she said, guilt twining around her throat. "Pressured by me, right? I wasn't trying to force her to change. I just wanted her to experience the joy of being one of God's people."

Chuza brushed a soothing hand down her arm. "I know, and I feel the same. I've been struggling to get her engaged in synagogue. But Leah had traumatic encounters with men of faith, first her grandfather, and then that rabbi. I think she feels that Jesus is asking more of her than she can give. If we push her, she'll end up shutting us out completely."

Joanna nodded once, hiding the self-inflicted accusation that if she had said or done the right thing, the young woman would have stepped past her pain and into peace. All Joanna wanted was to give Leah the confidence that she was accepted by God. But if Chuza hadn't made any inroads either, maybe the young woman would never be ready to take her place among God's people. Joanna swallowed around her failure.

Twilight was falling, casting Chuza's face in shadow. "I should take you to your friends," he said. "The wedding feast is tonight, and Antipas expects me."

Joanna wasn't ready to say goodbye. Fingers interlocked, they walked to the camp outside of the city. They stopped before reaching the secluded area, shadows wrapping around them and granting a last moment of privacy. Chuza pulled her into his arms, sharing a kiss both tender and regretful. She clung to him, squeezing her eyelids to stop the tears, then he turned and disappeared into the darkness. She lifted her chin as she rejoined the disciples. Somehow, someday, she'd pull all the pieces of her life together.

# TWENTY-EIGHT

Chuza reached the palace gates and blinked in the torchlight. He couldn't remember the walk back. He had been lost in thoughts of his wife, trying to solve the problem of Herodias. The guards waved him in, and he hurried to his room and changed his clothes, shifting to more immediate concerns.

The sound of revelry rippled down the halls while Chuza supervised the servants arranging the wedding gifts. Antipas wasn't disposed to generosity, but Chuza ensured that Salome's step-father would give her the proper honor.

He led the servants to the banquet hall, where the light of a hundred lamps and the harmony of skilled musicians beckoned them into the warm room.

Antipas clutched a golden cup as if it was permanently fixed to his hand. Herodias reclined at his side, pretending they were a happy couple. The bride and groom were beneath a canopy on a raised dais, framed by garlands of flowers and glittering beads.

Salome had changed into her bridal raiment, the cloth stiffened from rows of gold embroidery. Her kohl-lined eyes flitted nervously

241

around the room. Philip whispered to her, and Salome startled and looked at her groom. After a moment, she nodded.

Philip beckoned for a servant to bring a tray closer so he could select a delicacy. With a smile, he presented it to her. Salome hesitated, then accepted the morsel so she could taste what he offered. Philip leaned toward her as if waiting for her verdict, and then grinned at something she said. Salome's shoulders softened and she laughed tentatively. The sound soothed Chuza's conscience, and he took his first full breath of the day.

Antipas noticed Chuza's arrival and gave a nod. Chuza bowed before the new couple, sweeping his arm to present the parade of servants laden with cloth, jewelry, ornaments, and delicacies. Pleased with the gifts, Philip raised his cup at his brother.

Chuza's duty was done and he could escape to his room, but something held him in the banquet hall. He drifted to a quiet place along the wall, accepted a cup of wine from a servant, and watched the courtly display before him.

This was the way countries were managed, a dance between force and diplomacy. If Jesus was the Messiah, he would need to step into this dance. The ridiculous idea caused him to grin, picturing the wind-blown prophet playing for power like Antipas, Philip, or Herodias. No. If Jesus was Israel's savior, he'd be a different sort of ruler, that much was certain.

Joanna sat among the disciples, her emotions taut as she twisted her sash around her finger. The warm night air was mingled with the sweet scent of vegetation and the tang of smoke from the pagan temples.

Jesus had gone off to pray again. The mood in their little camp was subdued, as if everyone was holding their breath. It always felt empty when Jesus was gone, but tonight felt different, like pressure building before a thunderstorm.

She looked up at the sky, where the moon shone into their clearing, tinting everything in silvery light. Perhaps she was only imagining the tension, casting her own emotions onto the others. Chuza was so close, yet they could not be together. It wasn't fair.

She jerked as Jesus' voice broke the quiet of their camp. "Who do people say the Son of Man is?" he asked without preamble. He strode into their midst, his muscles coiled as if ready to fight or flee. In the moonlight, his eyes were dark and piercing. Instinctively, the disciples rose to their feet, and the air sharpened.

After a breathless moment, Maryam's son James answered, "I've heard some believe you are John the Baptizer."

Joses nodded at his brother. "Others say Elijah, or that one of the prophets of old has risen again."

Jesus leaned toward them in challenge. "But who do you say I am?"

Joanna's breath caught at the question. Everything she had done, everything she hoped, hinged on Jesus' identity.

Peter's voice echoed boldly through the clearing. "You are the Messiah, the Son of the living God."

A sunrise burst within Joanna's chest, and she stared at Jesus. Would he accept the title?

Jesus clapped his hands on Peter's shoulders. "Blessed are you, Simon son of Jonah, because flesh and blood did not reveal this to you, but my Father, who is in heaven."

In the pale light, Joanna saw the whites of her friends' eyes, the flash of teeth as others grinned in delight. With her pulse fluttering like a butterfly, Joanna wished Jesus would say it again. She had believed for so long, but that wasn't the same as Jesus declaring it aloud.

Jesus said, "You are Peter, and upon this rock, I will build my church, and the gates of Hades will not overpower it. I will give you the keys of the kingdom of heaven, and whatever you bind on earth will have been bound in heaven, and whatever you loose on earth will have been loosed in heaven."

Peter stared, and for once, the boisterous fisherman was too astonished to speak. Excited mutters circled the disciples.

"Finally, it's time!" an excited voice said, and Jesus turned to it.

"Don't tell anyone I am the Christ," he said.

"But why wait?" Judas said, stepping forward to face Jesus. "Why shouldn't everyone know that the Messiah has come at last?"

"Isn't it time, Lord?" Matthew said.

It had to be time. The image of Herodias cast from the position she worked so hard to claim curved Joanna's lips into a malicious smile. Perhaps she and Chuza would be together sooner than either of them expected.

Jesus kneaded his palm with the opposite thumb. "Do you still not understand?" Joanna's tension returned in force as Jesus' voice grew grave. "The Son of Man must suffer many things, and be rejected by the elders and the chief priests and the scribes." Joanna licked her lips, her mouth dry as Jesus met their eyes one by one. "He must be killed and raised up on the third day." It was as if a lightning bolt ripped across the sky, and the hair on Joanna's arms stood on end.

*Killed?* Joanna stared into her rabbi's face, her pulse loud in her ears. Jesus met her gaze, and instead of fear, worry, or resolve, she saw pity. Her stomach swooped. Pity for them? For her?

"If anyone wants to come after me, he must deny himself, take up his cross, and follow me."

A gasp escaped her lips. Crucifixion was so barbaric that many would not even speak of it. Her sneering words to Amichai about his revolutionary leader echoed through time. *Be careful you don't follow him right up a cross.*

She screwed her eyes tightly shut. This couldn't be right. Failed rebellions ended in mass crucifixions, not successful ones. And if Jesus was sent by God, there was no way he could fail.

Jesus was still talking, and she yanked her focus back to the present. "For whoever wishes to save his life will lose it, but whoever loses his life for my sake will find it. What does a man profit if he gains the whole world but forfeits his soul?"

She swallowed hard. What if, instead of watching Herodias pulled from her throne, Herodias saw her raised on a cross?

"For whoever is ashamed of me and my words," Jesus said, "The Son of Man will be ashamed of him when he comes in his glory, and the glory of the Father and his holy angels."

His words felt like an accusation. She and Chuza had so carefully kept Jesus' name out of the tetrarch's court. Besides Leah, Titus—and rather disastrously, Salome—they had not willingly shared the miracle-working prophet with anyone, or spread the message of repentance he brought. They believed they were protecting Jesus, but did he need their protection?

She was not ashamed of Jesus, but the idea of boldly speaking about Jesus' teachings before the court curdled her stomach. Facing the questioners was not much better than facing a cross.

"What hope do we have?" Maryam cried out, looking at her sons. Fear was written across her pale face, as if she already stood in the shadow of a cross.

Jesus stepped closer, and his face softened into a compassionate smile. "I say to you truthfully," he said, "there are some standing here who will not taste death until they see the kingdom of God."

Joanna's breath escaped in a rush, and she wasn't the only one. Shoulders eased and concerned brows softened. The danger dwindled before his assurance that the kingdom was still coming.

She nodded to herself, trampling her fears into resolution. Whatever was coming, it would be difficult. The Pharisees were growing bold in their accusations. When Jesus arrived in Jerusalem, it would be naive to believe his presence would go unchallenged by the Sadducees and priests. And it was reasonable to assume that those who followed Jesus would also face the priests' anger. Already she paid a price for following Jesus, as had others who left homes, livelihoods, and families. So when he spoke of them taking up crosses with him, he must be using an illustration. Making them count the cost. She drew bravery around her shoulders like a cloak and nodded. Jesus was honing their loyalty before they were tested by their enemies.

God promised forgiveness and restoration and glory through the line of Jesse, through a king, a son of God. The Messiah was the fulfillment of those ancient promises, and Jesus had taken on that mantle.

Determination stretched her lips into a thin line. Though hardship was coming, Jesus could not fail. Once Jesus was king, every sacrifice would be repaid a hundred times over.

# TWENTY-NINE

## 31 AD
## SPRING

Winter waned. Seeds sown in hope were nourished by the rain and sprouted. Shoots of tender green appeared among the brown fields, rising bravely despite the lingering risk of frost.

Jesus crouched to rub a delicate blade between his fingers. He smiled and tipped his face to the warm sun, as if enjoying its touch. Joanna matched his posture, closing her eyes against the brightness, a contented sigh escaping her lips. When she opened her eyes, Jesus was watching her. They shared a grin. She was sure Jesus loved the open fields of Galilee at least as much as she did.

The rabbi and his disciples broke their fast in a grassy field, and Jesus stood up, brushing crumbs from his robe.

"The harvest is plentiful, but the laborers are few," Jesus said. "Beseech the Lord of the harvest to send out his workers."

It was nowhere near harvest time. Joanna peeked at Maryam and raised her eyebrows in question.

Jesus smiled, meeting his disciple's eyes. "I am sending seventy of you on ahead. Go to the cities I will visit and prepare them for me."

Fishing for men. Harvesting men. Jesus was nothing if not poetic. Her humor dissipated as Jesus named disciples to stand up. To her shame, jealousy flickered up her throat as others were chosen. She knew in her head that she didn't need to prove herself to her fellow disciples, but her heart still longed to work for God.

"Mary Magdalene," Jesus said, and all the women sat straighter. Women were being sent out too? Longing crashed into Joanna like waves, and she gripped her fingers.

Mary rose, her thick, curly hair bound by a scarf. As he had with many of the other disciples, Jesus gave this Mary a nickname: Mary 'the Tower'. To go with Mary, Jesus chose Naomi, Zebedee's wife and mother to two of the twelve.

Joanna began counting those Jesus set apart. Seventy. Her disappointment settled like a pebble in her throat. It didn't matter that the twelve would remain with Jesus. Or that others weren't chosen, either. All she could think about was being left out again.

Maybe Jesus felt her faith was too weak for this task. Miserable tears burned the back of her eyes as Jesus instructed the seventy.

"I am sending you out like lambs among wolves," he said, his expression grave. "Carry no money belt, no bag, no extra shoes, and greet no one on the way. Whatever city you enter that receives you, eat what is set before you, heal their sick, and say to them, 'The kingdom of God has come near to you.'"

Her chest was too heavy to fill her lungs, weighed down by her longing. She searched her heart, trying to discern if it was pride or God's call that pulled at her.

Jesus continued, "But whatever city does not receive you, go out into its streets and say, 'Even the dust that clings to our feet we wipe off in protest against you. Yet be sure of this, the kingdom of God has come near.'"

Joanna jerked as a hand rested on her back. Maryam was studying her in question. Joanna hastily swiped a persistent tear away. She wanted to explain the ache to be used by God, but Maryam might think it was vain. That she should be content in any role. But where did contentment end and complacency begin?

Jesus looked at his seventy. "The one who listens to you, listens to me. The one who rejects you, rejects me. And he who rejects me, rejects the one who sent me." The silence hung long as they considered the seriousness of his words and the authority he claimed.

Jesus began dispatching the seventy to various cities he planned to visit in Galilee, Samaria, Judea, and Perea. As he sent them, they departed immediately, not gathering any supplies for the journey.

Joanna picked at her nail. Maybe Jesus didn't know that she wanted to serve. Hope fluttered its wings. It couldn't hurt to ask. She glanced at the others who were remaining behind, worried they would think she was putting herself forward, but conviction prickled at the back of her neck. Before she could talk herself out of it, she scrambled to her feet. As the last pair left, Joanna hurried up to Jesus.

"Lord, send me," she said breathlessly, clasping her hands to still their fidgeting.

Jesus assessed her with his probing gaze, and Joanna's inadequacies yawned wide. Her failings taunted her, one by one, and she wavered, knowing she was unworthy, yet still wanting to be sent.

"Are you sure, Joanna?" Jesus said gently, setting his palm on her shoulder. "The way is difficult."

Perhaps he thought life in court made her soft. If anything, the opposite was true. "I want to serve the Lord," Joanna pleaded. "It's all I ever wanted."

Jesus peered into her eyes and his expression was kind.

"Why do you worry so much, Joanna?" he asked softly.

She blinked, startled by his words, and even more by the compassion that underpinned them. It was as if he tipped over a rock, exposing the damp place where her anxieties hid, her fear of being overlooked. But she wasn't ready to examine what he found.

Jesus' smile was gentle. "My father has a plan for you." His gaze grew distant. "Will you be ready?"

Joanna seized the hope in his words, but she couldn't wait for some vague day in the future. "If it pleases you, Rabbi, I will go now."

Jesus nodded his assent, and Joanna sagged with relief. "Of course, my friend," he said. "But who will go with you?"

"I will." Maryam stepped forward and gave Joanna a warm smile.

"Daughters of Abraham," Jesus said, spreading his hands wide with approval. "Go."

Joanna strode away at once. A few steps later, she turned sheepishly. "Um, where should we go?"

Jesus laughed, his eyes twinkling as he winked at Maryam. Joanna laughed with him. Jesus liked to tease sometimes, but his humor was always edged with kindness, so it never stung like when Herodias or Dalia poked at her pride. When Jesus teased her, he made her feel like she was one of his friends.

Still grinning, Jesus directed them to a city deep in Samaria.

Joanna's zeal wavered. Samaria was not her first choice. Pilate governed the province, and Samaritans and Jews shared a difficult history. The Samaritans still simmered from bitterness because a Hasmonean king destroyed their mountain altar and relics, declaring the temple in Jerusalem the only correct place to sacrifice.

She glanced at Maryam, who raised her brows in question. Joanna drew her courage and said, "I won't let you down, Rabbi."

They strode away, and Joanna's relief at being commissioned for an important task lightened her steps. The sun rose higher, wrapping her in warmth as the birds flew overhead. After a time, she slowed, allowing Maryam to catch up and give her an amused grin.

"I am happy you came," Joanna said.

"We can't have you wandering off again," Maryam teased, her dimple deepening. "It is not safe for a woman alone, even among our own people."

Joanna faltered. Maryam was right, and Joanna's insistence to be sent out might lead Maryam into danger. The older woman seemed to read her mind.

"I am proud to go with you," she said, hooking her arm in Joanna's. "My sons and I will have many stories to share."

Miles passed under their feet, and they stopped at a farm as the sunset smeared pink streaks against the horizon. The farmer offered them supper and a place to sleep. Joanna, remembering what Jesus said, blessed the house as she ducked under the doorway.

As the housewife set bowls of lentil stew before them, she asked, "Where are you going?"

Joanna told her, then hesitated, adding, "We go to tell them that Jesus of Nazareth will visit them on his way to Jerusalem."

The woman's eyebrows shot up. "He sent two women to Samaria?" She clicked her tongue. "Well, I hope they don't toss you out on your ear."

Joanna glanced at Maryam. Jesus wouldn't have sent them out if the mission was impossible. Would he? She stared at her bowl, stirring the stew round and round. Jesus had made a few forays into Samaritan cities, but not all of them were successful.

They left at dawn and walked the whole day until they arrived at the small town Jesus had named. The sinking sun glowed low and orange, and the local women gathered at a well outside the city, drawing water and visiting.

"How about we start here?" Joanna said, gesturing at the well. "It might be easier to talk with women."

Maryam laughed. "To be honest, I'm not sure how we begin."

Joanna wasn't sure either. Mary Magdalene would know exactly what to say. Even Peter's quiet wife had shared wise words before.

Joanna drew herself up and murmured a prayer for guidance.

The Samaritans fell silent as two women strolled toward their town.

"Peace be on you," Joanna called, hoping her smile hid her anxiety. "May we have a drink of water?"

A woman hesitated, catching Joanna's Galilean accent, but she held out her jar. Joanna drank deeply. This journey forced her to lean on God's provision, which sometimes meant staying thirsty for longer than she liked. Joanna handed the jar to Maryam and wiped her lips on the back of her hand.

The woman peered behind them. "Where have you come from?" Her little daughter drew behind her, hiding in her skirt.

"My name is Joanna," she deflected. "What is your name?"

The woman hesitated a long moment. "Rebekah," she said at last, and her friends shushed her.

"What are you doing here?" one demanded, raking them with a distrustful glare.

Joanna looked at Maryam for support. "Jesus of Nazareth is coming to visit your city soon," Joanna said. The Samaritan women shared glances. Joanna gathered her courage. "Have you heard of him?"

"A little," one admitted. "He told my cousin's neighbor everything about her life."

A woman laughed. "Would you like your secrets revealed too?" She ducked as water flicked her way.

Joanna took courage from their jesting. "Jesus comes to proclaim the kingdom of God to you."

The women sobered instantly.

Rebekah set a fist on her hip. "If he's trying to convince us to worship in Jerusalem, he won't be welcome. We have our own mountain. If it was good enough for Abraham, Isaac, and Jacob, it is good enough for us."

"You can't believe the Jerusalem temple is better," a woman said, gripping her water jar. "They won't let women approach the altar."

"The priests have turned the temple courts into a market."

"Your high priest cares more about politics than righteousness."

Joanna held up her hands to stem the verbal assault. "The kingdom of God goes far beyond Jerusalem."

"And," Maryam said, "that woman you spoke about, well she asked him about the temple. He told her that a time is coming when we will not worship in Jerusalem or on your mountain, but in spirit and truth."

The Samaritan women glanced at each other blankly.

"I don't understand," one said.

Joanna spread her palms. "He will teach you when he comes."

The women muttered and gathered up their jars.

"We need to get home," one said with a frown. One by one, they began drifting away.

Joanna jerked with panic. Night was falling, and they had no place to stay.

Maryam returned the small water jar to its owner, her expression soft. "May I meet your daughter, Rebekah?"

Rebekah hesitated, but Maryam crouched. The girl kept her mother's skirt over her face, showing only her eyes.

"Leave her be," Rebekah said. "She doesn't like strangers."

Maryam glanced up. "That is too bad. I enjoy meeting little girls. I only have big boys in my family."

Drawn by Maryam's warmth, the girl let the fabric slip from her hand. Joanna smothered a gasp. The girl's smile was split up to her nose, dividing her teeth and lip.

Rebekah flushed scarlet, and glared at Joanna in challenge, daring her to comment on her daughter's appearance.

Maryam drew a slow breath and laid her palm on the child's head. "By the name of Jesus Christ," she murmured, "be healed."

"What are you..." Rebekah demanded, then let out a scream, dropping the jar. It shattered, the water splattering her clothes.

Rebekah dropped to her knees, heedless of the sharp fragments of clay, and gripped her daughter's shoulders. "Oh, dear God," she breathed. She ran trembling fingers over the child's perfect lips. "It's not possible."

Joanna stepped closer for a better look, but the other women came running back, pushing Joanna and Maryam away. Wailing in fear, a few ran into the village, abandoning their heavy jars. Joanna gripped Maryam's arm, searching her face for some sign.

"Did you…?" Joanna breathed.

"No, of course not," Maryam said. "I can't heal anyone. Jesus did it."

"But he's—"

"Distance is no barrier to him, is it?" Maryam tipped her head to the side. "He has healed from afar before. All it takes is faith."

Hands lifted the little girl's face to see her beautifully formed mouth. The child smiled at all the fuss, seemingly unaware that her life course had just changed forever.

Jesus commanded them to heal those that were sick, but Joanna hadn't really accepted what that meant. To see Maryam actually do it took her breath away.

A group of men marched from the town, glares preceding their heavy tread. Joanna and Maryam drew closer together as Rebekah showed the men her daughter's restored mouth.

All eyes turned against Joanna and Maryam, and a chill ran down Joanna's spine.

"What power have you invoked to do this?" one man demanded. His gray head and manner proclaimed him a respected figure in the community.

"It was Jesus of Nazareth who did it," Maryam said boldly. "He sent us to declare that the kingdom of God has come near to you."

The men did not look pleased. One of the younger men sneered. "He sent a couple of witches to speak to us?"

Joanna's temper flared. Jesus did not forgive blasphemy against the Holy Spirit. "We are not witches."

"The Nazarene heals by the power of demons," a man said, his scowl digging sharp creases around his thin mouth. "That's what I heard."

Rebekah looked at her daughter, torn between joy at seeing her whole, and fear that dark forces had touched her.

"No!" Joanna said, holding out her hands to Rebekah. "That is not true. We come with words of life. Of hope."

"You come with lies, witch!" a man shouted.

"Leave our city!" another one said. Others took up the cry. Shout layered on shout until they built an insurmountable wall of anger. Rebekah bit her lip, her gaze flitting between her neighbors and the strangers who healed her child. Her shoulders sagging, she turned her back, slipping through the crowd, her daughter in tow.

Failure burned the back of Joanna's throat and she tugged Maryam in the opposite direction. She ducked her head as a rock whistled past, her heart jumping into her throat. Hoping it was just a warning shot, the Galilean women abandoned dignity and broke into a jog, spurred onward by taunts and threats. It wasn't until they were a mile gone that Joanna realized they had forgotten to shake the dust from their feet.

Would they have been chased out of town if they were men? The accusation of witchcraft dug between her shoulder blades, and she glanced back at the city, tempted to march back and set the record straight. But even if Joanna was brave enough, she wouldn't risk her friend's life.

"You're all right?" Maryam asked, scanning her from head to toe.

"Physically, yes," Joanna said, straightening her palla. "But it wasn't what I expected."

"It could have been worse," Maryam said. Joanna pursed her lips. At least Maryam healed someone in Jesus' name. Joanna had done nothing. No wonder Jesus hadn't sent her out until she begged.

Self-pity rising, Joanna studied the countryside. The rolling hills of spring grass were tinted blue in the twilight. The first stars twinkled overhead, and soon it would be dark. No glowing windows beckoned them to find food and comfort.

Joanna asked, "Where will we spend the night?"

"Let's check over there." Maryam gestured to a grove of trees away from the road. The women explored it in the dim light and found a sheltered place to curl up beside one another, sharing their body heat.

"We made a mess of that, didn't we?" Joanna muttered, her empty belly protesting in uncomfortable rumbles. "They won't be ready to receive Jesus now."

"They might have rejected him anyway. And besides, that little girl's life is changed forever because we visited."

Joanna's conscience prickled. When they were told to leave, her first concern had been finding a bed for the night. "That's only because you were convicted to heal her. I did nothing."

"I wouldn't have been there at all if not for you."

Joanna stared at the starry sky, and the tiny lights blurred into long points. She blinked rapidly. Perhaps she had made a difference, even if it was second-hand. "I hadn't thought of it that way."

Maryam yawned, nestling deeper in her cloak. "And who knows? After she has time to consider, Rebekah might seek the truth. Her daughter will be a living testimony to that whole town."

"That is a comforting view," Joanna said, the knot in her core easing further. Gratefulness for Maryam's presence warmed her more than her cloak.

"Then sleep now, my friend. We have a long walk ahead of us tomorrow."

Joanna fell silent, and after a few minutes, Maryam's steady breathing accompanied the chirp of insects, the flap of bats flying overhead, and the wind whispering in the grass. More stars emerged while Joanna lay in the grove, staring at the sky. She thought back to Tamar's words in Capernaum and realized that once again, she had made Jesus' ministry about herself. About her strength and weaknesses. Beneath the awe-inspiring expanse of stars, she was reminded that God was so much bigger than her successes or failures. She covered her cold nose with her cloak, peace stealing over her. These were the same stars God commanded Abraham to count, promising numberless descendants, of which she was one. Jesus kept trying to reach the Samaritans, the outsiders, and the rejects, wanting them to be counted among these celestial lights.

Unspeakable gratitude flowed up in her like a well. Her own missteps could never be enough to thwart God's glorious plan. Not for them. Not for her.

257

# THIRTY

Antipas glared as his pleasure craft bobbed beneath his feet. The wind pushed waves across the Sea of Galilee, rippling the canopy and tussling his short hair, but it could not scour his simmering frustration. Herodias strolled down the pier, laughing at something her brother said. Cypros followed in their wake, a little girl on one hip and a boy walking between her and his nurse-maid. The boy, who must be three years old by now, strained for the water, but the women kept him firmly in hand.

Oh, what a happy family outing this would be. Antipas sighed. Herodias had suggested it, calmly stating that the people would expect to see Antipas supporting his new mayor. She neither wheedled nor whined, but he cursed her logic. By the stars, was every woman's purpose to boss men around?

Antipas swallowed his frown as the cheerful faces turned his way. He wouldn't suffer accusations that his grumpy mood ruined a lovely day.

Agrippa leaped sprightly onto the barge. He was tall and fit, and though his time away from society had added a few more lines to his face, he was as handsome as ever. Curse him.

Agrippa bowed with a flourish. He laughed, glancing at Herodias. "We were discussing if I should address you as uncle or brother. We decided just 'Antipas' was safe enough, if that is fine with you?"

"Fine, fine," Antipas said, waving his hand dismissively. He inclined his head in welcome as Cypros came aboard, her honey-colored eyes searching his expression. Her mouth tightened, showing her sensitivity to his bitter emotions. He drew a breath and offered a smile. It wasn't her fault Agrippa was an idiot.

Knowing everyone was waiting for him to growl or complain, he crouched before Agrippa junior. The boy hugged his mother's leg, eyeing him in return.

"Do you like boats?" he asked the child.

Agrippa's son stared, and Antipas shifted awkwardly. He spent very little time around children. He tipped his face up to Cypros. "Does he speak?"

"Oh yes," she beamed, her freckled face aglow with love. "He is quite chatty, but rather shy with strangers."

How charming. "Well then," Antipas said, slapping his knees and standing up. "Shall we push off?"

Servants bustled, helping arrange the passengers on comfortable couches. Oarsmen pushed the boat from the pier and took their places. The barge drifted under the sun, drawn by the soothing rhythm of oars.

Cypros kept her daughter on her lap, laying a blanket over the child's pudgy bare toes. The nursemaid led the boy to stand by the low railing. Antipas cast glances over at the child now and then, unaccountably nervous.

Cypros leaned toward him. "Don't worry, Eliza is very attentive. He will not fall overboard."

His cheeks warmed at his foolishness, and he nodded at the toddler in her lap. The girl had her mother's coloring. "Your daughter is a pretty little thing."

"Yes," Cypros said, smiling. "Bernice has been my joy and comfort. I never dreamed I would have two children so close together. They are only a year apart." She kissed the girl's silky head, and Antipas battled an unexpected surge of jealousy.

He had never known the weight of a child in his arms, never mind one of his own. He peeked at Herodias. When they fell in love, they had talked about her giving him an heir. He studied the cup in his hands. None of Herod's heirs—Archelaus, Philip, or Antipas—had produced children of their own. And now, here was Agrippa with two.

Herodias lounged near her brother, laughing prettily. Of course, if he wanted an heir, things needed to change. He had not summoned his wife to his bed since the fateful night of his birthday. She still refused to apologize for what she had done, insisting she executed John for both of them, to protect their marriage and his rule.

Antipas shifted in his seat. His lack of female companionship was wearing on him, and his wife had dressed with care. Her neckline dipped tantalizingly and his loins stirred.

As they drifted northward, Agrippa studied the cities along the shore with interest.

"Which one is Capernaum?" he asked. "I hear that is where the infamous prophet lives."

Herodias pointed it out. "The reports say the city turned against him. The local teachers were angry that he wouldn't adhere to their Sabbath traditions or some such thing." She wafted her hand to show her disinterest, and her perfume teased Antipas' nose.

Agrippa aimed his raised eyebrows at Antipas. "That must be a relief to you. A would-be-messiah on my doorstep would have me on edge—if I was more than a humble mayor."

"He is not a messiah," Antipas sneered at the title. "By all accounts, he is a rabbi."

"Who performs miracles," Agrippa said.

Cypros' eyes widened. "Those stories are true? He can heal and raise the dead?"

Antipas jerked involuntarily, a chill settling in his bones. "Raise the dead?" He scoffed. "That is ridiculous. What is he, friends with Hades?"

Agrippa laughed as if Antipas made the wittiest joke. "I've heard he's been accused of working in league with someone called Beelzebub. Who, from what I can gather, is some demon prince?"

"Something like that," Antipas said dryly.

Cypros' eyes were still gleaming. "But can this man really do what they say? Have any of you witnessed a miracle?"

Antipas frowned. "My steward claims to have seen him heal and then feed a crowd of thousands from a few loaves. He's never lied to me before."

Agrippa's eyebrows shot to his hairline. "Chuza saw Jesus of Nazareth?"

"Yes," Herodias said, sliding back into the conversation. "And he has counseled my husband to leave this prophet be, despite Antipas' desire to see him for himself."

Antipas glared at his wife. "Considering what happened last time I detained a prophet, Chuza thought it prudent to avoid inflaming the people."

The servant passed around a tray. Agrippa selected a choice piece of meat. "But if the people are turning against him on their own, this could be your opportunity to squash a potential problem —before it grows more out of hand."

Antipas glowered. Agrippa had been managing a single city for a few months, and now he believed he could rule a kingdom?

Cypros, captivated by her own thoughts, missed the undercurrent that flowed between the other three. "Where is he now?" she asked. "Is he still in Galilee?"

Herodias studied her cuticles as she spoke. "He spent the winter traveling and teaching, or whatever else he does. I've heard he's moving toward Jerusalem, though. Perhaps he will be in the city for Passover. Won't that cause a stir?"

Antipas stiffened. "Jerusalem is not my problem. If there is trouble during Passover, Pilate will have to handle it."

Herodias laughed lightly. "It would almost be worth the difficulties of an uprising if it highlighted Pilate's ineptitude."

Agrippa tapped his chin. "Though, some might criticize the fact that a Galilean prophet was allowed to grow his following for so long." He nodded at Herodias. "You were wise, sister, to snuff out that other prophet before his popularity grew to this level."

Herodias' gaze flickered. "Perhaps," she said, "but I have learned that one must be careful with prophets. You never know which powerful men believe in them."

Antipas' temper flashed. "If this so-called prophet becomes a threat, you think I wouldn't deal with him?" Herodias' doubtful expression enraged him further.

"You'd order him executed?" she asked.

Cypros' mouth hung open, confused by the sparks flying between Antipas and Herodias.

Antipas leaned toward his wife. "You don't think I have what it takes?"

Herodias matched his posture, her eyes sparkling with intelligence and confidence. By the stars, she was beautiful. "It's your advisors that I question, not you. I have known my whole life that you were destined to rule." Her words flowed like fragrant oil. "Your father saw it too. You were going to rule all his lands before others preyed on his weakened state and made him alter his will."

Antipas' chest warmed. She was not the kind of woman to pour empty flattery to win his affection, not like Phasaelis. Herodias was strong, clever, and not afraid to show it—even if it went against his wishes. She was as untamed as an Arabian filly, as spirited as she was beautiful.

His pulse leaped with desire, and her lips softened as her eyes blazed with reciprocating passion.

Suddenly, the boat could not return to shore soon enough.

After a frustrating hour of mindless drifting, they arrived back in the city. Antipas and Herodias walked side by side to the palace, not touching, yet he could feel her body like a furnace raging beside him. They accepted the bows of the staff as they strolled to Antipas' room, outwardly serene.

But as soon as the door was shut, Antipas yanked her into his arms, his lips finding her throat as he moaned for the months they spent apart. She yielded to his embrace, throwing back her head. He was drunk with her, the touch of her skin was a euphoric drug. Her hands cupped his face, and she returned his passion with equal measure. Here was a worthy woman, worth more than rubies. Here was a woman who saw him for what he was, and who he could be.

# THIRTY-ONE

The cavorting man shouted praises to the son of David, his joyful noise rippling through the sultry air. The crowds were as thick as ever, countless supporters joining with Jesus as he made his way to Jerusalem. Jericho's citizens flocked to the streets as the procession marched down the tree-lined road. The dancing beggar was causing quite a stir.

"Isn't that Bartimaeus?" Joanna heard. "Isn't that the blind beggar?"

Bartimaeus' joy tugged at her, but it couldn't infiltrate the tension that knotted in her core. She drew her palla higher on her head and tried to blend in with the other Galilean women. Surely Antipas had quit the city by now, but perhaps Herodias left spies to search for her.

Joanna nearly trod on Maryam's heels as the disciples halted. Jesus peered up into the branches of a sycamore tree.

"Zaccheus!" he called. "Hurry and come down. Today I will stay at your house."

Joanna stared as a short, well-dressed man scrambled down from the boughs. He was far too old to be climbing trees. A finger tapped her shoulder. Stifling a fearful gasp, she whirled around.

"Susanna?" Joanna said, sagging with relief. She pulled her into a hug. "It's just you."

"Just me?" Susanna said, raising a brow. "Should I be insulted?"

Joanna laughed, glancing around at the crowd, rubbing one arm with her palm. "Sorry, I'm a little on edge. Is Antipas gone?"

"Yes, he left a few days ago," Susanna said. "My sons and I stayed to wait for Jesus. They can't wait to see him for themselves."

Joanna spotted the two young men behind her friend and nodded in welcome. "So, you knew Jesus would come this way?"

Susanna chuckled. "I don't know if you noticed—" she looked pointedly at the vast crowd "—but everyone knows where Jesus is."

Which meant if Herodias suspected she was with the disciples, she knew exactly where Joanna was too.

Susanna's brow furrowed. "What's wrong?"

"Does Herodias talk about me?" Joanna blurted.

Susanna blinked in surprise. "No, not at all. Well, I mean, she did for a while." Color bloomed on her cheeks. "She enjoyed gossiping about whether it was you or Chuza who was more miserable in your marriage. If you left, or if he sent you away. But she got bored with that after a while, thank goodness."

Joanna considered this news. "So Herodias thinks I went home?"

"Even I thought you were at your vineyard," Susanna said, lifting her brows. "I should have realized that you'd never be content to grow grapes when there's a prophet on the loose."

Maryam came forward. She welcomed Susanna, then turned to Joanna. "Zaccheus is putting together a meal. We're going to his house."

"Alright," Joanna said, scanning the crowd again, searching for threats. Susanna seemed confident she was safe, but she could be wrong.

They wove through the streets, heading into a wealthy district.

"How is Chuza?" Joanna asked Susanna, a lump in her throat.

Their last conversation was months ago.

"He is well," Susanna said. "He left a message for you." She rummaged in her small bag and pulled out a sealed scroll.

Joanna accepted it as if it was a treasure. Her letters to Chuza had been vague to protect their secrets, and the few messages that found their way to her were so carefully written that half the meaning was lost.

"You go on," Joanna said. "I'll catch up."

Joanna let the crowds sweep past her, finding a bench under a tree. Casting a quick look around herself, she broke the seal and consumed the words like a beggar at a feast.

> *My love,*
>
> *We leave only days ahead of you and I feel I am leaving my heart behind in Jericho for you to collect. I miss you more than this pen can convey.*
>
> *I have good news. Herodias and Antipas have reconciled, and her jealousy of my position vanished. I pray that the threat to us is over. But you must stay hidden among the disciples until we are certain. Don't come to the palace. I'll try to seek you out—I'm sure Jesus will be easy to find. Part of me wants to tell you to run to your vineyard, run to safety, but knowing you are only days behind me, I can't send you farther away. I need to see you.*
>
> *Your devoted husband,*
> *Chuza*

He sounded so calm about her traveling with Jesus to Jerusalem. She doubted he would feel the same if he heard Jesus' repeated prophecies about the danger that awaited him. She rolled the scroll shut and wrapped her arms around herself.

Something was coming. Jesus left them in no doubt that there would be difficulties ahead. She was sure Jesus would finally face off against Antipas, throwing the tetrarch's sins in his face like a prophet of old. He might call down destruction from heaven if Antipas refused to repent, or perform a sign that showed all of Jerusalem that their messiah had come at last.

She swallowed hard. Even if Jesus did nothing but celebrate Passover in peace, she and Chuza weren't out of danger.

Joanna unrolled the note and read it again, shaking her head in disbelief. It seemed unlikely that Herodias had truly forgotten her jealousy. But why hide it, unless she had darker plans to enact?

If Herodias truly thought the steward's marriage had collapsed like Susanna said, she wouldn't be able to prove Chuza supported his wife. Joanna gripped the scroll tighter. Would she and Chuza have to hide their love forever?

Restless, Joanna jerked to her feet and rejoined the others. The women gathered in Zaccheus' large courtyard, where pots of greenery spilled around a sparkling fountain. Joanna accepted a cup of wine and sat beside Susanna, rubbing the pottery with her thumbs. Naomi was detailing the necessary preparations for the Passover, flustered that they didn't even know where they would eat the meal.

Joanna drained her cup and stared at the dark residue on the clay. She could go home, far from the threat of trouble in Jerusalem and the tetrarch's court. She fled Herodias once before, but that time she ran to Jesus, not away from him. It felt cowardly and dishonorable to abandon him now.

And Chuza waited for her in Jerusalem. She couldn't leave him to face the coming trouble alone.

Joanna stood at the crest of the Mount of Olives, staring across the Kidron Valley at the broad expanse of the eastern wall of Jerusalem. She studied the highest tower, remembering Salome and her powerlessness beneath Herodias' will. Her focus drifted to the four towers surrounding Herod's Palace—where Antipas and Herodias basked in luxury.

One last time, she allowed herself to consider turning back. But Jesus' whole being leaned toward his arrival in Jerusalem. Something was going to happen and she couldn't tuck tail and hide now, or she knew she would regret it forever.

Jesus was riding a donkey like the kings of old. Behind him swarmed crowds—men, women, and children who had joined his pilgrimage from Jericho. Jesus surveyed the city as if drawing breath before the charge. His disciples waited, tense with anticipation, but instead of a war cry, he nudged the beast and it ambled forward. The people fell in his wake, and the atmosphere vibrated with expectancy. The prophet had come to Jerusalem.

"Hosanna!" a voice called joyfully, and others took up the praise. "Blessed is the king who comes in the name of the Lord! Peace in heaven and glory in the highest!"

Hope prickled in Joanna's eyes as the shout reverberated through her chest, echoing her longing for God to rule their land again.

"Hosanna!" she shouted, even while her gaze flicked to the looming city walls.

Men laid their coats on the road for Jesus' donkey to walk upon. Crowds surrounded him, waving branches in a leafy bower, making the sunlight dance and sparkle. They sang their adulation as Jesus approached the holy city.

A Pharisee shouted to Jesus, "Teacher, rebuke your disciples!"

Jesus called back. "I tell you, if these become silent, the stones will cry out!"

The Pharisee muttered, and Joanna wondered if he spoke censure or warning. She cast a nervous glance at the city walls that contained the priests, Antipas, and Pilate.

As they drew nearer to the city, Jesus' voice thickened, drawing Joanna's attention. "If you had known on this day, Jerusalem, the things that lead to peace. But now they are hidden from your eyes. For the days will come upon you, when your enemies throw up a barricade and surround you, hemming you in on every side. They will level you to the ground and your children within you, and they won't leave one stone upon the other, because you did not recognize the time of your visitation."

The crowd pressed in behind him, rejoicing, oblivious of his dark prophecy. Joanna's chest tightened as if bound with chains. The Messiah was supposed to protect the holy city, so how could it be destroyed? She stared at Jesus. For more than two years she sat at his feet, funded his ministry, and prayed for the kingdom to come, yet now she wondered if she had any idea what he was going to do. Her palms dampened with the unknown.

Jesus dismounted at the steps to the eastern gate, and the masses followed him up. At the cusp of the doorway to the temple courts, Joanna drew a deep breath. No turning back now.

Jesus entered the courtyard and Joanna streamed in with the crowd, her emotions as twisted as a skein of wool. Excitement and anxiety, turn by turn.

The clamor worsened within the Court of Gentiles. Passover was just a week away, and the city overflowed. It seemed every pilgrim was crammed into the temple courtyard.

Jesus strode straight for the courtyard market. Joanna gaped as Jesus gripped the edge of a table and heaved it upward. Coins caught the light, spinning in the sudden silence, then rained on the tile floor in a tinkling cascade. The crowd surged forward. A shocked laugh bubbled out of her throat as Jesus began driving the sellers out of the temple. This was not what she expected.

Jesus' words echoed off the walls. "It is written that my house shall be a house of prayer, but you have made it a robber's den!"

A hand gripped her shoulder, and she jerked in surprise, turning to face a pair of guards she recognized. Antipas' men. Her mouth turned to dust.

"Come with us," one growled beneath the chaos of the crowd. "Now." Joanna tried to step away, but he caught her by the elbow, pinching her with his tight grip.

"Why?" she demanded, though, in her sinking heart, she knew.

"You are under arrest. By order of Herod Antipas."

Fear drove into her like a spear. Chuza and Susanna were wrong. Herodias was merely biding her time. Fighting panic, she gathered herself up to her full height, refusing to show her terror. As Jesus cleared the temple, coins rolling on the beautiful tile and birds flapping into the sky, her captor pulled her to the nearest exit. She glanced back and met Susanna's horrified eyes.

# THIRTY-TWO

As she was jostled through the busy streets, Joanna's thoughts moved like sludge, trying to foresee what would happen next, what horrors Herodias planned for her. Her step wavered despite her determination to be brave.

As she approached the palace gate, familiar faces gaped in recognition. Staff stared as guards dragged Chuza's wife through the courtyard like a criminal. Her innocence straightened her spine, despite the man gripping her arm like a vise.

"I wish to speak to Antipas' steward," Joanna asked, frustrated by the crack in her voice.

He drove her forward. "Our orders are to deliver you to Antipas immediately."

Servants whispered, hurrying away to spread the gossip. Well, she thought ruefully, Chuza would learn of her arrival soon enough.

The door to Antipas' receiving room was flung wide, and the guards' hobnailed sandals echoed in the deserted room. The dais stood waiting, the throne expectant. Frescoes on the walls danced in the illumination of golden lamps and the marble floor gleamed.

Joanna was jerked to a halt in the middle of the splendor, wearing her dusty clothes and flanked by guards. She swallowed hard and lifted her trembling chin.

The strained silence was broken by a multitude of footsteps. A guard emerged from another door, followed by Antipas with Herodias on his arm. They swept into the room in regal robes and glittering jewelry. Their courtiers trailed behind, intrigued by this scandal.

Antipas settled himself on his throne and Herodias placed a palm on his shoulder. As Antipas took her hand and kissed her wrist, Herodias met Joanna's eyes and smirked in triumph. Joanna's breath caught in her throat.

"Joanna, wife of Chuza," Antipas began, "you've been accused of sedition."

"By who?" Joanna flinched as her voice echoed unexpectedly in the room.

Antipas' eyes narrowed. "Your presence among the followers of Jesus the Nazarene speaks for itself, don't you think?"

"Yet," Joanna said boldly, despite the fear coursing through her veins, "of the thousands in the temple courtyard, I am the only one here."

Herodias took a half step forward, a sweet smile belying the hatred in her eyes. "Did those thousands also provide for this so-called prophet out of their means?"

The men and women in the room muttered, but Joanna ignored them.

"I do not keep an account," Joanna said. "Jesus teaches that when we give, the right hand should not know what the left is doing." A lesson that could have saved her a heap of trouble if she had heeded it.

Antipas laughed. "No wonder your leader requires financial aid from women." The room chuckled at his wit.

Herodias did not laugh. She leaned forward. "But you cannot deny that you gave money. You bragged about it to my daughter, trying to puff up the importance of women among the disciples. Isn't that right?"

Joanna's face heated at the portrayal of her intentions, but she would not lie about the facts. "I gave him money, yes." She let her gaze travel over the witnesses. "Because it was Jesus of Nazareth who healed me from my sickness."

Herodias blinked, and Joanna's lip quirked with satisfaction at surprising her. But Herodias quickly recovered. "So you admit it," Herodias said. "You believe this man is a prophet with the power to heal. You believe it so much that you gave him a substantial sum. Even though some call him the Christ."

"Yes," Joanna said, locking eyes with her foe. Despite her fear, it was a relief to confess her belief in Jesus to the tetrarch's court. Come what may.

Herodias glowed in triumph, but Antipas' brow puckered in thought. Herodias took another step forward and addressed the room.

"You are all witnesses. She admits to supporting Jesus of Nazareth, a man the crowds rally around this very moment, declaring him their messiah." She smiled as if amused by the ignorance of commoners. "But this is not Joanna's first act against her lord, Herod Antipas. No, no," she said theatrically. "She disobeyed her master's will by spiriting away his first wife, spreading lies of Phasaelis' mistreatment to King Aretas of Nabatea, and risking war."

Joanna's lips parted, but Herodias was not finished.

"My gracious husband was willing to overlook her... disloyalty... because he believed she was doing as she was told. But now we see the pattern. Whenever she can, the steward's wife contrives to work against Herod Antipas."

The people murmured, and Joanna surreptitiously swiped her damp palms down her robe.

Herodias looked at her husband and tossed her head. "We know about these crimes. Perhaps she has done worse. Or has fellow conspirators within the court." She paused, letting that sink in. "With your permission, my lord, I will have her questioned." She peered down her nose at Joanna as if she was a large bug to be squashed. "King Herod always said that truth can only be tested under torture."

Antipas' eyes grew wide, and this time Joanna could not hide the tremble that ran from her head to her feet. "God help me," she breathed. She prayed for courage to withstand, to protect those she loved.

Herodias smoothed her hand down her husband's arm. Her icy tones filled the silent room. "Your father rooted out many a deadly plot through the use of his questioners."

The others in the court shifted. Herod employed torture with a heavy hand, but Antipas had not continued his father's ways.

Herodias leaned closer to Antipas, preparing to pressure him further, but an angry tread dragged all their attention to the door. Joanna's knees weakened as Chuza strode into the room, his eyes sparking like flint. He marched up to her guards, glaring them up and down.

"You may wait outside," Chuza said, force ringing in his tone. The guards hesitated, but hearing no counter-order from the dais, they stomped away. Joanna had never seen Chuza flex his authority in Antipas' presence, and the rest of the court glanced at each other with raised brows. To her surprise, Antipas' fearful expression eased.

Herodias folded her hands, her features cold as ice. "Steward," she said. "I see you've come to defend your wife."

Chuza ignored her. He spoke to Antipas, "My lord, why have you dragged my wife before your court? She has done nothing to warrant this treatment. You cannot charge her with disloyalty, unless you wish to arrest thousands of your citizens, including me." Joanna's hope that she could save Chuza by insisting on his ignorance trickled away.

The court murmured and Herodias' eyes gleamed as he implicated himself, but Chuza plowed on. "You knew I sat and listened to this prophet's preaching, and I saw him heal. I told you that myself. Yet you saw no reason to arrest me or charge me with sedition."

"Your wife has confessed to giving the Nazarene money," Herodias said with a sneer. "Did you give her permission to do that?"

Still, Chuza refused to look at Herodias, speaking only to Antipas. "Throughout the Roman empire, wealthy women support playwrights, scholars—even physicians. Particularly physicians who healed them. Do you deny Joanna the right to become the patroness of the man who healed her?"

Herodias scoffed. "We are not in Rome. This man is no mere physician—"

"Then what is he?" Chuza challenged. "If he is dangerous, why does he teach in the temple courts? Pilate has not arrested him because he poses no threat. If you will not arrest the rabbi, you can hardly arrest his disciple."

Joanna's chest swelled with pride. God had gifted her husband with wisdom—and the skill to use it. Chuza's voice softened, and he addressed Antipas as if they were the only two in the room.

"My lord, Herodias has harbored resentment because Joanna was your first wife's companion." Antipas glanced sympathetically at his wife, whose face now glowed like a hot coal. "I would take her accusations for what they are—the words of a jealous woman. Comfort your wife. Remind her that she is the only one your heart desires."

Herodias swelled with rage as her careful allegations were reduced to a woman's tantrum.

Chuza bowed. "Now, if it pleases you, my lord," he said, "Joanna will go and stay with family for a time, so she does not disturb your lovely wife."

Antipas nodded, clearly eager to be freed from the distasteful duty of ordering a woman tortured. "Yes, yes," he said. "You may go."

Joanna, stunned by the sudden shift in her circumstances, turned to Chuza. He gave her a nod of assurance, and she forced herself to walk calmly by his side.

As soon as they were free from the throne room, Chuza pulled her around a corner and into his arms. He rubbed his hands over her back, shushing her, and it was a moment before she realized she was shaking. That had been too close. If Chuza hadn't been there...

He drew back and placed his hand on either side of her face, holding her as if she was fragile.

"I'm so sorry," he said, contrition on every line of his face. "I should have known she wouldn't forget."

Her hands felt like ice, and she slid them into his warm grip. "She tossed the dice against us and lost," she said.

Chuza glanced around. "We should get you out of here."

She nodded, her throat scraped raw. Hands clasped, they hurried across the courtyard.

Susanna rushed up, ghostly pale. "You're all right!"

"Thanks to Chuza." Joanna smiled weakly.

"Sorry it took me so long to get there," Chuza said, sharp creases between his eyebrows. "I planned to meet you in the temple courts, and then Titus had to chase me down."

"So you're free to go?" Susanna looked between them.

"Yes," Joanna said. But the thought of joining the jostling crowds in the temple courtyard made her nauseous. "But I think I'll go to my sister's house."

"Yes, go see your family," Susanna said, nodding in approval. "I'll let the others know you're alright."

Susanna hurried away, and Joanna and Chuza made their way through the Upper City. Joanna realized this was the first time she visited her family for respite instead of obligation for a long, long time.

She squeezed her husband's hand. "How did you know what to say?"

Chuza barked a bitter laugh. "Herodias thinks she understands Antipas because they've been married a couple of years, but I've known him most of my life. She overplayed her hand. Antipas hated torture," he said. "He remembers the screams during his father's reign." A shiver ran down her spine, and she did not press for more.

They reached Dalia's house. He raised his fist to knock, but she grabbed his sleeve. "So what now?" she asked. "Is it over?"

Chuza hesitated. "Herodias will need time to lick her wounds. She's going to desire revenge above all else. Until she is appeased, you should keep out of sight."

She nodded, drawing a shaky sigh, wondering if anything could appease Herodias' wrath now that they had humiliated her.

Standing outside Dalia's house, Joanna drank in the sight of her husband's face, craving the safety of his arms. She glanced down the busy street, craving privacy. "Can you stay with me tonight?" Joanna asked.

Chuza grinned. "Will your sister let me sleep under her roof?"

His attempt at humor drove home the reality that she had escaped Herodias' plot. Herodias had attempted to hurt her and supplant Chuza and failed. Her inner tension began to unwind.

Joanna raised her eyebrow in a coy smile. "I think the greater question is, will we be wedged between a dozen aunts and uncles?" Chuza made a face, and Joanna laughed.

She knocked on the door, and Alexander let them in, expressing welcome surprise. After Joanna explained her arrest and rescue to her shocked family, Dalia looked at Chuza with a new expression.

"So," Dalia said, tilting her head to the side. "The steward can stand up to his master after all."

Chuza opened and closed his mouth, unsure how to reply. Miriam rushed forward to hug Joanna. She embraced Chuza next, whispering loudly in his ear, "Dalia's starting to like you."

Joanna laughed, and Chuza and Dalia shared a tentative smile.

The house bulged with guests, but none claimed the loft above the small stable. Though it was only twilight, Joanna and Chuza bid their hosts good night and slipped away, ignoring the teasing behind them.

The stall was pungent with dung and dusty hay, but other than a drowsy donkey, they were alone. Joanna fashioned a bed in the hayloft and lay down, patting the place beside her. Chuza stretched out on his back, his arms folded behind his head. Unexpectedly shy, Joanna toyed with a loose thread on his robe.

She said, "Tell me everything that's happened while I was gone."

Chuza gave her a lighthearted account of palace life, and her chest twinged at having missed so many little moments. As much as she struggled to find her place in the tetrarch's court, it held people she cared about.

Propping her cheek on one arm, she ran her fingertips up and down his chest. "Do you get jealous of my time with the disciples?" she asked. "Do you feel left out?"

Chuza rolled toward her. His face was inches from hers, and her pulse fluttered. "Sometimes. There is a side of your life I know so little about. You have friends, memories, experiences that I do not share."

"I feel like that when you talk about Leah and Titus," Joanna said. "You're not just a mentor to them, you're like family. I want to be part of it." She ducked her head, her cheeks flushing. She was only a decade older than Leah and had always tried to be her friend, not her family. Perhaps that was where Joanna went wrong, and why it had been so hard to breach the wall Leah built around her heart. She peeked up and saw Chuza's love shining in his eyes, encouraging her to continue.

"I want to share this experience with you," she said. "Share everything." Frustration puckered her brow. "Why can't I have it all? Now that Herodias has revealed my secret to the court, maybe I can pull both sides of my life together."

Chuza hesitated, his eyes searching hers, bright in the dimness.

"I want that too," he said. "But we're not there yet."

She studied the weave of his tunic, knowing he was right. "Will you come with me?" she asked, barely daring to hope. "I would like you to meet the others—my friends."

Chuza considered, then nodded, running his palm from her shoulder, to her elbow, to her hip, drawing her closer. Her skin tingled at his touch. "I'll spend this Passover week with you."

Joanna's mouth fell open. "Will Antipas let you go, after...?"

Chuza chuckled, obliterating the space between them. He burrowed his face in her hair, his lips tickling her ear. "If Antipas misses me, it will be a timely reminder of my value in his court."

"So you're finally running away with me," she teased.

He leaned back. "Well, not quite. I'll leave a message for him, letting him know I've got certain business to attend to." His gaze was full of meaning as he murmured, "After today, I think I've earned a few days of pleasure." He gave her a roguish wink.

As she laughed, he slid his fingers into the hair at the back of her neck and covered her lips with his.

# THIRTY-THREE

Joanna blushed like a newlywed as they emerged the next morning, Chuza's fingers twined in hers. They ate with the family, Alexander and Chuza talking about local news, the women dividing duties that needed to be completed before Passover.

"Will you need my stable again tonight?" Dalia asked with a teasing grin.

Joanna shot her a dirty look. "Maybe. We're going down to the temple later, and I hope to rejoin the disciples."

"Is that wise?" Miriam asked. "If you're already under scrutiny, won't this cause more trouble?"

Chuza overheard and turned to his mother-in-law. "I don't want trouble, especially for your daughter. But if our people cannot gather in the name of our God, then we have greater problems to fear."

"Well said." Dalia gave an approving nod. "It is Passover, after all. Antipas can't deny our right to assemble."

Miriam frowned. "As long as it stays peaceful."

The others sobered, knowing how quickly a riot could break out—and turn deadly.

After they finished eating, Joanna and Chuza gathered their things and walked to the temple. The city hummed with new energy, and Joanna knew Jesus' arrival was the cause. A sudden realization jerked her to a stop.

"Should we get Leah from the palace?" Joanna asked. "What if Herodias goes after her in revenge?"

Chuza whirled around, panic flitting across his features. "You're right." He charged toward the palace, Joanna hastening to catch up.

Joanna waited outside the gate as he slipped inside. Twisting her sash around her fingers, she worried Antipas would see his steward and force him to stay. She exhaled a sigh of relief when Chuza hurried up with Leah in tow.

Joanna rushed to embrace the young woman. She expected resistance, but Leah squeezed her in return. Chuza was right, Leah had grown.

"I heard what happened," Leah said, shaking her head in disbelief. "Thank goodness you came back for me. I've been as nervous as a chicken in a pot."

"I left a note for Antipas, and I explained everything to Titus," Chuza said.

They turned to the temple once again. Making conversation was difficult in the bustling streets, but Joanna was amazed at how much Leah had to say. The young woman seemed determined to catch Joanna up on everything she had missed. Titus' name came up often, and Joanna couldn't help but wonder if Leah was nursing a youthful infatuation. The soldier had a certain allure, but he was still only a God-fearer. Leah must marry a true Jewish man.

The mood in the temple courts thrummed with celebration. Children skipped in a circle, shouting hosannas as their parents rose on tiptoes, trying to peer over the crowd. A man jostled Joanna as he pushed by, carrying his son in his arms.

Picking their way, they searched for a place to stand where they could watch and hear. An angry knot of priests, elders, and scribes glared at Jesus. Joanna pointed them out to the others.

"What happened?" Chuza asked a man nearby, gesturing at the priests.

"The Nazarene turned their own arguments against them," he muttered under his breath, apparently torn between admiration and outrage.

Chuza opened his mouth to say more, but Jesus' loud voice overrode all others.

"A man planted a vineyard, rented it to vine-growers, and went on a long journey. At harvest time, he sent a slave to the vine-growers for some of the produce, but they beat him and sent him away empty-handed. And so he sent another slave. They beat him too, treated him shamefully, and sent him away empty-handed. So he sent a third, but this one they also wounded and cast out.

"So the owner of the vineyard said, 'What shall I do? I will send my beloved son. Perhaps they will respect him.'" Jesus rose and turned in a slow circle, looking at the crowd. "But when the vine-growers saw the son, they reasoned with one another, saying, 'This is the heir; let us kill him so the inheritance will be ours.' So they threw him out of the vineyard and killed him."

A heavy silence fell over the courtyard.

Jesus said, "What will the owner of the vineyard do to them? He will come and destroy these vine-growers and give the vineyard to others."

His opponents began protesting. "May it never be!"

Jesus turned, fixing them with his stern gaze. "What then is this that is written, 'The stone which the builders rejected became the chief cornerstone?' Everyone who falls on that stone will be broken into pieces, but on whomever it falls, it will scatter him like dust."

The priests' faces turned purple, and they twitched their hands as if wanting to seize Jesus by the throat. But the wiser of their group nudged them and gestured at the crowd. Joanna released a slow breath. The priests couldn't arrest Jesus, no matter how he accused them. Not after the crowd saw his miracles.

As the sun dipped to the west, Jesus left the city and climbed over the Mount of Olives to Bethany. Joanna, Leah, and Chuza followed the disciples, Chuza looking uncomfortable among the close-knit group.

Manaen spotted them and hastened over, putting his arm around Chuza's shoulder. "I hear you saved our Joanna," he said. "You've always had a greater influence on Antipas than you believed. I'm proud of you."

Chuza shook his head, casting Joanna a weighted glance. "I've spent months fearing the worst, imagining every scenario and what I would say. I hate to think what could have happened if I was caught by surprise."

Manaen tussled Leah's hair. Though the young woman was past the age of childish teasing, she grinned anyway, which made him smile wider. His voice warmed. "I'm glad to see your face again."

"I'm glad to see yours too, new wrinkles and all."

Manaen pretended to be affronted, and the banter continued as they walked. Joanna watched Leah with wonder. Chuza said Leah had grown, but this was a transformation.

A man waited outside Bethany to invite Jesus to a feast in his honor. Jesus accepted, taking the twelve with him.

"Come on," Maryam nudged Joanna as Jesus strode away. "Let's help Martha prepare the evening meal."

They entered a house with a side courtyard and Joanna introduced Chuza to their hosts. "This is Martha and her brother Lazarus." She leaned closer to whisper in his ear. "Jesus raised Lazarus from the dead."

Chuza stared, but Lazarus pressed his lips together and looked away, as if heading off questions. Joanna squeezed her husband's hand. Lazarus suffered his share of animosity from the religious leaders, who assumed he was part of a great deception with Jesus. Perhaps it was understandable that he had become wary of attention.

Joanna glanced behind Martha. "Where is your sister?"

Martha rolled her eyes with good-natured annoyance. "There are chores and guests, so of course, Mary vanishes. That girl is as unbridled as the wind."

Jesus and the other men returned long after dark, and Joanna's nose twitched with confusion at the spicy perfume wafting around Jesus. Peter's wife and Martha's sister Mary followed in the men's wake, Mary clutching a small alabaster amphora to her chest.

Martha came forward, taking in her sister's tear-stained face and the opened jar with alarm. "What did you do?" she demanded.

Mary shook her head, unable to answer, so Peter's wife spoke up. "She anointed Jesus."

Martha blinked. "You did what? Why would you do such a thing?"

Tears spilled over Mary's pale cheeks. "I think you know," she said, her haunted gaze resting on each face, stilling their tongues. "We all sense what's coming."

Jesus' dark prophecy washed over Joanna's memory. Chuza nudged her in confusion, his brow puckered. She drew him aside. "Jesus told us we must pick up our cross and follow him," Joanna said. "He's expecting trouble. Something serious."

Chuza took a protective step closer. "He talked about crucifixion?"

Joanna's mind roved back over everything Jesus had said. His warnings. His predictions that he would be handed over to the chief priests. That he would be killed. She gave Chuza a wobbly smile. "He said a lot of things. But I'm not sure how we're supposed to understand them."

Chuza looked at Mary with concern. "She believes him."

Joanna followed his gaze to the distressed woman. Mary had been praised by Jesus for sitting at his feet to learn, and Jesus considered the trio of siblings his close friends. If Mary believed Jesus' words were about to come to pass, they needed to listen.

"Let's stay with the disciples," Joanna said, looking around the room. "Perhaps we can help."

Chuza nodded, his gaze far away, planning for a future they could not see, but one Jesus promised would be difficult.

# THIRTY-FOUR

Joanna ignored a tug on her sleeve, assuming it was an accidental bump from those pressing close in the temple courts, but when it came again, she frowned. Jerking her head around, she met her sister's tear-stained face.

"Dalia!" she said, and allowed her sister to drag her away from the crowd. Joanna glanced over her shoulder, relieved to find Chuza and Leah in her wake. Joanna pulled on Dalia's hand. "Slow down. What's going on?"

"You've got to help him," Dalia said.

"Help who?" Joanna asked.

"Amichai," Dalia said, stopping in a quiet spot by the wall. She leaned against the stone for support, her expression a mask of despair. "Pilate arrested him and some of his friends. They planned to free their leader and were caught smuggling weapons into the city."

Joanna gave her head a little shake, trying to understand. "Wait, Pilate arrested Barabbas?"

Dalia nodded, releasing more fat tears to roll down her face. "Pilate has charged them all as violent thieves and insurrectionists."

Joanna met Chuza's eyes, her mind reeling. For years she foresaw that Amichai's beliefs would land him in trouble, yet the moment found her unprepared.

"Please," Dalia begged, pulling Joanna's attention back to her. "I heard a guard talking about crucifixion." Joanna sucked a startled breath, and Dalia nodded. "Pilate wants to make an example while the city is packed with pilgrims."

No matter what he had done, she couldn't let her brother die—especially not like this.

"Will Antipas help us?" Joanna asked, gripping Chuza's arm.

Chuza rubbed a hand over his face and then behind his neck. "I don't know," he admitted. "We must play this carefully. He was angry when Pilate killed Galileans, and perhaps we can use that."

Joanna nodded and stepped toward the gate. "We have to try."

Chuza caught her wrist. "Hold on, you can't speak to Antipas. Not yet."

"He's my brother. I have to."

Chuza's expression was sympathetic. "You could make it worse."

Joanna opened her mouth to object, then closed it again. He was right. "Fine, but I'll come with you to the palace."

"Me too," Dalia said, wiping her face on her sleeve.

"No, I'll take you three back to the house," Chuza said. "I will speak to Antipas, then find you there."

The women protested, but Chuza was already heading for a temple gate. Joanna followed on his heels, her mind a muddle. Just a few minutes ago, she had been listening to Jesus teach and heal. Now her husband needed to save her brother from a death sentence.

Chuza left the women at Dalia's. The house felt deserted, the extended family exploring the town or visiting the temple. Miriam rose when they entered the courtyard, clutching her granddaughter in her arms. Samuel looked up from his toys.

"Oh, thank the Lord she found you!" Miriam gasped, swiping at her red-rimmed eyes. She peered behind them. "Where is Chuza?"

"Already gone to talk to Antipas," Joanna said.

Miriam nodded. "Alexander is outside the Antonia, trying to learn more."

They stood in stony silence, comforting words too weak to share.

"I'll make some tea," Leah murmured, and began poking around in the kitchen.

Joanna, Dalia, and Miriam sat in the courtyard and watched the children play.

"I remember when Amichai was that size," Miriam said. "So innocent." Tears leaked down her cheeks. "How did this happen?"

Dalia squeezed her mother's arm. "He's trying to honor the Lord."

Miriam looked at Joanna, seeking answers. "And is this the way? Is this truly what your rabbi wanted?"

"My rabbi!" Joanna's neck reared back. "What does Jesus have to do with this?"

"Amichai said Jesus called the men to take up their crosses and follow him. He believed it was a signal, that it was time to fight. Was it?"

Joanna stammered, "I-I don't think so. Jesus has brought no weapons, no armor, no... nothing. Just himself. He's healing and teaching in the courts, Mama. Healing and teaching."

Fat tears rolled down Miriam's cheeks. "So Amichai risked his life for an empty speech?"

Loyalty to Jesus made her defensive. "Jesus didn't call us to arms!" she said. "He asked us to count the cost."

"Which is what Amichai did. He is willing to die for our people. For our freedom."

The children were staring, and Joanna lowered her voice. "Did you know he was attacking travelers on the Jericho Road? Has he killed people?"

Miriam covered her mouth with a shaky hand, tears pooling. "I don't know," she whispered. "I don't know."

Leah brought over a herbal tea, the small pot exuding a calming aroma. She poured it into cups and stirred in generous globs of honey. Leah turned to play with the children, her voice cheerful but quiet as she distracted them from the grown-up problems.

Dalia watched Leah for a time. "I wouldn't let her hold my daughter," she said, casting Joanna a guilty look. "Back at your wedding. I saw it hurt her feelings, but I wouldn't relent. I didn't trust her."

"You didn't know her."

Dalia pressed her lips together. "But you did. I could have trusted your judgment."

"And listened to your little sister?" Joanna teased to cover the lump in her throat. "Impossible."

Dalia stared at her tea. "I listened to my little brother. Why him, and not you?"

"He is harder to ignore than a thunderstorm. At least you've remained close. Now your help can save him."

"My help." Dalia scoffed. "Alexander and I can do nothing. No, everything depends on your husband now." Joanna could see what that admission cost her sister and offered a small smile.

Miriam set down her cup and clasped both her daughters' hands. "Chuza will help. I know it."

"He's coming now?" Antipas said to his servant.

The servant nodded. "He's almost at your door."

"Good. Go!" Antipas hissed, waving him away. He reclined, taking up a scroll and slowing his breathing.

Chuza knocked and strode in, and Antipas glanced up, doing his best to exude boredom.

"Oh, it's you," he drawled, and turned back to his scroll.

Chuza bowed. "My lord."

"So? Where have you been?" Antipas asked, his unseeing eyes

moving over the page.

"I was spending time with my wife."

Chuza was pretending to be at ease, but Antipas knew better. Antipas smirked. "Oh, ho! So the steward finally takes his wife to bed. Was it worth the dance she put you through?"

Chuza's cheeks reddened above his beard. Let him feel embarrassed. It was the least he owed after abandoning the court with only a note for explanation. Chuza never disappeared like that before. It was unsettling.

"My lord," Chuza said, "have you heard that Pilate has made arrests?"

Antipas sighed, rolling his scroll closed and tossing it on a side table. The governor must wake each morning plotting how to make life miserable for everyone else. "What's happened now?" he asked.

"It seems some men were trying to smuggle swords into the city." Antipas' eyebrows rose. "Well, then. I'm glad they were captured."

"Pilate plans to have them crucified," Chuza said. Antipas' breakfast tried to rise. He'd seen enough crosses to last a lifetime.

Antipas cleared his throat. "That's his choice, isn't it?"

"At least one man is a Galilean. One of your citizens. Will you let Pilate kill your people again?"

Antipas frowned. Pilate was a dim-witted, heavy-handed idiot. It would be a pleasure to remind him that he did not rule the whole world. But if this situation was poorly handled, Pilate wasn't the one who would look like a fool. Antipas narrowed his eyes at Chuza. "How do you know this?"

Chuza hesitated. "One of the men is my wife's brother."

Antipas' jaw dropped, and he barked a laugh. "Your brother-in-law? A zealot? My, my, your marriage has come with baggage, hasn't it?" Chuza didn't argue, and Antipas ran his thick ring over his lips, enjoying the cold gemstone against his skin. Joanna certainly offered the court ample drama. In fact, until Joanna came into the court, life had been simple. Perfect. He plucked at his lower lip.

Herodias would give him no peace until she saw Joanna shamed, but Chuza would never let that happen. Unless...

He dropped his hand and smiled.

"If it is Joanna's brother," Antipas said slowly, "she should come before me to plead for his life."

Chuza looked hesitant. "My lord, your wife is still angry with her. I don't wish to stir up trouble—"

"Trouble?" Antipas cut him off, holding his hands out in disbelief, surveying his quiet chambers. "I see no trouble. Bring Joanna here, and we will discover what can be done."

Chuza met his eye, his expression akin to an accusation. Antipas shifted on his couch, but he would not be swayed. He was tired of the dramatics. It was time to end this. Finally, Chuza bowed and left the room.

Antipas grinned. Yes, this could solve everything. He summoned his servant. "Tell Herodias to dress and come here. I have just the thing to cheer her up."

Sweat trickled from under his arms as Chuza rushed back to Dalia's house. He knocked and let himself in before anyone could answer. Joanna rose to her feet, her hopeful expression falling as she saw his face.

"He wouldn't help," she said flatly.

Chuza dragged a hand through his hair. "He insists on talking to you first. He wants you to plead for Amichai's life."

Joanna nodded, her lips pressing together. "If he needs to humiliate me for his wife's sake, so be it. Perhaps if I fall on my knees and beg, Herodias will finally be satisfied."

Chuza's fist tightened at the idea of his righteous wife groveling at the feet of that woman, but it needed to be done.

Miriam caught Joanna's hand. "Be careful, my girl," she said.

"I need both my son and my daughter to come back to me, you hear?"

"Of course," Joanna said. Her swift steps brought her to Chuza's side. Together they strode toward the palace.

"Do you think this will work?" Joanna asked as the palace walls loomed ahead of them.

For the first time, Chuza had no idea what Antipas planned. Herodias made his master unpredictable. "I have to believe my long service to him will count for something," he said. He wrapped her fingers within his.

As they expected, Herodias had joined Antipas in his room. In sharp contrast to Joanna's simple braid and clothes, Herodias was dressed like a queen. Her haughty expression made Chuza's breakfast curdle.

"Joanna," Antipas called, spreading his arms wide as if welcoming an old friend. "How lovely to see you. I hear your brother is in some difficulty?"

Chuza's shoulders stiffened at Antipas' playacting, but Joanna told the story again for Herodias' benefit.

"My, my," Herodias clicked her tongue. "Your family has developed quite a taste for rebellion. Between your patronage of a so-called messiah and your brother following a zealot, we seem to have a pattern." She shook her head, as if sorry for Joanna's shame. "Can you image your mother's heartbreak if they crucify him outside the city gate?"

Joanna flushed as Herodias drew pleasure from her pain. Chuza implored Antipas with his gaze, begging him to bridle his wife's tongue, but Antipas looked away.

Antipas ran the back of his hand over Herodias' arm. "My dear, he's Galilean," he said. "Should I allow Pilate to kill one of my citizens?"

Herodias shrugged. "Why should you take the effort? If he was of some importance, maybe, but Joanna's brother sounds no better than a barbarian."

Chuza frowned as Antipas made a show of considering.

"Perhaps we could make a trade?" Antipas said, taking Herodias' hand and kissing it.

Joanna's voice was stiff. "What trade do you suggest?"

Herodias fixed Joanna with a level stare. "Your vineyard."

Joanna paled, and Chuza's heart sank. Joanna's vineyard was her home, her father's legacy, her mother's income, her brother's inheritance... and it was the place Joanna loved most. Everyone knew it, even Herodias.

"No," Chuza said, his anger rising. "Antipas, you must reconsider."

Joanna set her hand on his arm. She lifted her chin, meeting Herodias' stare. "You will release my brother? He will be absolved of all charges, free to go where he pleases?"

Herodias' victorious expression could have lit up a room. "Yes. He will be free to do whatever comes into his head. I suspect he will run straight into another prison."

Joanna kept her composure, though Chuza knew she must be dying inside. "Then I accept your trade."

Chuza closed his eyes, defeat washing over him.

Herodias raised a brow. "Oh, but you can't. You have no legal right to barter anything, do you? You are just a woman."

The phrase seemed to mean something to Joanna. Her head reared back. "The vineyard has been my responsibility for years—"

"But it is not legally yours, is it?" Herodias said with sickly sweetness. "You were simply the caretaker. I'm afraid if you want to save your brother, you'll have to get the head of your family to sign the papers."

Joanna flushed. "My brother-in-law will agree."

"Oh, I hope so," Herodias said. "But perhaps he feels a vineyard is worth more than a troublesome brother-in-law. Wouldn't you agree, Chuza?"

Chuza glowered at Herodias, hating every line of her simpering face. "I accept my wife's family as my own."

Herodias laughed. "You're braver than most. But you've never had a real family to compare them to, hmm?"

Chuza's lips parted at this barb, his temper bubbling beneath the surface of his calm facade, but Antipas rose to his feet. "Bring us the signed deed for the vineyard, and I will begin negotiations with Pilate," Antipas said. "Once both papers are in order, we'll make the exchange."

Chuza jerked a bow at his master, and he pulled Joanna out of the room. Without making eye contact, he led her to his office and away from curious onlookers before the reality of the situation hit her.

As soon as the door shut behind them, Joanna raised trembling fingers to her mouth, her eyes wide. "The vineyard! What have I done?"

Chuza tried to stifle his anger so he could console his wife. He pulled her into his arms. "What you had to. Herodias has found her revenge."

Joanna drew back with a gasp. "David! Tirzah! Where will they go?"

Chuza rubbed her upper arms. "As Antipas' steward, you realize I now oversee your vineyard, right? David and Tirzah will be fine."

Joanna sagged in relief, but fat tears slipped down her cheeks. Chuza's chest heated with frustration. If Joanna's brother had any sense in his thick head, this wouldn't have been necessary, but once again, Joanna paid the price for her brother's revolutionary ideals. Now, Joanna had nothing. She had given all her money to Jesus, and she was trading away her family home and livelihood.

But there was no help for it. Antipas was trying to appease his wife, and Joanna would front the cost.

After Joanna had calmed, they returned to Dalia's house to present Herodias' offer. Miriam and Dalia gave quiet assent to the plan, valuing Amichai's life over the land.

Chuza drew up the paperwork. He handled many deeds before, but this one was different. How feeble their friendship had been, if Antipas could turn his petty displeasure into crippling revenge. As Alexander signed the document, the contract of friendship between Chuza and Antipas was crossed out, line by line.

Amichai was freed the day of the Passover meal. Pilate was willing to lose one prisoner to keep peace with the tetrarch. He still had three men left to crucify, after all.

Chuza met Amichai outside the Antonia and brought him to Dalia's house. The young man had lost his bluster. His revolutionary ideals were smudged in dark shadows under his eyes. He was visibly shaken at his brush with death and grieving for what his friends would soon face. Before they joined the family, Chuza stopped him.

"You do realize what price they paid for your freedom, right?" he asked.

Amichai studied his palms. "I can't believe Joanna agreed. She must be furious."

"She will regret the loss of that vineyard to the end of her days," Chuza said, tilting his head until Amichai met his eyes. "But she did not hesitate to save your life. Do not throw away what your family has given you."

Amichai scowled as Antipas' steward dared to counsel him, but he nodded once.

As they stepped into the house, Miriam came running, pulling her son to her chest and weeping. Dalia hovered nearby, and her in-laws watched with mask-like faces. Amichai flushed under the scrutiny, his gaze darting back the way he'd come.

At last Amichai turned to Joanna. The feuding siblings locked eyes. After a long moment, Joanna gave him a stilted hug. They didn't say a word, but a layer of tension dissolved in the atmosphere.

"What will you do now?" Dalia asked her brother as Joanna stepped back. Amichai stiffened.

"I don't know," he muttered. "We were positive this was the time, but Barabbas is arrested, and now…"

"For now," Miriam said, "you will wait. Wait on the Lord, my son. You young people rush about as if it is you who will bring about Israel's glory. Wait on God's timing. Moses waited forty years! Surely you can wait a little while."

Amichai made a face at waiting four decades for God to free his people, but he nodded.

Dalia nudged Alexander and he took the hint. "You may work for my family," he said. "I need someone to source ingredients for our perfumes. You would travel and see the world."

Amichai nodded dully. "Thank you," he said, though it was clear Alexander's generous offer did not excite the young man. He came to Jerusalem to join a revolution, not a trade.

As the family planned Amichai's future, Joanna slipped away to the stable. When Chuza went in after her, she was petting the donkey, her back to him.

"Are you alright?" he asked.

"No," she said, wiping her face on her sleeve before turning. She drew a shaky breath. "Foxes have holes and the birds have nests, but the Son of Man has nowhere to lay his head." Chuza looked at her quizzically, and Joanna's lips quirked in a smile. "Something Jesus said. He also said that those who lose family or houses or farms in his name will be repaid many times over. I lost my family's inheritance, but Jesus promised we will inherit eternal life. Isn't that worth so much more?"

"Of course it is," he said. Though he would have preferred to have both.

She gripped the front of his robes. "The kingdom of God is all we have," she said, tears gathering again. "We can't lose that, too. Antipas and Herodias tried to shame us, but let us turn that shame into honor, and fully commit to serving the Lord."

Chuza wrapped her in a hug, running his hand down her back. "I'm not sure what that looks like," he admitted. "I made my vow to Antipas before God. I can't just walk away."

Joanna sighed. "I don't know either. But I think we start by following Jesus and let the rest fall as it may."

"It's nearly Passover, but we can rejoin him tomorrow." Beyond that, he had no idea how to balance his vow to a man he had come to despise against a prophet who called them to live for God.

Joanna sighed. "I wish I knew where they were staying for the meal. I would go to them now."

Chuza kissed her cheek. "I think your mother could use your presence tonight. Her son escaped a torturous death, and this is your first Passover together in years."

Joanna hesitated. "Let the dead bury their own dead."

Chuza's brow furrowed at the ominous words. "What?"

Her lips twisted to the side. "Another phrase Jesus said."

His stomach tightened. "It's all or nothing with him, isn't it?"

"It feels like it."

Chuza raised an eyebrow. "So we wander the streets, calling out for him?"

"I guess that would be foolish." She drew a deep breath and turned to the doorway. "Come on, I should help the women prepare. It's almost sundown."

He caught her hand and stared into her eyes, willing his words to be true. "We'll find a way through this together, all right?"

"Of course, we will."

# THIRTY-FIVE

The family gathered around low tables, the courtyard lit by flickering lamps. The scent of roast lamb mingled with the tang of bitter spices and unleavened bread. They sang the Hallal, the sound of praise reverberating off the walls and joining with voices throughout the city.

As the meal was eaten and the cups were passed, laughter and prayers intermingled. Joanna's own prayer rose to the heavens, asking God to show her and Chuza how to bring the fractured parts of their lives to God's glory.

She glanced around the table, her gaze resting on her mother and her siblings. They were only missing her father. Her throat ached with the unspoken wish that he could be here with them, but perhaps it was better that Ira was spared the loss of his vineyard. Chuza sat at her side, making conversation with Alexander. Leah ate with Joanna's niece in her lap. Despite the circumstances that brought them all together, Joanna was thankful.

The hour grew late, and children slumbered at the table. The stars shifted overhead in a cloudless sky.

A pounding broke through the family clamor, voices falling away as everyone turned toward the noise. Her heart in her throat, Joanna gripped Chuza's hand. Alexander answered the door. Several men rose, alert to trouble, and a startled baby wailed in protest of the tense atmosphere.

Alexander hastened back and murmured in Joanna's ear.

"Your soldier friend is here, as well as a man named Manaen. They said it's urgent."

She scrambled to her feet, Chuza on her heels. Something had to be very wrong if the unlikely pair would come during the feast.

She and Chuza burst into the dim street, lights flickering in the neighbor's windows. Manaen and Titus stood waiting, their faces anxious.

Manaen clasped Chuza's arm as if needing support. "I went to the palace looking for you," he said. "Your friend brought me here."

The look on his face sent Joanna's mind reeling with grim possibilities. "What happened?" she demanded.

Manaen scrubbed his bearded face with his palms. "Jesus has been arrested."

Joanna felt as if the ground beneath her opened up. "By who? Antipas or Pilate?"

"The chief priests," Manaen said, and Joanna stared, Jesus' prophecy sharp in her mind.

"Why?" Joanna said. "He's been teaching all week in their courts! Now they arrest him?"

"How long ago?" Chuza asked.

"Within the hour," Manaen said, his hands shaking as he balled them into fists by his side. "He was praying with three of his closest friends when a whole mob came with torches and weapons. They hauled him away like he was a violent criminal."

"What about the others?" Joanna asked.

Manaen's face showed his shame. "We scattered. We weren't prepared. Most of us were half asleep." His mouth twisted in regret and he rubbed his eyes as he mumbled, "Why didn't we keep watch?"

Chuza gripped his old mentor's shoulder. "If there's been no violence, perhaps they will release him in the morning. They can't have any real charges against him."

"Well, someone had a sword," Manaen said, brushing his palms down the front of his robe as if wiping away the touch of violence. "He struck the high priest's slave."

Joanna gasped. Amichai was not the only one ready to fight.

Chuza's expression was grave. "If he killed him—"

"No, only injured," Manaen said. "Then Jesus healed him. Jesus commanded us not to fight, and that's when I fled, like a dog with my tail between my legs." Shame-filled tears shimmered in the light from the open door. "Some of the others followed Jesus at a distance, but I hoped we could convince Antipas to intervene."

Chuza drew a breath. "Antipas has little sway over the Sanhedrin. If they decide to imprison or stone him—"

"They won't!" Joanna protested, refusing to follow that line of thought. "Antipas has always wanted to see Jesus. If we can somehow get him before Antipas, he can pardon him."

"But how?" Chuza rubbed the back of his neck.

Joanna opened and closed her mouth, her mind blank.

Chuza looked at Titus, who had watched the conversation. "Are you off duty?"

"I am," Titus said.

"Come with us. Let's visit the high priest's house and see if we can figure out what's going on," Chuza said. He turned to Joanna. "Hurry. Grab our cloaks."

Joanna rushed back inside, her family muttering in concern. Leah came up as Joanna donned her sandals.

"Just wait here, alright?" Joanna said. She didn't want Leah tangled up in trouble. "We'll explain everything later." Before Leah could protest, Joanna snatched up Chuza's cloak and ran back to the door. The men were deep in conversation with Alexander and Amichai.

Their words faded as Joanna approached, and Alexander ducked back inside.

"I'm coming with you," Amichai insisted. Joanna and Chuza shared glances, but there was no way to stop him.

"Come on then," Chuza said, swinging his cloak over his shoulders and nodding at the group. "Let's find out what's happening."

They slipped through dark streets in the Upper City, the Passover feasts winding down as the night turned to early morning.

As they rounded a corner, the high priest's bustling and well-lit house was an anomaly on the quiet street. They drew closer together as they approached the gate to the walled courtyard. Chuza murmured in the right ear, and the doorman allowed them to enter. Joanna scanned the space, not finding Jesus. Peter was hunched among a group of strangers, his hands spread before a fire. He looked as if he was trying to blend in. She realized he could be in danger, too.

Manaen saw a man he recognized. "Rabbi," Manaen said. "What's happening here? Have they truly arrested Jesus of Nazareth?"

The teacher nodded, looking uncomfortable. "I live two houses down and heard the commotion. To be honest, I am confused about this whole thing. If he is a blasphemer, why arrest him in secret?"

Manaen ran a hand down his beard and spoke carefully. "The people might riot if the priests arrested him in the temple."

The rabbi considered. "That may be so, but I still don't like it. Why bring him here? Annas has taken him inside for questioning. It's all quite irregular."

"Maybe he's weighing the risks before there is a public trial," Titus said.

"So they might let him go?" Joanna said, hope rising.

The rabbi frowned. "They've raged against the Nazarene for days. They wouldn't arrest him without a plan to see him sentenced." He shook his gray head. "No. This will not be over soon."

"Back off, woman!" a man's voice caught their attention, and Joanna turned as Peter snapped at a servant girl. "I told you, I don't know the man."

Peter turned back to the fire as the servant glowered. Another man leaned into the firelight, studying him. "No, she's right. I saw you with him. You are one of them!"

"Man, I am not!" Peter said.

Joanna drew her palla closer around her face. She shuddered, afraid of being arrested again—this time by men Chuza could not sway.

They drifted through the chilly courtyard, seeking answers and finding only vague rumors about the priests' intentions.

Movement at the door drew everyone's attention, and guards led Jesus out of the high priest's house and into the courtyard. They kept him surrounded, as if afraid he would fight his way free.

A livid bruise was rising on Jesus' cheek, and his clothes were askew. Hands bound before him, he sagged with exhaustion. Joanna struggled against a rising tide of powerlessness as the guards made Jesus stand in the predawn chill while the priests remained comfortably inside, deciding what to do.

Peter straightened to look at his rabbi, emotions warring on his face.

"You know what?" a man said, jabbing a finger at Peter. "I know this man was with him. He's a Galilean too!"

Peter scoffed, his bravado failing to conceal the fear on his face. "I don't know what you're talking about."

A rooster crowed in a neighboring courtyard, and Jesus turned to look at Peter. Peter trembled, his mouth parting in a silent plea. He fled without a word.

Joanna shared a startled glance with Chuza.

"What happened?" Amichai demanded in a hiss. "Was that some sort of signal?"

"Maybe," she whispered, biting her lip. Peter ran like the devil himself was on his heels.

As the minutes dragged by, the guards around Jesus grew bored.

Joanna cringed as they entertained themselves by mocking their prisoner. They soon grew tired of insults.

"Here!" one said, wrapping a strip of cloth over Jesus' eyes. They began slapping him, a cruel parody of the children's game.

"Who hit you?" they taunted, as Jesus stumbled beneath their blows.

"Stop it!" Joanna cried out, tears burning in her eyes. Chuza gripped her arm.

"You must be quiet," he said. "You're known as his disciple. Do you want to get arrested too?"

Stubbornness crashed against her fear. But she couldn't help Jesus if she was in prison with him. "I can't watch this," Joanna said, her body stiffening at Jesus' grunt of pain.

She fled across the street, her arms wrapped around herself. A few moments later, the four men came out to join her.

Amichai clenched his fists, his nostrils flaring. Titus stared back at the courtyard, and Manaen and Chuza were conferring.

"Can't we stop them?" Joanna begged, angry tears gathering. "That can't be allowed, can it?"

Manaen's face was haggard. "The priests are in no mood to rein them in. It's nearly dawn. I'm sure they'll start the trial soon."

"And that's a good thing?" Titus muttered.

Manaen sighed. "Well, at least the guards will stop toying with him."

Chuza pinched the bridge of his nose, squeezing his eyes shut. "We should prepare Antipas with what we know, which admittedly isn't much. It'll be a few hours until the trial."

Desperate for activity, they hurried through the city as rooftops glowed in the rising sun.

Joanna spoke to her brother. "Go back to Dalia's and tell them what's happening."

Amichai glared at being ordered by his sister, but he nodded once, and the group parted ways.

As they climbed the palace steps, a shadow stepped away from the guard tower and Joanna's stomach swooped.

"Leah, what are you doing here?" Chuza demanded.

"I want to know what's going on," Leah said, her jaw set with determination.

Joanna stared at her. "You walked here? Alone? At night?"

Leah crossed her arms. "So? You walked to Tyre alone."

Joanna growled under her breath, but she beckoned for Leah to fall in with them. Joanna explained the situation as they hastened to Antipas' apartments.

A servant held out his hands in protest as they neared. "My lord went to bed only a few hours ago," he said. "He does not wish to be disturbed."

Chuza stepped closer. "He will want to be awakened for this."

The servant hesitated, but Chuza pushed him aside and slipped into the room alone.

As the others waited under the servant's glare, Leah plucked at Joanna's sleeve.

"I still don't understand," she whispered. "Jesus walked on water, but he can't walk out of that courtyard?"

Joanna's throat burned as she answered. "I'm sure he could if he wanted to. For some reason, he's decided to stay."

Her mind tumbled with all of Jesus' dire predictions in the weeks leading up to Jerusalem. He knew there would be trouble, yet he seemed unwilling to use the Spirit to break free of it.

Chuza came out, his expression somber. "Antipas is dressing now." He looked at Manaen. "He doesn't know you've been with Jesus all this time, does he?"

Manaen tugged on his beard. "This isn't how I wanted to tell him."

Antipas kept them waiting for an hour. The sun cast its beams across the courtyard tiles before his body slave opened the door and let them enter. Leah and Titus waited outside, and Chuza, Manaen, and Joanna entered.

Antipas wore an elegant robe and his hair was curled above his bloodshot eyes. His glare held them, one by one, but he fixed his attention on his foster brother, his gaze raking over Manaen's over-grown beard and simple garb.

"Brother," he said flatly. "It has been too long. Did you visit your people in the desert?"

Joanna was impatient to turn the conversation to Jesus, but Chuza laid a warning hand on her arm.

"I didn't go to the Essenes," Manaen said. "I found a Galilean rabbi, and I have learned much from him."

"Oh?" Antipas said, feigning polite interest. "Is he as exciting as the Galilean who marches through my land performing signs and wonders?"

Manaen stepped forward. "My brother, you know he is one and the same. He is a man of God."

Antipas' eyes darkened at his brother's words. "So you lied to me. For two years, you lied."

"I did not lie," Manaen said evenly.

Antipas snorted. "You withheld the whole story, which is equal to a lie in my eyes." His chin worked and his voice wavered. "You have betrayed my trust."

Chuza cleared his throat. "My lord, Manaen has brought us troubling news. The high priests have arrested this man of God, Jesus of Nazareth."

Antipas' brows met over his red eyes. "On what charge?"

"They are keeping that quiet."

"Is this connected to Barabbas? Are they working together?"

"No," Manaen said fervently. "They are not. Jesus has caused no disturbances in the city."

"He made quite a scene arriving, though, didn't he?" Antipas sneered. "Riding in like the kings of old, the people shouting his praises."

"The priests did not welcome him," Manaen said. "They spent the past week trying to trap him with words, but they have grown impatient."

Antipas began to shake his head but then winced and rubbed his temple. "So why bring this to me? What do you expect me to do? This is a religious concern, not a matter for the government."

"If you talk to Annas and Caiaphas—" Chuza began.

"No!" Antipas' hand tightened into a fist. "I will not. You don't even know what he's been charged with, and you ask me to intervene, perhaps to my embarrassment?" He rose and unsteadily made his way to the sideboard to pour a large cup of wine. Joanna looked at her husband and saw her anxiety mirrored in his eyes.

After taking a sip, Antipas turned back to them, his lip curling as he surveyed them.

"Look at this," he drawled, then laughed darkly. "My three betrayers. You!" he stabbed a jeweled finger at Joanna, "foiled my plans with Phasaelis." Joanna fumbled for a reply. "You!" he turned his finger on Manaen "were supposed to be my real brother, but now you love this prophet more than you love me, don't you?" Manaen's expression broke, but Antipas had already turned away. "And you!" He jabbed at Chuza, his spittle flying. "You have fallen under the oldest curse of all. A woman." His disgust distorted his face. "You love your wife more than your master. You vowed to serve *me*!" he roared, and his wine sloshed.

Joanna cringed. This had been a mistake. Antipas was growing angrier by the second.

Chuza and Manaen shared a distraught glance. The silence hung heavy.

Finally, Chuza fitted his steward's mask in place. He bowed. "My lord, we will learn more and report back to you."

Antipas blinked, and before he could protest, they fled the room.

Leah and Titus fell in with them as they hurried to the palace gate.

"Well, that was an unmitigated disaster," Joanna muttered.

Manaen pulled his beard with both hands. "I shouldn't have gone in with you. I expected we would pick up our friendship where we left off. I was naive."

Chuza gripped his shoulder. "It wasn't just you. You heard him. He believes we all betrayed him."

When they reached the gate, Titus stopped. "I have to start my shift," he said. His expression was torn between duty and friendship, but Chuza clapped him on the shoulder.

"I'll find you later and let you know what's happening."

Titus nodded once and turned for the guard's barracks.

They fell silent as they entered the city and turned their feet for the temple complex. As they made their way to the tall building where the Sanhedrin convened, the relaxed mood in the temple courtyard was jarring. The early morning worshipers seemed unaware that a trial was happening beyond the council chamber's carved double doors.

Sanhedrin sessions were not open to the public. As they waited for news, Joanna scanned for the disciples. She spotted a small group of women huddled in the colonnade's shadow. Mary Magdalene, Jesus' mother, Naomi, and Maryam. There was only one man with them, Naomi's youngest son, John.

Joanna hurried forward, and Maryam stretched out her hands, her expression drawn. Joanna clasped her icy fingers and brought her head close.

"What's happening?" Joanna whispered.

"They've been in there for an hour," Maryam replied, her forehead pinched with worry. "We saw him as they took him in, bruised and exhausted. They're treating him as if he's already been declared guilty."

The door to the meeting hall burst open and the elders filed out, their faces grim. High Priests led the way, their white linen robes gleaming in the morning sunlight. The crowds stared, rising on tiptoes to see beyond the rows of temple soldiers and their long spears. Joanna caught a peek of Jesus' profile. He looked calm, and it gave her hope.

"Where are they going?" Joanna said.

The cluster of disciples followed the procession. As she saw where they were being led, Joanna's stomach flipped.

"The Antonia?" Manaen choked the word.

The priests led Jesus from the Jewish temple and into the courtyard of the Roman governor.

# THIRTY-SIX

Curious onlookers drifted into the courtyard of the Antonia as the soldiers marched Jesus to stand before the judgment seat, the full Sanhedrin arrayed against him.

After a few tense moments, the door opened and Pilate emerged with his own guards, an impatient scowl dividing his clean-shaven face. The sight of him in this courtyard sent a shiver through Joanna's body. At least he wasn't wearing his armor.

"What are you doing here?" Pilate demanded.

Caiaphas pointed an accusing finger at Jesus. "We found this man misleading our nation and forbidding the people to pay taxes to Caesar. He said that he is the Christ, a king."

Joanna's breath caught. The jealous priests moved past charges of blasphemy and claimed political crimes—treason against Rome on two counts. But despite the Herodian's and Pharisee's best efforts to trap Jesus between Roman law and Jewish faith, Jesus had made no declaration against taxation. As for being the Christ... Joanna swallowed hard. Only Jesus could prove that claim.

Pilate followed Caiaphas' finger to Jesus, a common-looking figure in simple clothes, bruised and battered, hands bound, standing quietly with enough guards to subdue a madman. Pilate's lip curled in amusement.

"You?" he spoke to Jesus in disbelief. "Are you the King of the Jews?"

Jesus looked him in the face. "You have said it."

Pilate burst into laughter, and the soldiers with him joined in. Joanna's chest burned at Pilate's amusement, but Jesus didn't react. She glanced behind herself as more people approached, curious to see what induced the priests to enter the Antonia.

The Sanhedrin stiffened at the governor's mockery, but Pilate tucked his thumbs in his wide leather belt, grinning. "This is what you Jews consider a king?" he jeered. "Well, then. I find no guilt in this man."

Annas stepped forward, his ornate staff gripped in his fist. "He stirs up the people, teaching all over Judea, starting in Galilee."

"So he's Galilean then?" Pilate asked, one eyebrow rising.

"He is," Caiaphas said. "You know what sort of men hail from Galilee."

Joanna bristled at his derisive tone, and she others murmured behind her. Pilate's gaze flickered over the growing crowd of witnesses.

"Well, if he's Galilean, he's not my problem." Pilate shrugged. "As someone recently reminded me, that is Herod Antipas' jurisdiction, and the tetrarch is here in the city. Send this man to him."

Joanna and Chuza shared a look of relief. Despite everything, Antipas was still their best hope.

"Do you think Antipas will let Jesus go?" Joanna spoke beneath the complaints of the priests.

Chuza glanced at Manaen. "Maybe. If Jesus pleases him."

"If he shows him a sign, you mean," Joanna said, and her chest squeezed with misgiving. Jesus had never performed on command.

Manaen gripped Chuza's arm. "We need to go back. Perhaps we can sway Antipas to make the right decision."

They split from the disciples and hurried toward the palace. Joanna looked over her shoulder at the young woman in her wake.

"Let's stop at Dalia's," Joanna said to Chuza. "I want Leah to wait at my sister's house."

Leah overheard and her expression darkened. "I'm not a child," she said. "If it was safe enough for me to follow him in Galilee, why should I hide now?"

Joanna stopped, and Leah stumbled into her. "Please," Joanna begged, gripping the young woman's wrist. Leah wasn't caught up in any of this yet.

Leah opened her mouth to protest, but as she stared back into Joanna's eyes, she nodded reluctantly.

The remaining trio found Antipas still in his room, but now Herodias lounged on his couch, eating delicacies from a platter. A musician plucked soothing music from a lyre. The scene felt contrived, Antipas showing his disdain for the worries of his foster brother and steward. The tetrarch scowled as they approached, but his wine-soaked eyes had cleared.

"You all look awful," Antipas drawled. Joanna smoothed her hair, but she hastily dropped her hand when Herodias smiled in amusement. "Do you have more to report?"

Chuza and Manaen shared a glance, and Manaen spoke. "Jesus of Nazareth is coming here."

Antipas' expression transformed immediately. "Here?" he repeated, sitting up straight. "Now?"

"Yes, now," Manaen said, working to subdue his impatience. "The Sanhedrin took him to Pilate first, but the governor insists Jesus is under your jurisdiction. He will let you decide what to do with him."

Antipas tossed Herodias a pleased smile, and she squeezed his arm. "See?" she said. "He is starting to respect you."

"We can use this situation to our advantage." Antipas' eyes flickered back and forth as he considered the possibilities.

Chuza cleared his throat. "What do you plan to do?"

Antipas rose and spread his arms grandly. "Meet him in the throne room, of course! It's about time he came before me."

He extended his hand to Herodias, and she glided to his side. Joanna's stomach clenched, knowing Antipas' mood could slide from one extreme to the other. If Jesus pleased him, the prophet's freedom was all but guaranteed. But if he did not— Joanna swallowed hard.

"Can we watch?" she asked as they stepped back out into the courtyard.

Chuza nodded, his expression grim. "I think Antipas wants an audience."

Word rippled through the palace, and by the time Jesus was led into the throne room, Antipas' friends and allies were gathered in their finery, eager to view the famous prophet for themselves. Antipas sat upon his father's throne, and Herodias was in her usual spot, standing at his right side. Antipas had arrayed a threatening row of guards along the wall, holding spears aloft.

With a jolt, Joanna realized Titus was among them. His face was carefully blank, but his knuckles were white on the shaft of his spear.

Joanna, Chuza, and Manaen stood on the sidelines, helpless to intervene as the priests pushed Jesus right up to Antipas, shoving him so he stumbled. Joanna blinked back tears. Her rabbi was mottled with bruises, his hair mussed, and his clothes were rumpled. This wasn't the dramatic confrontation between a fiery prophet and meek king that had lived in her imagination.

"So." Antipas leaned forward, a gleam in his eye. "The prophet has arrived. Welcome, Jesus of Nazareth."

Jesus refused to reply, and anger flitted across Antipas' face before he smoothed it away.

"I have waited to meet you for some time," Antipas tried again, his voice echoing throughout the chamber. "Tell me, what prophecies do you have for the ruler of Galilee and Perea?"

Jesus didn't move. Antipas scowled, and Joanna whispered a plea to Jesus. "Speak to him. Please him, just this once." But Jesus stood silently.

Antipas tried another tack. "If the Lord has no word for me, share some of your parables. Enlighten the court with your wise words." The witnesses waited with bated breath.

Jesus remained quiet, and the audience muttered.

Antipas gripped the arm of his throne, a dangerous glint in his eye. "Show me a sign, then. Prove to me that you are a man of God, a miracle-worker, a prophet, and I will let you go."

Jesus didn't move an inch. Herodias drew an incensed breath, and Antipas' lip curled.

"Do you not understand?" Antipas snapped. "I hold your freedom in my hand. Show me one little sign, and you can go back to Galilee. I can find a blind man, a cripple, or bring water for you to turn into wine. Whatever you want, I can provide."

Jesus glanced away, as if tired of this charade. Antipas' neck reddened. He barked question after question, demanding to know the truth about the kingdom of heaven, the future, how Jesus got his power, who were his parents, and on and on, but Jesus would not utter one syllable.

Finally, Antipas threw himself back in his chair. Herodias ran a soothing hand over his shoulder.

Joanna slipped her hand into Chuza's, her pulse racing. What would Antipas do now?

She jerked in shock as Antipas laughed, loud and mirthless, the mocking tones reverberating off the walls and his guard's shields. No one else joined him. Herodias glanced at her husband, concern puckering between her eyes. Antipas grew silent. "You have deceived me." Antipas sneered at the priests. "This is no prophet. He is the village idiot, too stupid to speak."

Scattered laughter answered Antipas' wit as the priests flushed.

Caiaphas stepped forward. "He's trying to escape justice with his silence. He is inciting your people to rise against Rome. How will inaction look to your friend, the emperor?"

"You have to set an example," Annas said, fixing Antipas with his sharp glare. "Will you permit your citizens to follow a blasphemer?"

Another priest shouted, "Your father rebuilt the temple, and this man threatens to tear it down!"

"He claims to be king! Will you let that stand?"

"His power is from the devil! We must be rid of his foul presence!"

Antipas glowered at Jesus as accusations rained like the arrows of battle. The air congealed with animosity, and Joanna clutched Chuza's fingers.

At last, Antipas held up his hand and the priests fell reluctantly silent. Antipas tipped his head to the side. "You know what? I have not given this king the proper welcome." His lip curled, and he snapped a finger at Manaen. "Fetch one of my best robes. Bring it here."

Manaen hesitated, but when Antipas glared, he jerked into action, hurrying away.

"What is Antipas doing?" Joanna hissed in Chuza's ear.

"I don't know," he said, his voice tight. "But whatever his game, I fear there is nothing we can do."

Manaen returned with a gorgeous purple robe folded over his arm. It was worth a year's wages to a common laborer.

"Yes," Antipas said as Manaen showed it to him. "That will do nicely. Put it on him."

Herodias' hand twitched to Antipas' shoulder, as if wanting him to consider the garment's price. Manaen carefully draped the robe over Jesus' shoulders, swallowing hard as he stood eye to eye with his rabbi, adjusting the robe until it hung straight. Jesus' lips softened, and he nodded slightly, as if Manaen offered him a gift. Manaen's eyes were wet as he stepped to Chuza's side.

Jesus, dressed in the robe of a king, stood before Antipas like a meeting between two rulers. But Jesus was bound, and Antipas was free. Joanna twisted her fingers until her knuckles screamed in protest.

"Now," Antipas said, rolling his hand graciously and inclining his head. "My soldiers will pay this king his rightful homage."

The captain glanced at Antipas in question, and the tetrarch gave a cruel smile and a nod. The captain marched forward and bowed low, then rose and spat in Jesus' face. Jesus flinched as the spittle struck his cheek, but did not protest. Joanna tried to draw a breath, but her ribs were like sharp splinters as the line of guards passed by, repeating the offense. The priests watched the parody in icy silence.

Chuza trembled, staring at his master, blinking rapidly. Joanna shifted closer, until she was shoulder to shoulder with her husband. Chuza leaned against her, and they shared their suffering in silence. Antipas had done many foolish things in his life, shown his faithlessness time and time again, and displayed his selfishness and pettiness. But this, this was as if every bit of evil in Antipas' soul consolidated in this moment, transforming him into a monster.

She dragged her eyes away so she could breathe, and realized Titus hadn't moved. As his companions spat in Jesus' face, Titus remained at his post, staring straight ahead. The captain of the guard stepped up to him, hissing in his ear. Titus shook his head once, and the captain's skin mottled with rage. He jerked Titus' spear from his hand, and Titus' face turned a sickly hue.

Finally, the mockery was over, and the room waited, unsure what to do. Annas' fist was white on his staff. Herodias stood with her chin lifted, seeming torn between pride and confusion. The crowd of courtiers had shifted closer together.

Antipas rose, his robes rustling in the silence. He descended from the dais, each slap of his sandal echoing. Standing toe to toe with Jesus, he searched the rabbi's dripping face.

"Welcome to your kingdom." Antipas sneered, and turned to leave the room. The priests glanced at each other in confusion, and

Joanna's heart leaped, hoping Antipas' anger was spent.

But then Antipas paused and looked back. "Take him back to Pilate with my thanks," he said. "The governor can do what he wishes."

He swept through the door, Herodias at his side.

Joanna stood as if frozen. The priests glared as their guards hustled Jesus from the room. Chuza spun on his heel and hurried after Antipas. Manaen fell into his wake, and Joanna hastened to catch up.

"My lord!" Chuza called, but Antipas did not slow as he swept across the courtyard toward his quarters. The gold threads in Antipas' robe gleamed in the sunlight and Herodias' skirt swished behind her. "My lord!" Chuza repeated.

Finally, Antipas paused and turned, a dangerous glint in his eye.

"Yes, steward?" Antipas asked coldly. "Do you have business to discuss with me?"

"Antipas," Chuza pleaded, holding out his hands. "We have spent our lives together, yet you speak with such hostility?"

Antipas' brow twitched, and he spoke with more calmness. "What do you want, Chuza?"

"Stop the soldiers," Chuza said. "Bring Jesus back here. Don't let a man like Pilate control his fate. You've seen how the governor treats our people."

Antipas crossed his arms. "I have already done you a favor this week." He looked pointedly at Joanna. "You're getting greedy, my friend. Besides, what do you have left to offer?" His lips twisted into a hard smile. "I have taken everything I want from you."

Joanna swallowed back bile.

"Please," Manaen begged. "The priests will not stop until Jesus is punished. I've seen his miracles. He is a real prophet."

"So was John, supposedly," Antipas said. "Yet he died like any other man."

Joanna's hand fluttered to her throat as Herodias' eyes gleamed.

Jesus could not die, he just couldn't.

Manaen stretched out his palms. "My brother, think of what you are doing! Don't allow the blood of another prophet to stain your hands."

"It won't," Antipas said with a confident smile. "It's on Pilate. Let him decide between angering the priests or the people."

Herodias cupped her husband's cheek with proud affection. "And if he decides Jesus is guilty of sedition," she said, practically purring, "then you have assisted Rome by purging the country of a false king. Pilate must speak well of you in his report."

Antipas took his wife's hand and kissed it. "If I can't be rid of the governor, I will make him my friend." He looked back at the horrified trio standing before him. "A wise plan, is it not?"

Manaen gaped as he beheld the depth of Antipas' hardness of heart. Without another word, he fled.

Antipas turned to Chuza, the tetrarch's expression dangerously mild. "Are you going into the city to discover the Nazarene's fate? I wouldn't mind an eyewitness report."

Chuza pressed his pale lips together. "As you wish, my lord," he said hoarsely. Groping for Joanna's hand, he led her back to the palace gate. There was no sign of Manaen, but Titus was slumped against the wall. He still wore his uniform, but his hip was oddly empty without his sword.

"The captain fired me," he said dully.

Chuza gripped his shoulder. "You did the right thing," he said. "It was... madness in there." Joanna shivered as if the malice that steeped Antipas' throne room clung to her skin.

Titus shook his head, pain sweeping across his features. "I had no other choice, but what am I going to do now? How can I—" he cut off the words, his neck coloring.

"Come with us," Chuza said. Titus nodded dully.

As they left the palace, Amichai ran to them. He glared at Titus' uniform, but Titus rubbed his empty palm with his opposite hand

and wouldn't meet his eye.

"Antipas would not help?" Amichai asked.

"No," Joanna said flatly. They had been foolish to believe a man like Antipas would offer any aid. "We're going to the Antonia to see what Pilate decides."

Amichai scrubbed his face with his palms. "Pilate has already tried and sentenced three of my friends to die by crucifixion today, including Barabbas."

Joanna shared a desperate look with her husband. There was no more potent warning to an unsettled populace than a screaming insurgent upon a cross.

But that couldn't happen to her rabbi. Joanna shook her head. "Jesus isn't like them. He was preaching and healing in the temple, not preparing for a fight. Pilate will have to recognize the difference." Chuza did not answer as the horror of a cross hovered above them all.

Amichai fell in with them as they hurried into the city. They neared the Antonia once again, and a crowd packed the courtyard wall to wall. Joanna's stomach back-flipped as the angry mob shouted at the platform where Pilate held court. It was so much like the day her father died that her feet stumbled, but Chuza gripped her hand and pulled her into the crowd.

Blood pounding in her ears, she glanced upwards as she entered the courtyard, up to the corner of the temple where she watched the riot with Phasaelis years ago. She hadn't understood what madness drove her parents into a crowd just like this, and now here she was, struggling deeper into the jostling bodies.

Pilate had changed into his armor, the metal glinting in the late morning sun. Jesus stood to the side, his shoulders sagging beneath Antipas' robe as if the weight of the world rested on them.

Pilate held up his hands for silence and the shouts subsided to a dull rumble. "You brought this man to me as one who incites the people to rebellion," he said. "I have examined him before you, and I found no guilt in him. Nor has Herod Antipas, who sent him back to us. He has done nothing deserving death. So I will punish him and release him according to the custom of the festival."

"We don't want him!" a voice shouted. "Release Barabbas instead!"

"Barabbas," Amichai breathed, and Joanna shot him a look. But the crowd took up the name, shouting for a criminal's release. It was madness.

Pilate commanded his soldier, who jostled Jesus into the Antonia. Pilate conferred with his servant as the glaring sun tracked its path across the cloudless sky. Joanna chewed a fingernail until it was ragged. Where was Jesus?

Finally, the soldier reappeared, and Pilate whispered to him. Pilate nodded and turned to the waiting crowd.

"I am bringing Jesus of Nazareth out to show you I have found no guilt in him."

Two soldiers dragged Jesus from the Antonia, gripping his arms to keep him upright.

Pilate swept a hand to Jesus. "Behold the man!"

"Oh, God!" Joanna cried out, tears springing anew. "He scourged him!"

The crowd stared, unprepared for the horrific sight.

Blood soaked through Jesus' clothes and coated his face like a mask, flowing in rivulets from a crown of thorns. As the people realized the political mockery, they protested.

A sob pulled the air from Joanna's lungs, and her chest was too tight to draw a full breath. Tears blurred her vision, but she could not stop staring at Jesus' mutilated figure. This must be enough punishment to appease the priests.

But Annas raised his staff and roared, "Crucify him!"

The people took up the chant. "Crucify! Crucify!"

Joanna's insides twisted with horror. The priest had gone insane.

Pilate's face darkened with anger, and he strode forward to shout at Annas. "You crucify him! I found him innocent."

Caiaphas shouted in reply. "We have laws. He must die because he made himself out to be the son of God."

Pilate stiffened and glanced back at the man he had ordered scourged.

Joanna turned to Chuza, desperate. "What do we do?"

"What can we do?" Chuza choked in reply as the priests worked the people into a bloodthirsty fervor.

After speaking with Jesus again, Pilate tried reasoning with the crowd, but the priests would not let the governor get in a word.

A temple official shouted at Pilate, "If you release this man, you are no friend of Caesar. Everyone who makes himself a king opposes Caesar."

And still, the crowd chanted, "Crucify! Crucify!"

The atmosphere wavered on the edge of a riot.

Joanna stared at her people in shock. These were the same ones who called hosannas a week prior, witnesses as Jesus healed and taught. This must be a nightmare, it was too convoluted to be real. Heat rose from her ankles, rushing up her limbs.

"I'm going to be sick," Joanna mumbled, her head spinning.

"We don't have to stay here," Chuza said, gripping her arm to steady her. Joanna shook her head and reined in her emotions with effort, swallowing bile.

Jostled by the screaming crowd, Joanna watched Pilate's face. With a throb of despair, she saw the exact moment he accepted the will of the mob. Pilate sent his servant away, and when he returned with a basin, Pilate washed his hands before them all, snapping a towel off the servant's shoulder.

"I am innocent of this man's blood," Pilate said. "See to that yourselves."

A man shouted in reply, "His blood shall be on us and on our children!" Others clamored their agreement. Pilate shook his head in disbelief.

Minutes later, a man, grimy and grinning with wild-eyed delight, was released.

The crowd recoiled as he passed by. As he made his escape, Barabbas noticed Amichai. Joanna's hands tightened to fists by her side as the highwayman pushed toward them.

"You're free as well?" Barabbas exclaimed, clapping his palms on Amichai's shoulders, his broken nails black with filth. "Good! Come on, let's regroup with the others."

"No!" Joanna cried out.

Amichai took a step with Barabbas, then glanced back at his sister. She shook her head, pleading with him to consider his choice.

"Amichai, think," Chuza said. "She sacrificed everything to set you free. We have nothing left to help you a second time."

"Ha!" Barabbas said, his sneer raking over Chuza's expensive robe. "Did you release me as well? No! It was the Lord's doing, proof of his approval. God will take care of us, right?" He looked at Amichai, and Joanna saw the conflict warring on her brother's face.

"Please!" she cried out, reaching her hand to him. "You need to stay!"

"For what?" Amichai's voice broke. "I have no inheritance, nothing to keep me here. How can I live indebted to my sister's husband for employment and shelter? There is no honor on that path. And Jesus—" he gestured weakly at the platform "—well, he's not the one we hoped for, is he? I need to be ready for the real messiah when he comes."

Joanna released an angry sob and squeezed her eyelids shut against burning tears. When she opened her eyes, Barabbas and Amichai were gone. She would never forgive him for this.

Her heart splintered beneath the combined weight of Jesus' death sentence and her brother's betrayal. Joanna battled her way out of the courtyard. She sensed Chuza's presence behind her, a silent guard on her flank.

She emerged on the street, panting as she spun in a circle, trying to catch her bearings. Jesus was supposed to take down the corrupt rulers—not the other way around. Her gaze landed on the same small cluster of disciples. She stumbled to them.

"Is it true?" John asked, supporting Jesus' mother. "We could hear some of it—"

"Pilate sentenced Jesus to crucifixion," Joanna said, the words heavy on her tongue. "The crowd would allow nothing less."

The women clamped hands over their mouths in horror.

Chuza set his hand on her arm. "We should go report this to Antipas," he said.

"No," she snapped, fierce heat clawing up her throat. "If I see him, I will slap that smug smile off his face. He could have stopped all of this! I'm staying here, with them."

Chuza tried to draw her away from the others, but she would not be moved. "It'll be horrific," he pleaded. "Is this how you want to remember him?"

Joanna wavered for a moment, but shook her head. "I must see this through. I failed to help him. I owe him this." She moved to stand with the other women, trying to hide her trembling lips. Leah's words from long ago rose to taunt her.

*One day you'll let Jesus down and your whole life will fall at your feet.*

Chuza dragged both hands through his hair. "Remain close to them," he said hoarsely. "You will be safer if you stay in a group."

Joanna stared after him as he walked away, his expression numb, slipping into his familiar role. Titus followed, his silent shadow.

The soldiers began shoving to make way for Jesus, a cross beam cradled on his maimed back, his battered face unrecognizable. Joanna's mouth opened in a silent scream, and she wished she left with her husband.

# THIRTY-SEVEN

Chuza's fingers and lips were numb as he walked. Jesus' fate was too horrible to be true, and Amichai's treachery was the final stab. Joanna gave up everything to save her brother's life, and he was throwing it away without a thought. Chuza feared this second betrayal would haunt Joanna for years.

From the start, he and Joanna had been trying to catch the wind in a sack. Nothing they did made any difference. His insignificance pressed on Chuza's shoulders until he stumbled, barely catching himself before he sprawled on the street. Titus stepped closer, but Chuza waved him away.

"Why am I here, Lord?" Chuza whispered, the words cutting at his raw throat. "What good have I accomplished in your name? I have served my master, tried to honor you with my life, and yet everywhere I turn, I come face to face with my failures. How can you let the world continue? How can you allow evil to win?"

Tears were running into his beard by the time he reached a red door. He blinked. He hadn't meant to walk to Dalia's house. All he wanted was to throw himself on his bed and let the pain bury him.

Without knocking, he went inside. Leah was at his side in a heartbeat.

"What's happening?" she demanded, and then looked past him. "Where is Joanna?"

Chuza hesitated, unsure how much to tell the young woman. Leah had experienced enough suffering in her short life. She spoke to Titus instead. "Where is she?" Titus looked at Chuza.

Chuza swallowed hard. "Pilate has sentenced Jesus to crucifixion," he said, his dull voice unfamiliar in his own ears. "Joanna remained with her friends. They wish to stay with him until... until the end."

Leah stared at him, the blood draining from her cheeks as she absorbed his words.

"I should be with her," Leah said, moving to pass him.

Chuza caught her arm. "No! It's not something a young woman should witness."

She jerked against his grip. "You can't tell me what to do!" Angry tears gathered on her lashes. "You're not my father!" Her truthful words hit him with unexpected pain. "I belong to Joanna, not you!"

"And Joanna would say you don't belong to anybody but God," he snapped.

She yanked against his grip a few times before giving up. "Fine," she said. She glared pointedly at the fingers wrapped around her arm. Chuza released her.

"We should—" Titus began, but then jerked as Leah raced out the open door. Chuza was not quick enough to stop her.

"Leah!" Chuza roared, dashing into the street, his stress rising in a surge of anger. "Get back here!"

Titus slapped Chuza on the shoulder. "I'll go after her." He charged after the fleet-footed young woman, running into the city.

"Wonderful," Chuza muttered darkly. He smothered his face with his hands, wishing against reason that this day was a nightmare. He dragged his fingers down his skin, ripping at his beard. Everyone he loved had scattered, and his master awaited.

As he approached the palace, mournful cries rose like a sickly stench, mounting in an overwhelming wave. Almost against his will, he turned for the aqueduct bridge. Steeling himself, he peered over the balustrade. Crowds lined the main road, more running from side streets as if gathering to view a royal procession.

Jesus was leaving the Antonia.

Guards spread out around the prophet, preventing anyone from intervening. Jesus shuffled forward with a cross beam on his shoulder, bearing the instrument of his own torture and death, bloody footprints in his wake.

Women lamented, their mourning songs sharper on tongues that sang the Hallal only hours prior. One of the chosen people was handed over to pagans to suffer and die. The crowd murmured their confusion. Isn't this the prophet? The man of God?

As Jesus heaved the cross under the aqueduct, Chuza saw blood soaking the back of Jesus' simple clothes. The royal robe Antipas gave him had been stripped away.

Antipas' role in this man's execution buckled Chuza's knees. He slid down the balustrade to sit on the ground, pressing his fists into his eyes. Jesus' enemies mocked him as a king, but Chuza had bowed before kings. None of them, not even the emperor of Rome, could stand before the power and authority of Jesus. Jesus was filled with God's Spirit, but God turned his face from his prophet.

Chuza wept, his mind churning with confusion. He couldn't go to Joanna. He would be an intruder to the disciples' grief as they mourned a friend and rabbi. But he shuddered at facing Antipas.

"What do I do, Lord?" His prayer was muffled by his palms. "What do I do?"

Joanna clung to impossible hope. She followed Jesus as he limped in humiliation and pain toward an agonizing death, sucking air through his teeth with each step. Two criminals walked behind him, one of them sobbing in fear. He was Amichai's age, and unlike Barabbas, he had not escaped a rebel's fate.

Everything was moving inexorably to the end, but Joanna refused to accept it. Any second now, Jesus would rise up and throw off his cross. The power of God would burst from heaven and smite his enemies. He was the Messiah! He had declared it with his own lips.

Jesus stumbled and fell, pulling a strangled cry from Joanna's throat. His lifeblood soaked his clothes and dripped from his face. The soldiers roared in Jesus' face, insisting he continue. Jesus tried to rise, but he was too weak.

"Help him!" Peter's wife screamed at the guards. "Please, help him!"

The centurion looked at her, weighing her plea. He chose a man from the crowd and ordered him to take up Jesus' cross. The man heaved it up, his muscles straining with his grisly burden. The procession moved on.

Wails filled Joanna's ears. She shuffled along, dragged by the current of Jesus' suffering. Susanna was among the crowds lining the road, her face soaked with tears. Jaban stood at her shoulder, his arms wrapped around his sons, trying to shield them from the cruelty of the world.

Jesus paused and faced the lamenting women of Jerusalem, and Joanna held her breath. He held out a stained hand, pleading with them, as if broken more by their sorrow than by his suffering.

"Daughters of Jerusalem, stop weeping for me. Weep for yourselves and for your children. For behold, days are coming when they will say, 'Blessed are the barren, and the wombs that never bore, and the breasts that never nursed.'"

Joanna's heart twisted in her. Even now, as he swayed in pain, his concern was for the people. His cry was the same. Repent! But their religious leaders were wolves amid the sheep, tearing apart the good shepherd and inciting the sheep to help. If they did this evil while the Spirit of God walked among them, no hope remained when Jesus was gone.

A soldier shouted, and Jesus resumed his limping journey. Joanna kept with her friends, those who had served and followed and loved him. United by his life, now they would be bound together by his death.

The procession left the city, the crowds falling away as the soldiers led Jesus to a place called Calvary—'The Skull'. The space was barren, the soil tainted with rotting garbage and the blood of Rome's enemies. A road passed nearby, close enough that travelers would not fail to see the crosses and avert their gaze at the victims' shame.

As the crowds drew back, unwilling to witness the barbarous practice of crucifixion, Joanna still clung to fragmented hope. Jesus could do it. He could walk away. Over and over he had escaped danger.

The man dropped Jesus' cross and retreated as the soldiers closed in for their grisly work.

Each blow of the hammer attacked her hope. Jesus writhed as nails drove deep into his hands and feet. The soldiers heaved him into the air, stripped, bloodied, and fastened to a cross, mocking words scrawled above his head.

Her hope finally died.

As he trembled in pain, Jesus called out, "Father, forgive them, for they do not know what they're doing."

A gaping hole ripped inside of her, and she sobbed, each inhale searing as if she drew flames instead of air. Jesus shepherded the lost and healed the broken. He was their messiah, and those he came to save were killing him. She shook with disbelief.

The robbers were crucified on either side of Jesus. Their screams failed to penetrate the horror that scoured Joanna's mind like a wind storm in the desert.

The soldiers crouched in the shadow of the crosses, casting lots for the clothing. She twisted her hands in her palla, the cloth cutting off her circulation. They quibbled over linen and wool while men hung dying above their heads.

Then the insults began—priests and scribes, elders and officials, all jeering at Jesus, taunting him to use his power.

"If you are the son of God, come down from there!"

"He saved others, but he cannot save himself!"

The women wept around her.

"Have they no mercy?" Maryam sobbed.

One criminal heaved himself on his wounded feet, his ribs protruding as he arched against the pain. He drew breath to hurl curses at Jesus. "Are you not the Christ?" the criminal shouted. "Save yourself and us!"

The younger man roared at his friend, "Do you not fear God? You are condemned to die too! We deserve this, but this man has done nothing wrong." He sagged, weeping uncontrollably.

The truth of his words made Joanna squeeze her eyes shut, hot tears burning her lashes.

The young man turned his face to Jesus, his voice cracking with agony. "Jesus, remember me when you come into your kingdom."

The man had lost his mind. It was impossible for Jesus to claim his kingdom now.

Jesus heaved himself up to draw breath, the effort making his limbs shake. "Truly I say to you today," he rasped, "you shall be with me in Paradise."

Joanna couldn't look anymore. She crouched to the ground, hiding her face, shutting out the horror. A gasp lifted her head, and she blinked at the sky in confusion. It was too soon for nightfall. Darkness fell over the land like a shroud, and the crowds murmured in fear.

Wiping her cheeks with her sleeves, Joanna dragged a shaky breath and stood with the other women, strengthening her spine. She came to witness with them. She would not turn away from Jesus, not now.

Shadow blanketed the grim valley, and torches were lit as one hour passed, then two, with no light on the horizon. The jeering grew quieter and the people shifted, discussing what this sign in the heavens meant. John led Jesus' mother up to the cross so she could speak to him. Fresh tears ran down the women's faces, and Maryam tipped back her head and wailed at the sky, sharing the grief only a mother can know.

After three hours of darkness, a shout split the valley. All eyes turned to Jesus.

"My God, my God, why have you forsaken me?" Jesus cried out.

The crowd murmured. Joanna blinked her gritty eyes. His words sounded familiar. A Psalm. But she couldn't drag the memory through her sludgy thoughts.

A man soaked a sponge and put it on a reed, offering it to Jesus. Jesus tasted it but then turned away. Joanna clenched her teeth as he sagged again, too weak to hold himself up. Time seemed to unravel as he hung there.

Then, with trembling limbs, he heaved himself up again.

"Father!" Jesus shouted hoarsely. "Into your hands, I commit my spirit." His head fell forward with his exhale, and did not rise again.

The crowd stared, and Joanna held her own breath. As the moment stretched, she realized: Jesus was dead.

"No," she choked, her body convulsing.

The ground heaved beneath her feet, and Joanna stumbled, crying out with the others as rocks were split and pebbles rattled across the ground. Then a hush swept through the valley like a sigh, and the darkness rolled away.

A centurion stared up at the cross, his arms limp by his side. "God almighty!" he gasped. "This man was innocent."

The crowd murmured, disturbed by the heavenly signs. Joanna glared as a few lamented, beating their breasts. Now they understood? Too late. Israel had rejected another prophet.

# THIRTY-EIGHT

Chuza sat on the aqueduct road. His backside was numb and he was cold, but he could not move. He stared up at the sky. The late afternoon sun had returned. The mysterious darkness was gone. Each thought came slowly, like a drip from a cracked jug.

Hasty voices widened the crack in his mind. "Torn? Are you sure?"

"That's what the priest was shouting. He went in to offer incense, but the veil was ripped in two."

The men hurried on and Chuza's reasoning tried to catch up, though his body refused to move.

Voices came from the other direction. "I'm exhausted. I can't remember a day like this."

A man gave a weary sigh. "At least it's over."

"I heard Caiaphas requested they be killed before the Sabbath. I'm surprised Pilate agreed."

"I'm surprised Caiaphas offered mercy."

A snort of agreement. "Maybe he's worried Jesus' disciples would help him escape."

"Didn't you see him? There's no recovering from wounds like that."

Chuza waited until the men walked by, their sandals scuffing the cobblestone. After a long moment, he rolled his neck, his muscles protesting. He straightened one leg, then another, letting the circulation return. Gripping the balustrade, he struggled to his feet.

His fingers tightened, and he leaned on the stone, surveying Jerusalem. Against all logic, it looked normal. They called themselves the people of God, but today they let a prophet die.

Guilt settled on his shoulders. He should have convinced Antipas. Said something to set Jesus free. He hit the railing, pain shooting up his wrist. All his life, he had served Antipas. But he should have done more to steer him toward faith.

Time and time again, he had humbly insisted he had no influence over Antipas, but in the rawness of his heart, he admitted his humility masked his cowardliness. He still craved his master's praise, despite everything Antipas had done. Joanna prayed that Chuza would be freed, but he didn't know how to live as anything other than Antipas' slave. It was who he was.

Chuza squeezed his eyes shut, self-loathing churning through his veins. Afraid of censure, he had protected himself, and now a prophet was dead.

Chuza shuffled to the palace, clueless as to what he would do when he got there.

No one stopped him as he climbed the wide steps and crossed the courtyard. The palace was hushed, the servants scurrying about their evening duties, unusually quiet.

Chuza pushed open the door to his office and blinked in the dimness. Leah sat on the couch, weeping into Titus' chest. They turned to him, and in their eyes, he beheld the horror of Jesus' death.

Leah threw herself into Chuza's arms, knocking him off balance.

"He forgave them," she wailed. "Even as they killed him, he forgave them. How?"

He stroked her hair and made shushing noises. He wished she had listened to him. This day would haunt her for years.

Titus rose to his feet, his face drawn with sorrow. "He was a true prophet," Titus said, his words like wind rasping over rocks.

Chuza nodded.

"And your priests, your scribes, and the elders of the people, they killed him."

Again, Chuza nodded, shame twining up his legs like hot water.

Titus' nostrils flared. "I came to Jerusalem seeking God, but now I see there is no more righteousness in this city than there was in Antioch."

He strode past Chuza and out the door.

"Titus, wait!" Leah pleaded, abandoning Chuza's arms and reaching for the soldier, but Titus marched away without a backward glance.

Leah sagged against the door frame, weeping, but Chuza did not call his friend back. He had no comfort to give, no defense to make. Jerusalem was not a holy city on a hill. Today it was a den of thieves and murderers.

A man passed Titus in the opposite direction. Manaen.

Her head bowed, Leah slipped into the private room in the back. Chuza and Manaen embraced for a long, silent moment.

Chuza moved to his side table and poured wine. He offered a cup to his friend. Manaen held the drink as if unsure what to do with it.

"Why aren't you with the disciples?" Chuza asked.

Manaen looked up. "I feel too guilty. I should have done more."

Chuza's grip tightened, tears smarting as Manaen echoed his pain. His emotions surged, and he hurled his cup across the room. The pottery smashed against the wall, wine staining the plaster and dripping to the floor. Unleashing his temper didn't bring the relief he expected.

He laughed mirthlessly. "Me and you both." He looked at his mentor. "So now what? How do we live with Antipas?"

Manaen shook his head, his gaze haunted. "I don't know if I can stay."

Chuza stared at his shaking palms. "I don't know if I can leave."

Joanna stared at the tomb's entrance, tracing the outline of pale rock circling a shadowy hole. Her father's hasty burial in a borrowed tomb echoed like a recurring nightmare.

The sun was sinking too fast. There wasn't enough time to anoint Jesus properly. The men had carried Jesus' linen-wrapped body inside and laid it on a stone shelf, and they were now murmuring the funeral prayers.

Is this what it meant to be called by God? As Joseph of Arimathea began a song of grief, Joanna's memory wandered through the stories of her people, the suffering of the ancient prophets with their hunger and thirst, their embarrassment and isolation. Their pain and despair. She thought about Elijah running from Jezebel so soon after proving God's power over Baal. How he had laid down and wanted to die. Reading about Elijah's trials, they had seemed like part of the glorious adventure—until she was in the thick of them.

"Whose tomb is this?" she asked, the words slow on her thick tongue. Jesus' family tomb would be far away, back in Nazareth.

"It belongs to him," Maryam said, gesturing to the singing man. "He's the reason Jesus will not be buried among the criminals."

"Thank God," Joanna murmured. Jesus had endured enough.

The last rays of sunlight stretched their fingers over the mountain as the men rolled the stone over the entrance. As the grating rock slid into place, Joanna's hopes were entombed with Jesus. "What do we do now?"

A tug on her sleeve drew her forward, and she joined the others walking back to Jerusalem.

They drifted down subdued streets and arrived at a large house with an enclosed courtyard and a staircase that led to an upper level. Naomi led them up the stairs and knocked on the door. Martha opened it a crack, studying them with puffy eyes. She hurried them inside before bolting the heavy door behind them.

The room was full of disciples, the air close with tears and fear. A large table was still littered with the remnants of a Passover meal.

Joanna scanned the faces, relieved to see so many. "Have there been any more arrests?" Joanna asked Martha in an undertone.

"Not yet," Martha whispered. "They may be waiting for the right time."

"But the twelve are safe?" Joanna said. As Jesus' chosen apostles, they were at the greatest risk.

Martha blinked. "You don't know? Judas betrayed him!"

"Not Judas the apostle." Joanna glanced around the room in disbelief.

Philip overheard, and said dryly, "The one and the same."

Joanna's eyes widened. "But why?"

"Who knows?" Philip said. "During supper, Jesus spoke of a betrayer, but I never thought—"

"None of us did," Andrew said, gripping Philip's shoulder and sharing a heavy glance. "I believed we twelve would rule with him, just like he said."

"And yet we all deserted him," Peter scoffed from the background.

John flushed, his shoulders hunched. "I ran too. I'll be ashamed until the day I die." His mother squeezed his arm.

"That's not as bad as my betrayal," Peter said, his eyes scarlet with self-loathing. "He told me I would deny him three times before the rooster crowed, and I did." His face crumpled. "Oh God, he heard me deny him!"

Mary Magdalene twisted her arms against her chest. "How can Jesus be right about everything and still be dead?" Her voice rose in pitch. "He said the kingdom is coming, so where is it?"

Jesus' mother cleared her throat. "If my son said it, then it is true." She spoke boldly, though her lower lip trembled with restrained emotion.

Joanna twisted her fingers. She wanted to believe. "Increase our faith," she whispered.

Martha offered a sad smile. "All we need is a mustard seed."

Joanna wasn't sure if she could manage even that.

# THIRTY-NINE

Joanna woke in the gray predawn with a jolt, realizing her husband didn't know where she was. She whispered to Martha and let herself out of the house, inhaling the cool, fresh air—sweet after the closeness inside. The sky turned from pink to blue as she hurried through the city streets.

It was the Sabbath, and the city churned slowly. She expected to hear Jesus' name on every lip, but as she wove through the streets, she caught no hint of the shameful proceedings the day before. No one wanted to dwell on torture or injustice—at least not in public.

She nodded curtly at the guards at the palace gate. The staff would have plenty to whisper about her and Chuza now. And once Herodias learned Amichai had returned to Barabbas, she would not stop laughing for a week.

Joanna slipped into Chuza's office, shutting the door behind her. The air was thick with sleep. Chuza snored on the couch, still wearing his robe from yesterday.

She smoothed a curl from his face, then peeked into the bedroom. Leah slumbered on Joanna and Chuza's bed, her clothes rumpled and her hair in wild disarray. Joanna silently closed the door.

Enough light shone through the window to illuminate a scroll, so Joanna selected one from Chuza's collection and sat at her husband's cluttered desk. On top of receipts and contracts, she unfurled the writings of Jeremiah. Jesus had been compared to this prophet, and there was a passage she needed to read.

She whispered, "Thus says the Lord God of Israel concerning the shepherds who are tending my people: 'You have scattered my flock and driven them away, and have not attended to them; behold, I am about to attend to you for the evil of your deeds,' declares the Lord."

Joanna swallowed around a painful lump. The priests were supposed to lead their people to righteousness, but they had come among Jesus and his flock like ravenous wolves.

"'Then I myself will gather the remnant of my flock out of all the countries I have driven them and bring them back to their pasture and they will be fruitful and multiply. I will also raise up shepherds over them and they will tend them, and they will not be afraid any longer, nor be terrified, nor will any be missing,' declares the Lord." Joanna swept her tangled hair aside and pushed on, eager to get to the part she craved.

"'Behold the days are coming,' declares the Lord, 'when I will raise up for David a righteous branch, and he will reign as king and act wisely and do justice and righteousness in the land. In his days, Judah will be saved, and Israel will dwell securely. And this is his name by which he will be called, the Lord our righteousness.'

"'Therefore, behold, days are coming,' declares the Lord, 'when they shall no longer say, 'As the Lord lives, who brought up the sons of Israel from the land of Egypt.' but, 'As the Lord lives, who brought up and led back the descendants of the household of Israel from the north land and from all the countries where I had driven them...'"

She trailed off. They just celebrated Passover, remembering the day God rescued them from Egypt. Jeremiah anticipated a miracle even greater, the true restoration of God's people.

It seemed impossible with the sorrow weighing on her chest, yet hope flickered and leaped at the idea.

"You promised us," Joanna whispered, tapping her fingers on the papyrus. "Lord, you promised us this. When will it come to pass, and how?"

A rustle of fabric drew her attention from the page, her husband was rousing. He groaned as he sat up, then jerked as he realized a figure perched at his desk. Joanna tucked the scroll away and sat beside him on the couch.

"Are you alright?" she asked, searching his face. Dark shadows were smudged beneath his eyes.

"I ask you the same question." Chuza reached over to clasp her hand.

"We witnessed to the end." Joanna swallowed a painful lump. "I saw him laid in the tomb. The disciples are safe. They are afraid and confused. So am I."

Chuza squeezed her hand tighter and stood up. He wobbled, pressing fingers to his forehead. "I need to eat," he said. "Is Leah still here? Wake her too."

Joanna gently shook Leah, who woke with a gasp. She saw Joanna and her face crumpled. "Oh, Joanna," she said, bursting into tears. "I should have listened to Chuza. I shouldn't have gone."

Joanna's heart fell. "You went to Calvary?"

Leah nodded, tears rolling down her cheeks. "It was so awful, yet I couldn't look away."

"But how did you get there?"

"Titus took me." Leah averted her gaze with a flush. "I convinced him that Jesus would perform a miracle, that he would not die. We expected to witness a wonder from heaven, but we saw a vision of hell instead."

Joanna swallowed hard. She would have spared Leah if she could.

Joanna held out her hand. "Let's get something to eat."

"I'm not hungry."

"I don't care," Joanna said, her patience stretched thin by emotional exhaustion.

Leah hesitated, but then swung her legs over the bed, trying to arrange her hair into some semblance of order.

They met Chuza and walked to the kitchen.

"Where is Titus?" Leah asked. "He said he lost his job. Where did he go?"

"I haven't seen him since yesterday," Chuza said, sounding too weary to search him out.

The kitchen felt empty without the bustle of preparation, but the long tables were arranged with platters of cold food. In the courtyard ovens, pots stayed warm over beds of coals. Hearing their footsteps, Michael strode into the room. He studied their exhausted faces, and Joanna again wondered what the servants were saying about them.

"Good Sabbath," he said out of habit, and Leah burst into tears. Micheal drooped with regret. "Leah, my girl," he pleaded. She stepped into his arms, and his large, scarred hand rubbed her back.

Joanna and Chuza shared a glance. Leah was no stranger to grief, but witnessing torture was completely different. Joanna feared all of Leah's recent growth would be cut away before it had a chance to truly bloom.

After a few moments, Leah drew back, wiping her cheeks.

Michael gestured that they should sit and brought them bowls of sweetened porridge and bread. At the first bite, Joanna's appetite leaped to life, and she ate ravenously.

Michael slipped into the courtyard, leaving the three of them alone.

Joanna wiped her bowl with her crust and ate the last piece. A full belly rekindled her determination. "I'm going back to the disciples today," she said. "We're going to mourn at the tomb tomorrow morning."

"I will stay here," Leah said flatly.

Joanna met Chuza's eyes. She couldn't make Leah go, but the young woman needed to grieve. Chuza pressed his lips together and nodded.

He leaned toward Leah. "You should be with Joanna and the disciples."

"Why?" she demanded.

"Because they knew Jesus like you did. They share your grief."

"You grieve," Leah retorted.

Chuza rested his hand on hers. "I grieve for what could have been. For how low Antipas has fallen. I grieve for another Jew slain by our oppressors. I grieve for the man who healed my wife. A prophet. But the others grieve for their rabbi and friend."

Leah picked at her bread. "But I left him. I wasn't with him the whole time, like the other women. I'll be an intruder."

"No you won't," Joanna said. She gave her a nudge and a small smile. "They will love to have you back."

"I don't know." Leah shook her head.

"We won't be far away," Joanna promised. "And you can return the day after tomorrow, if you'd rather be with Chuza."

"And then what?" Chuza asked. "What happens now that it's… all over?"

Joanna splayed her palms on the wood table, the wood glossy from generations of use, from thousands of servants and countless meals. Palace life would churn on, as it always had. But she was changed.

Joanna spoke slowly. "He told us the kingdom of God is near. I refuse to accept that this is the end. That it was all for nothing." She locked eyes with Chuza. "I am not the same person I was before him, and I won't go back to how I was."

Chuza folded his hands, staring at his knuckles. "I know what you mean. My vow binds me to serve Antipas, but it does not bind my tongue to silence. I can no longer allow Antipas to transgress the law without telling him the truth. If he is angered, so be it. If he casts me out—"

"We will praise the Lord," Joanna interrupted, and even Leah gave a half-smile. Joanna reached over and clasped her husband's hands, pity rising as she studied his face. She prayed he would not take on the shame that only Antipas deserved. "I'm sorry," she said. "I know Antipas has been a big part of your life. Perhaps he can change."

Chuza swallowed hard. "Even if he doesn't, I must. I don't know how the kingdom of God can arrive in a broken world, but I believe Jesus wanted more for our people. Jesus stood for restoration, for righteousness, for a true kingdom of men and women who love the Lord and serve as a holy priesthood, as Moses foretold. Jesus died before he could bring that kingdom to us, but I want to live as if he succeeded."

Joanna's throat thickened. "Well said."

Michael came into the kitchen and the mood shifted. Joanna and Leah left to change their clothes, and they met again at Chuza's office.

"Find Titus," Leah said, fixing Chuza with a stern glare. "Make sure he's all right."

He nodded, and the women walked into the city.

Chuza stood at the top of the stairs and watched the women until they disappeared. Though he meant what he said in the kitchen, his mind tumbled with questions. Who was Jesus, and why had God sent him? To heal and teach and then die? Jesus had saved Joanna, but he refused to save himself.

He shook his head and went to the barracks, asking for Titus.

One of the soldiers shrugged. "He collected his things and left."

Chuza furrowed his brow. This wasn't like Titus. "Did he say where he was going?"

"No, but the captain refused to give him a letter of recommendation. I'll bet he's drowning himself at a tavern."

Chuza's chest tightened with pity for his friend. Titus must know that Chuza would help him find another position, but perhaps the soldier needed a little time to wallow first. He hadn't just lost his job, his burgeoning faith had taken a heavy blow.

As Antipas' steward, Chuza had plenty of opportunities to see the priests' flaws as they succumbed to petty quarrels, jealousy, and posturing, but he supposed an outsider like Titus might have assumed the priests had risen above such sins. But ever since the priesthood became a political tool rather than an ordained calling, their righteousness was always in question.

Jesus had seemed different. Remorse pressed against his ribs as he regretted not taking more time to listen to Jesus, to form his own opinions rather than leaning on the faith of his wife. But it wasn't too late to fix things in the court.

He returned to his office, half-wishing Antipas would summon him and announce some dishonorable plan so Chuza could prove that he was changed. That he wouldn't stand aside anymore.

But today was the Sabbath, and there was no business. He drew out a scroll and shored up his faith, like a man securing his house against a storm churning on the horizon.

Late that afternoon, Manaen knocked on the office door, inviting him to pray in the temple. As they strode through Jerusalem, Chuza saw the familiar city as if for the first time. His perspective shifted yesterday, and now he refocused on the fickle citizens and the smoke rising from sacrifices offered by men with hands stained by treachery.

"We can't go back, can we?" Chuza asked. Manaen glanced over in question. "We've come face to face with our unholiness, our unworthiness to be called children of God. We're naked in Eden once again."

Manaen considered as they crossed the Court of Gentiles and entered the inner court. "Many will forget," Manaen said. "But those that repent and return to the Father will be restored as heirs." Manaen's eyes drifted to where the priests bustled about their business. His eyes darkened. "But not everyone will celebrate when the prodigals return."

# FORTY

Joanna shifted, easing her hip away from the hard floor. The rumble of sleeping filled the upper room. She squinted at the curtained windows and the crack of pale light that filtered through. It was almost dawn.

A shuffling lifted her head. A curly silhouette was tiptoeing to the door. Another woman stood to follow, and realization settled like a rock in Joanna's stomach. Joanna nudged Leah, who slept at her side.

"What?" Leah's shadowed face scrunched in a scowl.

"It's time to go."

"I just fell asleep," Leah groaned, tugging her blanket higher. "I'm too tired to move."

"It'll do you good to say goodbye." Joanna's throat tightened around the words.

Leah hesitated. "I can't do it," she said, her knuckles white on her blanket. "I can't see him all cut and bruised. I can't."

As much as Joanna wanted to order her to come, Leah was old enough to decide for herself. "Alright," she said, patting her ward's shoulder. "I'll be back soon."

Leah nodded. Joanna wrapped herself in her palla. She picked her way over prone forms and glanced over her shoulder. Leah made no move to follow her, so she scooped her sandals from beside the doorway and slipped outside, pausing at the top of the stairs.

Her mind cleared in the dewy air. A single bird sang to its mate, calling it home. Over the pale houses, clear gray sky claimed the east while a sprinkling of determined stars held the west. A beautiful morning for a grim task. Joanna hurried down the steps and shared tight, commiserating smiles with the gathered women in the courtyard. Maryam clutched the spices they had prepared to anoint Jesus' body.

"Everyone ready?" Mary Magdalene said.

Joanna nodded with the others. Mary led the way out of Jerusalem, down empty streets and past silent homes. They slipped through the city gate as the watchmen snuffed their torches. Their sandals crunched on the road.

The stars faded as they climbed the Mount of Olives and turned onto the narrow path that wound around whitewashed tombs, bright in the rosy glow that preceded the sunrise.

As they wove through the trees, retracing their steps, Joanna's legs grew heavy. Jesus had been in the tomb for days. He might not look the same. He might smell. She shivered as if a cold breeze brushed over her skin, though the morning was calm.

She remembered her father throwing her in the air when she was a little girl, catching her in his muscular arms while his face glowed with laughter. Now he was nothing more than bones. She recoiled from the dark reflection. To dust her father returned, but his soul lived on.

Jesus promised the criminal that he would be with him in Paradise. She clung to the image of those she loved someplace warm and beautiful, rather than rotting in a cold, dark tomb. And maybe, if souls were conscious in the afterlife, her father could meet Jesus after all.

She turned to the east as the sun burst over the horizon, shooting beams of warmth across the earth. As she squinted in the light, the sound of grating rock traced a shiver down her spine.

"What was that?" Naomi whispered.

"Hush!" Mary hissed back at them. "Something is happening up ahead."

Joanna's stomach contracted, and she fell in with the others as they crept forward, her attention darting through the deserted garden.

"The tomb is open!" Mary wailed.

Joanna jerked to a stop. The heavy stone was pushed aside. Who would disturb Jesus' resting place? Mary raced ahead, heedless of danger, and Joanna rushed to catch up. The priests would not steal his body, would they? Not when Pilate gave them permission to bury Jesus. Fear that Jesus' ordeal was not over sickened her empty stomach.

Mary ducked through the doorway. Joanna drew a breath for bravery and charged in after her. She gasped in shock. Jesus' body was gone.

"Where is he?" Mary cried out. "Who took him?"

The other women rushed into the tomb, wailing in dismay. Joanna's chest cinched. The funeral linen was folded neatly and set aside. Why would—

A flash shattered the shadows, and Joanna cried out, grabbing Maryam in fear. The light faded, revealing two men. Their clothes were bright as lightning, filling the tomb with their splendor. Joanna fell to her knees, fear lancing through her as she bowed her face to the ground.

"Why do you seek the Living One among the dead?" The voice pulsed through Joanna like thunder, and she realized these were no mere mortals.

The angel spoke again, his tone rich with power and joy. "He is not here, but he has risen. Remember how he spoke to you while he was still in Galilee? He said that the Son of Man must be delivered into the hands of sinful men and be crucified, and on the third day, rise again."

Like a lamp shining on a dark corner, the words illuminated Joanna's memory. Jesus prophesied his resurrection, and she had been too thick-headed to understand.

She dared to lift her face. The tomb was shadowed once more, and the angels were gone. The sunrise cast golden light at the entrance, beckoning them out of the cold tomb and into the world of the living.

Mary scrambled up, her chest heaving.

Maryam hovered beside the stone shelf and stared at the neatly folded linen as if the shroud held the answers. "He's alive?" she choked out the words. "Really alive?"

"We have to tell the others!" Mary exclaimed. She spun around and ran from the tomb.

The others hurried after her, but Joanna studied the abandoned stone slab. She reached out a hand, then hesitated. Holding her breath, she lay her palm on the coarse rock. A hint of warmth remained, as if Jesus sat while he folded the funeral cloth. A tremble shivered from her crown to her toes, and she yanked her hand away. Logic rebelled against what she knew in her soul to be true. Jesus, who she had seen tortured and brutally killed, was alive.

She tipped back her head, tears trickling down her cheeks and into the neckline of her robe. God had not forsaken his son after all.

She chased after the other women, ducking around low-hanging branches, her palla trailing, her long legs eating the distance. She caught up as they raced into Jerusalem. The town was awake now, women striding to the well with their jars, men preparing for a day of work. They charged past a yard of snowy geese that honked and flapped their wings in consternation.

They burst into the upper room.

"He is risen!" Mary gasped without preamble.

Dozens of eyes stared.

"What are you talking about?" Andrew demanded.

Mary doubled over, catching her breath. She continued between gasps. "The body is gone, I don't know where it is. The tomb is open. An angel spoke to us." She gestured at the knot of panting women, and as frowns raked over her with doubt, Peter charged from the room, seeming intent on seeing for himself. John gripped his mother's shoulder, then raced after Peter.

Joanna searched for Leah's face. Leah had to know. She spotted the girl across the room.

Joanna drew herself up to her full height and spoke loud enough for everyone to hear. "Jesus foresaw this. He told us this would happen."

The silence dragged. Eyes turned to Mary, the mother of Jesus. Her face shone from within, tears shimmering with love and hope.

"Then where is he?" James asked, crossing his arms. "If he is alive, where did he go?"

The women glanced at each other. "I don't know," Mary Magdalene admitted.

"You're confused by your grief," Andrew scoffed. "You say he has risen, and then you say that the body is gone. Which is it?"

Mary Magdalene pressed her lips together and wordlessly strode after Peter and John.

The rest of the room stood in shocked silence, and Joanna wanted to shake them. Didn't they understand? Jesus was risen from the dead!

Leah remained at a distance, a dark scowl shadowing her face. Joanna stepped around others and reached for her hand. Leah jerked away.

"Why are you doing this?" Leah said. Her red-rimmed eyes bored into Joanna painfully.

"It's true," Joanna said, wishing she had forced the young woman to come to the tomb.

"You always wanted to be special. Chosen for some purpose," Leah sneered. "Now you make up an angel?"

Leah was right. Joanna spent the last few years worrying that God would overlook her. But like Elijah on Mount Horeb, she now knew that the God of indescribable glory saw her. God was with her, even though the past days had been like walking the valley of Sheol. Suffering may be the price of being used by God, but there was wonder and glory and purpose too.

And now God tasked her with telling the disciples that Jesus was alive! Joanna yearned to leap and dance like David before the ark of the covenant, but Leah's curled lip stilled her feet.

"I'm not making this up," Joanna said, catching Leah's cold fingers. Leah scoffed and tried to pull free, but Joanna gripped tighter. "Listen to me!" Joanna cried out. She lowered her voice, pleading with her. "It's real. We all saw them." She gestured to the women who were recounting the miraculous events to the doubtful disciples again. Leah's scowl flattened into a thin line.

"You're in denial. Do you know how many times I pretended my parents were still alive? I would wake up in the morning and keep my eyes shut, straining my ears, praying that I would hear my mother preparing breakfast. That I could run to her and let her soothe away my bad dream." Her brow crumpled as she fought back tears. "But it never happened. They're dead and gone forever. And Jesus is too."

Joanna's heart broke for the young woman's suffering, and she tried to draw her into a hug. Leah resisted.

"I want to go back to the palace," Leah's voice cracked. Joanna retreated a step, and Leah wrapped her arms around herself like a shield.

"Of course," Joanna said. "I need to tell Chuza the good news."

Leah rolled her eyes, an expression Joanna hadn't endured in months. The young woman stomped to gather her things, and Joanna let her go. She couldn't force someone to believe. And if Jesus reappeared, soon all of Israel would buzz with the news.

She and Leah moved to the doorway, passing the other women who were growing more frustrated by the moment.

Martha caught Joanna's sleeve. "Where are you going?" she asked in alarm.

"I'll be back," Joanna promised. "I must tell Chuza and Manaen what happened."

Martha hesitated, then released her grip. "All right, but I wouldn't reveal this to anyone else."

Joanna furrowed her brow. "Why not?"

Leah scoffed. "Because they'll think you're insane?"

Martha shot Leah a withering glance, one Joanna admired for its effectiveness. "Until Jesus tells us what to do next, we don't want to cause an uproar. We may still be in danger here."

Joanna scanned the packed room. For three days they had hidden out, afraid of more arrests. She nodded once. "All right. We'll be back later today."

The bolt slid into place behind them.

Joanna and Leah crossed the city, the streets bustling with the start of the work week, oblivious to the wondrous miracle just outside the city walls. They made their way from the Lower City, through the Upper City, and up to the palace gates, Joanna's eagerness increasing with each step.

"You're sure it's safe for you to be here?" Leah asked, concern cracking through her bitterness.

"Herodias thinks she won," Joanna said, passing the guard with her chin raised in defiance. "They took my vineyard and handed my rabbi over to be killed. I'm pretty sure she's too busy congratulating herself to bother me."

They hurried across the courtyard to Chuza's office, and Joanna was relieved to find both men she sought.

Chuza rose, compassion on his face, and Joanna's chest swelled with her good news.

"You're back so soon?" he asked.

355

Leah put her hand on her hip, her brash voice startling the men. "And just wait till you hear the story she's brought back."

Chuza blinked in confusion, but Leah flopped on the couch, crossing her arms and legs. Joanna shot her an exasperated glance.

"We visited the tomb at dawn," Joanna said. She told them about the encounter with the angels, her tongue savoring what she had witnessed. "He's risen, just like he said he would," Joanna said. She studied Chuza's expression, wondering if he would accept her words or side with Leah.

Chuza held his breath, his eyes closing. His gaze softened, and he reached out his hand. "I believe you," he said. Joanna's heart took flight. She gripped his fingers, and he pulled her into a hug. United in their faith in the resurrected Jesus, her heart was full to bursting.

Manaen wrapped his arm around them both, squeezing the air from their lungs. "Praise God!" he said, and Chuza's chuckle tickled Joanna's ear.

Leah laughed derisively. "You're all fools," she muttered.

Manaen released them, and Chuza sat beside Leah on the couch. Leah stared straight ahead, her body rigid.

Chuza leaned toward her. "Why are you afraid?" he asked.

Leah jerked and whipped her head to glare at him. "Afraid?" she scoffed. "I'm not afraid. Well, unless you count my fear that my mistress has lost her mind."

Joanna's lips parted, but Chuza held up his hand, requesting silence.

"Leah, talk to me," he said. "We can see that you're hurting. Tell us why."

Leah burst into tears, her hands flying up to cover her face. Joanna was caught unprepared for this outburst of emotion, but Chuza put his arms around her. Leah collapsed onto him, and her words were edged with rage. "Most people die and never come back. It's just the way it is. Joanna should know this."

Chuza glanced at Joanna, and she shared his look of sympathy, her lips pressed together.

Chuza picked each word with care. "You're right. Your family is gone. Joanna's father still lies in his tomb. My family..." He paused to clear his throat.

Leah pushed herself upright and stared at him. "You don't understand how ludicrous Joanna's claim is. You didn't see him." Leah shook her head, splattering thick tears on Chuza's robe. "He was mangled. No one recovers from scourging like that. Every time I close my eyes, he's back on the cross. Bleeding. Suffering. Dying at their hands, and he's forgiving them." She squeezed her eyes shut. "How could he?" She twisted her mouth in disbelief. "Yet, despite his unfathomable goodness, he's still dead," Leah said flatly. "Imagining that he somehow came back—no. It's impossible."

"So," Chuza said carefully, "maybe you're afraid to believe Joanna's testimony? Afraid to hope, in case the grief comes crashing back, worse than before?"

Leah pressed the heels of her palms into her eyes, sucking a breath through her teeth. "When my family was sick, I clung to hope, praying that God would save them. But God let them die, just like he allowed Jesus to die on that cross. Jesus cried out to him, but God did nothing!" Joanna's throat burned as she remembered Jesus' anguish, his cry to his Father. Leah shook her head. "If God wouldn't listen to the prayers of a man like Jesus, why would he raise him from the dead?" Her shoulders were taut with bitterness. "The world is broken, demented, and cruel. Jesus is better off in Paradise."

Joanna sat on Leah's other side and drew a deep breath, searching for the right words. "Jesus is alive for a reason," she said. "All along, he's been telling us to prepare for the kingdom of God. God's kingdom is not broken or cruel."

Leah glared at her. "How do you know that?"

"Because of Jesus. He said that when we see him, we see the

Father. If Jesus loves and restores and calls us back to righteousness, then God does too."

Leah wove her fingers together, gripping until her knuckles whitened. "I can understand that part. But I cannot fathom why Jesus had to die like he did. Why would God allow it?"

Joanna swallowed hard. Leah was right. There was too much senseless suffering in the world, but there must be a reason for Jesus' agony. "I don't understand either," she admitted, "but I'm sure Jesus will tell us."

Leah stared into Joanna's eyes, her gaze darting back and forth as she searched for answers. Joanna held her breath and refused to look away. The silence dragged, and no one moved.

Hope flickered in Leah's eyes. "There really were angels?"

"Yes," Joanna said, relief rushing into her like a wave. "They declared that Jesus is alive."

Leah pressed her lips together and nodded, her shoulders sagging with exhaustion. "It still seems impossible. But I will wait and see." Joanna drew her into a hug, rubbing her back.

It wasn't the full acceptance Joanna hoped for, but she reminded herself she was asking Leah to believe something so incredible it could change everything. Her hope bloomed like a desert flower as she considered what this would mean. Perhaps it was time for the kingdom of God to arrive. Her lips curved with a smug smile as she pictured Herodias' and Antipas' stunned expressions when they beheld Jesus, alive.

Manaen took a turn wrapping Leah into a hug and Joanna's chest warmed with gratefulness for the people in Leah's life. Joanna gripped Chuza's hand. It would take all of them to restore the girl Joanna rescued, to give her a family.

"Come on," Joanna said, rising to her feet, pulling Chuza up with her. "Let's join the disciples. When Jesus is ready to reveal himself, I'm sure that's where he'll go first."

# FORTY-ONE

Chuza gripped his wife's fingers as they approached the house in the Lower City. Anxiety fluttered in his chest as Joanna opened the courtyard gate and led him up the steps to an upper room. Chuza glanced over his shoulder. Manaen was completely at ease, expecting a welcome among these cloistered disciples. He was one of them. Chuza, on the other hand, was on the fringe, if even that.

A man cracked the door to peek out, then ushered them in. Chuza blinked as he was struck by the ripe smell of too many warm bodies. Men sagged over furniture or leaned against walls, exhausted with grief and disappointment. He hadn't been sure what to expect, but this wasn't it.

"Thank goodness you're back," Maryam said, hurrying over. She darted a glance at Chuza, then leaned closer to Joanna. "Mary Magdalene went back to the tomb. She saw him."

Joanna's eyes widened, and Chuza heard the yearning in his wife's voice. "She saw Jesus? Did she speak with him?"

Maryam nodded. "She did, and he sent her back to us." Joanna looked at Chuza with marvel and questions written in her eyes.

Maryam looked at Manaen. "Where have you been?"

"Hiding in shame," Manaen admitted, a crooked smile splitting his beard.

"Haven't we all," Maryam sighed, flicking her wrist around the room. "They've been trickling in the past few days. And some have left."

"Left?" Joanna asked, glancing at Leah. "After what happened this morning? After Mary saw him?"

Maryam swiped her damp brow. "John came back from the tomb. He believes and says that Peter does too, but Peter hasn't returned. His wife is still here, so I think he's just taking some time." She looked at Manaen. "Cleopas returned to his home in Emmaus." Manaen looked disappointed.

Chuza's brow furrowed as he scanned the room. Joanna told him some doubted, but these men were completely deflated. "So the others think the women lied?" he said.

Andrew overheard Chuza's accusation, and he crossed his arms. "Do you believe your wife?"

Chuza stiffened, and Joanna set a soothing hand on his arm. Chuza stuffed lingering doubts far down. "You have a man raised from the grave standing before you." He gestured to Lazarus, who reddened as dozens of eyes turned his way.

"Lazarus didn't raise himself," Andrew said, thrusting his chin forward.

"The tomb is empty," John insisted. "Peter and I saw the linen wrappings. Why would someone unwrap a body to steal it?"

"If Jesus is alive, where is he?" another man demanded.

The room rumbled with contention, and Maryam shook her head. She beckoned to Joanna and Leah. "Let's leave them to run around in circles again," she said, her tone laced with scorn. "The women are in the courtyard, preparing the midday meal."

Joanna slipped back outside with Leah, casting a reassuring glance at Chuza. He inched closer to Manaen. Manaen led him to a bare patch of floor and they sat.

Chuza flinched as a man stared at him, his eyes burning coals. "You are Herod Antipas' steward, aren't you?" the man said.

"I am."

The accuser leaned forward. "How do we know you're not a spy?"

Chuza cleared his throat, glancing at Manaen. "My wife has been among you. Her life is as bound up in this… situation as yours."

"Unless you sent her to be your eyes and ears."

Chuza scoffed. "Then why would I need to be here?"

The other man wobbled his head, mocking Chuza's logic.

"Peace, Bartholomew," Manaen said. "Jesus welcomed Joanna among us, and we all benefited from her help. I know her to be a woman of strong faith."

Bartholomew folded his arms. "Jesus welcomed Judas Iscariot, too. Then Judas betrayed him, selling him to the priests."

Chuza blinked in shock. "One of the twelve did this?" Joanna had spoken in awed tones about the twelve men Jesus chose, as if they were giants among the other disciples.

The door burst open, and everyone blinked at the silhouetted figure. As he closed the door, Peter emerged, staring at them all. Astonishment was painted on his features.

Andrew jerked to his feet. "Simon!" he exclaimed, hurrying to his brother. "What happened?"

"He appeared to me," Peter croaked, dragging his fingers through his hair.

After a heartbeat of stunned silence, the room erupted with questions, men leaping to their feet, crowding around their friend. Chuza hung back as Peter raised his palms to calm the deluge.

"He spoke to me," Peter said, his voice thick with emotion. "But that's all I can tell you right now."

Protests rose at his refusal to explain. A diminutive woman followed him through the door, pushing through the crowd to join her husband. Peter wrapped her in a hug, murmuring in her ear, and squeezed her tighter.

As the men clamored for details, Peter hunched, overwhelmed, his gaze still far away. Peter's wife turned, one fist on her hip, her expressive brows narrowed in consternation.

"It's time to eat," she said, her voice soft but firm. "Perhaps if you let him fill his belly, he'll be more open to conversation."

The promise of food soothed angry voices, and the men drifted to their seats. A group of women entered with bowls and bread. The tantalizing aroma of cumin and coriander teased Chuza's nose as Leah approached, holding out a dish of beans smothered in a savory sauce. She had added a portion of brined olives.

"You'll have to share your bowl." Leah nodded between Manaen and Chuza, passing the dish to Chuza, who balanced it gingerly, the pottery hot. She handed two rounds of unleavened bread to Manaen. "We're a bit short on dishes."

"This smells fantastic," Manaen said, wafting the steam closer. "Did you have a hand in making this?"

"Maybe a little," Leah said, a grin dashing across her face before she returned to the courtyard. The girl was calmer now, Chuza saw with relief.

He placed the bowl between himself and Manaen and ripped a piece of bread to scoop a generous mouthful.

The room settled into appreciative murmurs as the men ate, though Chuza noticed more than one set of eyes staring at Peter. The fisherman kept his attention fixed on his dish, but his relaxed posture and hidden smile hinted at calm assurance.

Chuza wished he felt the same. He refused to fall into the trap of disbelief that almost prevented Joanna from being healed two years ago. But it was one thing to believe his wife received a message from heaven, another to know beyond a doubt that Jesus was alive.

When they had swiped their bowl clean, Chuza returned the dish to the courtyard kitchen. It was a sunny space with pots of herbs, a mill, and a stone oven. The fresh air was a relief after the shuttered living quarters, though the space was almost as full. The women were eating their meal, and Leah rose when he approached.

He set his bowl down by the empty pots and scanned the women's faces. The mood here was brighter, more expectant.

"Why are you all out here?" Chuza asked Leah. "I mean, I know a few men could use a bath—" he winked "—but I don't remember this segregation before."

Leah flushed. "Some of the men were quite vocal in their doubt. Like I was." She pressed her lips together. "I imagine that if I saw a miracle and everyone insisted it was a figment of my imagination, I would be hurt, too." She glanced at Joanna, who sat between Maryam and a woman with a long, silvery braid. "I should probably apologize to Joanna."

"That would be wise," Chuza said, and squeezed her shoulder. "I understand how grief can overpower your good sense. I hope, next time, you'll share your struggles rather than lashing out."

"Hopefully there isn't a next time," Leah muttered, looking away in embarrassment. "I should have accepted my loss by now."

Chuza's grip tightened on Leah's shoulder until she met his gaze. "Grief never leaves, my girl. Not completely. But it is easier to bear when we share it."

She laid her hand on his with a grateful smile. "Thank you, Chuza. You've done so much for me these past months. More than I realized." She hesitated. "I'm sorry I said you aren't my father. I wish—" She cut off her words, her cheeks blooming.

Chuza tilted his head closer. "You are part of our family, Leah." Her expression glowed, warming him from within. This young woman was special to Joanna, and she had become precious to him too.

He cleared the emotion from his throat. "Joanna and I will be proud to act as your parents. Even after you leave to start a family of your own."

Leah studied the floor. She spoke with forced nonchalance. "Have you heard from Titus? After the way he stormed off, I'm worried about him. I feel awful for insisting he take me to Calvary." A shudder rippled through her, and Chuza's chest squeezed. No one should ever witness a crucifixion.

"I'm sure he'll find his way back to us," Chuza said. "And if Jesus is alive—"

"If?" she said archly, crossing her arms.

Chuza chuckled. "*When* Jesus reveals himself, Titus will find comfort, too. His faith took quite a blow."

"That happens when our spiritual leaders let us down," Leah said. She drew a deep sigh. "But God raised Jesus from the grave, despite the cruelty of the priests and elders." A smile brightened her face, though her lips trembled. "God rescued me, too. Using Joanna. And you."

A tear shimmered in the corner of her eye, and she flicked it away. "But enough of this. I have dishes to wash."

"Can I help?" Chuza asked. When Leah raised her brow, he jerked his head back at the shadowy house and whispered. "Take pity on me. I am a fish out of water in there."

She chuckled. "All right. Go fetch the rest of the dishes."

As he gathered up the dirty bowls, he earned more than a few odd glances. He ignored them. They already thought he was an outsider.

"Bit overdressed for a servant, eh?" a man quipped.

Peter's voice cut across the room. "Who is greater, the one who reclines or the one who serves?"

Chuza blinked at the strange statement, but the other man flushed as if reprimanded. Peter gave Chuza a nod of acceptance. It loosened a knot in Chuza's chest.

The afternoon slipped by, and Martha and her younger sister returned from the marketplace with a basket of salted fish.

"Mary thought we should have something special for supper,"

Martha said, looking guilty at the expense. "We got a good bargain."

"Oh, excellent!" Leah said. "I know just how to prepare them!" She reached for the basket and then flushed with embarrassment at her presumption. "I mean—"

Martha chuckled. "I have sampled your cooking. I am happy to entrust you with this task." She held out the basket. Leah hesitated, then accepted it, her mouth a line of determination. Chuza grinned. No pot would be more carefully attended tonight.

Leah set the salted fish to soak in water, then began gathering herbs, crushing them between her fingers and bringing them to her nose. While the other women baked stacks of unleavened bread, Leah bedded coals in the central fire pit. She liberally coated the two cook pots with golden olive oil and set them to warm. Once they were hot, she tossed in a chopped onion, placed the drained fish with careful fingers, and sprinkled the pale meat with the herbs. A delightful aroma filled the courtyard. After turning the fish, Leah drizzled it with honey.

Chuza realized he was not the only one watching. Joanna and Maryam stood side-by-side, wearing matching smiles as Leah was lost in her work. Leah used a towel to protect her hands as she slid the pots away from the coals.

"It's ready!" she announced, looking around the courtyard. She blinked in surprise to find herself the object of attention.

Martha bent over the pot and inhaled. "It smells heavenly, my dear." Leah flushed, ducking her head.

Leah filled the stack of dishes. With dismay, Chuza realized they would need to be washed all over again. Leah offered him a bowl with tender chunks of fish. As the women carried food to the upper room, Manaen came down the steps and joined them in the courtyard. He sat near Leah, engaging her in conversation.

Joanna pulled herself away from her friends to sit beside Chuza. He set his bowl between them.

"You and Leah seemed to be having a serious talk earlier," she said, raising her eyebrows with curiosity.

"Oh, you know," he said with feigned boredom. "Discussing our role as her guardian—and a possible betrothal."

Joanna narrowed her eyes. "A betrothal? She and Titus aren't... serious, are they?"

Chuza chuckled, bumping her shoulder with his own. "Just because you waited until you were an old maid doesn't mean Leah will."

Joanna shot him a dirty look. "That's not the issue, and you know it. If Titus is the man in question, there are other concerns to consider. Will he take on the full rites of Judaism?" Circumcision prevented many Gentiles from embracing the full Jewish faith, and Titus was no exception. But Chuza knew that the soldier was a good man.

"He learned a lot these past few months," Chuza deflected, then hesitated. "Though recent events might have put a damper on his zeal."

Joanna considered, then nodded. "If he's willing to embrace all the laws, then I don't see an issue, except..." she trailed off, studying her bowl. "Should we be planning her future? We're not really her family, are we?"

Possessiveness surged like heat. "We have become her family," he insisted.

"But her real family is still out there. We should try to find them." Her eyebrow rose at his annoyed expression. "Maybe we should talk about this later."

"Or not," he muttered, too low for her to hear. Would God lead them to help Leah and then take her away?

The sky grew dusky as he and Manaen ate amid the women in the courtyard. Twilight painted the calm courtyard in rosy hues and the sounds of the city were muted. Despite the strange events of the day, Chuza felt at peace. He leaned against the wall and admired the streaks of vivid pink amid the hazy blue.

The sound of hurried footsteps on the street shattered the stillness. He tensed as the gate burst wide and two figures rushed in, their faces split with eager smiles.

"Cleopas!" Manaen exclaimed, rushing forward. Cleopas and Manaen embraced. "I'm so glad you came back," Manaen said. "We have wonderful news. The Lord has really risen, and he appeared to Simon!"

Cleopas didn't look surprised, as Chuza expected. Chuza rose to his feet, and Joanna stood beside him.

"I know. We've seen him," Cleopas said, his expression glowing. His wife nodded. A stunned silence stretched to fill the courtyard. Jesus had appeared to Peter, a man who denied him, now he revealed himself to those who left, full of doubt. He glanced at Joanna to gauge her reaction. She arched her eyebrows at him, smiling as she shrugged.

Cleopas led them all up the stairs and into the upper room, declaring his joy to all who would hear it. "Jesus is alive!"

The disciples gathered closer as Cleopas was hustled into the center of the room. He beamed around at all of them.

"Well, don't just stand there," Andrew broke the silence. "Tell us what happened!"

Peter kept his encounter close to his chest, but Cleopas seemed eager to share his experience.

"We were walking to Emmaus, and overtook another traveler," Cleopas said. "He overheard us discussing everything that happened and asked what we were talking about." Cleopas widened his eyes. "I asked him how he, of everyone who visited Jerusalem, was unaware of the things that occurred these past few days." Cleopas chuckled with wonderment, and the group leaned forward, drawn to his humor after the weight of their confusion and grief. "He said, 'What things?'"

"He really didn't know?" John said, sharing a look with his brother.

Cleopas held out his arms in an exaggerated shrug, and then let them fall. "So we told him about Jesus of Nazareth, who was a prophet mighty in deed and word in the sight of God and all the people. And how the chief priests and our rulers ordered him crucified."

Joanna stiffened at his side, and Chuza wrapped his arm around her waist.

Cleopas grew serious. "We explained our hope that Jesus was going to redeem Israel." His gaze encompassed the room, and some nodded. "And then, we told him that this is the third day since all this happened. Some women went to the tomb early in the morning." Cleopas' voice grew hushed. "They saw a vision of angels who said he was alive." Men shifted.

Cleopas gestured at Peter and John. "I told him that others went to the tomb and found it empty, but they did not see him." The moment stretched, heavy with anticipation.

Cleopas grinned. "Well then, it was his turn to talk. He said, 'You foolish men, slow of heart to believe in all that the prophets had spoken! Wasn't it necessary for the Messiah to suffer these things and to enter into his glory?'" He paused, allowing his audience to murmur at this bold statement. Chuza furrowed his brow at Joanna, trying to remember where a suffering messiah was prophesied.

Cleopas nodded in agreement as confusion spread. "Just like you, we were surprised by his words. And then, starting with Moses and with all the prophets, he explained everything concerning the Messiah in the scriptures."

Chuza would have given much to have heard that explanation.

"As you can guess, we were amazed," Cleopas said, his awe coloring his tone. "So when we arrived in Emmaus, we urged him to stay the night. He sat at the table to eat with us and blessed the bread. He broke it and gave it to us." Cleopas paused, and the air vibrated with expectancy. "As we accepted the bread," Cleopas said, "our eyes were opened, and we recognized him. It was Jesus!"

"No!" John's exclamation spoiled the awed atmosphere.

Cleopas laughed, nodding at the young man. "But before we could recover from our shock, he vanished from our sight."

"That's incredible," Andrew said, his jaw slack.

Cleopas shared a knowing glance with his wife. "We should have understood sooner." He tapped his chest. "Our hearts were burning within us while he spoke on the road, explaining the scriptures to us. After we came to our senses, we realized we had to come back immediately and tell you."

Suddenly, as if stepping through a veil, Jesus stood before them. Men threw themselves backward and a woman screamed in alarm. Chuza's chest compressed at the shock, preventing him from drawing breath. Joanna's hands flew to cover her mouth.

Jesus wore a simple robe, and he looked the same—yet different. After giving them a second to compose themselves, Jesus nodded in greeting, an affectionate smile on his serene face. "Peace be with you!"

Leah rushed to Chuza's other side. The three of them stood in astounded wonder. Jesus seemed to be alive, but he was disappearing and appearing like a ghost.

Everyone was quiet, staring at Jesus. Andrew was making eyes at Peter, as if pressing him to speak first. Peter surreptitiously shook his head.

Jesus took in their frightened expressions. "Why are you troubled?" he asked, his head tipping to the side in question. "Why do doubts arise in your hearts?" He shook back his sleeves and extended his arms. "See my hands and my feet, touch me and see!"

Chuza swallowed hard. Holes marked Jesus' hands, smoothed into scars.

Still, no one moved, and Jesus took a step forward. "A spirit does not have flesh and bones, and you see that I have both."

Leah gripped Chuza's arm until it hurt.

Jesus chuckled. "Have you anything to eat?" he asked.

Eyes turned automatically to Martha. She jerked into action and hurried out to the courtyard. She returned, holding out some fish with trembling hands. Jesus pointedly took a bite, and, as one, they leaned forward, watching him chew. The room was so quiet, Chuza heard him swallow.

As Jesus licked off his fingers, the fear soaking the room drained away, and joy rushed in to take its place. The disciples crowded around him, but then, just as quickly as he appeared, he vanished.

The room quaked with exclamations, and Chuza released Joanna so he could pry Leah's fingers off his wrist before he lost circulation. Leah's focus was far away.

"Are you alright?" he asked.

She turned slowly, blinking at him in a daze. "Jesus ate my fish."

Joanna burst into laughter. Chuza's arms came around them both, and they all laughed together, a sound of rejoicing that drove into his heart with truth. Jesus had risen from the dead.

As the disciples' clamor filled the upper room, Chuza wondered what could possibly come next.

# FORTY-TWO

Chuza strode through the palace courtyard with a wax tablet pinned under his arm. Antipas was strolling through the garden with Herodias. The couple studied him, their expressions uneasy. Chuza's peaceful expression confused them, but he didn't care. A dead man came back from the grave with nail holes in his hands and feet. Chuza witnessed him eat fish like a mortal and vanish like a spirit. Jesus' three days in the tomb changed the prophet into something —more.

The disciples were gathering. Those that missed Jesus' first visitation received another. Hope swelled as weeks passed and hundreds more reported Jesus appearing, encouraging, teaching, and explaining the kingdom of God.

Chuza wondered what he and Joanna would do when Antipas' court moved on. Jerusalem felt like the epicenter of everything, and to leave now was to walk away from something life-changing. But even those worries could not break the peace that filled him like a calm sea.

Joanna approached. "Any word from Titus?" she asked.

Chuza shook his head, waves rippling across his inner calm. Titus' disappearance was the one mar on their happiness. The soldier had vanished, and Chuza began to fear he had left the city, maybe even Judea. Hopefully, Titus would hear the good news and return.

Whispers of the empty tomb were trickling already, running through the streets of Jerusalem. Chuza had no doubt they would become a flood as the pilgrims returned to their homes. When Titus learned about Jesus, surely he would come back—unless he dismissed the rumors as hearsay. Chuza kneaded the back of his neck. The priests were employing counter-measures, spreading the lie that the disciples had stolen Jesus' body away.

Joanna leaned closer. "Jesus has appeared again. We are supposed to gather tomorrow near Bethany."

Chuza warmed with a new feeling, one he hoped would become his baseline—joyful expectation. "We'll be there," Chuza said. "Have you told Leah?"

"Not yet. We can tell her at supper." Now that Joanna was home, the three of them ate supper together nearly every night. Joanna hooked her arm in his, and they strolled side by side. "Have you given any more thought about going to Alexandria?"

Chuza pressed his lips together. Joanna was determined that Leah should search for the family she left behind in Egypt. The trip was lengthy and expensive. Not to mention rife with emotional dangers.

"Alexandria is an immense city," Chuza said. "What if we do not find them?"

Joanna studied him. "But what if we do? What if we hear news about your family, too?"

Chuza looked away. "I don't need to find them," he said. "I have a family. You, Leah, Manaen, Titus."

"Yes, Titus," Joanna said wryly. "Another important reason to locate Leah's people. I don't think we can plan for her future unless she faces her past."

But that presented a new difficulty, one that tightened his chest.

"But what if we locate them and Leah decides to stay?" Chuza said.

Joanna studied his face. "We have to allow her that choice. We both know what it is like to have our choices stripped away, our futures stolen. Let us give Leah the gift that neither of us had."

Chuza's heart rebelled against the idea of losing Leah. "We will think about it. Too much is happening for us to leave now."

"You're right," Joanna said, smiling, "and we don't have boat passage yet, anyway."

"We could walk," Chuza teased. "You've had some practice."

Joanna laughed. "I have walked the length and breadth of Israel, but Egypt is too far!"

They rose before dawn, and Leah brought a breakfast tray to Joanna and Chuza's room. Chuza ate with gusto, but Joanna's stomach was too unsettled to eat. She counted the days again. There was no doubt about it, her monthly courses were late. She hesitated to voice her suspicions, but her hope was like a lamp glowing in her chest.

Joanna, Chuza, and Leah arrived in Bethany as the sun peeked over the horizon. A small crowd of disciples was waiting.

Peter took the lead. With his strong, fisherman's voice, he hollered for everyone to follow him. He brought them to a secluded place to wait for Jesus' arrival. Birds sang praises in the sweet summer air. The sky hung like blue tapestry above the verdant grass and the swaying branches of silvery olive trees.

Once again, Jesus appeared in his mysterious way, as if he stepped through an invisible veil. Gasps echoed, and Joanna's joy clogged her throat. She squeezed her husband's fingers, rejoicing that they shared this experience.

Jesus' gaze swept over them, beaming. "You must not leave Jerusalem," he said. "Wait for what the Father promised, which you heard of from me. John baptized with water, but in a few days, you will be baptized with the Holy Spirit."

Joanna's mind fluttered with possibility. She felt the Spirit when Jesus healed her. She witnessed Jesus' miracles, made possible by the Spirit that filled him and empowered him to do wonders. The Spirit granted the disciples the ability to heal and cast out demons. But this sounded like something else.

Excitement pulsed through the disciples and voices clamored, asking Jesus if now was the time to restore the kingdom to Israel. Joanna ached with longing, ready for Jesus to make everything right in her world.

Jesus held up his palms for quiet. "It is not for you to know the times or epochs the Father has fixed by his authority, but you will receive power when the Holy Spirit has come upon you; and you shall be my witnesses in Jerusalem, in all Judea and Samaria, and even to the remotest parts of the earth."

She blinked. Gratitude and joy bubbled up like water, ready to overflow with the good news of Jesus' resurrection.

Jesus lifted his hands and blessed them. As he spoke, he rose, hovering in the air. They stared, transfixed, as he ascended higher and higher. Then, in the blink of an eye, he vanished.

Silence hung in the little clearing, birdsong and the buzz of insects an earthy backdrop to a heavenly moment.

"Men of Galilee," a voice jerked Joanna's attention back to earth. Two men in gleaming white linen viewed the dumbfounded disciples in amusement. Joanna realized her mouth was hanging open and snapped it shut. "Why do you stand looking into the sky? This Jesus, who has been taken up from you into heaven, will come in just the same way you watched him go."

Joanna glanced at Chuza. Jesus had gone to heaven? Wonder mingled with a stab of loss. Her mind flew to her hero Elijah, who was swept up in a chariot of fire. Elijah had not returned to Elisha, leaving him to carry his mantle. Tears smarted in her eyes.

But Jesus couldn't be gone for long. Antipas was still tetrarch.

Pilate was still governor. Rome still held sway over her people. Like so many others, she and Chuza were stuck in a strange place, believers in an unbelieving world. She turned to the white-robed strangers, desperate for answers, but they had vanished. Marvel rippled through the disciples.

"What just happened?" Leah said, turning to Joanna. "Why did Jesus leave? Why send us to preach the kingdom of God instead of going himself?"

Chuza twisted his lips ruefully. "I don't understand most of what's taken place the past few weeks. Why should this be different?"

Joanna surveyed Jesus' disciples, an idea forming. Elisha had picked up Elijah's fallen mantle and done greater deeds than his master. Maybe they were supposed to be like Elisha, who received a double-portion of Elijah's spirit. Her heart leaped, but the idea was too daring to speak aloud. She tucked the thought into her heart and prayed she would rise to the task God placed before her feet. She had been called, and now she was being sent out. Her chest swelled as if the sun had lodged itself between her ribs.

Peter raised his palms to catch everyone's attention. "Let's go back to Jerusalem. We can talk more when we get there."

The large group wove through the narrow streets of the Lower City. Joanna swiveled her head, jarred by the normalcy of city bustle after what had transpired outside the city walls.

They took the stairs to the upper room. The large space had grown hot, and Martha opened the shutters to let in a whiff of breeze.

As the last disciple filed inside and the door was closed, Peter stood at the front of the room. "We should pray," he said. "I'm sure we all remember how Jesus devoted himself to prayer. Disappearing at odd hours, gone before dawn and in the middle of the night." He grinned, his tanned face crinkling at the eyes. Joanna chuckled with the others. Peter grew serious. "We need to imitate him."

In that dim upper room, they stood together, lifting hands as they took turns praying aloud, murmuring in agreement, nodding, and praising God. Wiping a bead of sweat from her upper lip, Joanna peeked around the room. So many familiar faces. So many shared experiences. Changed lives. It was as if Jesus spent his ministry winding a cord from one to the other, binding them together.

The sunbeams shifted their glowing track across the floor and faded away before Joanna, Chuza, and Leah prepared to return home. Joanna yearned to remain among the disciples, but there wasn't enough space for everyone to sleep. At the doorway, Joanna rested her fingertips on the mezuzah and cast a longing gaze over the crowded room. She couldn't wait to return.

As they walked through the city, Joanna noticed Chuza's somber expression.

"What's wrong?" she asked.

"Do you think Jesus included me in his words? Back on the mount." Chuza paused, his brow furrowed. "I did not witness his ministry."

"You witnessed his resurrection," she reminded him. "You've seen him appear, heard him teach."

Chuza still looked troubled. "But others have followed him for years. Why should I be accepted equally with them?"

Jesus' words rose in her mind. "The first shall be last and the last shall be first," she said. He frowned at her statement, but she patted his arm. "Jesus welcomes all who come to him, and they all receive the same promise. There is no partiality with God. The man beside Jesus on the cross was ushered into Paradise, though he only understood in the moment of his death."

"But it doesn't seem fair—"

Joanna cut him off. "Faith is not about fairness. It's not about who earns it. Who of us can say we deserve the gift Jesus has promised?" She smiled at her husband. "Peter denied Jesus three times, yet Jesus has called him to lead his flock. There are highly educated Pharisees among our number, yet Jesus picked a fisherman to shepherd us. Jesus does not judge by outward appearances. He sees our heart."

Chuza still seemed hesitant at taking up the mission Jesus gave them. Leaving her husband to consider her words, she put her arm around Leah's shoulders, giving her a squeeze.

"And what about you?" Joanna asked. "How do you feel?"

Leah leaned against her. "I like the new atmosphere among the disciples. I feel... like I am home."

Joanna and Chuza shared a long glance, and Joanna swallowed hard before smiling at their young ward. "Me too."

# FORTY-THREE

The Day of Pentecost dawned as golden and warm as freshly baked bread. Joanna looked with approval at the perfect loaf Leah made for them to present at the temple.

Because it was a festival day, there was no work, and Chuza and Leah breakfasted together. Joanna nibbled on plain bread and drank a cup of ginger tea—remembering a conversation with Phasaelis and Susanna in what felt like another life. Chuza watched her, and her cheeks warmed. Did he suspect what she began to hope?

Her nausea faded as they crossed the aqueduct road, joining the throngs of people that funneled into the vast complex. They met up with Susanna, Jaban, and their sons in the temple courts. Joanna had taken the good news of Jesus' resurrection to them, and they responded with joyful acceptance. Joanna prayed that the whole city would believe as quickly.

The mood in the temple courts was celebratory. For those who had made a once-in-a-lifetime pilgrimage to Jerusalem for Passover, it was a time for worshipful praise before they departed the holy city for their homes.

Everywhere Joanna turned were fluttering sheaves of wheat and loaves of bread. So much bounty, yet the stalks represented only a fraction of the harvest. Chuza added their loaf to the pile as a priest spoke the benediction. They prayed in the courts as priests offered the sacrifices. Joanna watched it all with a flutter in her stomach, eager to join the others in the upper room. If it was true what they hoped, the promised Spirit was coming soon.

The world had experienced the Spirit in new ways over the past three years. But now the disciples expected something more. If the Spirit had been a stream weaving through their land, Joanna believed it was about to become a flood.

After the service, they made their way through the packed streets of the city. As they climbed the stairs to the upper room, the hum of voices beckoned, and her soul reached out to join them.

She knocked and grinned as Cleopas let them in. The room was shadowy after the bright morning light, and disciples filled the open space. She saw Jesus' mother and brothers, Mary Magdalene and Maryam, along with the other women who accompanied Jesus from Galilee. The apostles were all together, twelve once more, having added Matthias to their number. Peter was praying aloud, the room murmuring in agreement.

The very air shivered with holiness. Joanna had just come from the temple and experienced the smoke rising from the sacrifices and the hum of thousands of voices joined in prayer. Yet that was nothing compared to the sanctity that filled this room. Emotion rose in her throat, a longing, a need to join.

Joanna led the way to a small open space, and she, Chuza, and Leah stood together, letting the world slip away and joining into this flow between heaven and earth.

Matthew was praying aloud now, fervently beseeching God to send what Jesus had promised, asking the Lord to prepare their hearts to receive the outpouring of the Holy Spirit.

Joanna pressed her hands to her chest, craving the Spirit the way she craved each breath of air. A mingled tapestry of Jesus' and her father's voices rose in her mind. Both men filled her with a hunger for God's word and a desire to be a tool in his hand, used to show God's glory to the world.

Leah rocked back and forth, abandoning herself to prayer. She murmured her wonder at the risen Christ, asking that everything he promised would come true. Voices rose in pleasing harmony on every side as more than a hundred disciples gave themselves to worship.

The air crackled and hummed with power, and the hair on Joanna's arms stood on end. She never imagined she could feel anything like this. She experienced holiness as a tangible presence, a force, a taste on her tongue.

The prayers rose louder, higher. And then something changed. The sound of a rushing wind filled the space, and Joanna and Chuza locked eyes, communicating their amazement.

Leah laughed aloud, the rapturous noise bubbling out of her like a spring as she lifted her hands to heaven.

The sound increased to a roar, as if they stood in the midst of a storm, the pressure increasing and crackling in the air until Joanna couldn't take any more. But then more came. Fire streaked into the room, brilliantly white, flickering without heat. Joanna cried out as flames swirled in an intricate dance and then split. She sucked in her breath as a tongue of fire came to rest on her, dancing along her skin like a caress. Squinting through the dazzling display, she saw the same thing happening to everyone. Her eyes burned with tears as she once again felt the Spirit touch her, burning through her with indescribable light. She threw back her head and reveled in God's presence. If this was a touch of heaven, there was nothing to fear in death.

Others sobbed while some joined Leah in laughter. The flame gave a pulse, thrumming through her chest, and Joanna cried out praise to the Lord with the others as the Spirit drove into them with overwhelming power.

Joanna prayed with abandon, declaring the wonders of the Lord. Leah and Chuza rejoiced beside her, and the others in the room were praising God aloud—but wait.

Glancing to the side, she heard Maryam speaking in a language she didn't know. Joanna caught bits of other languages flowing through the room, ones she could not place. Something strange was happening.

After precious, holy minutes, the fire faded and the wind died, leaving heaving chests and wet cheeks in its wake. Joanna swiped her face with her sleeves. Peter stood up among the others, and Joanna gazed at him in wonder. The fisherman had always been eager in his faith, but now his face bore strength and confidence that made his earlier, boisterous manner seem childish by comparison.

As the room quieted, the rumbling of a crowd pushed through the shutters. Surely the entire city had witnessed that wind. James threw open a window, and the voices grew louder, demanding an explanation.

"What is going on in there?" a man called. "We heard a terrible noise, like wind!"

Another man shouted, "Someone is praising the Lord in Egyptian, and this man says he heard perfect Latin!"

A woman's voice came next. "I heard a woman speaking of the mighty deeds of God in the dialect of my village in Pontus."

Joanna looked at Chuza and her awe echoed in his shimmering eyes. They stared at each other in wonder as the crowd demanded that those in the upper room explain themselves. Chuza gripped Leah's shoulder. The young woman's face was illuminated like the rising sun. Jesus' mother had her eyes shut, her chin resting on folded fingers as she swayed back and forth, her sons flanking her on either side. The apostles stood taller, sharing knowing glances.

Peter drew a deep breath. They had been holding back the good news for over a month, and now God proclaimed Jesus' glory. With a determined nod, Peter led the way out the door. Joanna hurried with the others, down the steps and into the crowded street to share the good news.

Peter plunged the woman beneath the water, baptizing her in the name of the Father, the Son, and the Holy Spirit. The woman was lifted, her hair and clothes streaming water, and she joined the growing crowd of believers. The numbers were staggering. Matthew was keeping a tally, and he was in the thousands. Thousands of men and women were praising God and accepting Jesus as their savior.

Joanna glanced up to the temple mount and her stomach tensed. White-robed priests gathered on the steps like a storm cloud on the horizon, but they did not intervene.

As the sun set over the city and the crowds dispersed, Joanna's stomach growled. Many of the newly baptized refused to leave the disciples. Maryam was trying to organize meals for the sudden increase of believers who jostled like a joyous family reunion.

"Joanna!" Maryam called, waving her arm. "We could use your husband's help!"

"My help?" Chuza said, glancing at Joanna as if for confirmation.

"Yes!" Maryam laughed. "You're a steward, aren't you? Help us get these people organized and fed."

Joanna understood as Chuza's face brightened. She was sure that his skin still tingled from the tongue of fire, a declaration that God had chosen them to be witnesses of the risen Lord. And their role was just beginning.

# FORTY-FOUR

Antipas stood in the palace courts, watching the servants haul his luggage to the waiting carts. Sweat beaded on his brow, but he didn't move for shade. He couldn't get out of Jerusalem soon enough.

The day of Pentecost had shaken the city. Some people—gluttons for miracles—insisted a sign from heaven occurred at a common house. Something about the spirit of God coming in force and filling people. Whatever that meant. It was said that the witnesses went half-mad and thousands were baptized in the frenzy. The priests could not protest at this outpouring of devotion, but they bristled as knots of these baptized believers gathered daily in the temple courts to pray. No one knew what this group stood for, other than their stubborn insistence that Jesus of Nazareth had risen from the dead.

A chill brushed over his arm despite the sun's glare. He was innocent of the man's death. And besides, the absence of a body didn't prove he was alive. Antipas scoffed to himself. The disciples rather conveniently declared Jesus had gone up to heaven. Alive, of course. They insisted he was coming back, but they did not know when. If Jesus employed a steward, he would be furious at this lack of organization.

Antipas frowned as his own steward strode toward him, wearing his traveling cloak. Antipas eyed him with suspicion. He stripped Joanna of her vineyard and refused to help their prophet, yet Chuza continued his faithful service without bitterness.

"Nearly ready, my lord," Chuza inclined his head. "But I want you to know that after I've arranged things in Sepphoris, I will return to Jerusalem."

Antipas blinked, and sweat trickled into his eye. "What?" he asked, wiping his face. Chuza had been asserting his authority since the moment Herodias foolishly tried to torture his wife. Herodias awakened a side of Chuza that Antipas would rather have left dormant.

"Don't worry, my lord," Chuza said. "I will perform my duties as thoroughly as always. My sense of honor demands it."

"Yes, but—"

"With the troubled history between my wife and yours, Joanna and I feel it is better if we put some distance between us and the court."

"Distance? But—"

Chuza patted Antipas' arm with a frustrating calmness. "I will spend a few weeks with you at each stage of your yearly progress, but the court won't be my home. Surely you see how this will make both our married lives happier."

"I suppose—"

"I'm glad you agree. Of course, now that I'll travel separately and live with my own household, I require an increase in my stipend. Unless you are unhappy with my services as the steward of Galilee and Perea, I will give myself a substantial raise." He lifted his eyebrows.

"By the stars," Antipas snapped, "do you plan to hold this against me forever?"

Chuza blinked with feigned innocence. "Hold what against you, my lord?"

Antipas glowered. "You know exactly what I'm talking about." Chuza stubbornly retained his puzzled expression, and Antipas rolled his eyes. "Your wife. The vineyard. The prophet."

Chuza's face relaxed. "Oh, well, the situation with Jesus was a matter beyond your control," he said with confidence. "He submitted himself to the cross so that God could raise him up to his right hand. And Jesus isn't dead anymore, my lord."

Antipas stared at his steward. The calm, calculating man had always carried his faith close to his chest. Now he stood here, in Herod's Palace, and brazenly admitted he believed Jesus rose from the dead. And not just that, that the Nazarene was sitting at God's right hand. Antipas worked his mouth, unsure what to say. Perhaps he should be honored that one of his Galilean citizens achieved such status.

He rubbed his face with his hands and dragged the dampness through his hair, not caring if it stood on end. "You're insane, like the rest of them," he muttered.

Chuza chuckled. "It seems like insanity to those on the outside, but if you experienced what I did, you might feel differently."

A twinge of jealousy pulled Antipas' lips into a frown. He had always longed to touch the spiritual realm, to receive a prophecy or some sign from God. But disciples of a dead rabbi were rather too spiritual for his taste.

Clearing his throat, he waved his steward away as if he didn't care what his longest serving slave, his advisor, his old friend, did. "Do what you must. Oversee my kingdom in whatever manner you see fit, but do not neglect your duties. You are still my bondslave, Chuza," he said, dropping his voice in warning. "You vowed to serve *me*, remember?"

Chuza smiled politely. "How could I forget?" He bowed and went to supervise the loading of the final luggage.

Herodias came from her room, drawing her palla over her hair to block the sun's glare.

"I'll be glad to be gone from this city," she said. She tucked her arm in his. "Our visit has been fruitful, but I am ready for a rest."

"Yes," Antipas said, leading her to a waiting cart. "It is definitely time for a change."

As he handed her into her seat, he cleared his throat. "Oh, and by the way," he said, "I spoke to Chuza. I've asked him to keep his wife away from court. He will divide his time between his new household and serving me. He's not happy about it, but I put my foot down."

Herodias glanced to where Chuza was directing the staff and murmured conspiratorially. "You are so wise, my lord. Your steward will serve you all the better because you enforced a little professional distance."

Antipas smiled to hide his unease. "You are right, as always."

Joanna wove through the courtyard, nodding at the staff as they bustled by, arms laden with baskets and wooden chests and satchels. Antipas was finally leaving the city. It was unfortunate that Chuza must accompany him, but he was still bound to the tetrarch.

For years she dreamed about an end to Antipas' unrighteous reign, but Jesus had seen fit to let Antipas rule—at least for a while. Perhaps she should be more upset that her hopes to serve in a godly court were dashed, but Jesus did more than she ever dreamed possible. Not content with ruling the promised land, he was determined to bring the whole world into Israel's blessings. A miracle beyond Passover indeed.

But before her husband left to serve the tetrarch, she needed to tell him her news.

Chuza was speaking with Michael. He waved at her, and Joanna hurried over.

"Still not returning my best cook to me, then?" Michael asked, looking past her, searching for Leah. The young woman remained with the disciples, helping to feed the masses of poor believers.

"Not yet," Joanna said, "but she misses you already."

Michael grinned and held out a slip of papyrus. "The recipe she's been begging for." His lips twitched with suppressed emotion. "I told her she wasn't ready to learn my last secret, but I want her to have it now."

Joanna took the recipe like it was gold. "Thank you," she said, holding his gaze, "for taking her as an apprentice and restoring Leah's belief in herself. Your friendship has been a treasured gift."

Michael wiped his eyes with thick fingers as Chuza clapped his shoulder in agreement.

As the cook ambled away, Joanna stepped closer to Chuza. "Ready to go?" she asked.

"I spoke to Antipas." He pressed his lips together and puffed out his breath. "I thought I would vomit with nervousness, but he agreed to everything."

Joanna blinked in shock. "Everything? Praise God!"

Chuza nodded in agreement. "It's more than I hoped for, but now I can divide my time between the believers and Antipas. He sees no threat in the followers of a dead rabbi. And you are free of Herodias' jealousy."

Joanna's joy faltered. "Someday, you'll be free, too. I know it."

Chuza took her hand, braiding their fingers together. "For now, I will run Antipas' estate with righteousness and pray that I can influence him to godliness as well."

"A worthy mission," Joanna said, though she wondered if the tetrarch could change. But Antipas' selfish ways no longer held the threat they once did. Antipas and Herodias couldn't diminish her assurance that she was serving the Lord—in more ways than one. "Before you go," she said with a grin, "I have an important job for you."

Chuza's brow furrowed in question. "Have the disciples asked me to complete a task?"

Joanna smiled coyly. "No, this responsibility comes from me—and you."

"What are you talking about?"

She leaned forward and whispered her secret in his ear. As she stepped back, he stared at her, dazed.

His hands fluttered over her middle, searching for proof. "I hoped... I suspected... Are you sure?"

She laughed and nodded.

"When?"

"This winter," Joanna said.

His expression softened with joyful expectation.

She cupped his cheek. "You will make a wonderful father to our child," she said. "And we'll raise them in a world where the Holy Spirit is moving."

Chuza, careless of watching eyes, seized her, pinning her against his chest as he kissed her until she was breathless.

A servant hooted, and Chuza shot him a mock glare. "Can't a man have a moment with his wife?" he said. His eyes searched hers. "Be well, while I am gone," he murmured, running his lips over her cheek, his beard sending shivers down her spine. "My days will slip past like pearls on a necklace, knowing you wait for me, pregnant with my child."

A groom led Celer from the stable. Chuza kissed Joanna one last time and swung into the saddle. Joanna watched him ride after his master. Her palms pressed into her middle, though it was still flat and smooth. They'd need to find some sort of home, a place to raise their child. But it was early yet, and she had plans to enact before she held a baby in her arms.

She arrived at her sister's house and knocked briskly. One of Dalia's sisters-in-law answered. She let Joanna inside and gestured to the courtyard where Joanna heard women chattering.

Joanna paused in the doorway to the courtyard, taking in the domestic picture. Her mother and Dalia were busy at a large loom, sitting side by side as Dalia's children played on a blanket nearby. Other women were spinning wool into thread. It was the sort of scene that once would have made her feel left out. But now there wasn't room in her heart for jealousy. The community of witnesses filled her completely.

Dalia glanced up and saw her with surprise. A shadow passed across her eyes. They had not spoken since Amichai abandoned them a second time, leaving with Barabbas. Joanna smiled, trying to show she was coming with peaceable intent. Miriam hurried to embrace her.

"I thought you left without saying goodbye!" Miriam exclaimed. "We heard Antipas' retinue is on its way for Sepphoris."

"He has left the city," Joanna said and raised her brows mischievously. "But I have left the household."

Dalia and Miriam split a concerned glance, and Dalia asked, "What about your husband?"

"He will go back and forth as necessary. We will have our own home. Chuza insisted on it."

Dalia's mouth fell open. "But where are you staying now?"

"I have a room with friends," Joanna said, hesitating to share too much too soon, in case she overpowered her sister completely. "Do you have time for a visit?"

Dalia shook off her confusion. "Of course. Let's go on the roof."

Miriam and Dalia gathered up refreshments, and they took the stairs to the top of the house where the breeze fluttered the shade canopy and the height afforded them a pleasant view. Joanna accepted a cup of water freshened with mint and a sweet cake. She drew a deep breath, deciding there was one topic they needed to tackle before she gave her news.

"Have you heard from Amichai?" she asked.

Dalia and Miriam looked at each other.

"No," Miriam sighed. "Not since he left. Again." The word hung between them.

Dalia pressed her lips together. "I suppose you're furious at him, after giving up the vineyard to earn his freedom."

Joanna dusted crumbs from her lap. She should be furious with Amichai. This second betrayal was worse than the first. Instead of just risking the vineyard, his actions caused a total loss.

But Jesus' trial and crucifixion overshadowed her anger. His resurrection swept her bitterness aside. A corner of her heart throbbed with pain over losing her home, but it was small compared to the joy that sealed her days.

"Well, I'm not happy with him," she admitted. "But if I had to do it again, I'd make the same choice. The important thing is that he's alive and well."

Dalia sat back. "You've changed your tune."

Joanna smiled wryly, remembering angry words spoken long ago. "I still don't agree with his choices, but I recognize that he's trying to do the right thing. I know what it's like to follow my convictions wherever they lead."

Miriam squeezed her hand with pity. "Yes, about that. I am sure you must be heartbroken. We were upset to hear the prophet died."

"Yes," Joanna said, gripping her mother's fingers, praying she would be open to the truth. "He died. But he didn't stay dead."

Miriam and Dalia shared a weighted glance.

Dalia spoke slowly, "So you're one of *them*? The ones who insist that Jesus rose from the dead?"

Joanna nodded. "I am. I saw him."

Miriam pursed her lips. "I don't want to belittle your experience, but that's impossible. The priests have been quite clear about what happened."

"They're lying," Joanna said, and Miriam flinched. Dalia scowled at Joanna's bold accusation. Joanna raised her hands. She had no desire to return to the animosity of the past few years. "I believe their intentions are to protect the people. They are afraid of Jesus and what he teaches."

Miriam looked troubled. "Well, I guess we'll have to wait and see. If Jesus is alive, we'll have proof of it soon enough."

Joanna's eyes flicked between these two women she loved. "If my testimony is not enough, you may never believe," she said. "Jesus has risen from the dead, and after appearing to many, he ascended, alive, into heaven." They glanced at each other as if afraid she had gone mad. She folded her hands in her lap. "It sounds impossible, but wasn't Elijah swept up to heaven alive?"

"Not after being crucified," Dalia said flatly. Miriam flinched as if Dalia uttered a curse word.

Miriam leaned forward. "Why would God allow him to die on a... in such a way, just to raise him from the dead?"

Joanna spread her palms. "For his glory. And for all of us."

"Glory?" Miriam nearly choked on the word. "What glory is there in that kind of death?"

"In accepting and overcoming it, though he was innocent," Joanna said. "By believing in him, we can be saved." Miriam still looked confused.

"Saved from what?" Dalia asked.

"Sin. Judgment," Joanna said. "God's righteous wrath."

"We're Jews," Dalia said, crossing her arms. "We have Torah to save us from sin." Miriam nodded in agreement.

Joanna knew she would have to tread with care. "Our generation is wicked and perverse, despite our many teachers, our priests, our synagogues. Our treatment of God's prophet brings that into sharp clarity. We need to repent and be baptized in the name of Jesus."

Dalia and Miriam were unconvinced, and Joanna sensed it was not the time to push. She had planted the seeds, but only God could make them grow.

She shifted in her seat. "But that's not all I came to say. I have two pieces of exciting news. First..." she hesitated, a smile teasing at her lips. "I'm pregnant!"

The transformation on her mother and sister's faces was comical. Dalia leaped forward and threw her arms around Joanna with an eager squeal.

"Finally!" Dalia said. "I can't wait to be an auntie!"

"But you're a mother already," Joanna said with a laugh. "Don't you already have babies to kiss and hold?"

"Yes, yes." Dalia waved the words away. "But it's different to be an aunt. I can hold and cuddle and spoil and then give the baby back to you for the hard work."

They discussed symptoms and pregnancy and childbirth with far more ease than they discussed sin and salvation.

"But wait," Miriam said. "You said you had two pieces of news to share."

Joanna nodded, hoping that they would receive her other announcement with equal enthusiasm. "Chuza and I are going to Alexandria. We'll be gone a couple of months."

Miriam and Dalia stared. "Egypt?" Miriam exclaimed. "What on earth takes you there? Has Antipas demanded it?"

Joanna shook her head. "No, this is for us. We are searching for Leah's family." And Chuza's. But that hope was so meager that she kept it safe in her heart.

"But I thought her family was gone?" Dalia said.

"She has a grandfather, aunts, uncles, and cousins."

Miriam shook her head. "I don't understand. Why hasn't she returned to them before?"

Joanna smiled at her mother. "She's ready now. We leave in a few weeks. We want to be back in Jerusalem well before my time."

Miriam's brow puckered. "And then what? Where will you raise my grandchild? The vineyard is gone." She cast an awkward glance at Dalia, and Joanna could see her sister was about to offer her home—as tight as the accommodations would be.

"I'll stay with the disciples."

"With a baby?"

"We plan to rent a room nearby."

"But—"

Joanna held up her hands for peace. "We are taking it one day at a time. Why worry about tomorrow? Each day has enough worry of its own."

Dalia's lips puckered. "Wise words, I suppose."

"A prophet's words," Joanna said.

Joanna saw her continual references to Jesus were making the other women uncomfortable. She had become accustomed to speaking freely of Jesus and the Holy Spirit. She turned the conversation to simpler topics and watched them relax. When Joanna rose to go, they followed her to the door.

Joanna took her mother's hand. "Look, I know you don't accept everything I am saying. But if you would visit the disciples and see their love and their earnestness to serve the Lord, you'd understand." Joanna gave directions to the house where the disciples met, hoping her mother and Dalia would investigate for themselves. She had learned her lesson with Leah. She couldn't force someone to believe, but she could love them either way.

# FORTY-FIVE

31 AD
SUMMER

J oanna's jaw fell open with wonder as they sailed past the towering Pharos Lighthouse. Built with pale stone, it dwarfed the small island supporting its bulky base. Able to withstand the crashing waves of storms without a shudder, the tower was a sentinel guarding the sprawling city of Alexandria. A polished metal mirror pointed out to the Great Sea, beckoning ships into port.

"At night you can see a fire at the top of the lighthouse," Leah said at Joanna's elbow. The sea breeze tugged a long strand free from her braid. As Leah tucked her hair behind her ear, Joanna recalled the skinny girl with the shaved head. She had grown so much.

The women leaned on the railing of the ship as the crew bustled and the captain shouted orders. The merchant vessel sailed around the T-shaped harbor and into the southern port. As they turned toward the city, the shallow water smoothed, protected by a wall of sand and stone. Across a narrow strip of land, military ships were anchored in the northeastern port, their tall masts like a forest of stripped trees.

As their ship glided to the dock, Joanna gripped the railing, stunned as she took in the sprawling capital of Egypt. Alexandria was the second-largest city in the world, superseded only by Rome, but she had not known what to expect.

"How will we find anyone in a city so large?" she said, her stomach sinking. For the first time, she understood how alone Leah had been, orphaned and separated from her extended family.

Chuza came up to her side, handing her and Leah their bags. "We'll go by landmarks," he said with a determined smile. "Leah will remember things as she sees them."

Leah frowned with doubt. "It's been a long time."

He gave her a nod full of confidence. "You'll remember."

The gangplank slid into position as sailors secured the craft with thick ropes. The trio joined the queue of travelers eager to depart. As her feet hit solid ground, Joanna wobbled, and Chuza reached out a hand to steady her.

"What's wrong with my legs?" she said in alarm.

Chuza chuckled. "They're waiting for the earth to pitch and roll like a ship."

"Mine feel fine." Leah shrugged with an impish grin. "It must be because I'm younger." Joanna shot her a dirty look that made Chuza laugh.

Joanna gave her husband a wry smile. She was thankful his spirits were high, despite their purpose. Too often on their voyage, he stared across the water, battling his desire to go home and avoid the emotional dangers ahead. She shared his worry about the possibility of leaving Leah behind. But, despite the fear, she still prayed they would find the young woman's family. Leah deserved the chance to face her past.

Joanna wobbled her way through the noisy port full of rough-mouthed sailors. Foremen directed the loading of merchandise onto wagons that would flow into the city, bearing goods from every corner of the world.

By the time they made it to the paved streets, Joanna's legs had adjusted. She ran a hand down her middle out of habit, cradling the soft rise between her hips. Her morning sickness left during the voyage, thanks, perhaps, to the bracing sea air. For that, she was grateful. They had only two weeks before they must find a ship for home, and she didn't want to slow the search down. Antipas begrudgingly paid for them to travel by ship, not out of generosity, but because he wanted Chuza back as soon as possible. The threats of war with Nabatea were rising once again.

But as they wove down the packed streets, she realized two weeks may not be enough. She glanced at Chuza, conveying her anxieties with her expression.

They reached an open square filled with a bustling market and stopped to buy food. As they ate crusty bread and soft cheese, they tried to figure out the best way to track down Leah's old neighborhood, a place she hadn't visited since she was a child of eleven.

"You said you can see the fire of the lighthouse at night?" Joanna asked, an idea dawning. "Was that from your house?"

Leah nodded. "On the roof."

Chuza's eyes lit up with understanding, and he peered back to the harbor. "What direction was the lighthouse from your house?"

Leah hesitated, following his gaze. "I think it was more to the left?"

Chuza bobbed his head. "Then let's go north. Perhaps your home is in the old Jewish quarter."

"We have our own quarter?" Joanna asked in surprise.

"Well, not so much anymore," Chuza said. To prepare for this journey, he visited a synagogue in Jerusalem made up of Alexandrians, Greek-speaking Jews who had their own traditions and theology and formed an exclusive community. "There are synagogues all over Alexandria as more Jews gain Roman citizenship, but a large cluster remains on the northwest end of the city."

"This doesn't seem like a lot to go on," Leah said, frowning.

"Don't give up before we've even started," Joanna said staunchly, though she was becoming more overwhelmed with every step.

Chuza wrestled with his emotions as days crept by in fruitless search. He wanted Leah to find her family, but he feared what would happen when she did. Surely the animosity that excluded her father from the synagogue was forgotten. Which meant they might welcome Leah back as a long-lost daughter and expect her to remain.

His throat tightened. He befriended the girl at God's prompting, and over the past months, she became part of his family. But maybe God had used him to prepare Leah for this moment, and to help her return. His chest cinched at the thought, and he begged God to make him strong enough to endure another parting.

They visited synagogues, inquiring about Leah's relatives. At Joanna's pressing, he asked after his own family as well. He felt foolish, considering three decades had passed. He couldn't be sure that they even made it to Alexandria.

Leah grew moody after days of heightened emotional stress. Joanna kept prompting Leah to see if she recognized anything, but she was never sure.

Finally, they struck gold.

"I know this place," Leah said as they approached a synagogue.

Joanna darted her a look. "Is this the one where you—"

"Not the one I stole from." Leah's expression was tight. "I remember coming here with my family."

Chuza's stomach churned with mingled hope and fear. Drawing his courage around him, he led the women up the steps and entered the cool, shadowy building. A synagogue official was sweeping the floor.

"Peace be on you," Chuza said in Greek. "We are visitors to

Alexandria, seeking a family who attends this synagogue—or at least they used to." With a peek at Leah's pale face, Chuza gave her grandfather's name.

"Yes, I know the man you're talking about," he said. "Joash is an elder in the synagogue. His house is just three streets from here. Are you relatives?" He studied them with curiosity.

"Yes," Chuza replied, speaking on Leah's behalf.

"It is good you have come." The man grew grave. "I must tell you, he has not been well, and he rarely leaves the house."

Leah's lips trembled, and Joanna put an encouraging arm around her shoulder.

They followed the man's instructions to a pleasant house. The shutters and door were painted a deep red, and flowers and herbs sat in pots along the sunny wall. They could hear voices within, men talking, a woman scolding, and children's laughter. The house exuded familial warmth, but Leah froze as she studied it, taking in each detail.

"I never imagined I would be back here," Leah whispered. Her hands trembled as she tucked her hair behind both ears. "They might not even recognize me."

"Then we will explain," Joanna said, offering a compassionate smile. Joanna nodded at Chuza, and he wondered how she could be so calm. Drawing a breath, he knocked on the door.

After a few moments, the door swung open. A man glanced between them, skipping over Leah.

"Yes?" he asked politely.

"Peace be with you," Chuza said. "We have come from Jerusalem, and are seeking the family of Joash ben Moses."

"Yes, that is my father." The man gave them a closer inspection. "What do you want with him?"

Leah stepped forward, her voice shaking as she said, "Uncle Levi?"

He did a double-take, then his eyes widened in shock. With a gasp, he disappeared back into the house, leaving Leah wilting in the hot street.

Leah turned to Joanna, tears of rejection pooling. Joanna held out her arms, but before Leah could seek comfort, the noise in the house rose in pitch, and a parade of people rushed out the door.

"Leah!" a dozen voices shouted.

Leah was hugged and passed from one set of arms to another. Young children ran and shrieked in delight at the chaos.

Chuza purposefully shoved down any inkling of jealousy. He stifled his old dreams of joyfully reuniting with his family in a scene just like this.

He stepped closer to Joanna and twined his fingers with hers. Clearly, Leah had been missed. This was her real family. Where she belonged. The idea of returning to Jerusalem without her burned his throat, but he determinedly kept his face serene. Joanna looked at him with damp eyes, and he clutched her hand in shared turmoil.

Eventually, the noise subsided enough for the trio to be invited inside. Levi led them to an inner chamber where a man lay on his bed. A thick shock of silver hair crowned his head, and his hands and face were yellowed from illness.

Chuza opened his mouth to protest as Levi pulled Leah right up to Joash's couch, not considering she might be fearful after the way they parted. Joash stared at her. Cushions supported his frail frame, and a blanket covered him despite the warmth of the day.

"Grandpa," Leah whispered, kneeling by his side. "I've come home, though I am not worthy to be called your granddaughter."

Chuza thought his heart would break at the pain and regret in Leah's voice.

"Oh!" Joash cried, fingers covering his lips as tears gathered. "My prayers have been answered!" He reached trembling hands for her, and she went into his embrace, both of them weeping, releasing years of unresolved anguish.

Chuza sucked a breath, willing himself under control. Leah's reunion with her family would have to be enough for both of them. Joanna wrapped her arm around him, sensing his churning emotions beneath the calm of his exterior.

At supper, Joanna and Chuza sat in places of honor as the whole family gathered around a long table. Joash lay on his couch, presiding over his large household despite his illness.

"What happened to you?" Levi asked Leah. "We received word everyone died, all except the oldest girl, but we searched and could not find you."

Leah flicked a guilty peek at Joanna. Over and over, Leah had insisted no one missed her.

Leah drew a breath and explained what happened. Chuza admired her bravery. She did not hide her shameful attempt to steal money from the synagogue, the fear of being sold as a slave, or her abandonment at Petra. Her story shocked her family, and a few of the women dabbed away tears.

Leah's history took a brighter turn as Joanna came into it, and grew happier as she spoke of traveling between the palaces and Joanna's beautiful vineyard and being accepted as an apprentice to the palace cook. Chuza was captivated, seeing their lives through Leah's eyes.

Then Leah recounted her experiences with Jesus. From a few shared glances, Chuza could tell that stories of the famous prophet had made their way to Alexandria. But they came as rumors, not eyewitness accounts. Leah's family listened, spellbound.

Leah's eyes dampened as she told them about Jesus being sentenced to death, and seeing him on the cross. She cried happy tears as she revealed how she witnessed Jesus alive and well, risen from the dead.

A stunned silence filled the room, and Chuza prayed the Lord would reward Leah's boldness in declaring the good news to a family she had not seen for five long years.

"You did all that—saw all that—since leaving home?" one cousin said in awe. She was close to Leah's age, and they shared similar facial features.

"I did," Leah said and offered a small smile. "I guess it sounds like a wonderful adventure now, but there were many times that I believed God abandoned me. I thought he rejected me as one of his people." A few peeked at Joash, and his deeply creased brow showed his regret.

"I want you to understand," Leah said, her lips wobbling, "I was full of darkness. Full of hate." She ducked her head, her cheeks crimson. "I thought God was punishing me for my father's sins by letting me be sold into slavery, but now I don't think so."

"What do you think now?" the same cousin asked, leaning forward.

Leah weighed her words. "I understand now that I was just a child in a difficult situation." She looked at her grandfather, and forgiveness shone in her eyes. "I think about how our people were forced into slavery in Egypt. Pharaoh made them slaves because he was wicked and cruel and did not know the Lord. Our people suffered, but then God used that suffering to show all of Egypt his power. Through his signs and wonders, he rescued those slaves from bondage and made them into a mighty people."

Leah glanced at Joanna, who was working to hold back tears. "I don't think God sent me to slavery," Leah said, "but I believe he was with me in slavery. And even amid the hardship, he was working everything for my good. He brought me to Joanna, Michael, and Chuza, and they have become a family to me. My struggles led me to Jesus, so I could see the wonders and signs of the Lord for myself. Witness his immeasurable forgiveness for those who hurt him." She paused to blink rapidly, and Joanna gripped Chuza's hand.

Leah smiled, and it was like sunlight through the rain. "And now I have experienced the indwelling of his Spirit, which is given freely to those that believe." She glanced around, her expression growing shy. "I think he worked in my suffering so I could share that good news with all of you."

No one spoke as they shared uncertain glances. Levi looked at his father, but Joash remained silent as he considered his long-lost granddaughter's testimony.

"Well," Levi said, breaking the awkward silence with a warm smile. "You've given us much to think about, and even more to thank the Lord for. Praise God's goodness for bringing you home!"

The family invited Joanna and Chuza to stay as their guests, and Chuza accepted. But once he and Joanna were alone, he drew his courage.

"We need to leave Leah here for a while," he said quietly, though each word stung like a wound. "She needs to reconnect with her family without us distracting her. A chance to decide if she wants to stay."

Joanna's face crumpled, and he pulled her close. "I want what's best for her," Joanna whispered as she leaned her cheek on his shoulder. "But how can we leave without her?" Chuza swallowed hard. He had no idea.

The next morning, he and Joanna gathered their things. Leah's face grew panicked as Joanna explained the plan.

"I'll come with you," Leah said, grabbing her bag.

Joanna caught her arm. "We will not leave Alexandria without coming back here. Stay with your family and get to know them again. You have a place with us forever," Joanna said, casting a pained glance at Chuza. "But you need to slow down and think about your choices."

Chuza set his hand on her shoulder. "Whatever you decide," he said, "don't make your choice out of fear. Pray. Let the Holy Spirit show you what to do."

Chuza and Joanna spent the rest of their allotted days searching the city for any hint of his family. They spoke often of Leah, wondering what she would decide. Before Chuza knew it, their time was nearly up. He was exhausted and hoping Joanna would let him stop the search, but Joanna insisted they make good use of their last day. They entered a small synagogue, and the synagogue official came out of the backroom to speak with them.

Chuza asked, "Do you have anyone among your congregation who would remember a family who came to Alexandria thirty years ago?"

The official pursed his lips, then sent them next door to ask one of the elder's wives, a woman in her sixties with an impeccable memory.

The woman welcomed them into her home. Chuza relayed the same story he had told for the past two weeks, giving his parents' names and explaining how they came here looking for work.

Her focus grew distant, and he felt a jerk behind his navel as she nodded slowly. "I remember a family like that. The boys were Rael and Caleb, and there was a daughter too, yes?"

Chuza's ribs tightened at the names of his siblings, and he could not draw a full breath. This was impossible. "Yes," he said, choking on the word. "That's right."

Startled at his reaction, the woman looked at Joanna for an explanation. Joanna gripped his fingers, and he squeezed her hand so tight he worried he was hurting her. "It's his family," Joanna said. "They have been... separated for a long time."

The woman nodded, her faded eyes softening with compassion. "They weren't here very long. I only remember them because of the mother." Chuza swallowed hard. "She was so very sad, a woman grieving. She spoke often of the son they had to leave behind." As Chuza's shoulders shook, she spoke slowly. "I guess that was you."

Chuza's breath seared like fire, and Joanna pressed her arm against his.

The woman said, "She was clinging to the time when she could go back and get you." Her gaze roved over Chuza's face, seeing the tears that he barely contained. "But they didn't go back for you, did they?"

Chuza shook his head, and his shoulders trembled under the strain of confining his emotions.

The woman leaned forward and patted his knee in a grandmotherly way. "It's alright, honey," she murmured. "You can cry in front of me."

Her warm sympathy burst the floodgates open and Chuza wept for his family as Joanna wrapped around him, whispering comforting words. He cried for his mother, who had grieved for him, missed him, and wanted so much to come back and get him. The confirmation both soothed and tore his heart.

Joanna asked what he couldn't. "What happened to them?"

The woman sighed. "I don't know," she admitted. "They didn't find what they needed here either, and quietly moved away. I never got to say goodbye, and it's that lack of closure that made your mother and her grief stay with me all these years."

Chuza collected himself, and they thanked the woman and went back to the inn where they were staying.

In their booth around the inn's central courtyard, Chuza and Joanna snuggled together on their thin bed. Chuza drew a deep, cleansing breath. He rested his cheek on his wife's chest, taking comfort in her heartbeat as he laid his palm on Joanna's middle, soothed by the swell beneath his fingers, the hint of his son or daughter. Joanna ran her hand up and down his back.

He propped himself on his elbow to see her face and saw tears of sympathy.

"It's not the answer I wanted," he said, "but at least I know I was not forgotten."

"Your mother loved you very much," Joanna said, her eyes liquid. She put her palm over his, the two of them cradling the new life that grew there, the symbol of their love. "I cannot fathom the pain of giving up a child."

His throat ached. "The knowledge of my mother's love will need to be enough. I can't dwell on the past. I need to look to the future, and there's a lot to see there."

"Yes," Joanna said, a warm smile brightening her eyes. "I am eager to get back to the disciples, to help spread the good news."

"And then there's the threat of war with Nabatea," Chuza said with a sigh.

"And our growing family." Joanna squeezed his hand. Her happiness faded. "I wonder what Leah will decide?"

"We'll have to give her our full support if she stays," Chuza said, determination overshadowing his anxiety. His own family was lost, but Leah had a second chance. "These are her people, and they seem loving."

Joanna nodded, and he nestled his head back on her heart, his own torn in two.

Joanna woke after a restless sleep. She dreamed Leah had flown away like a bird, and Joanna chased her, begging her to come back. The panic she felt seemed foolish in the light of day, but she was worn down with worry. She needed to know what Leah had decided.

She and Chuza broke their fast with simple fare prepared by the innkeeper's daughters. The innkeeper approached their table and spoke to Chuza. "I hear you're looking for a ship going north. There's one leaving when the winds are favorable, if you want to book passage." Chuza looked at Joanna and her anxieties bobbed to the surface. Today Leah would decide not only her future, but theirs.

Joanna and Chuza were welcomed into Joash's house with less chaos than their first arrival. Leah hurried forward, a bright smile on her face, her cousin just a few steps behind. Bittersweet pain clutched Joanna's throat. Leah was happy here.

"Is it time to go?" Leah asked.

Joanna blinked in confusion. "You're coming with us?" She worked to hide the excitement in her voice in case she misunderstood.

Leah nodded, her expression peaceful. "I talked with my family and explained how much I feel at home with you, and that I want to be on hand to help when the baby is born. I want to live close to Jerusalem, so I can be a part of the disciple's work."

"Your family says you can go?" Chuza asked, glancing around at the household filling the room—Leah's aunts and uncles, and her many cousins. Joash watched solemnly from his bed.

"They tried to change my mind," Leah admitted, and turned to her cousin, who gave her a sad smile, "but they will agree if you become my adoptive parents."

"Yes!" Joanna gasped, pulling the young woman into her arms. "Of course, we will!"

Chuza stared around the room at the gathered family, as if ensuring himself that they accepted Leah's decision. Levi met his gaze and gave a single nod.

"Leah told us you have loved her as your daughter," Levi said huskily. "My brother would be grateful if you would raise her as your own."

Leah released Joanna and turned into Chuza's arms. He kissed the top of her head, blinking back tears. Joanna's heart surged with joy. Chuza had lost his family, but now he gained a beautiful daughter. And maybe another one on the way. She rested her hand on her middle. Sometimes life was harsh, but even so, God was good.

Leah said a tearful goodbye to her extended family, knowing full well she might never see any of them again. But this time, it was her choice, and she wasn't leaving alone.

The trio turned their faces to the port and the ship that would take them back to Jerusalem and the family of fellow believers. The future was uncertain, but with the Spirit that Jesus had sent them, they would navigate it together.

The story continues in:
*Court of the Tetrarch - Book Three*
*Herod's Steward*


COMING 2023


To be the first to hear about upcoming releases and enjoy exclusive content, subscribe to Katrina's website at katrinadhamel.com

# AUTHOR'S NOTE

I hope you enjoyed the continuation of Joanna and Chuza's story. More skilled hands than mine have tackled the gospel story as a novel, but I am proud to add my contribution. This story is very dear to my heart, and I pray it touches yours.

These notes address a few historical facts.

*The Characters*

All the characters in this novel are fictitious, including the ones we find in scripture or history books. I say this because they may have been very different than the way I present them. (And I hope they don't mind my taking creative license!)

Joanna, Chuza, Manaen, Susanna, Maryam (one of the Marys with an alternate spelling) are all mentioned in the New Testament, as are Herod Antipas, Herodias, John the Baptizer, Pilate, Jesus, and many of his disciples. Titus and Leah are purely from my imagination, as are Joanna's family.

Antipas' family history is absolutely crazy—a soap opera of

murder and intermarriages on the royal scale. I gathered my information about the Herods through the ancient writings of Josephus. Not everyone agrees with Josephus, but he gives a detailed history of their many intrigues and scandals. Josephus gives Herodias' daughter her name, and he also provides information about Pilate's grisly, often violent, political mistakes.

### Cultural Sensitivity and Authenticity

I have done my best to be respectful to Judaism. As Christians, we feel some claim on their history, and I hope that I have not offended anyone in my presentation of first-century culture. First-century ways were different than modern or orthodox Judaism, which were necessarily modified after the destruction of the temple and have continued to evolve over the centuries. There is much we don't know about daily life in the first century, and many traditions were not written down until later.

### God-fearers

According to my research, God-fearers were considered righteous Gentiles. They were not expected to undergo circumcision or adhere to Sabbath rules unless they took the next step and became proselytes and full converts. God-fearers were to follow the seven rules that the rabbis believed Noah gave to Gentile world: keep from stealing, murder, adultery, idolatry, blasphemy, eating live animals, and they were to uphold a system of justice.

Jews believed that such God-fearers would be accepted by God in the world to come/final judgment.

It was difficult to learn if God-fearers were fully welcomed in Jewish circles. It seems as if the early church was entirely made of Jews or Jewish converts until Peter's encounter with Cornelius. The shocking revelation to accept uncircumcised men into the church caused quite a stir! To me, this hints that there was still some pretty big separation between Jews and God-fearers. I have showed some of this tension with my character Titus.

*Sending Out the Seventy*

There is a little scholarly kerfuffle over Jesus sending out the seventy in Luke 10:1-16, as some manuscripts say he sent out seventy-two. I played on that debate in my novel. We have no solid evidence of who made up the seventy (or seventy-two). Some have suggested that women could have been among the number. After all, women (including Joanna) were mentioned by name in Luke 8, traveling with the twelve and supporting Jesus' ministry. Others have insisted that women disciples would have been scorned in a patriarchal culture. While I wanted to show that Jesus welcomed women, I didn't want to gloss over the struggles they might have faced.

*The Thief on the Cross and Barabbas*

Crucifixions were not for small-time criminals, but for enemies of Rome. Considering that Pilate had Barabbas in custody, I decided that these two thieves on the cross would be part of Barabbas' group. This is conjecture drawn from the circumstances.

In Luke, Barabbas is complicit in a riot. In John's gospel, Barabbas is called a bandit, and the Greek word for 'bandit' is the same one that the historian Josephus uses to describe revolutionaries. So these thieves/bandits may have been actively fighting against Roman influence in the land. They could have been precursors to the group later titled the *sicarri* by their Roman occupiers.

*Scriptural Accuracy*

As I'm sure you noticed, scriptures are sometimes paraphrased to continue the conversational tone of this novel. They are not intended to replace the biblical text.

This book gathers inspiration from Jesus' ministry from all four of the gospels and the opening chapters of Acts. My intention is to inspire and encourage, not replace sacred writings.

I believe each gospel writer was very intentional in selecting how they would present the gospel, and they have each emphasized different elements of Jesus' life and ministry.

As someone who loves research and the Bible, it is an emotional challenge to accept that the gospels are difficult to put on a timeline. As I took my women to the tomb, I had to decide how to show those poignant scenes. Do they see angels sitting outside or inside the tomb? One angel or two? Do several women see Jesus right away, or just Mary? When does Simon Peter have his private encounter with Jesus that is alluded to in the gospel of Luke?

I have not attempted to create a complete narrative of the crucifixion and resurrection in this novel, but instead chose to focus on Luke's timeline. I hope it touched your heart with the wondrous knowledge that Jesus is truly alive.

### Scriptural References

Elijah is mentioned frequently as Joanna's hero. You can find him in 1 Kings, starting in chapter 17, when he flees from Ahab and stays with a widow and her son in Sidon. He calls down fire from heaven in 1 Kings 18. You can read about Elijah passing his mantle and a double-portion of his spirit to Elisha in 2 Kings 2.

Other stories mentioned are Hannah and Eli by the tabernacle in 1 Samuel 1, Jonathan and his shield-bearer in 1 Samuel 14, David and Goliath in 1 Samuel 16, David dancing before the Ark in 2 Samuel 6, and David and Bathsheba in 2 Samuel 11. God's call for a kingdom of priests and a holy nation is in Exodus 19:6.

### Women in Ministry

A few of my early readers felt uncomfortable with Joanna leaving her husband behind. Others found her inspiring, wondering if they would follow Jesus over their husbands if forced to choose. The Bible mentions Peter having a wife in 1 Corinthians 9:5, and perhaps other disciples did too. Their wives might have been quite upset that their men were suddenly running after a prophet, abandoning their jobs and family responsibilities.

I have never heard someone say that Peter should have stayed home with his wife instead of following Jesus. If a modern-day woman is called to ministry, but her husband isn't, what should she do?

## Egalitarian Christian Couples

Chuza and Joanna are a team. Joanna helps Chuza with his job, he lets her lead when she has more experience, and Chuza steps into the emotional gaps Joanna struggled to fill with Leah. I love Chuza's servant-heart despite his authority and position, and Joanna's deep yearning to be used by God. I think they make a stellar couple and am excited to conclude their story in the final book of the series, 'Herod's Steward'.

If you're interested in egalitarian Christianity based on scripture, I suggest you check out Marg Mowczko's website. You can also visit out my website, katrinadhamel.com, for some articles on women in the New Testament era and some of my research on Herod's family.

## Discussion Questions

1. What is something you love about biblical fiction? Is there any aspect of this genre that you find challenging?

2. How did you feel about Joanna repeatedly leaving Chuza behind to follow Jesus? Do you feel Chuza should have made more of an effort to go with her?

3. Joanna and Chuza begin by keeping Jesus a secret from Antipas in an effort to protect him from being arrested. Do you feel Christians try to protect Jesus, the Bible, or the church today? Does God need us to defend him?

4. What do you think it was like for women who followed Jesus? Do you think it's possible they could have been part of the seventy that Jesus sent out?

5. Joanna married Chuza with the hope that they could do good in Antipas' court. Do you feel Christians should seek employment with unrighteous people in power?

6. Do you feel sympathy or frustration with Leah? What would you say to someone who has become jaded towards faith because of someone in the church?

7. When Joanna goes back to Jesus the third time, Susanna does not go with her. How did that make you feel?

8. What did you think about Titus? Have you ever considered the challenges Gentile God-fearers would have faced?

9. Joanna's attempts to share her faith often end badly. Have you tried to share the gospel and failed? What helped you try again?

10. What did you think about Herodias and Salome? What do you think motivates Herodias, and why?

11. The author chose to focus on the tetrarch's court in this series. Did you gain any new perspectives on the gospel as you saw it from this angle?

12. Dalia and Amichai are quite harsh in their exclusion of Joanna. Are they justified in feeling betrayed that their sister serves the enemy? How do we hold to our convictions when our loved ones don't understand?

13. Did you learn anything new about Pilate? Based on his violent history toward the people he governed, what sort of a man do you think he was?

14. When reading about Jesus' death and resurrection, were there any scenes the author left out that you wished were included? Did you experience any part of that well-loved story in a new way?

15. Chuza feels loyalty to his master, despite Antipas' failings. It isn't until Jesus' resurrection that Chuza begins to distance himself from Antipas. What changed for him?

16. Do you feel Joanna's yearning to be used by God was fulfilled? How? In what way has God called you to serve him? Are you living out that calling?

17. When Jesus is resurrected, Joanna and the others are full of questions. What do you think it was like in those early years, before they had the gospels and the letters to turn to for answers? What should we do with our modern-day questions that are not easily answered?

18. Where do you think the story will go next?

# ACKNOWLEDGMENTS

God, thank you for calling me to write. I give it all back to you, and pray that you would use my stories to encourage others to seek a deeper relationship with you.

I have deep gratitude for my wonderful husband and kids who supported me with unlimited patience as I worked on this project.

A huge thank you to my early readers: Jenna Kosters, Jillian Sevilla-Sales, Melissa Robertson, Shari Hamble, Jennifer Q. Hunt, Addison Lea Brannon, Rebecca Tellez, and Melissa A. Buffaa. I truly appreciate you reading the rough draft and giving me valuable feedback and encouragement!

Big thanks to Cay Danielson for creating the amazing map of Joanna's world.

Thank you, dear reader, for allowing me to share this story with you. Your support means more than I can say.

The grace of our Lord Jesus Christ be with you all.

Katrina

# ABOUT THE AUTHOR

Katrina lives in Alberta, Canada, with her husband, four children, two cats, and their Cavalier King Charles. She began her indie-author career in 2019 with her debut novel Dividing Sword, and is grateful for the book-loving friends she has made and the expansion of her mind through her research. She welcomes comments and questions on her website:

katrinadhamel.com

## Biblical Fiction from Katrina D. Hamel

Dividing Sword

As the Stars

## Court of the Tetrarch Series

Joanna

Wife of Chuza